The Egyptian Wife

Windsor Cole

ISBN: 1492924008
ISBN 13: 9781492924005

THE GODDESS WENUT

She was about 14 inches tall, with a slender stylized body of a woman, the head of a rabbit, or hare. She was rarely seen in this combination, because this style was from the very beginning of ancient Egyptian history. Her nickname from the earliest of times was 'the swift one' and she once likely had the head of a snake, before she assumed this softer look. Later in time this goddess would change again and become one of the common people's best loved 'daily' gods, called Bes. There were hundreds of little sculptures of Bes found in the ruins of excavated homes, temples, and tombs. But representations of her earlier style were beyond rare, and usually just shown in flat pictographs on walls. Such as on the walls of the temple at Dendera, dating from around 2250 BCE.

There was only one 3 dimensional sculpture of her older form in all the world.

Until this one had been discovered in 2009.

The sculpture had been sitting in one of the vast underground basements of the Cairo Museum for at least 6 decades, in a group of artifacts from 18th dynasty, from the 1400's BCE. This was the dynasty of Nefertiti, and her husband Amenhotep, and their son King Tutankhamun. The little sculpture goddess had never been chosen for study because she was so very plain compared to the many important pieces for that time period, often stunning artifacts covered in shining gold and sparkling jewels.

A request to study the little piece was granted easily, without any curiosity by the Regents of the Museum. Why would someone wish to concern themselves with such a minor piece? But in truth this simple sculpture was incredibly precious. The stiff little goddess had been lovingly made for someone who wished to honor her in the deepest past, thousands of years before Christ.

And she had been so cherished and beloved that she had been honored and saved and passed down from ruler to ruler though the millennia, to be finally included in the tomb of the boy king, Tutankhamun. To bring him good luck in his passage to the afterlife.

ONE

It was an odd dream, about looking through a cabin window in the motorboat, watching the shimmering light of the early sun on the river, as they floated over the water. There were a few ripples on the water's surface suggesting calm and peace. And it was very quiet. She was the only thing moving, not even a bird floated in the dawn sky. The boat slowly pulled past a few feluccas, the traditional Egyptian sailboats, sitting motionless, tied up to their docks. It was a beautiful morning on the Nile, but something was terribly, terribly wrong.

Suddenly there was a screeching, a ripping that seemed to be almost inside her head, and then a jolt threw her forward as a jagged piece of metal came bursting up through the cabin floor at her feet, followed by a crush of billowing water. She heard crunching. She heard screaming in the air all around her. It must be a nightmare. She had to wake up. But everything began to fade away and she thought it might have been her own voice screaming.

Something was tickling her back. This was odd, Della thought, as she tried to come awake. Could there be something in her bed? But she wasn't in bed, she realized, as she felt a sloshing around her legs. Had she fallen asleep in the bath? When she opened her eyes, she was looking up into a clear blue morning sky. Raising her head, she saw little red points sticking up in front of her. Her red painted toenails. She giggled. It felt oddly comfortable, carried here on whatever water this was, and surrounded by her floating cotton abaya and reeds. Reeds! Like the baby Moses at the edge of the river. She felt the rush of her pulse throbbing, and as she looked down again at her toes, her heart

1

pounded in her throat. Did she see two yellow points of light blinking out in the river beyond the curve of her left foot? Yellow eyes. She had to get out of here. The crocodiles could be anywhere.

She struggled to put her foot down through the reeds, finding mushy muck below, and almost passed out as the entire universe spun around her, punctuated with bright red spots. She knew she was going to vomit any minute, but still she stretched out her hands to grab hold of some of the tall greenery beside her. Sudden pain shot up her left wrist as she touched the stiff green bristles. Something there must be broken.

Remembering that snakes also loved the reedy shore of the Nile, she made herself struggle forward, dizzy and slipping as she tried to stand up, moving towards what seemed to be the muddy bank, refusing to think about what she might be stepping on. Moving was torturously slow, and as the vomit came, she sank down into the shallow murky water to hold on until she could stop heaving. Bile rushed into her mouth and into her nose. . .

She ached everywhere with pain, but more so in her stomach, and arm, and her head. Della knew she had to choose to not look too closely, not to think about this, and pulled herself up and began to wobble forward again. She wasn't sure how long all this was taking. Was she moving fast enough? Each tickle on her ankle could be the first brush of the massive bite of a crocodile or the stinging puncture of a snake's fangs. Would she even know it when she was bitten, she wondered, as she tried to stay level and keep moving? Would she just notice the sleepiness as the venom took effect? Would the first sign of the deadly bite be the relief of the pain in her arm and stomach as the venom coursed through her bloodstream and dulled her senses?

Soon she began to feel more solid earth beneath her feet and she fell onto her knees and crawled up the muddy, sandy shore, and then slowly, so slowly, up the bank. She couldn't put any weight on her left arm because the pain was too intense. So she crawled lopsidedly, like a big wounded crab, up the bank out of the reeds. But she knew she still wasn't safe here. A crocodile could easily pull her off such a low rise. She stopped to catch her breath.

Ahmad ! . Where was he? Was he injured, too? ? It was hard to focus her eyes in the pain and the new dawn brightness, and as she turned, the dizziness came back with a rush. But she could see the river behind her, and there was nothing there. No sign of a boat. ? ?

"Ahmad!" she cried out, but as she heard the sound, she knew he wouldn't hear her even if he was ten feet away. Her voice was as weak and wavery as she felt.

"Ahmad!" she tried again.

Della noticed that something was moving at the edge of the reeds near the open water. Was something riding by on the current? No, it was swimming. It was coming towards her. She had to go.

She crawled higher up the bank and kept on crawling. She had to keep moving. ? . Her abaya was shredded and coming off in pieces and slowing her down, so she pulled what bits she could away from her. Maybe the croc would be deceived by the black cloth she left behind. . . She kept crawling, dragging herself, mostly using her right hand.

There was a regularly traveled road ahead, she thought. It went between Luxor and Aswan, and if she could get to the roadside, someone would see her. But how far was it to the roadside? The pain and dizziness came again in a big wave.

Della came awake to discover that she was prone, her face in the dirt and the hot sun beating on her back. Thirst twisted itself up through her aching chest and throat, and she looked around for some kind of shade. . Ahead of her was stand of date palms, maybe. Three of them together. How far were they? Fifty meters? It might as well be a mile. But she must get out of the sun, so she couldn't think about the distance. What time was it? Was the sun directly overhead? She didn't dare look up towards the sky to check, because if she got dizzy again and passed out, she would fry out here. She began to inch forward.

The next time she woke, she was on a bench or bed, and it was bumping up and down and moving. She was on her back, with her head on something soft. She opened her eyes and saw the padded ceiling of a car. Then she tried to turn onto her side so she could sit up and she heard herself groan with pain.

"Is she waking up?" The words were in Arabic.

"Maybe. Take a look." A second man.

Della rolled her head and looked towards the front seat. A dark head full of hair and tbrown eyes peered over the seat at her. She could see the top of a dark beard.

"Yes, she's waking up. How far is it yet?"

"Not far. Maybe 30 kilometers. It will be fine."

The windows were open. No air conditioning. In June, in southern Egypt. And the seat back in front of her was taped together and stained. Who were these men?

She made a decision and asked in English, "Where am I and who are you?" She could barely hear herself.

The driver answered her. His English carried a British accent. "We found you out by the side of the road under a palm. We are taking you to Aswan to get help. Were you in an accident?"

"Yes, an accident, in the river."

"The river is a long ways from where we found you. How long ago?"

But the woman on the seat didn't answer. She had fallen back asleep or passed out again, and Nigel watched her off and on, in the rearview mirror, rocking gently on the backseat of the van as he kept driving.

They were late, and Nigel knew Gamal would be upset. Gamal was always upset when any little thing didn't go perfectly. Which was very funny, Nigel thought, because things were rarely perfect, much less on time, in this part of the world. But they could hardly have left her there. And if they had tried to call for a rescue, they might have been identified, and he knew that Gamal would not want that to happen. He thought there was a hospital just outside the north end of Aswan, and they could take her there on the way to the warehouse. Gamal would never need to know about it.

They had almost missed her and would have driven right past her if Youseff hadn't needed to take a leak. The stand of palms looked like a good enough place for a little bit of cover, and there she was, lying on the ground under the tree farthest from the road. At first he thought she was dead, but when he kneeled down to check her wrist, she stirred. He tried to wake her, but the best he could do was to get her to mutter some nonsensical words in English. She called out some Arabic names and then faded back into whatever dark reality she was trapped in. Nigel had seen symptoms like these before, of course, in the desert, from the effects of extreme thirst. But severe dehydration usually didn't occur so near the river and human habitation. And he had never seen a red-haired white woman in that condition.

He and Youseff got several mouthfuls of their warm bottled water into her and then got her into the backseat of the panel van. They were too far from Qena to go back, but it was better to take her to Aswan anyway. She looked young and strong and not really likely to die on them. They would drop her off at a hospital there. With any luck she would never know how she got there. The plane in Cairo had landed behind schedule too, so that had made them doubly late, and when he had called Gamal to let him know, he had been even terser than usual.

"What was the delay?" he parsed out across the wireless space from Aswan.

"Pietor said that the weather was bad in London and everything was delayed. He just had to wait his turn."

"*Min falak*," said Gamal. "It is always bad weather in London. What is different?"

"Not sure, Gamal, but it is early summer up there and that usually means big rain storms, you know."

Gamal had trouble understanding northern European weather, or wet weather at all, for that matter. He had been born and raised in Egypt and rarely left. He had been to London and to New York but in each case was happy to get back home and away from all the infidels and the craziness. Gamal, like many Egyptians, was just fine with 120° searing heat, but he froze if it the thermometer dropped below 75.

Nigel had had to build up a resistance to the heat, and it took him several years. On a lark, he had gone along on a cheap trip to Egypt with some school friends from Wales during winter holiday. And it changed everything. He returned to school to change his major to Archeology and never looked back. That was 17 years ago, and now he loved these old brown hills and the magical colors of the desert. But mostly he loved the thrill of the search for artifacts, for remnants of what was one of the world's greatest civilizations: his beloved ancient Egypt.

The mystique he felt on that first visit was only slightly lessened by his need to make a living. After all there were plenty of artifacts, he knew, and many more likely than had been discovered. The museums couldn't keep them all – they would have to erect buildings miles wide to store them. It was just as well that he and his colleagues made some of the ancient treasures available to wealthy individuals around the world. And who was to say that they would not care for them more lovingly than some museum, visited by crowds of uneducated and unappreciative groups, old fat tourists with more money than sense. The people who ended up with the treasures Nigel found knew about the glory of ancient Egypt, they knew about the details of the eras and the reasons that each item was precious. They appreciated the artistic delicacy and nuances of the pieces. And they loved the items well enough to pay very, very well to own them.

He first met Gamal at a government reception for the new British ambassador and immediately disliked him. Gamal gave off the air of the sort of Egyptian who thinks he is of a superior class. Nigel had seen this attitude before, particularly in Egyptian taxi drivers in New York, and he didn't like it. It was true that the ancient Egyptians were the first to develop an amazing civilization, but that didn't mean that today's citizens could take credit for it. Hardly. Although he did wonder if the country would have as many problems with crime and corruption and poverty if they were still governed by the softly gloved bronze fist of a strong pharaoh. Of course, Nigel had to admit he had seen the same attitude in some of his British countrymen, who still thought they were part of a world- dominating British Empire.

There were lots of stories about Gamal, hints of things that were never actually talked about. It was rumored that when he was a boy, his wealthy father was frequently visited by King Farouk, and that he took quite a liking to little Gamal. Gamal, had, as expected, gone into his father's lumber business but then tried his hand at acting and had become somewhat famous, thanks in no small part to his roughhewn looks and smoldering chemistry with leading ladies. His career was to have included some significant western films, but then he had had to move to London because President Nasser's international travel restrictions interfered with his ability to get to the sets. That was when Gamal apparently realized he hated cold wet weather and had no tolerance for western thinking. Nigel knew that at least part of this story was true, but Gamal had long since found other ways to make a living in his "superior" homeland.

At the end of that first party, he had brushed by Gamal as he was leaving and Gamal had stopped him.

"I didn't realize that you worked for the Oxford *Journal of Archeology*," Gamal said. "I thought you were just another of those useless archeologists that have infested our country."

"So it is alright if I'm an archeologist as long as I write about it in scientific journals?"

"Yes, it is a good living."

"Well, not really. But a little better, I think, than most archeologists."

"We must talk about that some time."

"Really? Why?"

"I may have a story for you to report on. A story that will pay very well."

"OK, what sort of a story? Are you aware of some new discoveries?"

"I must go now. I'll call you to set up a meeting."

"When?" Nigel called out to the closing door of the SUV as it pulled out into Cairo traffic.

Nigel didn't hear from Gamal for six months. Then one day, while he was sitting at an outdoor café near his flat on the outskirts of the Ma'adi district, enjoying his English newspaper and his morning coffee, Gamal quietly sat down at his table.

"Would you like to take a drive today?"

"Well hello there, Gamal. What brings you to this café this morning?"

"It isn't the coffee. I can take you where the coffee is much much better."

"I like the coffee here, Gamal."

"You will like the coffee where I'm taking you even more."

Gamal was a tall, well-built man with a full moustache. He had a full head of closely clipped pale gray hair: salt and pepper with more salt. His still dark brows set off his eyes, which were almost black. The whole impression was slightly sinister, slightly aristocratic. If eyes were the windows to the soul, Gamal had one-way glass in his. Nigel could see that this was a powerful man who was used to controlling and who expected to have his way. When he offered up a disarming grin with perfect white teeth, Nigel found himself intrigued.

"Okay, then. Let's take a ride." Gamal's smiled.

Nigel was still not sure why he had trusted Gamal enough to go with him. But it was a good thing he had.

Gamal was at the wheel of the Land Rover, no ubiquitous Egyptian driver today. As they drove, Gamal began to ask Nigel questions about his work and why he stayed in Egypt year round and didn't travel back to his British home-land like so many other rcheologists. He queried him about his knowledge of Egyptian history and turned to smile, once, while the Rover hurtled forward over the bumpy highway at 90 kilometers an hour, saying, "You seem to know your stuff, Nigel. Why didn't you take a job in a museum or teaching?"

Nigel grabbed hold of the gripper above his passenger window and said "I'd rather be out in the sunlight and real air, instead of trapped in a lab or classroom. I did my stint in those places and I'm done with that. Besides, even though it is hard work, it would take me years to work up to the money I make now, freelancing."

"I hear that this kind of work can be feast or famine as they say."

"Yes, I suppose. But so far I've found the world is always hungry for more information on ancient Egypt. So while it hasn't been exactly feast, it hasn't been famine – so far, anyway."

He looked at Gamal. "I've heard rumors of some new discoveries that the museum in Cairo is going to announce soon."

"Really?" Gamal flashes him a Cheshire cat smile. And then he started laughing. "Those are nothing compared to what is still out there."

After navigating the Cairo traffic, Gamal had driven them south down the Maryouteya Road past the exit to the Saqqara region, then along the El Marazeek-Dashoor Highway out into the desert, leaving the plush green of the Nile valley behind. The passed the Dahshur Red pyramid to the south, and after a few more kilometers they turned south on a smaller, sandy road. A few more kilometers and they left the road altogether and plowed westward over the open ground, gently rising over a very low hill, and then cresting a small rise, down into a shallow valley.

They came to a stop at the beginning of a little wadi, a steeply banked gully that transected it. The area had once been much wetter, and greener, it was believed, but in the last six or seven thousand years, it had been extremely dry. Anything buried within, or beneath, the sandy earth during that time tended to be preserved. While in other parts of the world mold and mildew destroyed artifacts, Egypt's extreme dryness mummified everything.

Gamal parked near the mouth of the wadi, which was now mostly filled with sand, although there were still bumpy remnants of the gravelly bed. "Let me show you something," he said, as he got out.

"I daresay we are not going to get any coffee out here."

"Better. Coffee is later."

Gamal led the way and after 20 meters or so the wadi turned a little to the left and some bigger rocks were spread along one bank. In the bright sun the crevices between them were in deep shadow, and then Gamal stepped down between two rocks and his head began to lower into the earth. Nigel walked over and watched as he descended into a very deep hole, and when his eyes were level with the edge of the hole, he motioned for Nigel to follow.

"A tomb? Here? "

"You will see."

What Nigel saw, after following Gamal down the rope and wood slat ladder, was a long square tunnel, with floor, walls, and ceiling made from precisely carved giant blocks of stone. The seams between the blocks were almost perfect, and the bl0ocks. were smooth and undecorated. Gamal led the way in, away from the bright shaft of sunlight, and turned on his flashlight, shining it on the walls for Nigel to see.

"It is beautiful. When did you find it? Were there any artifacts?"

"Three months ago. It appeared to be empty until we found the small chamber behind a false wall. No one had gotten there before us. It was very exciting – some lovely pieces. I'll show you later."

"Where are they? They're not here?"

"No, they were removed. Otherwise we would have round-the-clock guards."

"The construction almost looks 2nd dynasty."

"Yes. Very late 2nd dynasty."

"Wow, that's quite rare. And here of all places, so far from Abydos. What a find! Do you think it's an unknown pharaoh or royal official? What is the date range?"

Gamal turned from his crouch and faced Nigel, holding his flashlight so that the light made a circle on the stone floor.

"Our experts have dated the tomb to about 2675. After Khasekhemwy. But there is no official date range because the tomb has not been reported."

Nigel stared back at Gamal. He said nothing for several minutes. He knew that Gamal couldn't have reported the artifacts either, because it was required by Egyptian law that each artifact had a location and complete data on who had found it, who funded the find, and how it was handled. Even digging in the first place required official pre-approval. And there were the permits. Lots of permits. Permits that took lots of official time to acquire. It also occurred to Nigel that he was very likely committing a crime by just standing here.

Gamal continued to crouch and wait, saying nothing.

"Why exactly am I here, Gamal?"

"Well, I was simply hoping that you might be able to provide some information."

"Information?" The anger was creeping into his voice, but Nigel knew his only way back to Cairo was standing in front of him.

"Just some names."

"What names? Let me guess. You need the names of some ancient Egyptians who might be connected to this region from the 2nd dynasty."

"Close." Gamal smiled his disarming smile again, but only with his mouth. His eyes stayed clear and cold. "But not quite. However, the names of some modern non-Egyptians who would like to be connected to artifacts from the 2nd dynasty would be excellent."

"Of course. And, I suppose, these names should have the resources to pay well for such precious things."

"That's the idea. Yes."

"Just names?"

"Just names. And, of course, contact information."

Nigel had to think about this. He could be thrown out of the country, a disaster for someone who made his living reporting on archeological research in Egypt, or worse he could be thrown in jail and not allowed to leave the country. Either way this would be a catastrophe. On the other hand, after all his years of reporting, he knew that illegal trading of unofficial artifacts was very big business. The government tried to prevent artifact theft, but there were so many things buried in the sands of Egypt and so many people who wanted to own a piece of this civilization, that it was almost impossible to keep it under control. Nigel also knew that, because it was a dangerous business, a list of names might pay very well. "And how exactly would I be involved?"

"Ah, that's the best part. You would not be involved at all. I would give you an initial deposit, and then you would get a small bonus'for each sale. Only that. Nothing more would be required of you. No one will even know where we got their name."

Nigel wondered still, to this day, that he had fallen for it. Because of course there had been more, much more.

Nigel refused to give Gamal an answer while he was trapped in the empty tomb, and. Gamal was gracious and took him to a café near the Khan al-Khalilil bazaar in Cairo, and then he drove him back to Nigel's tiny flat.

Nigel waited a full week to call Gamal back, and by the second day, he wondered if he was being watched. One morning, while having his usual coffee and the standard Egyptian breakfast of fava bean dip with flat bread, he looked up from his table and saw a man he knew he had seen the day before over near the Hilton Hotel – a different side of town. Perhaps it was his imagination. Or nerves. He wasn't used to thinking like a criminal, after all, and had probably watched too many cop shows.

It wasn't so much that Nigel actually knew the people on the list he would be giving to Gamal, but more that he knew who they were after years of reading and writing about and for them. And he had access, through his scientific colleagues, to names of university research donors as well as sponsors of events to show off and therefore to raise money fo, field operations in Egyptology. He had just met his deadline for on an article in the JEA on the heated debate about the chambers beneath the Giza plateau when he decided to go ahead with it. It was only a list of names, after all.

"What kind of percentage should I be expecting, Gamal, from this list?"

They were meeting again over drinks, but this time it was late in the day and they sipped cups of strong tea flavored with crushed mint.

"Very small, Nigel. It is only, after all, a list."

"What is very small, Gamal?"

"Perhaps 5%."

"Of what?"

"Of the net proceeds from each sale."

"How will I know what is sold and how much is paid?"

"You won't. And it is better that you don't know. You must trust me."

"No offense, Gamal, but I hardly know you. Why do you think I should trust you?"

"Ah, a good question. I have thought of that. I'll make a small deposit, to secure your confidence."

"After I give you the list."

"No, now. In fact, I have already done it. I have the receipt with me."

Gamal dug into his brown leather case and pulled out a crumpled piece of paper. It looked as though it had been run over with a dirty tire. He handed it to Nigel.

"Put this away and look at it later. It isn't good to be surprised in public. You never know who is watching."

Nigel knew that, if he did prepare this list and opened this relationship with Gamal, that he would need to look over his shoulder from now on. And he almost decided then and there to forget the whole thing. But when he got home, he pulled the piece of paper out of his jeans and saw that it was a deposit slip for his London bank account. Gamal had put the equivalent of 10,000 pounds Sterling into his account two days before.

He delivered the list to Gamal a week later.

Gamal left him alone for six months and then asked for a "small bit of help" with the identification of an unusually tiny canopic jar and lid. The jar was from a much later time period than the 2nd dynasty, and so Nigel now knew that Gamal must have other resources besides that one tomb.

Five years later Nigel wasn't just providing names of potential buyers and an occasional date estimate. He was sometimes helping to arrange the transport of certain items to and from certain buyers. He also provided expert authentication and, using a pseudonym, signed ersatz certificates as to the date and authenticity of some of the artifacts. But lately he had had the feeling that this wasn't all that was going on. He suspected that Gamal's operation was much wider and broader than what he personally knew about. Of this he was alternately glad and worried. Better that he know as little as possible about any of this, he thought, thinking it might be possible to claim ignorance if he ever got caught. But sometimes he worried about what Gamal's other agendas could be. There had been hints, Nigel thought, of darker things. Gamal had a militant side to him that Nigel had glimpsed a few times. It had scared him.

Now the woman in the back seat began to moan and call out words again, some in English, some in Arabic. Some that he didn't recognize. They were just coming to the outskirts of Aswan, and he would get off the road and ask about the hospital.

"Call Gamal, Youseff. Tell him we are coming into Aswan and will be there soon."

Nigel knew that Gamal would wait for a few minutes and then raise the corrugated door to the warehouse so they could drive inside without stopping. It would hardly matter if the door stood open for a few extra minutes.

TWO

The undercover agent gently moved the frayed draperies around the front of the thick black cylinder. The cloth was crumbling and ripped, filled with dust and dirt, but he was careful to keep them clear of the concave glass of the telephoto lens. He reached down and gently pushed on the tripod to see if it was stable. No movement. It was solidly in place in spite of the uneven floor. Reaching for the timer cord on his right, he connected it to the back of the camera and reviewed the whole setup one more time. He turned on the camera. Nothing happened.

He stood back from the apparatus and waited for perhaps a minute, although it seemed longer. He was sure he had set it up correctly. He moved to the back of the small dim room, where the kettle was coming to a boil over the little fire he had built in the ring of concrete pieces. He squatted and poured hot water into the dirty glass he had filled with tea leaves and waited while it steeped. Still nothing. He reached into a pocket in his backpack and found a packet of honey and added the whole of it to the tea.. He settled down cross-legged on the floor, cupping the glass in his hands, to savor the feel of the hot liquid on his lips, his tongue, his parched throat.

Click.

So he must have set the timer to start later than he had thought.

He continued to sit, unmoving except to raise the tea to his lips, in the dusky empty cave-like room, hearing only the occasional vehicle pass by outside on the quiet industrial street.

Click.

Soon he would rise and pick up his canvas backpack and quietly slip into the hall, then climb the stairs to the roof and walk over to another flat-topped roof where he would disappear beneath laundry hanging motionless in the mid-day sun. But first he would wait just a little longer and finish his tea.

Click.

He smiled softly to himself. He had accidently discovered one of master-mind Gamal's warehouses. This information would be worth a great deal of money to his clients in Tel Aviv. He would have the proof very soon.

Nigel pulled over to the side of the road.

"Youseff, ask someone where the hospital is."

"Okay, but I think it is on the other side."

"Just ask, okay?"

"Okay yes."

There were few people walking in the street. It was still mid-day break and most were holed up in their homes or shops, resting through the crest of the heat after the main meal of the day. Nigel pulled up in front of a storefront whose doors were still open. It looked like the store sold sundries, which was probably why the doors were still in the open, up position. Youseff got out and disappeared into the dark cavern of the entrance. He came out a a few minutes later.

"Other end of city. "

"But isn't there a new hospital on this side?"

"No. Other end of Aswan. That way," he said and pointed in the general direction of the dam."

"Damn."

Youseff said nothing. Nigel knew that Youseff was used to his swearing and that he didn't approve. He was a very religious man. Nigel wasn't sure how Youseff justified being a devout Muslim and also working for Gamal, but he didn't question him. He just stopped to let Youseff pray whenever he asked.

The cell buzzed.

"Gamal," said Youseff, hitting the button.

Youseff listened and then turned towards Nigel. "How long now?" he asked. At first Nigel didn't answer. He continued to drive along looking for stores that didn't have their metal doors pulled down. Maybe they could get a better answer if they asked someone else.

Then Nigel took the phone from Youseff and put it to his ear.

"We are almost there. No, I'm looking for a hospital. Well, not exactly. We found a woman, by the side of the road, half-way down from Qena. Yes. No. No, she seems to be English. Not sure. White with red hair. It seems it is on the other end of town. Ah! You're probably right. That would work. We'll come right away."

Gamal had pointed out that if they went to the hospital, there was the possibility that someone would write down their license plate number. Nigel hadn't thought of that. He wasn't used to subterfuge, he realized. And he also realized that he was tired of trying to remember to think that way.

The woman in the back seat had been quiet for the last half hour. Nigel was beginning to wonder if he had really screwed up. What if she didn't make it? Would she have had a better chance if they had just driven by and left her there? No. She hadn't even been visible from the road, and they had only found her by chance. The likelihood that she would have been found before she slipped into a coma from severe dehydration was slim.

They pulled the van off the main road and wandered through a number of side streets, down a narrow street that would have been considered an alley in a western city, and then turned right, and there it was, just as Gamal had said: an open door into a warehouse. It had been a hot trip and Nigel was glad when they pulled into the cooler interior of the big room and heard the grinding of the creaky metal door come down behind them.

The only light inside came from high windows to the roof on a mezzanine above them, above a misshapen metal catwalk. There were large crates spread around the sides and the back of the darkened space, stacked ups, and a number of huge burlap bags arranged in front of the crates. There was a strong fragrance in the air. Spices! Nutmeg, clove, cardamom, and cinnamon — and what else? Peppercorns? Nigel hadn't realized that Gamal also traded in spices. But it made good sense. Large burlap bags full of fragrant seeds and bark would be excellent packing material for fragile ancient artifacts. And who would want to dig around in one of those massive bags, taller than most men, to inspect it?

"She is young." Nigel realized that Gamal was standing by the side of the van and looking through the open window at the woman.

"Yes. Let's call a taxi and have them take her to the hospital."

"Let's move her first."

"Move her? That sounds risky. Where?"

"There is a good place just down the street."

"You propose we carry an unconscious woman through the streets? We'll be seen."

"No. We'll use carpets. I have carpets."

On the other side of the warehouse were stacks of carpets, carpets intended for sale to tourists.

Nigel looked at the face of the young woman as the three of them carefully pulled her from the back seat and moved her to the stack of carpets. She was very pale. Her jeans and blouse were dirty and torn, she had bloody patches on the ripped denim over her knees, her bare feet were scratched, grimy, and dusty. There were bruises on her face and neck and one arm. But there was no telling what else was wrong with her.

Just then she opened her eyes and looked up at him. Her eyes were an arresting deep green. Suddenly Nigel was afraid she was going to scream, but instead she opened her mouth wide and smiled up at him – a wonderful wide smile – and mumbled "thank you" in Arabic. Her eyes were dilated, and the expression on her face was serene. Was she lucid or perhaps only partially aware of what was happening to her? She seemed fragile and beautiful and he couldn't imagine how such a lovely creature would have found herself under that palm. Her eyes closed again, as she sunk back into unconsciousness. He tucked her hair around the back of her head, as they centered her on a carpet that was half again as long as she was and then, before he could stop himself, he whispered, "Don't worry, it will be alright. We are getting you some help." He didn't think she heard him, her eyes remained closed, but Nigel had a profound and strange feeling in his gut as if she was very important to him, even though he didn't even know her name.

Nigel asked Gamal if he could take her to the hospital and tell them that he was just out doing some photos for an article. But Gamal and Youseff were already moving the rolled-up carpet and Gamal didn't answer him.

They pulled up the door and Youseff and Gamal carried the bundle several stacked and rolled carpets down and across the street to what had a tenement house. It was abandoned now, probably condemned. Gamal had gestured for Nigel to stay behind, and Nigel knew it was because he had sandy blond hair and Nordic blue eyes and would be too noticeable in this area, even wearing his keffief,. Youseff and Gamal came back in less than ten minutes with the carpets, and then Gamal phoned someone who would call the hospital and report a white woman who was injured and lying on the floor of the old building.

Nigel sat near the wall of the warehouse on the stack of carpets watching Gamal as he made the call and then watched him as he walked towards him.

"We have worked well together," said Gamal, "but if you ever do anything like this again, that's the end. You will never see me again. Ever."

"Gamal, we couldn't just leave her. She would've died."

"Ever."

"It is hardly likely to happen again, Gamal. There isn't a thing to worry about. She doesn't know us and we don't know her."

"My friend, I'm very <u>very</u> serious. Remember what I say. Never."

"Got it."

"Now let's go. Take the parcel you brought with you. Youseff, there is a stack of wood in the corner. Bring two long pieces."

"Are we going to carry the crate? We had to move it ourselves in Cairo and the damn thing is really heavy."

"There is no need to swear, Nigel. It isn't necessary."

"Alright, then. But it really is VERY heavy."

"Yes. But we leave immediately and we can't leave it behind. Put it on top of the two boards – like a stretcher."

The crate that Nigel and Youseff had driven down from Cairo was clearly handmade, a little more than a meter and a half square, and it easily weighed at least 100 pounds. It was both very heavy and very awkward. Gamal insisted it was very fragile and that it could absolutely not be dropped. Nigel had to admit that strapping the crate to the two long thick boards would provide much more stability than just his and Youseff's arm strength had at the Cairo airport in the middle of the night. Was that only last night? It seemed like a week ago.

After getting the box lowered onto the boards and tied down securely with rope, they rolled twelve carpets and slid them into the van, filling up more than half of the cargo space. Gamal insisted that they look at the back seat of the van in case there was anything that the woman left behind.

"Like blood?" asked Nigel. "She wasn't bleeding."

"Look, please, carefully."

And sure enough, they found six long red hairs on the seat and on the floor. Gamal took them, folded them into a scrap of brown shipping paper, and placed it on top of the crate.

The three men went single file, with Gamal leading and Nigel and Youseff carrying the stretcher, through a small, back door into a very narrow alley, one that had recently been used for a toilet. Stepping over what was clearly human offal, they edged their way slowly along the back of the warehouse in the stifling, reeking heat. They came to a street, but instead of proceeding, Gamal led them around into another even narrower alley, where they continued behind several more buildings until they came to a staircase that jutted out from a wall and led toward the roof of one of the buildings. The rise of the stairs was very deep, about 24 inches each, and the stairs themselves were narrow and not level, but the men were able to maneuver and juggle the awkward parcel up the incline, with Gamal continually saying "Careful, be careful! Fragile, I remind you!"

The weight seemed to have increased since they started, but Nigel knew it was just the heat getting to him. It could easily be 120 today, especially between the walls of the buildings in the narrow alleys. Just past half-way up the staircase, there was a little alcove, which seemed from below to be a wider stair but turned out to be a low door into an attic room. It was larger than it looked and Nigel could see some other crates and what looked like sculptures in the shadows around the edges. They were just able to move the crate and themselves inside past the iron grate that was wedged open and get out of sight when they heard someone walk by in the alley below.

The three men sat on the cement floor, under the low ceiling, dripping with sweat and catching their breath. Nigel looked over at Gamal, who was staring at him with his penetrating eyes. Nigel knew that he didn't want to be part of this business anymore, but he didn't think that Gamal would allow him to simply disconnect and walk away. Unless it is his idea, he thought. Was Gamal's threat to dismiss him only the anger of an always tense man whose plans had been disrupted? Perhaps there was some hope of getting out of this arrangement. As they sat sweating and trying to slow their breathing in the stifling room, Nigel was glad he didn't know what was in the crate.

The pale pink wall came into focus. Della noticed the itch of the IV line in her arm at the same time that she heard the quiet clicking of the machines above her head. She was in the hospital. She vaguely remembered being moved in an ambulance. She had just gotten here, she thought, today. But she was confused. Why was she here? And had it just been yesterday that someone lifted her from a gurney onto this bed? Maybe a day – two at the most. The last thing she remembered was riding home from the office with the driver. Ahmad was driving. They must have been in a crash. A bad one.

Hers was the only bed in the room, but there were some chairs that looked like they had been moved around. And a cabinet in the corner had two bouquets of flowers. Had Sameh brought them? The window that went across the whole side of the room had curtains that were pulled, but since no one was around, Della decided she would get up and go over to the window. She would be able to look out over Luxor, because the hospital was on a slight slope at the edge of the city. She slowly sat up and was able to move her legs over the side of the bed, then began to get up, when she was stopped by the pull of the IV line. It was connected to a rolling pole, and stretching her arm out, she pulled at it a little and it moved towards the bed. All she needed to do was lean on the pole, hold onto the bed, and edge towards the window. This wasn't going to be too hard.

She almost made it around the end of the bed, maybe three or four steps, before she fell to the floor, pulling the pole and the bag of fluid with her. She made lots of noise as she fell in the silent hospital. As she tried to sit up, she saw three sets of feet coming toward her. She looked up at the women in their bright scrubs and tried to smile. Their faces were crestfallen and frightened. .

"I want to looked out the window," she said.

"You need to push the button for help, Mrs., please. You're still very weak, and we'll be happy to help you." The head nurse had spoken to her in English. All three women helped her into bed and pulled up the bed rails. Two of the aides left the room and the younger one, the one who had almost smiled, brought her a warm blanket and fluffed her pillow for her.

"Okay. Can you take me now?" Della was surprised that Arabic was coming out of her mouth. But she noticed that she was talking very slowly. It seemed like a long time since she had talked in any language.

"We have put a call into Dr. Habibi. He will decide."

"May I talk to him?"

"Yes. He will be here later this evening."

"Is Dr. Habibi the blond man with the blue eyes?"

"No, Mrs. He is Egyptian. He isn't blond. We have no blond doctors here."

"Then who was the blond man who helped me?"

"Perhaps someone at Aswan, Mrs."

"Aswan? I was at Aswan?"

"Yes, Mrs. And now you're here, in Cairo. You will feel better soon."

"Cairo?"

"Yes, the Dar el Fouad Hospital. It is the best hospital in Egypt."

The nurses couldn't reach Dr. Habibi and they refused to let her go over to the window, even in a wheelchair, but they did agree to open the curtains. And the friendly young aide helped her to sit up, with pillows to support her, so that she could see out, and there, spread across the whole window was the jeweled city. She wished she could remember coming here. She wished she could remember what had happened.

She was offered some soup and ate a little but then was very tired again. She was on the verge of sleep when Sameh arrived, carrying a big bouquet of red Shasta daisies. Her husband knew that she loved red flowers. Walking in behind him was her father, who began to cry as he came to her bedside and took her hand in his. Della pushed down her surprise. He looked tired and worn, but a little better than he had before his bypass. It was wonderful to see him smile at her.

"We thought we'd lost you," he whispered as he bent down to kiss her cheek. Seeing her father standing there weeping scared her. She knew there had been an accident and she knew something was wrong with her, but when she looked into her father's eyes, she realized that whatever had happened was bad.

"What is wrong with me?"

"Nothing that time won't heal," said Sameh. She turned to look at her husband. He was giving her that warm grin he usually saved for when he was teasing her. Was it relief she saw in his eyes?

Sameh was holding her hand and rubbing her palm. She smiled for him. Hello, Sameh. She realized she had only thought these words, not spoken them out loud, and so she tried again.

"Hello, Sameh. They are beautiful flowers." It took a lot of effort to speak.

"Hello, my sweet Della. You have been through a lot but we have found you and now all you need to do is rest. Your father will stay and visit with you for a few more days, so if you need to sleep now, sleep. We are both here and you're safe now."

She thought maybe there was something else that she should ask Sameh, but what was it? .

"You must not worry about anything, Della. You're going to be just fine. You will have the best care possible."

She turned back to her father. "Dad, I'm so sorry you had to come so far. I promise I'll be okay." Now she felt tears coming into her eyes. She wished she could hug her father. She hadn't realized how much she had missed him. She loved him so much.

Della knew she was fading again, and she felt her dad squeeze her hand and Sameh on the other side patting her arm as she fell back to sleep. They are both such good men, she thought, and then she slipped back into a lovely dreamlessness.

She awoke with a start to find herself alone again. Ahmad! What had happened to Ahmad? Ahmad had been driving. Loyal and devoted Ahmad. Had he survived the accident? Where was he? Was he here in this hospital?

Della found what she thought must be the nurse's call button and pushed it, and after a while a nurse in pale yellow scrubs came in.

"Do you need something?"

"Ahmad."

"Who is that, Mrs?"

"He was with me in that car crash and I need to know if he is alright."

"There was a car crash, Mrs?"

"Yes, that's how I was hurt."

"No, Mrs. You were found in Aswan. There was no automobile accident. They found you in an old abandoned warehouse. A very dirty one, I have been told. With vermin."

"A warehouse? What happened to me?"

"No one knows. You had many bruises and internal bleeding. The doctors are not sure what caused them."

"But, how can they—"

"Mrs, please. You can ask questions another time. It is the middle of the night now and time for you to sleep. You need to get lots of rest. You almost died."

"Is my father here?"

"No, Mrs. He has gone home to get some sleep too. He has been sitting by your bedside for two days and nights waiting for you to wake up."

"Two days?"

"Yes. Now please sleep, Mrs. Would you like me to bring you a pill to help you fall asleep?"

"No, thank you, nurse. But could you open the drapes again, please? I want to look out at the lights."

As Della tried to fall asleep, she watched the flickering lights of sleeping Cairo below her windows and she wondered where Ahmad was. She prayed that he was safe. She hoped that Allah was looking after him.

The next morning Merina came flowing in the door like a fresh breeze. She dropped shiny shopping bags on the floor, put a a bouquet on the table, leaned over Della, and then stopped. Hovering there, her beautiful face turned from a smile to a questioning look.

"Will it hurt you if I hug you?"

"No, Merina, I don't think so."

"Wonderful! I'm so relieved to see your smile and to know that you're going to be alright. I've been worrying about you."

Next she was pushing Della into the pillow with her tender hug, her luxurious red hair streaming around Della, who could smell the mango and jasmine scent she wore. Pulling back, Merina threw her arms and hands wide into the air beside her, the positions of her upraised fingers similar to a yoga position.

"There! I feel much better now!"

But then she was moving again, unpacking bags, taking things to the table in the corner, bustling about in her usual cheerful, in-charge style. Soon, catching her breath, this laughing chatting woman, this blessing of a mother-in-law, began to recite her litany of items in the bags: sachets for Della's sheets, lotion for her skin, several pretty pajama sets with a matching silk robe, two pairs of slippers, four books, an iPad Mini and a KindleFire HD in case that was easier, a hand-tooled leather cover for the iPad – red of course , three oranges, a banana, a few strawberries, and a business card for a manicurist who would come and do her toes and nails as soon as she made an appointment. And the name of the massage therapist who had already contacted the nurses to see when he could come and give Della the gentlest of massages to ease the frustration of being stuck so long in bed.

Della didn't know what to say. This woman was so different from any woman she had ever known, and she felt awkward about being showered with this much attention. It would be pointless to say something like "you shouldn't have." Merina simply wouldn't understand. She might even be hurt. Of all the people in the world Della didn't want to hurt, it was Merina.

Soon her mother-in-law had pulled a chair to the bedside and was talking about her daughters and the antics of their brothers, about a guitarist who was going to come and play and sing for her in the room, and something about Silva preparing a favorite dish for her, but Della had trouble following it all. She found she was drifting in and out. So when she looked up and saw Merina's face close to hers, she understood she must have fallen back asleep.

"Just rest, my dear. Very soon you will be home and we'll have such fun together. The girls are saving movies for us to watch together. And Ptolomy is all ready to sit in your lap and purr loudly for you. He has always loved you best, you know. But now, just rest. It is so wonderful to know you're doing better and better each day."

The last thing Della remembered was Merina patting her hand softly. Her hand had been warm and so soft. Just like Merina herself. Again Della had a nagging feeling that she should ask Merina something, but now she would rest until her father came again.

Wael Abbas looked up from his reverie. His son Masud was looking down at him with exasperation. He had been reading through some of the crime reports he had brought home from the office.

"What?"

"Did you hear what I said?" said his son.

"Well, no. Sorry."

"I'm going over to Zamir's to do homework, and I'll be back for dinner. I have my cell phone."

"Where is Rehema?"

"She's in her room doing her math assignment."

"Okay. But after dinner I have to go back to the office, so you will need to stay home with Rehema. I have to go to the office."

Wael had been trying to cut back on his hours at work so that he could spend more time with his children now that he both mother and father. But police work was crisis-driven, and as soon as they got one crisis under control, another would appear. It wasn't that there weren't intervals, times when things were quiet with only petty crimes coming across his desk, but it seemed like there was never enough time to write all the reports. His bosses loved reports. The chief of police, in particular, personally read every report that Wael wrote, which meant that Wael had to be sure to turn them in.

In fact, most of the chief detective job was routine in Luxor. Wael had an excellent list of the usual suspects for the standard petty thefts and robberies, and he had a great network of informants that he had slowly built up over his 15-year career. But every now and then something really interesting happened, and Wael got to flex his detective mind and use the skills that had gotten him his promotion seven years ago. And that's why he had to go back to the office this evening.

An interesting coincidence occurred in Aswan recently. The American wife of a prominent Luxor resident was found in a condemned building in Aswan, with abdominal injuries. She was severely dehydrated and near death. And on the same street, just a day later, a man was found strangled in another abandoned building. The man was bound and gagged and then strangled with some kind of a camera cord. No camera or ID was found. There was a burned-out fire on the floor with a metal pot on it. Surprisingly, it hadn't caused a fire. It seemed that that might have been the intention. The strangled man wasn't Egyptian, it seemed, but with no ID this couldn't be proved. He had desert-weathered skin, was bald, and wearing a kerif. But underneath his clothes he had very pale skin.

Manar, Wael's friend and the chief of police in Aswan, had called to inform him of the American wife, since she was a resident of Wael's city, Luxor. And then he called again to share the finding of the strangled man. And then he called a third time to ask Wael if he would like to help him with the either or both cases.

"Unofficially, of course," he had said.

"Of course," said Wael.

It was quite coincidental, Manar said, to have two incidents in one week on the same block in quiet Aswan. Wael had long since ceased believing in coincidences.

THREE

When Sameh walked into the chamber, Khalid Salama was standing with his legs wide apart. He was naked and facing the arched entrance while two servants rubbed his body with fragrant oil. Eucalyptus and clove scented the air. Both of the servants were very young men, almost boys, and both were wearing only tight thin Speedos. Sameh knew that Khalid knew he had entered the room, but he continued to lean his head back with his eyes closed.

Sameh was instantly furious and aroused.

Khalid was a beautiful man. He had a face like the famous Saleh Salim, with a broad brow, high cheekbones, and slender chin. His full lips had a permanent pout. His longish, silken hair was combed back across his head. Khalid was very proud of his walnut brown hair.

The proportions of his body were those of an ancient Egyptian tomb guard: a magnificent sculpture. All he needed was the headdress. He had a broad chest, a tight flat stomach, and a tight rounded ass that now protruded as he turned and bent over a little to allow one of his servants to rub the top inside of his legs.

"Stop this, Khalid."

"Why? It is very pleasant. Does it bother you?"

"Send them away. I want to talk with you."

Khalid opened his eyes and looked up to give Sameh a sharp look.

"So NOW you want to talk! Well, I'm busy at the moment, my dear Sameh. But if you want to talk, then talk. I can listen and enjoy my massage at the same time."

But Khalid did change position, turning his head to speak to one of the young servants, "Bring a towel and some pillows, Nasim. I wish to have you massage me while I'm lying down." He put his hands on his bare hips and then raised one arm and fluttered his fingers in the direction of the other room as the young man left to get the pillows. "And bring some rosemary oil."

Sameh knew that this whole scene was for show. Khalid likely had his spies alert him that Sameh would be arriving soon and then set the scene so that Sameh would be jealous and angry. And it had worked, thought Sameh, who was struggling with both his anger and a growing erection.

"Bring Khalid a robe, Nasim, and leave us," Sameh directed.

The two servants, whom Khalid had hired, were paid for by Sameh. They all resided in the rooms that Sameh paid for as well. And all of them knew this. In spite of this, the young servant Nasim looked to Khalid for approval before he turned to bring the robe. This brought more red into Sameh's cheeks. Khalid just smiled and then waved his hand and fluttered his fingers again and said, "Go. Do as our master commands."

"I'm not your master, Khalid. Don't speak this way to me."

"Why are you here? Is that wife of yours coming home soon?"

"She is still in the hospital. She will spend another week in a rehabilitation wing and then come to the family home in Cairo."

"I suppose that you will have to go home to her at night when she is here and not come to me. I'll hate that. I don't intend to be a good sport about it, just so you know."

"Khalid, this is very important for me. And that means it is important for us. Please understand that this is beyond my control. Of course I'll see you whenever I can, but I also have my family and the business to attend to. "

"I'll find a way to keep myself occupied when you're too busy. "

"Is this what I get for taking care of you?"

"Taking care of me? You won't even let me travel with you so we can have more time together!"

"I have explained this before! When I'm away on business, it is often with my father or with important clients, and it is essential there be no hint of scandal. No hint of a relationship such as ours. And my father, as you know, is hoping to get into the National Assembly this coming year, and it is critical to avoid any rumors. "

"You could always just tell him you have a male lover."

"He would have me shot. Or run me through with one of his antique swords. He would surely find a way to get me out of the family business. And then how would I support you, dear Khalid? How would I be able to provide you with the little trinkets you so love to buy?"

Sameh slid his fingers along Khalid's arm, lightly touching the golden arm bracelet that he wore. Khalid didn't usually wear jewelry, except for an earring sometimes, but this was a special gift from Sameh, and Khalid loved it. It wound around his arm just above his elbow, and was solid gold and beautifully crafted. It looked like it had been made for an ancient Egyptian prince. And it had.

"Your dear mother. That's the key. She will protect you."

"She can only do so much, Khalid. Besides, she liked it better when I was interested in many men and having discreet affairs. She used to arrange for me to meet prominent men, you well remember, because she introduced us. That was when she thought you had some influence, of course. She knows many secret things about the elite in this country, including who would like to have a secret encounter with a safe man. This is part of her plan for power, you see. She isn't at all happy that I have become so devoted to you. And she doesn't yet suspect that I have put you here, in this apartment. She would prefer that I remain available, of course, and that I have liaisons with rich, powerful men. You don't have money, Khalid, and you don't have power. Remember that."

"And you, my dear Sameh, remember that I'm hung, and gorgeous, and you love me, you want me." Khalid lay down on the pillows that Nasim brought, lay on his back, and began to stroke Sameh's ankle, as he stood over him, and to move around, raising his buttocks up in the air while doing little practice thrusts with his penis, which had become wonderfully large and stiff. He watched Sameh's eyes begin to glaze, looking down on Khalid, first at his cock, then into his eyes, as he felt the hand rubbing his ankle.

"Yes," Sameh said as he gazed down at Khalid's surprisingly large organ, much bigger than would be expected for such a small man. Sameh's lips parted and he bent down to stroke Khalid's cheek, then his bare hip, circling around his groin. Now Sameh kicked off his Moroccan leather slip-ons, then slipped off his black slacks, then his briefs, and kneeled barelegged in his t-shirt, placing both of his knees close together between Khalid's legs.

The two servants left the room and stood just outside the door. Nasim peaked around from one side of a drape as Sameh began to lick and then suck on Khalid's cock. He continued to watch as Sameh took off his t-shirt and rolled over to pull Khalid on top of him, and the two men made love on the pillows and on the floor, with Khalid's fragrant oils getting all over the parquet and the silk pillow fabrics.

Nasim loved working here, and he loved to watch Khalid having sex. When Kahlid had discovered that he had watched him with another of his lovers, one that Sameh didn't know about, of course, he had just laughed and said "You can watch and learn, my little one. And later I'll give you a test." Nasim had loved that test.

Later, as Sameh and Khalid rested, exhausted, towels, robe and clothing scattered everywhere, Khalid said, "I'm the only one you want, Sameh. Even though you may think you're fooling me, I know you're mine."

"Yes. It is true, Khalid." Sameh spoke softly, almost with regret.

"Except that part of you that belongs to your wife, I suppose."

"A wife is necessary for business and political status. You know this. It is important to have a family and a family life. In Allah's name, think about your own father. He is a perfect example of too much public philandering and not enough discretion."

"Please be kind, Sameh. You know you can say anything you want about my father, because I hate him. But I wish you would not. I hate to think about him. I wish he did like boys, rather than doing all those little girls. He is a very stupid man. He should have been a little careful, at least."

"Ah, just so. We have to be discreet, Khalid. Our future depends on it."

Sameh rose and went to the opening in the draperies to request that some tea be brought to them, so he didn't hear Khalid say under his breath, "Your future, Sameh, not mine."

Wael and his colleague Manar Ammar met in the street in Aswan where the two terrible events had happened. There was little to see in the abandoned tenement where the beggar had found the American wife. The bare room had dirt and rat feces on the floor, and a musky lemon smell that could be of snakes but little else. And if there had been any evidence of possible value, it was long gone, as the police didn't get back to the location until two days after Della was taken to the hospital. It had been a holiday week and Aswan, though now a city of almost a million, still had the relaxed style of the much smaller city it had once been.

The strangled man was found when the police searched the area nearby. Manar's men were close to finishing their routine canvassing when they discovered the body stretched out in an empty room in a building down the block. The room was one of many that had long been empty, because it was now a warehouse district, although decades ago people had lived in the rabbit warren tenements. Now they were empty and covered with big signs reading "danger of collapse" and "do not enter.". That didn't keep the squatters out, of course, and Manar dreaded the day when one of the buildings would collapse and kill people camping in them.

On the other side of the street, some effort had been made to reinforce the the salvageable buildings and the spaces were bigger, and so it was possible, even with poor construction, to make them safe enough for use. They were not supposed to be for living space, only for the storing of goods. Of course, as with much of Egypt, there was usually someone living in the warehouse for security reasons. Now, walking along the street, Wael pointed above and to his right and asked Manar, "So this window is the room where they found the man?"

"Yes, behind that window."

"Did you get a call? Did someone report the body?"

"No."

"How do you get to the second floor?" The only door to the building was boarded up and had barbed wire nailed across it.

"The stairs have collapsed, so you go to the next building, up on the roof, cross over, then down. The upper level stairs are still good enough to use."

"Have you figured out what he was doing?"

"No. No clues so far. Only the ring of concrete pieces that had a little fire in it."

"What about the cord? What kind of a camera does it go to?"

"It isn't really a camera cord, just a cord used to hook up electronic components. A very common item. It could be used for many things."

"Such as?"

"Anything on a timer. A light, a camera, a gun."

"But your first impression was that it was for a camera."

"Yes. But I don't have any basis for that. It is just a feeling."

"What is across from the window, here, behind this door up ahead of us?" The corrugated metal door the two men were just coming to was like most of the others in the region. It hadn't been painted for many years. He couldn't see a lock of any kind on the outside. Perhaps there was one inside. He knocked on the door. "Open up, police."

"It is just a warehouse. We have already been in it. Marble and stone, honey and spices, and a few other things. It is a small outfit."

"Who owns it?"

"A man named Faizel Wallah. Has a family on the other side of town. He inherited this space from his uncle. He drives a taxi for tourists and does a little trading business on the side."

Wael knocked again.

"We already interviewed him."

"And he wasn't there when these things happened, I suppose."

"Yes. He was working with a tour group from Sweden the whole week that these events happened. He knows nothing."

The creak of the door surprised the men. It moved up noisily, about one and half meters above the dirty gravel of the street, and a small dark head looked out from under the crinkled metal curtain of the suspended door.

"What is your name?"

"Poshti Al Kareem. I'm guard here. Work for Faisal Wallah."

"May we come in, Poshti?"

"Yes, come, come." The man bowed under the door and then the door moved up another meter or so and stopped.

After waiting about a minute to be sure that the door would not fall on them, Wael and Manar went into the warehouse. They had already noticed the strong odors that floated in the air of the open door and out into the street. The fragrance of spices. As Wael's eyes adjusted to the dimness, he noticed many large burlap bags of spices, beside which were buckets and small crockery jars. Along the back of the deep space was a large handmade wooden workbench, with stacks of flat cloth bags, scales, and several bolts of string. Around the edges of the two story walls were large crates, some of which were completely inaccessible because of the bags of spices. He saw an old panel van parked along the opposite wall. Its windows were down, and it had been hand-painted with white paint. The license plate looked to be the only up to date thing about the vehicle, which was probably 20 years old. But then he noticed that the tires looked new. There was dirt in their deep treads.

Poshti offered to give them a tour of the warehouse, and because it was cooler here inside and partly because of the wonderful smell, they agreed. He showed them the little office and some pieces of marble that he said there was more of and then, one by one, he showed them ten kinds of spices, some in only one bag, some in two or three. The local spice sellers come two days a week, he explained, filling the smaller cloth bags for their market stands.

"Would you like to have a sample?"

"No" said Manar, almost at the same time that Wael said "Yes."

"Just a small bag, for my sister-in-law. She loves to cook."

Poshti went to the work bench and got two bags, and then went to two of the largest burlap bags and using a scoop, placed one dollop of cardamom in a bag and then one scoop of nutmeg in another one.

"These are our best. She will like them!"

"How much do I owe you?"

"No charge! Just tell your sister-in-law to ask for "Spices from Faisal.""

Wael and Manar thanked him and turned toward the door. Out of the corner of his eye, Wael thought he saw something around the back of the parked van.

Poshti was reaching up to pull down the door when Wael said, "Excuse me. Are those rugs?"

"Rugs?"

"Carpets."

"Ah. Yes, carpets. We have also carpets. Most excellent carpets. Best in Aswan. Do you want to see?"

Wael had been hoping to find a good bargain on a carpet for his front room and had recently been trying to put aside the money to buy one. He hadn't found anything that he both liked and could afford, but perhaps he would find one here. Before it went to the bazaar and was expected to get a retail price.

"Yes, please." Wael noticed that the top one had a lot of blue in it, or so it seemed in the dimness as he stepped back inside the warehouse. He had been hoping to find a carpet with lots of blue.

"I go to get a light so you can see the color better," said Poshti, moving away from them into the other side of the cool fragrant cavern.

Wael immediately loved what he could see of the carpet on the top of the stack. It was a perfect size and color. He wondered, as he waited for Poshti to come back with the light, if he would be able to afford it.

The round cone of light from the flashlight shone on the weave and it was clear that this was likely a Karistan. Just perfect, Wael thought.

"Do you know how much?"

"No. My boss Mr. Faisel will have to give you very good price."

"When can you talk to him?"

"Maybe today, maybe tonight. He is driving. I try to call on his cell."

"Thank you, Poshti, I'll wait while you call him," said Wael.

"Maybe take a long time. You come back, or maybe I give you his number. You call Mr. Faisal."

"Yes. I can call. But I'll wait here, too."

Wael would wait because there, on top of this beautiful blue carpet, in the beam of the flashlight, he was looking at two very long red human hairs.

Della was moved to the rehabilitation wing and began to have regular physical therapy. She was feeling better but her strength lagged behind her determination. Sameh came to see her every morning and every evening, and he brought new flowers almost every day. Della's father stayed for a week and supervised her move to the rehab floor, but then he had to go home. He and Della had talked with her mother in Kansas on the phone twice, but it became apparent that things were not going well back home. Della overheard him talking with his employees, and then with his neighbor, and at least once with a teacher at her brother's school. Apparently hehad been skipping school but no one could be reached at home.

She hated to see her father leave, but more than that, she hated knowing that he was going back to so many problems. Her old anger with her mother was there as usual, but now she wondered if her father felt something similar about her mother, his temperamental and erratic wife. She had never thought of his life that way, but now she had to question what kept him going. It made her even more angry with her mother that her father should be so trapped.

Merina and the girls came to see Della every few days and brought her magazines, and make-up and some new earrings. They even played a little Scrabble one afternoon until Della fell asleep over the letters in her lap.

One afternoon, Della was sitting in bed, dozing, when an aide came to take her for a walk as part of her new physical therapy routine. As they turned the last corner and were heading back to her room, down at the end of the hallway she thought she saw a man she recognized. Could it be Ahmad? The PT aide was surprised that she wanted to walk down the corridor again, but he agreed. She felt weak but the man looked so familiar, she had to get a closer look. As she approached the man who was sitting in a chair in the tiny floor lounge, she realized that he was a stranger, but there was something about him, a title of his head, his posture, that arrested her. Then suddenly a scene came flooding into her mind like a movie; she saw her husband passionately, sexually, embracing a young man. A very handsome, even beautiful, young man. She gasped out loud. As suddenly as the image came, it left her mind and she stood, confused, flushed, her knees suddenly quaking. Where had this image come from? She had no idea why she was seeing this. Perhaps she had some brain injury in the crash. Would that explain it? If she told her doctors, they might make her stay in the hospital.

She realized that the PT aide was looking down into her face, holding on to her tightly.

"Are you alright, Mrs.?"

"Ah" was all she could get out.

The aide insisted she not move and called for a wheelchair on his radio. It arrived quickly. As he was pushing her back to her room, Della felt a knot growing in her stomach. Something was wrong. Something about Sameh. What was it?

"We did too much today, Mrs. Tomorrow we'll take it easier."

Sameh came into her room an hour later, smiling. "You look wonderful, Della! I think they will let you come home soon. Your face is almost glowing."

Della said nothing, but sat looking into his face. Who was this man, her husband?

Then Sameh's grin became sheepish, and he looked towards the door before he pulled a small brown bag out of his case. "You must not tell anyone about this. You must hide it." It was chocolate. Della loved strong dark chocolate.

She looked up into his eyes. He was smiling at her with his same wonderful wide grin, as he gently patted her arm. He was a kind man, perhaps even a good man, and he was her husband and he loved her and she had to be wrong about that vision. It was her mind playing tricks with her memory. The doctor explained that it was normal for all the short-term memory to be obliterated by a trauma. "It was waiting to be put into long term," he said, "and it just never made it. It is usually lost forever. This is often a good thing. The body is protecting itself from the terror of bad memories."

Della wasn't so sure. This vision seemed so real, like a true memory. But there was no context, just the scene. Sameh was talking to her but she hadn't been listening. She was afraid to think about it. And she was sick of the hospital. All she wanted right now was to see Merina and the girls and the cat Ptolomy and to be away from tubes and the anesthetic smell of disinfectants. "I want to come home, Sameh."

"I'll ask the doctor again. I think he might say yes today!"

The doctor did say yes, as soon as Sameh assured him that there would be help at home for Della until she was stronger. She would continue with physical therapy at home. She would check in regularly.

On the mid-July day that Della came home, the family compound in Cairo was decorated with red flowers, and Silva had prepared her favorite dish, koshari, and the girls had gotten movies that they were sure Della would love and planned to make popcorn and watch videos with her all evening. After all the anticipation and the paperwork and the SUV ride and the happy greetings of staff and family, Della was so tired that she fell asleep at 5 o'clock, missing the movie evening and having only a few bites of Silva's delicious stew. But the next day was easier, and the next, and within several weeks she was ready to follow Silva to the market in the morning again.

Sameh stayed in town, curtailing business travel, insisting that client dinners in Cairo were as much as he was prepared to be away from home. He moved into his old room, the room of his youth, insisting that Della should have interrupted sleep during her recovery. It seemed that business was doing well, as the family company had just signed two new huge Saudi client companies. Sameh's father, Omar, had formally announced his candidacy for the National Assembly. There was a rumor that President Mubarek would appoint him to one of the ten coveted positions. Omar was endorsed by the National Democratic Party and the Editors of *Al Ahram*, the biggest and most popular newspaper. They said he was the best possible candidate.

Merina was planning a series of parties for the more elite members of the party, and she also began to attend some business dinners for important clients, hosting a separate dining room for the wives, where she provided little fashion trinkets for each guest and brought in tasteful musicians to entertain. She was developing a reputation as an excellent hostess. It was rumored that she had the ear of not only the president's wife, but also many other important wives in the government. People rarely declined an invitation to one of the Makram-Ebeid parties, if they were fortunate enough to get one. Omar couldn't have a better partner for a wife.

Because Omar spent more and more time on politics, it was left to Sameh to be sure all the aspects of the business were managed. Sameh had always expected he would be an apprentice, but instead he felt like he had been shoved into the pilot's seat. His learning curve was steep and frightening, but it also revealed things he had trouble believing: things that were part of Omar's business practices that would be considered unethical, immoral, and likely illegal. As Sameh's suspicions grew, so did his contempt. It was always a battle to get Omar to spend more than 20 minutes at a time with him, but one day Sameh was surprised to find Omar not only in his office but agreeable to a meeting. He entered the plush corner office with a stack of papers and his ongoing list of questions. He had just started to ask his first one when Omar stopped him.

"What have you found out about Della's accident?"

"Only what the police have learned."

"You need to learn more. Call a man named Mahmoud Salam. His contact information is in our system. Tell him we need the usual service."

"Why?"

"It doesn't add up. We should have found some remains of Ahmad by now. What if the boat exploded *before* it hit the bank at full speed? That would mean someone was trying to kill your wife. She is your property, and when someone is trying to take away your property, Sameh, there must be repercussions. They must be swift and brutal, and people must hear about them and be shocked or your family will never be safe."

Sameh was able to ask a few more questions before he was dismissed, wondering what his father meant when he said "brutal."' But he thought he knew what it might mean. It was a glimpse of a side of his father that he had heard about. He wondered how much of the rumors were true.

The shocking scene of her husband embracing a man hung in the back of Della's mind, returning suddenly to her at odd times: in the middle of a conversation, while she was reading news on her iPad, or playing a board game with the girls. She felt like she almost recognized the location, almost recognized the other man, but she knew for sure that it was Sameh. But that was all: that scene, no before, no after, no explanation. Was it a memory?

Della found Merina in the salon one afternoon, her head down over a partially checked-off list, a phone in her lap.

"Merina, are you busy? Can we talk?"

"Sweet Della, please sit down. You must not tire yourself, dear. Of course I am never too busy to talk with you. Now tell me, is something wrong?"

"I don't know."

"That sounds curious. Do you mean you have some symptoms that have just shown up?"

"No. Well, yes."

"And?"

"I have a picture that keeps coming into my head. But I don't know where it comes from."

"A picture?"

"A scene, a memory maybe, except that I don't know if it IS a memory."

"Of?"

"You must forgive, me Merina, this is going to sound crazy."

"Try me."

"It is of Sameh kissing a man. Passionately. I don't understand why I would imagine this and yet I can't make it go away."

"Oh, poor Della, it is likely another after effect of your accident. Sameh is always away working, and your subconscious is playing tricks on you. I would not give it any thought at all, dear."

"I don't know if I can, Merina. It's so vivid."

"I know it has been a rough start, dear, here in Egypt, but it will get easier. Any time you move into a culture as different as this one is from America, there are subtle differences that take a while to adjust to. I had trouble, when I first came from the UK, understanding that Omar was going to be gone all the time. But when you adopt a new culture, you have to accept all of it, and soon I did adjust, as will you. Sameh cherishes and cares for you, dear Della, and I would not tell you that unless I was absolutely sure of it. Don't worry about this vision or whatever it is. Just put it aside and keep on being your wonderful self. You know, Della, we love having you here, in Cairo, the children and I. We'll be sorry to see you move back to Luxor. Perhaps someday, when you have babies, you will move back from Luxor and live with us again."

Babies. She would love to have a baby.

One hazy, stiffling morning in late August, Della decided to go with Silva to the market, to feel the bustle of the vendors, and to get outside of the house for the second time since the accident. She loved to watch Silva haggle with her favorite merchants, accusing them of charging outrageous prices even though she shopped there three or four times a week. It was a game Silva and the merchants both seemed to enjoy.

Standing behind her, suppressing a smile at the servant's fake outrage, she saw a man in the crowded aisle beyond the booth. He looked familiar. It was Ahmad! He was here, walking around, safe, and in Cairo! She felt a rush of joy, relief, and then, a strange sense of fear. Why had he not come back to the family?

Della jiggled Silva's arm, even though she was just winning her price war.

"Silva, look there. It's Ahmad! See?"

"Where? I don't see him?"

"There. Standing by the hanging ropes, see?"

"No, Mrs. I don't see him."

And neither did Della. The man had disappeared. But she was sure. It was Ahmad.

Della and Sameh and Silva moved back to Luxor a month later, in late September, just when the summer heat began to abate. The primary tourist season was ahead, but because of the magic of ancient Egypt, the tourists never really stopped coming, even in the hotter months of the year. Della returned to her job and the staff and her colleagues threw her a little welcome-back party at the central office area. The university had made it clear that her PhD candidate research position would be waiting for her, and in fact her program had been put into limbo until her return. The regents of the university had sent flowers and cards several times during her convalescence and even personal handwritten notes saying that they looked forward to her return.

Any memory from the days immediately before the crash, or anything about her ordeal, still hadn't returned. The doctors assured her that this was really normal, and she might never remember what happened and that it was probably best. The fact that there had been a crash had unfolded from the evidence, but she couldn't pull one shred of that day or the ones before or immediately after out of her mind. She remembered coming home from the office, on a typical day, and then waking up in the hospital.

It troubled her not to remember. On some days Della felt the creeping up on her of a deep dread, as if she was missing something important. But she couldn't figure out what it might be. She had asked the doctors about the blond doctor who had helped her, but no one knew. How could she remember that and not remember anything else? The police had found no evidence of how she had gotten from a boat ride on the Nile to Aswan. Her doctors, very patiently, continued to explain, "As we have told you, Mrs. Makrem-Ebeid, it is very common for people who have had endured traumatic events to lose all memory of it." And, Dr. Habibi had added, it was a blessing and she should be grateful, for based on her condition when she had been found, it must have been quite an ordeal. It would be better to never remember any of it, but just to enjoy being alive.

Fragments of the boat had been found, but quite a ways from where it was thought to have run aground. It likely drifted downstream towards Luxor. No report of Ahmad had ever surfaced. Had she really seen him in the market with Silva? Maybe her mind was just grasphing at straws. His absence wasn't spoken of by the family. Since ancient times people had disappeared into the Nile, when hippos were an even bigger threat than the crocodiles. There had been no way to find out who had picked her up or how she got to Aswan. There was a detective in Aswan who was working on the case but so far no clues had been found. Dr. Habibi recommended a therapist to help her accept her feelings of losing the memory of part of her life, but Della, taking the offered business card, knew she would never make that appointment. She was used to managing on her own, to getting through things without help. She would do it again.

Back in Luxor she started going to the office late every day and coming home early. After a month, however, she was falling back into her old routine, working a little too much, perhaps, particularly with Sameh back to traveling all the time for business.

She was stopping to pick up some oranges on the way home one afternoon, on an early November day, a mild day in one of the best months in this climate, when she saw the man across the market street from the fruit stand. She stood, her hands on an orange, and stared, just watching him. She wasn't sure, but she realized he reminded her of the blond doctor. But more than that she knew he was important to her. She had a powerful feeling about him. He had Nordic blue eyes and short shaggy blond hair and he seemed to be waiting. People and carts went by between them, but Della kept looking at the man, mesmerized. He was wearing western khaki pants and a light cotton shirt. Della realized that he was very handsome, but his face registered in her mind as much more than that. He was leaning on the side of a building near a man on a stool smoking a shisha pipe. Then he turned and saw her. He stood up straight and seemed to hold his breath for just a moment as he looked back at her. He looked directly into her eyes. Then he turned sideways and disappeared into a marketplace alley behind him.

FOUR

It was a full minute before Della moved. Then she began to run, zigzagging across the street, through the carts, cars, and pedestrians to get to the mouth of the alley. Hanging dresses and shawls crisscrossed on ropes over her head in the narrow walkways, hiding the view of the man she saw ahead of her. She kept going. Rushing past stalls with clothes, then racks of shoes in the open air, next a stall with white bags of rice and beans. All around her merchants were standing beside their scales shouting "Best price" and "Buy now," as she hurried by.

Della crowded around a donkey cart full of onions and squeezed by a group of women haggling with a vegetable seller, stumbling for a moment when a laughing little boy ran into her knee. She didn't think she was going to catch him. The white shirt and khaki pants would be almost impossible to distinguish in the pageant and color of the market chaos, but wait, did he turn left up ahead?

As she got to the place where she thought he'd turned, she could see a narrow hallway, which led into a honeycombed cavern of interior shops, and as she slowed down to look at more corridors with more shops and more people hustling by with their bags, she suddenly stopped. What was she doing? He could be anywhere. She might have already passed him. She didn't even know who he was. She was crazy to chase a strange man through the bazaar. Even if she did find him, which was very unlikely, what would she say to him?

But he recognized her. She remembered his eyes. And she remembered seeing those eyes before, somewhere else, and she wanted to understand. For an instant there was a flicker of memory - a scene - but then it sunk back into the morass of her vacant remembrance. Had she looked up at his face in that lost scene?

Della wound her way back out of the maze of shops and found the fruit stand. The vendor was still holding the three oranges. As she took her change, she realized that the pursuit of the man had winded her. She would find a small cafe, an ahwa and have some tea or cold coffee with cream to cool her down before she walked home. She could call Mohammed, the new family driver, of course, but it was good for her health to walk and she usually slept better if she got some exercise. Not the running kind, she smiled to herself, the walking kind.

El Kamar Street angled away from her usual route home, but it had lots of ahwas, and she would take that today. After a little rest the walk home would be easier, as the heat of the day would have subsided some. She kept her abaya and hajib close around her, in spite of the heat. Egyptian men would leave her alone if they thought she was an Arab woman going to the shops. If they noticed that she was a single western woman, it was more likely that they would bother her. She had learned that if she called out *"Hl D'wh 'Mk Dhlk?"* in Arabic ("Would you call your mother that?"), that would usually stop rude comments. But even better, if she kept herself fully wrapped up, the comments would not begin.

She found an ahwa that looked clean and had a small private area inside, beyond the customary outside tables under an awning. She went inside and found an empty table and gathered her abaya around her to sit. But she stopped midway into the yellow plastic chair. For there, across the room, was the man she had been chasing. His back was to her, but she knew that it was him. He was sitting, sipping his tea, reading a newspaper. *the Luxor News* in Arabic. Della had a moment of doubt, because for some reason she was sure the man was British or English and seeing the Arabic paper made her wonder. But she had to know. She picked up her oranges and walked over to the man.

"I mean you no harm." she said, softly, in Arabic, from just behind him.

He turned sharply and looked up at her.

"You speak Arabic," he said in English.

"And you're English, I think."

"Yes. Wales originally."

Della just stood there looking down at Nigel. And he looked up at her. They said nothing: neither of them moved. Feeling the stalemate, Della took her chance.

"I'm Della al Makram Ebeid and I feel like I know you."

"Nigel Sutherland, and I'm afraid I don't remember meeting you." Nigel spoke these words very slowly, very carefully. Very matter of factly. He didn't move his eyes from her face.

Della was sure he was lying.

And then he suddenly, as he stood and motioned for her to sit down, added "Are you one of **the** Makram Ebieds? I wasn't aware that they married outside of the Egyptian culture."

"Yes, and yes they do. My husband is Sameh, the son of Omar, who I believe you're referring to when you say "**the**" Makram Ebieds."

Wow, Nigel was thinking. Not only is she not English but she is probably the only American in a powerful Egyptian family. And so much more beautiful than he had remembered.

"You didn't answer, Nigel."

"Sorry, what did you say?"

"I was saying that I remember reading an article in the *JEA* about the Giza subterranean cavity controversy and it was written by someone named Nigel Sutherland. Is that you?"

"Yes. That's me. But how is that you read an article in the *JEA*?"

"It was quite good, I thought. You handled the difference between the politically correct opinion and outside academic opinion much more deftly than I thought possible. I almost sent an email to tell you this, but then, well, I was distracted by other things."

"You must be an archeologist."

"Yes. I am. I have a doctorate in Egyptology but I'm getting another PhD from Cairo University. I'm based here at the Luxor satellite campus."

"I had heard rumors that there was a campus here, but I wasn't sure there actually was one."

"Well, it is more like a facility than a campus, as it is mostly for research and rarely used for classes."

"I have never met anyone who was based there. It sounds like a wonderful place to do your research."

"Yes, I suppose it is. I love my work here."

As they sipped their tea, their conversation circled around to the writing projects that Nigel was currently preparing and then to some of the rumors about other professionals in their field in Egypt and beyond. Both of them slowly relaxed into this area of expertise that they were both comfortable with, and soon they found themselves laughing at the gossip and even an Egyptian tomb joke. They agreed tha archeologists, and especially Egyptologists, were an odd lot, many with strange habits or who took themselves far too seriously, so there was lots of lurid and odd facts to laugh about.

The conversation wove on through the recent discoveries in Saqquara and the political machinations of the Department of Archeology and its world-famous media-savvy chairman. The afternoon slipped into early evening, and they were still talking when Della realized that she was very late and that Silva would wonder what was going on. She usually called her when she worked late so that Silva would not worry or hover around a dinner that would be cold when Della came in.

"I need to go home. Silva will worry about me."

"Silva is your sister?"

"She is my helper, my assistant, I think you could call her. She will have made dinner for me and she hates it when I forget to come home and eat."

Nigel couldn't help himself "And your husband? He must eat dinner, too."

Della looked at him and saw the lovely blue of his eyes and the slight wrinkles around the edges from being overlong in the desert sun. But his face lit up when he smiled and even his eyes were smiling. She couldn't help smiling back at him.

"Sameh is doing very well in business. I think he may be in Jordan this week. His famous father needs to have him do much of the work now, so he can stay in Cairo and entertain the VIPs and attend important meetings. You may have heard that Omar is running for election to the National Assembly."

"Yes, I have heard something to that effect."

Nigel rose to walk Della to the street and waved down a taxi.

As he was opening the door for her, she turned to him, "Please let me know if I can help with any of your writing projects. We have artifacts from many periods represented in our vault here in Luxor, and I could arrange to let you see anything we have."

"Thank you, Della. It was a pleasure to meet you."

After she sat down, she looked up at him, holding her bag of oranges. "I hope you will call." Her voice was softer now, almost timid. "And I know that I have met you. I almost remember you. I believe you helped me. Maybe some-day you will tell me about it."

As the taxi took off into the traffic of the Luxor twilight Nigel stood very, very still and watched it disappear down the crowded street.

Manar picked up the receiver on the old black desk phone. It was, as always, warm and a little dirty. He wiped it down with his handkerchief before he put it to his ear. There was never enough money for new phones for the police.

"Yes, this is Manar. Who? Okay, yes. How can I help you, sir?" He listened a moment.

"Yes, I can meet here with you tomorrow, but I don't know if my colleague, Wael, can come. What is this about? And why do you need to talk to him, too? Is this something to do with Aswan, because I'm the chief detective for this district. Wael is from another city, north of us, Luxor, or Qena as it is usually called."

"I see."

"In that case I'll call him and tell him to be here. If he can't come, how can I reach you to let you know?"

"Ah, I understand. He will definitely be here. We'll both be here."

Manar was surprised to hear from someone from Interpol. He had never talked to anyone from that organization before, even though he somehow knew that it was better than its somewhat murky reputation. He did know that they were based in Europe, and so it was a mystery as to why they would be coming to talk to him here in southern Egypt. At first he didn't believe it, thinking it must be some kind of joke. But when the man gave the name of the Egyptian Federal Secretary of Police, who was also coming to the meeting, Manar sud-denly believed it all. Everyone knew that man's name and no one would make a joke about that one. He was suddenly worried. Had he done something wrong? Stepped over some kind of line he didn't recognize? Exceeded his authority? He could think of nothing that he might have done, so when he called Wael, he was unable to explain it to him.

"I don't know, Wael. The agent, as he called himself, would not tell me anything. He said they would explain everything tomorrow and that we were not to speak of this meeting to anyone else. I told them you would be here, 11 a.m., at my office. I have been trying to think of a reason, or some infraction, but can come up with nothing. But if our beloved secretary of police is coming, you know it is serious business."

"True. I have only seen a few photos of him. I have never seen him in person. But I have heard the rumors. A velvet glove over an iron fist. An iron fist with an electric charge in it."

Manar hung up the phone and thought about what to do to prepare for a meeting he didn't know the subject of. He called his wife to tell her he would not be home for dinner and in fact would be quite late. He cleared off the coffee table in his office. He called in two of the administrative assistants and told them to bring him a list of all the cases they had worked on in the last three years. And then to bring the lead case file folder for each of them. No, change it to the last five years, he added. Manar also asked them to bring him some strong mint tea. Then he sat down to begin going through the files.

He would begin with the cases that were still open. He would look first for any irregularities, then would remove any papers or notes that were not explicitly proper procedure. There was still time to burn anything that might be incriminating in the trash cans out back of the police offices. But he would wait until the middle of the night to do that, of course, by himself.

The day was a busy one for Merina, because she and the two girls and the younger two of her sons had just come back from a week at the family home at Sharm el-Sheikh. It was the December winter school holiday, and the weather at the resort had been warm, if not hot. It had been a long trip back even though they had left quite early. It wasn't the airport in Sharm el-Sheikh so much as the traffic coming in from the airport in Cairo. Omar had been too busy to join them, so Merina had let each of the kids bring a friend, and they had spent the days swimming, riding the jet skis she had rented for the week, playing badminton and boogie board, and staying up late watching videos and playing board games. Merina remembered the slumber parties of her childhood and set up the dining room so that the kids could snack as late as they could stay awake. She took two of the family servants with her, giving them each several days off to enjoy the seaside pleasures of the beautiful resort. The family home was part of an elite resort compound, with a semi-private beach, and Merina enjoyed watching the kids freely laugh in public, something they would never do in Cairo. Because of the privacy, the girls could wear western style swimsuits and splash and dive and jetski as much as they pleased.

Back in the compound in Cairo, the driver had just taken the children's friends to their homes, all tired and happy, dragging with each of them small presents for their mothers that Merina had made sure they purchased at the resort shops.

Omar had left word that he was going to be in a number of meetings, wasn't to be disturbed, and should not be expected home today at all. But he also called just after the guests had left to welcome her home and ask how the children's friends had enjoyed the trip. It was Omar's idea to encourage the children to choose friends from the families of prominent ministers, and he was hoping that the girls, particularly, were developing friendships that would be socially profitable for him.

"You will be pleased to learn that Nylla and Nabila were perfect hostesses, and both their friends had a lot of fun. We chose a nice gift for each of their mothers, and I included a note from us thanking them for sharing their daughters with us. Zaki's friend has invited him to go skiing in Austria next winter, as a direct result of this visit. Of course I said that you and his father would work out the details, but that he would love to go. So the trip was quite a success."

"Excellent, Merina. I hope you have a good evening. Please do get some rest, as shepherding a flock of young children must be tiring. Perhaps a bit like supervising unruly clients."

"I will, Omar. I did have a lovely time, though, and would like to do it again."

"That will probably be fine, but of course, we should see how things go. We might want to choose different guests next time, depending on the political winds."

"Yes, I understand, but I hope the girls' guests can come again, because they really got on well."

"Of course. We shall see."

"Omar, when do you think you might be home?"

"I can't say, Merina. Perhaps tomorrow, perhaps the next evening. It is hard to predict."

"Very well. I'll be patient. But it will be good to see you. It seems like we have been apart for a long time – but then, it was I who was away, after all."

"Yes. Get some rest. I'll let you know when I know."

Merina ordered dinner for 7:30 and then retired to take a long bath. She lowered herself into the deep sunken tub and relished the absence of the children, savoring the suds and the bath pillow, rubbing her body with tangerine-scented bath gel. Her iPhone, sitting on the tiled edge of the tub enclosure, rang again, and she dusted the suds from her fingers and pushed the button.

"Yes?" she said, wondering what Omar had forgotten.

But it wasn't Omar. It was Gamal. Merina hadn't heard his voice for some time and she was surprised at how soft and pleasing it sounded. Yes, she said softly, she would be able to meet next Thursday at Sofitel. She would call to make an appointment at the spa for that morning. Lunch would be lovely. She would tell him about her recent trip to the coast with the children. It was beautiful, there. Yes, she remembered the number.

As she clicked off, she smiled, sensing a soft flower of anticipation flow all the way down through her, down to her pink painted toes.

Della was still waiting for the second carbon dating report. It had been one of the first things she had done after she came back to work. It wasn't quite overdue, but it should arrive soon.

Sitting at her computer in her office one long afternoon, over a cup of no longer hot tea, Della thought again about her argument with Sameh about the dating report for this statue, so many months ago. It was the day before her accident and she remembered it clearly. Recently she had begun to think again about why the first dating report on the little sculpture had come back with such a different timespan than she expected. Because of the presence of wood, this kind of date discrepancy was unlikely to be a simple mistake. Did that mean the error was intentional? If so, why would someone want to do that? She could think of only one reason that someone would deliberately give the wrong date, and that reason could only be to distract Della's interest away from the study of the sculpture and to cause her to lose interest in the project. But why? She felt like she was being paranoid and yet she could think of no other explanation. She had submittedher request through the Antiquities Department at the University, which was the usual way to send out requests for dating. Perhaps she should send the data out independently, at her own expense.

Not long after getting the first dating report, Della had received an email from a lesser official at the Cairo Museum, informing her that they would be picking up the little ancient sculpture for return to the vault in Cairo. She responded that she had written permission to continue studying the piece and that she wasn't ready to return it. And then she did something uncharacteristic for her, something she couldn't explain to herself: she had hidden the little sculpture. More than just hidden it. Rather than the climate controlled storage area under the Luxor campus, where artifacts were supposed to be stored, she put Wenut behind the stacks of paper reams in her private supply closet. She had requested her own cabinet because she had some supplies that she preferred over the standard issue from the university. Wenut fit perfectly behind the reams, carefully wrapped in soft Egyptian unbleached cotton, always with at least one set of medical plastic gloves wrapped with her.

Hiding an artifact in this manner was against every university and museum protocol. And what was worse, Della didn't have a real reason. It was true that she had heard rumors about artifacts disappearing, artifacts that were supposed to have been returned to the vast vaults under the Cairo Museum but had somehow been "misplaced" after they were taken there. It was generally assumed that the artifacts were still there but just placed in the wrong area, and because the immense collection was overwhelming and the vast network of vaults were crammed and crowded, an occasional missing item wasn't considered a cause for concern. But still, something told Della to hide Wenut. The decision wasn't only not scientific but it was based on pure instinct, and she would be loath to have to explain herself to anyone.

In spite of her protests that she wanted to keep studying the statue, an official courier had come for Wenut when Della wasn't there and left a note asking to reschedule. Della had taken the note home and thrown it away with the household trash. She waited for another email, or visit, but so far neither had come. Or at least no visit that she knew about. Wenut had stayed hidden until two days ago. Looking at her, Della was always surprised at how much she loved the pale remnants of the beautifully painted hare's eyes. Those eyes seemed, in the artificial light in this interior office, to be smiling at her.

FIVE

Nigel watched the taxi pull into the evening Luxor traffic and then stood still, his heart and breath the only thing moving, for a full five minutes. How odd to meet the woman he had picked up by the side of the road on the way to Aswan. Whom he had tried to take to a hospital. If he had been an ancient Egyptian, Nigel would have thought that the gods were playing with him. He still remembered when she opened her eyes and looked up at him smilingfrom that carpet, still remembered her saying thank you"

It was a thank-you he hadn't deserved. It was a treatment she hadn't deserved. It was a filthy kind of guilt he felt, because he had been raised to respect the women in his life, to cherish them, to look out for them. He could never reveal the story of that day, never look into those green eyes and tell her that horrible truth. And yet he hated to have to lie to her. It would clearly be best if he never talked with her again. And that was something that could easily be managed, for although they were in the same small and club-like Egyptian archeology field, it would be simple to just leave the scene if he noticed her at one of the events, lectures, or conferences. Or perhaps acknowledge her from across a room, briefly, and then move on. She would never have to know.

Except for the fact that he wanted to see her again, wanted to enjoy their conversations, wanted to ask her opinion, wanted to see her smile. And that made him nervous. More than anything he had done for Gamal, this small red-headed scholarly woman made him uneasy. He wasn't sure why. It wasn't her pleasant pale face with its freckles, or her professional competence, or her tentative confidence. It was something more, something deeper, something that he couldn't exactly describe. And suddenly he knew with deep certainty that he would never be able to walk away from her, in any room, in any place, ever.

Nigel walked back to the flat he had leased for three months while he worked on several local assignments in and near Luxor and made himself a dinner of odds and ends. Then he checked his email and worked on the article about the new theory of the effacements at Karnak. It was going to be the most challenging of all his current projects so he worked on it a little every day. He finally went to sleep around midnight and dreamt about his sister. In the dream, they were playing in the blossoming pear trees behind their old stone farmhouse in Wales. They had made a little tree house out of a couple of old woven wicker laundry baskets. There were three of them sitting in the little hut wedged into the fork of the tree, surrounded by blossoms, looking out at the spring day, watching the robins hopping in the grass below them. There were three of them because his sister had brought a new friend with her today, a pretty girl with long red hair and freckles and beautiful green eyes.

The three young boys seemed to be following Gamal through the crowd as he wove around the vendors, the carts, and the flowing white robes for sale. Moving behind him, they could have been a procession, he the lord and they his attendants. His clenched jaw softened as he thought of his own youth, and he reached into the pockets of his cargo jacket and turned to toss some coins toward the boys. Then he chose his gruff voice to say "Go away." Two of the boys answered "Yes, mister. Thank you, mister" as they grabbed the change from the cracked concrete and turned quickly to run in the opposite direction. But the third boy, the shortest of the three, stood holding his coins and watched Gamal as he turned and continued his walk towards the El Tahrir. That boy is like me, Gamal thought. He won't be bowed.

Gamal walked with strong legs, his lean shape moving beautifully in his western clothing, with the self-confidence of a pyramid. He paid no attention to the white afternoon sun pouring like a waterfall over the market street, instead he received its power as his ancient ancestors had accepted the power of Ra, their Sun God.

The boy had looked so Egyptian, Gamal thought. But he probably was of a mixed lineage. Gamal knew that he himself was the rare exception today, because he was directly descended from a line of ancient Egyptian architects who had served the later Pharaohs. His family had never had any Greek inter-marriage, no Hittite, not even Jordanian or other Arab type. His lineage was pure. This was his homeland more than most of his fellow residents, even those simple citizens in the little countryside towns whose families had stayed on the same land for millennia. And that gave him certain rights. He was an authentic citizen of the most amazing civilization that had ever graced the earth. It was his burden to interact with others with the demeanor and grace of his pedigree.

It was often a struggle. Particularly with those ingénues, those novices, those archeologists who studied his history, took liberties, made up stories, invented absurd parables to explain things they didn't understand. Fortunately he had learned how to be gracious, how to employ his God-given charm to work with them. Alas, they could never really fathom the eternal mind of a true blue-blooded Egyptian. And of course, their adoration was completely understandable.

As a rule, Gamal preferred dealing primarily with the politically powerful men of Egypt, and he knew he was very good at it. He had many relationships with ministers and commissioners and directors. He was always respectful, as a good servant of the pharaoh would have been, and he was careful to provide generous donations in the correct currency. Most wanted a simple envelope of money, but some wanted favors of different kinds, and a few wanted him to remember them when he was able to get certain kinds of artifacts. It was understood that he would keep his business *sub rosa* and honor and respect the power and glory of Egypt, both of the past and in these modern times. But every now and then he would come across a minister or director who was a problem. And Omar Makrem-Ebeid was turning out to be just such a person.

The Makreim-Ebeid family business had recently purchased yet another freight and shipping entity, a small one that had been quite strategic for Gamal in the shipping of his articles, which were usually described as spices or carpets or marble pieces. Gamal had always been respectful and had taken the trouble to be sure his true shipments were well disguised and packaged so that the shipping company would have plausible deniability if trouble arose. Gamal was happy to provide the owners of this fast-growing company with an annual party and generous envelopes of cash and an occasional favor. However, when Gamal had sent his intermediary to arrange a payment to the new owner, Omar Makeim-Ebeid, he had been sent to the son, Sameh, who had refused to name a price. Sameh was 25 years his junior and clearly new at business, but his father had apparently been too busy with his political machinations to instruct the stupid child on how to gracefully accept a deserved bribe. This was very inconvenient. His business depended on the smooth shipment of contraband items anywhere in the world. Omar had always understood this. They had worked together for many years.

Gamal had hoped things would continue as before after Omar moved into politics full time. He had met Omar's wife, the regal and fascinating Merina, and had become intrigued with her. Truth be told, he could not get her out of his mind. He was making some progress on developing a friendship with her. Gamal was used to having his sex with subordinates, with women of lesser morals and sophistication. But this was something different. In fact, Merina was completely different from any woman he had known. And he had discovered that she was attracted to him. She was nervous to admit this, he knew, but he could sense it.

It had started for Gamal as a sort of challenge, to see if he could conquer such a beautiful, well-educated, and powerful woman. But their secret lunches together had exposed a deeper feeling, one Gamal wasn't sure he could name. He only knew that he wanted to be the one she wanted. She had allowed him to first kiss her and then to caress her, and he knew she was approaching the point of wanting much more. He needed to be very very careful, because not only was she in a position of political power, but he found he was becoming obsessed with her: her interesting ideas, her quick wit, her insight into Egyptian politics, and yes, her full breasts and wonderful body. He wanted to explore that body, to bring great pleasure to it, to make her cry out for him and long for him in the night. He imagined her beneath him as he relieved himself with other women. But the others were just shadows to him because he longed to see Merina's red hair streaming out around her full pale body beneath him. He longed to make her whimper and moan for him. It had become an obsession.

So his problem was complicated. He needed to get Sameh to accept his tribute and let his shipments go through undisturbed. Gamal shipped artifacts, it was true, but there were other things, such as weapons, that he needed to ship. How was he to influence Sameh? He had heard rumors of Sameh preferring men in the past, but after he had gone to the US for his doctorate, Gamal had heard that he had married. Probably some arranged marriage with a submissive Egyptian girl from a good family in the countryside. Someone who would take orders. But usually when someone preferred men, they continued to do so on the side. Gamal would have some of his people see what could be found out. Perhaps something that would help him to influence the foolish young man. There was always the back-up plan of a private conversation with his father about the publication of certain photos, but he would prefer not to be so callous.

SIX

"Really, Merina, I'm surprised at you." Omar's face revealed the tediousness of his attempt at patience.

"Because I'm angry?"

"It isn't as if you didn't know any of this. Since Sameh has taken over, money has been down, you know this. He will learn, I'm sure, but he has a ways to go."

"How is that my fault?"

"I'm not blaming you, but you were the one who wanted me to go into politics, who wanted me to start going to parties with the government leaders and the important ministers. It was your idea."

"That isn't true. Yes, I wanted you to meet them, and for them to know you, but that was because I thought it would be good for business. It was *your* idea to take it farther than that. You know that I support you completely, but I deny that I asked you to change our lives so you could enter politics. "

"Merina, at this point it really doesn't matter how it all started. I'm in the game now, and I'm not going back to selling freight. I want so much more. And I need for you to work with me to get there."

"But I'm helping in every way I can!"

"I need more from you. We really need to economize. I cannot borrow any more money just now, not until several of our clients pay us. We need to economize for a few months. That means you need to find a way for us to live on less, without having it show, of course. "

"Of course."

"You can be sarcastic if you want, but I have provided you with beautiful clothes and jewelry and a spacious home and rarely ask any sacrifice of you. I suggest we just accept invitations for a while and not entertain ourselves. So postpone that party you were thinking of having. No big vacations to the beach with guests for a while. Of course I'm glad that you took the children there last week, but that's even more reason to wait a while. Let others invite our children. But this will pass. We have a number of quarterly contract receipts coming in, so I think maybe two, maybe three, months, and we should be back to normal."

Merina sat quietly on the bed, her favorite teal silk robe around her, her long fox red hair hanging undone over her pale arms, pale soft bare feet hanging over the edge of the bed. She would say nothing more. She would do as Omar asked, and they would be fine, of course. And she would have a little talk with Sameh about working harder. She would not think of the lunch meeting she had agreed to later in the week.

Omar straightened his tie and began to leave the bed chamber, then stopped and turned back towards her. Handsome with his dark suit and his flashing eyes, she was reminded of other times when he had turned back from leaving for work, and they had embarrassed the servants. And then he had had to dress all over again and rush late to his meeting. But that was so long ago, and now those feelings were like the memory of a lush green hillside in the middle of the desert: true but not quite really believed.

"There is one more thing I need for you to do for me."

"Yes, dear Omar." She smiled up at him as he ignored the soft sarcasm behind her attentive smile.

"I would like you to take Mrs. Ahmed Nazif to lunch this next Thursday. The prime minister tells me his wife feels isolated and finds little company she can trust among the ministers' wives. I told him that you used to feel that way, too, and that you would enjoy spending time with her. I made reservations for you at the Semiramis Grill at the Intercontinental. It will be a company expense so no need to worry about cost in this case. And before you say anything, I *know* you never felt isolated but I wanted to give you a basis to develop a relationship with Mrs. Nazif. It is the minister himself who has had trouble trusting anyone, of course. He is devoted to his wife, so this will help a lot. Just do your usual thing of making people love you. "

Merina just stared at him. Did she always do that? It was a moment before words would come off her tongue.

"Anything else?"

"No, that's it."

Reclining on the bed, Merina watched him move out the double doors and down the wide hallway, the sun streaming onto his silhouette as he walked past the wall of windows to his right. It was a long hallway and she enjoyed looking at him, knowing the working of those glutes, hidden beneath his silk slacks; he was sleek and handsome even from the back, with long strides and a confident step. He didn't look back.

When Merina met Omar, she knew immediately that he was going to be part of her life. Looking up into his aristocratic face, she wasn't only completely unintimidated and at ease, but also riveted by his eyes. And she had a strong premonition: she would come to know him very well. In fact, he would some-day belong to her and she to him. He must have sensed it, too, although he denied it until after they were married. She had stood before him, a mere girl, and was aware of her power over him and aware that he knew it.

Her father was a history professor at Oxford and periodically hosted receptions for visiting historical experts. Even though she was barely 16, her father asked her to attend the reception for the famous Egyptian scholar and philosopher Abdel Wahab Elmessiri because her mother, who usually helped her father as hostess, was away visiting her family. Merina was reluctant, even afraid, and awed by the sophisticated conversations of her father's typical guests. When historical experts came to dinner, her mother and father would talk about so many things she didn't understand, things, in fact, she had never heard of. As she grew older, she began to ask her father questions after the guests had left. He encouraged her to learn more about history, but she was still painfully sensitive to the limitations of her knowledge. She noticed that some of the men who visited clearly noticed her but she found that they often spoke to her as though she were a child, asking simple questions while looking at her breasts and not really expecting answers. It seemed to Merina that they knew something about her – that everyone knew something about her – that she didn't.

But the night Omar was a guest of one of the scholars at the family table he had introduced himself and asked her what she thought of living at Oxford.

And then he had listened to her answer. She found herself telling him about how she was fascinated by history and recently aware of how much more she had to learn. They talked about the way England worked, and how Egypt was different, and about Merina being part of the implied nobility of the Oxford faculty, and knowing she wasn't entitled, like the real nobility, to carry on her father's status. She wondered if she ever would understand the discussions at her father's table.

You can go far beyond this, Omar had said, gesturing to take in the entire room, maybe the whole of Oxford. He looked down at her with his sparkling eyes and then took her hand gently. "You can go _far_ beyond this. And I think you will be a brilliant asset to some very fortunate man."

As she looked up into his face, the warmth rose in her own, and she experienced her first deep awareness of her sexuality, and she knew he felt it, too.

After the party Merina asked her father about the guest from Egypt. That led to discussions about the wonderful legacy of ancient Egypt and Egyptology and the beauty of the artifacts that existed, as well as the mystery of so many that were surely undiscovered. She learned that the guest was studying on campus and that he was from a very prominent family. Merina decided she wanted to study this amazing civilization, ancient and still continuing, and to develop some credentials of her own. She threw herself into her studies, excelling time and again. The next time she met Omar, she would be more worthy. He would see that she was the brilliant asset he had spoken of. She would capture him with her mind and her body.

Ah, but that was so long ago. She smiled when she remembered that young girl who was so determined to catch the gorgeous Omar. And to live the dream of being part of a famous Egyptian family, one that insisted it could trace its lineage back to Amemenheb, the military commander who saved the life of the famous warrior Pharaoh Thutmose III, when he was charged by an elephant.

It had been a dream come true for the first years: a wonderful marriage, different from those of any of her friends. Omar had treated her like a queen, loving her thoroughly, spoiling her with his attentions, and surprising her with his affection. She was enchanted by the luxury of their lifestyle, but even more, she was in love with her husband. In traditional Egyptian culture, even in these modern times, it was unusual for a man to dote on his wife and to even occasionally touch her in public. But Omar would sometimes, perhaps forgetting that they were not still in London, hold her hand or smiling down at her, give her a kiss on the cheek. A long lingering kiss. At home he wasn't the least concerned about what the servants thought, and there were many evenings and afternoons, when the servants had to dismiss themselves as Omar and Merina became consumed with each other. Her marriage was far beyond her parents' formal and stiffling marriage, so much more than she realized a marriage could be. If only they could have held onto the magic of those first few years.

Omar did very well in business, working dutifully with his father in the family company, which had been started by his great grandfather with a few wooden wagons and some camels. When his father decided to retire, Omar took over in the traditional fashion of the young lion assuming most of the responsibility. It wasn't long after this that Merina realized that she had a rival now. Omar was excited to have an opportunity to run the company his own way, after respecting his father's wishes for so many years. She watched him as he became more and more successful, and then more and more daring, expanding their freight services to other countries, and then upgrading their fleets of vans, of trucks, even their flocks of camels, and then buying one, then another, cargo ship. And Omar thrived. It was easy to see that he loved building his freight empire, showing everyone – his father, his sister, himself – that he could do it better than anyone had expected. Anyone but Merina, who had always known he would go far.

The children came along, one after another, five in all, and Merina loved being a mother. The teaching part was her favorite part, and because she had some excellent servants to do the daily housework, she was able to dote on the children, taking them to museums, to the theater. Playing games in the evening when Omar was gone, which was often, urging them to be studious, to challenge themselves to excel. Listening to them, encouraging them. The children developed excellent manners and respectful attitudes, which was of great pride to her. They did well when she took them to London to visit her family, doing their best to behave and to blend into the English culture, which was so different from their own.

Omar continued to build and expand. He was soon vying to become the third most successful freight company in the region, competing with the ighty worldwide shipping companies, in spite of the reputation as a home-grown regional organization.

As the children grew up, spending more and more time in school and sports, and with Sameh, her first-born, off at college and Omar rarely at home, Merina began more and more to seek out the solace of friends. A close girl-friend invited her to join a book club and it was there that she met a number of the prominent wives in Cairo, including the wives of the leading ministers and the president's wife. Omar would come home from his business trips and share how wonderful his new contract, or client, was going to be, and Merina would tell him that she had had lunch with the president's wife.

Omar and Merina began to be invited to a number of very elite parties, and Merina made sure that Omar was in town for these. She asked him to be the gracious man she had met in London and to leave the business in the back-ground, no matter how tempting it might be to talk about it. Omar laughed and said, "It will be a relief to take a break from talking about cargo holds and truck fleets and routing problems." Merina knew better. She also knew he would keep his promise – at least at first.

Merina was surprised when Omar took an interest in politics. He had always had an in-depth understanding of many of the socio-political issues of his country because of the influence those issues had on his business. But he had loved building his business so much that she didn't expect him to ever be distracted from it. But there were many things that he now felt should be changed, modernized, about his homeland and he began to believe he was the right person to do that. He loved his country deeply, wishing to see it become much more than the tourist Mecca that it was. Maybe because of the blood of famous ancient Egyptian leaders running through his veins, he began to believe that he could bring the majesty and greatness of ancient times to life again. The country that was responsible for the famous Library and the Lighthouse in the harbor of Alexandria, and the architecture of the great pyramids and the hundreds of ancient temples, could rise again, now, in the 21st century. Omar wanted to be one of the ones who led the way.

And so Sameh, graduated and married, was expected to take over most of the business duties. And that was turning out to be a problem. When Omar had taken over, he had had ten years of apprenticeship, whereas Sameh had had less than three and that included three summers between school years. Merina knew her son was determined to be successful, even if he still needed to sort out some of his personal issues, but Omar wasn't patient with him. He was determined that Sameh live for the company as Omar had for so many years. It was Sameh's responsibility to step up and do his duty to his family. Merina suggested that Omar wait for a few years until Sameh had a more solid grounding in this vast new empire that Omar had worked so hard to build, but Omar was adamant: Sameh could and would take over now. Omar needed enough time in politics to advance. There could be no waiting. Sameh knew all he needed to know; he just needed to work harder.

Merina had confidence in Sameh, but she knew he wasn't ready. He was still immature. He had been trying to keep his inclination towards sex with young men under control, she knew, but she also suspected that he was still involved with Khalid, that scoundrel son of the ousted minister of finance. That could be what was distracting him. Whatever the reasons, she had to admit that the transition had been rocky. Omar had been hearing back from some of his oldest clients that Sameh was too tense, and didn't know how to treat his clients to good hospitality. Sameh wasn't very good at bringing in young women to entertain his guest clients when he had important business meetings. He was great at the administrative side, and he was getting better at finding new clients.

But he was still weak in the social side of things. The social side was a key element of the way business was conducted in all of the Middle East and particularly in Egypt. Perhaps Sameh had spent so much time in the US that he had forgotten this. Omar had built a reputation for always providing suitable companionship for his clients. He had tried to teach Sameh good guidelines on how help clients relax before they talked about pricing and contracts. Tradition was important. Everyone knew this. Sameh would have to put his American ideas aside and learn to do this well or the whole family would suffer.

Merina had come to understand this underside of business for years, even though Omar never discussed it with her. It had been difficult to not resent his business sexual entertainment practice, in spite of tradition. She clung, for years, to a lingering expectation that her spouse would remain monogamous, that she should not just be first but only. She knew this was naive. Omar might not have honored the only part but that he did put her first, always, and had never done anything that would embarrass her or the family. Unlike many other businessmen, she had to admit.

The truth was that Omar had been an excellent husband, providing for her in every way, giving her children, and physically satisfying her whenever he was in town and she was in the mood. And thus she had decided long ago not to ask him about his business sex, and that had led them away from talking about sex at all. It was a door that was long since closed between them. In spite of her regret, it was too late to change things between them, she knew.

Merina could feel that she was changing. With Omar enthralled with his freight empire, and now politics, she found herself feeling more and more at loose ends. She felt so much more energetic now that her youngest was in high school and demanded less of her and found that she had developed a kind of romantic curiosity. Of course she had lots of personal time. But maybe, also, she had developed a stronger self-confidence than she had had as a young woman. At parties she came to understand that she was still very attractive, maybe even more so than when she was young. How would it feel to be kissed by another man? Someone, of course, that she could completely trust to respect her.

She found that she was musing on this subject more and more often, as she kissed the children goodnight and retired to her bed with her book. But how would she go about meeting someone who might want to be here *friend?* Someone who was safe, who would never reveal her identity for gain? But ah, then too, she thought as she read another chapter into the deep of the night, he should be good-looking virile, and with lots of life experience. Lots of sexual experience. Someone interesting. Of course he would need to have money to provide a location to meet and the means to treat her well. Someone who would not expect her to be responsible for thinking of details like money. She laughed at her list of requirements. She would certainly be safe from temptation with that list.

But perhaps there was some prominent man who might do. A relationship that perhaps might even be socially beneficial for her husband. It could even be just a friendship, a safe flirtation. Someone who might be able to share some inside information about the social elite in Cairo and Egypt and maybe beyond. Someone whom she could talk to.

Resting on her silky cotton sheets, she saw that it was again 2 a.m. and she wondered where Omar was tonight. He would call her from wherever he was staying or working, but usually he preferred to call her during the daytime. As

he often worked very late, it would be a shame, he said, to call and wak
from her beauty sleep. She was accustomed to this. He used to go back
office after dinner when they were a young couple, and she would be s
asleep and wake up in the middle of the night and find him there next to her.
He was a man of amazing energy. When they were younger he used to wake
her up sometimes, in the middle of the night, to tell her about a new project he
had won, or a new client he had sealed the deal with. He wanted to share his
accomplishments with his biggest fan. She was so proud of him.

But that idea of a forbidden kiss with another lingered, as she closed her
book and turned out the light. And, she thought, falling asleep, she might
have already met a candidate. Gamal Muhammed Naguib. She had met him
at Omar's side two years earlier at a benefit party. Since then, she has seen
Gamal coming and going at a number of very high-level events, and it took a
while before she understood that he was flirting with her. At one formal state
function, Gamal, had brazenly winked at her across the room, and when she
looked around, she was surprised there was no one observing. After the wink,
there were looks, and then a comment and a smile, often in the middle of a
crowd with her husband at her side talking to others around them. But she
began to see in his smile that there was more. And then he had sent a private
courier with a message asking her to have lunch with him. She had naturally
rejected his invitation.

But why not, she thought. I could just go to lunch and see how it feels. If
he asks again, I'll accept, as long as our lunch will be in a very private place.

And he did ask again and this time she said yes. After her driver dropped
her off at the spa, a car took her to the private entrance of a small restaurant.
Gamal was waiting there, standing beside the only table, with lush purple flowers on it, good-looking in a craggy sort of way but with eyes like sparkling
magnets. They sipped wine, he asked her to tell him about her beloved England
and about her family and her love of archeology. It was 3 before she thought
to return to the spa.

"My dear, it has been an exquisite pleasure to visit with you."

Gamal was such a gentleman. He reminded her of the young gallant Omar.

As she settled into the heated towel wrap and mud pack a little later, she felt
exhilarated. That wasn't so terrible. It was a wonderful lunch with an interesting
man. Perhaps she would do it again if he asked.

They began to meet once a month. They talked about many things, including some excellent inside information he shared with her that she was able to tell Omar she had heard from one of her women friends. The last several times they had had lunch he had walked her to the door after he had called for the driver to come and pulled her close and kissed her. She was expecting to feel electrified, but it was more than that. Was it possible that she couldn't remember feeling that way before? If so, it had been very long ago. He gently released her and with the back of his hand ever so lightly touched the top of her arm, and then passed slowly over to her breast, and then down to her waist. She felt a tingle, a kind of shimmer, all over. When she was walking away with the driver, she turned to see that he was standing perfectly alert where she had left him, watching her leave. She saw desire in his face. And then she knew that she had gone too far. She felt the desire too.

Merina had decided she must bring herself under control and wait a few days before responding to his next message. But it was he who waited. Two days passed and then a week and he didn't send his courier. A month passed and then another. Many nights, in bed with her book, she wondered what was going on. She remembered his look as she turned back. Had something had happened to him? And then, like never before, he called her on her iPhone while she was soaking in her tub. Would she have lunch with him on Thursday?

Yes, she said. Yes. Without taking a breath.

And now Omar had changed her plans.

Della had the flashback again. It wasn't like an image, exactly, but more like the negative of one. It floated in her almost memory on the periphery, like a reflection in a pond or a window, but she couldn't pull it into focus. She had tried so many times. It was a face: a warm and friendly face with electric blue eyes and concern on the features. The face was looking down at her as she…what? Lay? Rose? Was carried? The face in her almost-by-not-quite memory had sandy hair and was surrounded by a glowing white light and, through a kind of watery atmosphere she heard the words: "*Don't worry. It will be all right. We are getting you some help.*" And then a glimmer of a smile, a smile to reassure. And that was all. She couldn't remember more. And the memory, if she tried to pull it back, skittered away from her like a tiny mouse, gone without a trace. She could never bring it back at will; it only came on its own schedule, unbidden, tiptoeing into her mind when she was completely off-guard.

And now she thought she had seen that handsome and warm face, those electric blue eyes again. But had she?

Wael was surprised.

His old friend, a detective in Cairo, had called him back. Wael knew that the American wife found in Aswan had been taken to Cairo to the hospital. He asked his friend to find out where her family lived so that he could ask for an interview with her, now that she must be recovered from her ordeal.

The detective had found the address of the family but also found out that she was no longer in Cairo and had moved back home to Luxor. She must have recovered quickly.

He had just talked to a woman named Silva at the home of Mrs. Makram-Abeid. Yes, she would be happy to give the Mrs. the message. She would come to his office day after tomorrow, here in Luxor, after his trip to Aswan tomorrow. He would be sure to make it a casual meeting. Low key. He would be sure she felt safe and comfortable and could build a trust in him. That way she would relax, and he would get better information.

And Wael thought it was very likely that he would need to talk to her more than once. His instincts told him that there was more, much more, to this situation. He had no idea what else, but he had a feeling deep in his gut that it wasn't going to be good.

Gamal was a man who was always in control. He had learned that it was best to remain cool and calm, and always pause and look into the other person's eyes, before replying. He always focused on living in the moment, not letting things distract him. He was proud of his ability to compartmentalize, focus on his objectives, whether for business or pleasure.

His business was complex, and he needed to keep parts of it separate and unknown to the others who were part of it. For instance he had a number of people who aided him, such as that foolish Welsh archeologist, who had no idea of what else he was doing. Perhaps Nigel, and others, saw him as a clever artifacts dealer with a singular focus: money. He had to remember, when he was with them, to wear that persona and act the part. Sometimes he slipped out of that role and found that he was looking into the face of a person who had shock in their eyes. He had done something to scare them: given them a slight hint as to the other type of person he could be. Well, it couldn't always be helped.

Perhaps it was just as well that they feared him a little. They would be more manageable if they were a little afraid. But just a little. He had had to socialize a bit with Nigel. He had gone down to Luxor and taken him out for a few drinks and talked about soccer with him to try and get him to relax. Nigel had been acting oddly lately, and Gamal wondered if perhaps he had been too hard on him in Aswan. He would leave him alone for a while and then give him something easy to do. Something non-threatening. Which was really funny considering what Nigel had driven his wooden carton down from Cairo to Aswan. He would never know what was in that little crate. Gamal smiled to think how frightened Nigel would be if he did.

But Merina had become a problem. He was worried that he couldn't control her. He had always been too busy to consider a real relationship with a woman. Not to mention that he rarely met women who were interesting and also well connected. He saw the wives of the Cairo elite at the parties and functions that he attended, and most were either ugly, or fat, or if they were beautiful, they were hard and stupid. This was regrettable because Egypt had many beautiful women, smart women, but they somehow didn't find their way into the marriages of the top echelon. He naturally preferred Egyptian women, not those strange-smelling foreigners. At least until he had met Merina. His desire for her was unsettling.

Gamal had two authentic Egyptian women who provided him pleasure. Both were as close to pure Egyptian blood as he could get. Seha was a housewife and her husband was paid handsomely for her favors. She was always very accommodating, and she would to do things with Gamal that were adventurous, as long as he thought of them. She wasn't very creative. The other, Neela,

had been on the streets before he found her. She was a sweet thing, b
although she said she was older. She was grateful to Gamal for the apa
and money he provided and she was always available. She assisted him with a
few of his clients, too, as long as they weren't too violent. Neela was creative
and open to unusual sexual experimentation, and so much less boring than
Seha, but she was also an airhead and you couldn't talk to her, unless it was
about body parts or fucking.

What troubled Gamal lately, however, was how much he found himself
thinking about Merina. Everything about her bothered him: she wasn't Egyptian,
or even from the Middle East; she was the wife of one of his business partners,
one who probably was aware of many secrets about his work. She was as smart
as any man he had ever met and she clearly was attracted to him. At first he told
himself this was a good business move – to have a secret friendship with the
sacred wife of such a popular and fast-rising political figure. It could be a kind
of insurance in case Omar became a key leader in the country.

But the lunches had been an awakening. Besides being smart and sexy and
funny, Merina kissed him a way that was electric. A kind of electric Gamal
hadn't experienced. When they had kissed, he looked into her eyes and they
were open and it was clear that she was completely aware of what she was
doing. His desire for her was becoming harder and harder to control.

Gamal was no stranger to danger, but the danger of angering a senior government official was irrational and unnecessary. It could lead to unpredictable
things. He knew it would be best to just keep to his business, with all the right
people happily accepting their bribes, including getting Sameh to come to his
senses, and having no one feeling the slightest bit threatened, and not get into
further trouble. But oh, he was so tempted. To see this amazing infidel revealed
to him, giving herself to him. Once would be enough. Just once. Surely that
would be enough to stop this longing.

SEVEN

Gamal hated waiting.

He paced slowly as he smoked, lifting his hand with its monogrammed shirt cuff and its gold link bracelet, again and then again to his lips, pulling on the rich deep smoke of the Turkish cigarettes. He usually smoked Egyptian cigarettes, but sometimes he allowed himself the luxury of Turkish ones. He looked out from the windows of his office onto one of the main streets of the Ma'adi district of Cairo three stories below. Many of the men and women walking on the street wore western clothing. He kept his office here because it was good business to have a richly decorated office in an expensive area. But the strong western influence on the streets was annoying and he longed to go back to his compound, in the far north of Cairo, where the people were more traditionally Egyptian.

He hadn't been surprised to find out that Sameh had a male lover. There had been rumors of this long ago. But he was surprised to learn that this American educated son of the freight tycoon was stupid enough to provide his lover with a fine apartment and was paying for his luxurious lifestyle. He was a perfect target for blackmail. Especially since Khalid wasn't the kind of man to keep a low profile. It had been easy to find out, as Khalid was happy to brag about his situation to his friends. Omar would be outraged if this were to be printed in the newspapers. And that might be arranged soon, thought Gamal, as he paced. But first he would see what he might be able to learn from the vapid and pretty little Khalid.

Gamal had sent three of his men to talk to Khalid, to help him to understand it would be in his best interest to provide them with a little information, now and then, about Sameh's business. Gamal no longer cared to be directly involved in violent things, except in some of his sexual adventures, and therefore he had others take care of this more sordid part of his business, others who truly enjoyed the violent side. Because they enjoyed it so much, they had developed great skill at causing fear and pain without leaving a lot of bruising. It was an art that took years to perfect, and he was happy to pay well for this service. And best of all these men were loyal, and he could trust them to not get carried away and accidently kill the man. That had unfortunately happened a few times when Gamal was a younger man, and it had been a mess. He had to rearrange all his plans as a result. Getting rid of the body was the least of the problems. Getting all the players back into place, suspicious and distrusting of all the other players, had been the hard part. It had taken him months to catch up. Now he kept the two duties entirely separate. There were the kind of men who were talking with Khalid now, and there were others who knew how to take a man into the desert and to kill him quietly and leave no trace. Two different kinds of thinkers. One passionate, who loved to watch others beg in agony, and one cool and sure like the inside of a tomb.

There was a knock.

"Yes?"

"The boy is finished. He is resting."

"And?"

"He is happy to help. He will contact me twice a week by cell phone and then we'll meet."

"Do you believe him?"

"Yes. He was so scared he pissed himself. He was afraid I would shove my gun up his ass and so I let him think I would until I shoved something else up there instead. It was hilarious."

"Hazim, I'm not interested in the details of your methods. The only thing that interests me is if you believe he will cooperate."

"Yes, sir. He will. He is resting, but I'll take him home in an hour or two."

"Good. Drug him first. Knock him out for a while."

"Sure. It will be my pleasure."

"And Hazim, don't do anything to him when he is passed out that you will regret. Am I clear?"

"Yes sir."

"Good, you may go now."

He would never have to give those instructions to the men who were in his camp in the Sudan. But the men like Hazim had their purpose even if you had to watch them carefully.

Gamal would see what information was collected for a while, a few months, and then he would decide if he should perhaps arrange for the pretty little Khalid to take an excursion and then see how much Sameh would be willing to pay for his return. There were so many business opportunities to consider. And perhaps Hazim would like to visit him somewhere very quiet and remote where no one could hear Khalid scream. Gamal knew Hazim would jump at the chance.

Della felt sorry for Sameh. He had assumed he would follow the pattern of his father, who had all that experience before taking over the helm. But Omar had suddenly become passionate about politics and expected Sameh to step into his shoes. Omar relented a little while Della was recovering, but now he was adamant that Sameh should have his hand in everything that happened.

She tried to think of ways to help Sameh, to give him some kind of moral support, but she didn't know anything about the freight business. Della wondered if Sameh was up to the challenge. He was much more of a big-picture person than his father. Also, Omar, the powerful and tough business warrior, loved conflict and tension. Sameh didn't.

Over the next months she watched Sameh soldier on, doing his best to keep his clients happy, his fleets running, his shipping on time, and spending any extra time he had working to develop new clients. He had lost 20 pounds since he had become the acting CEO. He seemed to always have a worried look, no longer the enthusiastic and confident student she had met. He rarely smiled when he saw her, and when he did, his eyes didn't join in. He seemed to be taking on the physiognomy of his father more each day.

When he came home to Luxor, Sameh began to spend his nights in another bedroom, saying he would not disturb Della when he had late night calls or tossed and turned with worry.

"But I miss you, Sameh," she had blurted out one Saturday afternoon. "I see you so little, I would enjoy knowing you're tossing and turning beside me."

"You're so sweet, Della." He came over and leaned down to kiss her on the forehead. "I'm so glad you're all right and back at work. It brings me great peace to know that you're safe and doing something you love."

"But you will come sleep with me soon, after things settle down?"

"Of course, my dear. Of course."

But the months passed and Sameh continued to reside in his room, and she in hers. Sometimes when he was home for dinner, she would tease him about sneaking up on him in the middle of the night and seeing what would happen. He would laugh and say that would be a nice surprise but tonight would not be good.

One evening she told him she really needed him to make love to her, that she was feeling lonely and abandoned. He had hugged her after dinner, and smiled and dutifully come to her room and had stayed for a while afterward, until she had almost fallen asleep. She watched him through her eyelids as he left her bed. The next morning the driver took him early to the airport on another business trip. She had never thought that he might have been trying to plan an important business negotiation the night that she insisted they make love. She would ask, next time, before she insisted.

Della talked to her father every few weeks by phone, and they texted in between. Things at home were more or less the same, and Della didn't miss Kansas, only her father. She asked if he was going to any conferences in the coming year, thinking she could meet him there. But he was not. He had had to cut back on expenses in order to get through the recession and he had told his staff they were not going anywhere, so he was setting an example of belt-tightening.

In January she signed up to attend an upcoming conference in Paris with the title "New Archeological Methods Being Implemented on Deep Bas-Relief in Egypt". She hoped she might run into a few of her old colleagues, friends from her graduate school days, but none of them planned to attend. Many were now mothers and had husbands and young children. When she looked on Facebook, she didn't know what to say in response to all the photos of babies and family vacations. But of course it was still Paris. Paris with the amazing Egyptian collection at the Louvre. Della's old favorite professor, Dr. Nabil Kawass, was one of the speakers, and as soon as he found out she was coming, he invited her to speak.

Should she talk about Wenut? Did she dare describe what she believed was a mis-dating and her conviction that the artifact was really very ancient and precious?

Manar was prepared to be impressed. But the men from Interpol were not at all what he expected. Instead of several burly intimidating men with coats that could hide weapons, there were only two men, both slightly built and dressed like western tourists, with black work-out jackets and khaki pants. They drove up in a compact car with one driver. No black SUV of detective series fame. No weapons to be seen. They carried one brief case between them, a black canvas bag that also held a laptop. They were distinctly un-impressive.

Manar had finished going through the last of his files just as the dawn's light had crept over the distant brown mountains. His trashcan fire was almost burned out when he added the last little batch of paper, watched the pages turn to flame, then smoke. He covered the ashes with several buckets of sand and carefully distributed a bag of regular trash over the top of the sand.

Wael arrived shortly after 9:30, and they had coffee together and talked about why Interpol would send anyone to this southern Egyptian town, one that many native Egyptians had never even thought of visiting. Manar still worried that he had personally done something wrong, but Wael told him not to think that way. Manar was unconvinced. "Wael, I have never heard of the head minister of the security police visiting for a good reason."

"But, you see, Manar, I have heard that things have changed. The bad old days are over, and it is different now. The minister has become widely known outside Egypt, in the whole Middle Eastern region even, and so now he has a reputation to uphold. It is harder to carry on shadowy activities – easier to be caught involved in things that are considered inhumane to our allies. I have heard he has even traveled to foreign conferences and publicly pledged his cooperation with principles of humane incarceration with all our neighboring countries, except with Israel, of course. Actually, I have even heard rumors he has even cooperated with them in return for some, ah, favors."

"I don't believe he has given up his old ways, Wael, although maybe he is being much more careful."

"Exactly. He won't bother us unless he can get something from us that will give him an edge. Are you hiding something, Manar?"

Manar laughed. "No," he said, "the only thing I'm hiding is my usual incompetence, or what they could call incompetence, if they wanted to get rid of me."

"My advice is to resign immediately if you suspect that's the case. Plead family illness."

But the head minister of the security police hadn't come after all. No helicopter landed with his sniper-armed bodyguards, no caravan of SUVs arrived with guns pointed through the windows. Just the two men who looked like tourists.

The men showed Manar and Wael their credentials and then sat down in the office where Manar had worked all night and started to talk. It took the men a few seconds to realize that they were speaking in perfect Arabic rather than English.

Manar reached for his tablet and his pen, planning to take notes during their meeting.

One of the men, the taller of the two, raised his hand and said, "No notes. Today you will take no notes."

The meeting lasted for a little more than two hours, and then the men from Interpol, politely declining Manar's invitation to lunch, got in their compact car and left.

Manar had the administrative assistant bring in lunch, and he and Wael sat at Manar's desk and silently ate their food together, each thinking over what they had learned. After lunch, Wael thanked Manar for the food and left to drive back to Luxor. He didn't say goodbye.

At 5, Manar was still sitting at his desk, thinking. He hadn't taken any phone calls or done anything at all all afternoon. He was trying to decide what to do. The men from Interpol had shown very convincing evidence, reports that seemed to be extremely accurate, and aerial surveillance photos that were clearly real. They had offered their support and assistance. They said that the federal minister of intelligence also offered his support and assistance. They were confident that the item had probably already been taken over the border into the Sudan, to its most likely destination, to one of the terrorist training camps hidden in the eastern mountains there, but they couldn't verify this so they were being cautious. They thought they knew who was behind the operation, although they couldn't share his name until they were sure. Also they were close to finding out the names of the people who drove the box down from Cairo in the old panel van.

The men had told Wael and Manar they should not worry about anything, because arrests were coming soon. They had many sources who were trying to find out what happened to the box, to verify that it had been moved on past Aswan. But since so far they couldn't confirm this, caution was recommended. There were undercover operatives working the case, and of course Manar couldn't know who they were because they would be compromised. However, if he had a lead, please to let the Interpol men know immediately, day or night, and they would put him in touch with the local agents within minutes.

Manar and Wael should be looking for a wooden crate that could be lifted by two or three men, approximately the size of a largish suitcase but unusually heavy. There might be a smaller package with it, and that would be not as heavy. That would be the C-4, which was likely to be a pink orangey color. It might have already been broken into smaller packages. But it was the bigger crate that was the problem. There was no way to identify it and know that they had found the right one, so care must be taken. The only thing that might identify it was that it had shipped from the UK, so there might be some markings or writings in English. But the dirty bomb could have been put inside another kind of container by now. The reason it was called a dirty bomb was because it could cause a lot of radiation after the initial destruction of the blast. It was hard to tell how much damage could be expected. Possibly half the town. Not counting the radiation, of course. That was much harder to estimate. It was best not to think about that. And this was all precautionary, of course, because they expected to locate the bomb shortly.

As Manar left the office to go home for dinner, he was sure that the bomb must still be in Aswan. At least Interpol must think it was still in Aswan. Interpol would have not made the trip if they were so sure that it had moved on. He wondered if he would even recognize it if he saw it. Before it blew him and everything around him into the afterlife.

EIGHT

A month later, PowerPoint presentation well honed, Della found herself sitting in the waiting room at the Cairo airport, bound for Paris. She was trying to remember a song about April in Paris. But did the song say it would be raining or that everything would be green? She was arriving a few days ahead to adjust to the time difference, visit the Louvre, do some shopping, and perfect her presentation. Della hoped to have a chance to talk to some of the other archeologists who were doing early dynasty research.

She had told Sameh that she was going, but he must have forgotten, and she didn't remind him. He might not approve, insisting that it would be better to take it easy and continue to heal. She would call to check in from her hotel. Having four days to herself in Paris to rest and work and shop sounded peaceful. Sameh would check on her, of course, but that was okay. If she didn't mention that she was in Paris, he might not even notice, just doing his usual brief phone call, letting her know that he was wherever he was and that he was in charge. Chances were he would not even ask about her. Actually he might just text her and not even call.

Waiting in the boarding area, book in hand, she looked up to see a man standing across the waiting area with his back to her. He looked familiar. Then he turned and she could see it was Nigel. He was standing 30 feet from her, holding his carry-on, looking at his phone. Of course he would be attending the conference, too. Dressed in western style clothing, jeans and a lightweight sweater, for the journey, Della was reminded of how different the circumstances were when she had met Nigel in Luxor. And maybe before.

He didn't see her, and she waited, holding onto her closed book, wondering if he would see her and if so what she would do. And then he did. He slowly walked towards her. She was suddenly not sure she would be able to speak to him. She had forgotten how alluring his eyes and sandy hair were.

"Is that a 'no'?"

"Pardon?"

"May I sit down next to you? Unless, of course, you're expecting someone else."

"No. Please." She had been distracted by that face, that puzzling face. Clearing her jacket from the seat, she motioned for him to sit.

As they talked, Della learned he was going early because of some meetings. He was flying coach. Della asked the steward if they could upgrade him to first class, so that she and Nigel could sit together. They talked for the entire flight into Charles DeGaulle.

As they parted at the baggage claim, Nigel asked where she would be staying, and she told him of her small suite at the Hotel Plaza Athenee Paris, overlooking the Avenue Montaigne.

When he called the next morning and asked if he could show her some of his favorite sights, Della wasn't really surprised. They took the Métro to Montmartre, then to Chicken Street, Sacré Coeur. They had lunch at Chez Plumeau. They walked the streets of Paris into the early evening, when Della pleaded weariness and went to her room. Later that evening Nigel called to say he had arranged a surprise for her for the next day. They met for coffee and then took a taxi to the Louvre, entering at the professional entrance, where they met Henri Latourette, the curator for the Egyptian collection. Nigel had arranged for them to have to a private tour of the hidden, archived Egyptian collection in the basement. There was a tour offered to the attendees at the conference, but this was something more, a small private tour.

Della had long known about the extent of the collection, but seeing it in person, it was almost overwhelming. It was the closest thing she had seen to the collection in the Cairo Museum. Napoleon had taken an amazing number of artifacts back to France when he left Egypt in 1799. She could only imagine the vast caravans he had needed to move the extensive artifacts and mummies to Paris. She knew that many of them never arrived at the Louvre. She saw at least a dozen things she would suggest that the Cairo Museum request to be returned. But she didn't mention them, so as not to embarrass Nigel. Today she was the companion of a respected professional archeological journalist.

Everyone wants to be written up in a positive light, Nigel told her, and the Louvre is like all the other great museums: they use every resource possible to market their image. Nigel would write a short piece about the visit and send it to one of his publications, as well as post part of it on the museum's Facebook page as a thank you for their hospitality.

After the tour the curator invited them to wander through the restricted areas at their leisure, coming to his office at the close of the business day. Nigel stood beside Della, who, stopping to contemplate each item, seemed to be recording everything in her mind. She took no notes, but Nigel watched her mumble things under her breath as she followed him to the next aisle or around the next hall. When he asked her later what most surprised her, she took a long time to construct an answer. And the answer amazed him, because she spoke of the beginning of a new theory about the political structure of the Middle Kingdom. She had come to the idea before today, but because of the styles she had seen, it solidified in her mind. She also told him that the Louvre had made some mistakes on their dating. And Nigel looked into her deep green eyes as she told him this and knew she was probably right.

Della wasn't ready when Nigel said that it was time to leave, and she looked up to find him laughing at her. He knew she would prefer to stay for days in these musty vaults, carefully evaluating each item for the time and place it had been made, its provenance, maybe even the thoughts of the ancient artist.

As they were walking back to her hotel, she asked him if he would look at her presentation and give her his feedback.

"Could you look at it from a kind of pizzazz perspective for me? I'm excited about my little goddess, but I always feel like my presentations are dry and this is one time I don't want to be boring."

"Of course. But, Della, I think your enthusiasm will keep the presentation from being boring."

She and Nigel planned a late dinner that night nearby, after a brief strategy session to look over the presentation. Della hadn't presented at a major conference before, never on a new find. She would essentially be notifying the world of her possible discovery.

They sat in the sitting area of her small suite, with Della pulling her tired bare feet up under her on the Louis IV wingchair across the room from the little marble-topped desk. She told Nigel the whole story. How she had come across the little sculpture in the vaults and immediately recognized that it didn't belong with the other artifacts it had been grouped with. How she had requested it for a research project in Luxor and sent a tiny sample out for carbond dating. How the museum had tried to get it back, even tried to take it back. How the carbon dating report had come in all wrong, and how her husband had insisted that it must be she who was wrong. How she had sent out for a second dating report., but this time not through the museum. Nigel listened, and then he read through her presentation on the laptop. He took a long time.

"And you have the second dating report?"

"No, not yet, but I think I have a good case to present my theory anyway."

Nigel was quiet for quite a while longer, going back again through the presentation.

"Based on the time you're taking, I gather that you think it needs lots of revision." Della shifted her weight to relieve her toes on the gold damask of the chair.

"No, not really. It's very good, actually."

"Then what?"

"Let me think about my answer and we can talk about it over dinner. I made reservations at the Restaurant 9 New York, between the Eiffel Tower and Champs Elysees. I hear it's very private and has wonderful food. We'll be able to talk there."

As Nigel and Della walked out onto the Paris sidewalk, he was calm, but he was almost sure Della was in trouble. Had someone interrupted the testing process and sent her a fake report? It would have to be someone who knew how to fake one well enough to be believed. This could only mean that the person who did this had power and access. And that the little sculpture was worth the trouble. Considering the amount of effort it would have taken to fake the report, the statue was worth some serious money. Nigel was pretty sure that after this presentation at the conference, the little sculpture would be long gone before Della even left the conference hall. The attempt to pick it up confirmed his fears. If someone were not yet sure the piece was worth the hassle of getting around what must be very high security at the mysterious

Luxor campus, there would be no doubt after this presentation. A cell phone call from the conference and the statue would be gone within an hour, at best. And, of course, no one in Luxor would remember seeing anything. It was the miracle of bribery.

Della might be underestimating the rareness of the artifact. Nigel could only think of three people who would know that Della had the piece. One of those was a director inside the Cairo Museum system. He had been selling Gamal artifacts for years right out of the museum cellars. He would have them carefully packed and brought to his office, where a courier would pick them up. Incredibly lucrative theft in broad daylight. Nigel had only learned who the man was by accident last fall. More than a fox in the hen house, the man had been working at the Cairo Museum for 20 years, was highly respected, and had the ear of the world-famous national director of antiquities. He was completely above suspicion. Gamal referred to him as a "sourcing specialist." Della's little sculpture would be worth a fortune to this specialist. If Gamal was involved and because Gamal was aware of any and all artifacts being smuggled in Egypt, this was also quite dangerous. Nigel found himself wondered how many million Euros were involved here. Enough for a villa on the Riviera? And a yacht?

How could he help her? Surely she was aware of the smuggling market. It would be impossible not to. But perhaps she did not recognize their power. Almost absolute power. Nigel walked along the Seine and thought of the fragrance of Della's soft red hair, and her smile when she learned of the private tour of the Louvre basement archives. She was so gifted in her skill at Egyptology and at the same time so naïve. How could he tell her that he knew so much about the dark underworld of smuggling artifacts? How could he warn her without saying too much about his own past? She was smart, and she would catch on quickly as she grew in her profession. How could he help her now?

After they sat down, Nigel excused himself and called a friend in Cairo. He asked him to do a small favor for him, to just make a few calls and text him back. Nigel returned to the table hoping he would know more by the time dinner was over.

Della had worn a new dress she had found in Le Printemps. It was a radiant green, and even though modest by western standards, the style set Della's skin aglow. The colors in the silk defied their cool palette and washed the creamy skin of her neck and face with a glowing rose blush. She wasn't pretty in the Hollywood sense, but when she smiled, her face lit up, making people want to stop and watch her. Stop and listen. Stop and hope for another smile.

Nigel waited until they had had some wine, and then he began.

"Della, I think you're taking too big of a chance."

"Because Wenut is so valuable?"

"Yes. Have you hidden your sculpture well?"

"Yes, I have, I put her................. "

"No, please don't tell me."

"Should I be afraid of you then?"

"No, never. I just don't want you say it out loud. Don't tell me. Don't tell anyone. In fact, I think it would be better if you just talked about something else entirely in your presentation."

"That bad?" There was hurt in her eyes.

"No, the presentation is great. The sculpture is an exciting discovery and a great story. That's the problem." He took a deep breath. "I think you suspect that someone is trying to trick you. And I agree. They probably don't think you know what you have, and so they can wait for you to get careless. If you announce to the world that you understand the rarity of this piece, your little artifact will be gone within a day. In fact, maybe within a few hours. And by gone, I mean gone."

Della just stared at him. He waited for her rebuke.

She had had a strange flashback. It shot into her mind and was just as quickly gone. Perhaps it was the wine. "I just almost remembered when I first saw your face. In the van."

"My face? What van?"

"Right after I was in the accident."

Nigel stopped and took a sip of his wine. He looked at Della calmly, using all of his composure. "Della, I know you think that we met somewhere before, but we didn't. And I don't know anything about an accident. I'm sorry, but I don't."

She just stared at him, and then said, softly, "I've told you before. I know you helped me. I just now remembered looking up and seeing your face. I'm not sure why it bothers you, Nigel, but it seems very important to me. And because I have not been able to remember anything more than just your face, it is even more important."

Nigel slid his hand across the linen tablecloth and grasped one of hers. She looked down at his hand and hers together on the table, and then back up into his face.

For a moment he didn't speak, sensing the warmth of her skin against his and the throb of her heartbeat through her soft fingers."I'm flattered that you think I have helped you. But I truly don't remember any accident. But please, please, let me help you now."

Della held her breath as she held his gaze. Although she knew he was lying to her about the memory, she sensed that he had almost relented, almost had decided to tell her, for just a moment, before he changed his mind.

"So you feel pretty sure that someone is trying to steal Wenut – to sell her into the artifact smuggling underground?"

Nigel was surprised to hear her say these words out loud in public. Their table was private and no one heard her speak, but it made him realize how careful he had become since working with Gamal.

"Even though my artifact is locked inside an official government Museum compound. It would be very hard to get into the campus at Luxor. We have excellent security."

"I have been reporting on Egyptian antiquities for 15 years, and I have heard things, things I wasn't intended to hear. Things I cannot verify or confirm. Just things I believe are true. That I know are true. Bad things that have turned out to be very real."

"Such as?"

"Such as the people doing the stealing are the insiders or at least they are helping. You have heard rumors, too, I know."

"Yes, but I don't believe everything I hear."

"I don't either, but I know this is happening."

"Then have you reported it to the authorities?"

Nigel smiled. He had almost laughed. He saw that she was smiling back at him. She knew as well as he that 'authorities were often the problem.

"I have no proof. No evidence. So it would be hearsay." Except, that, of course, he did have proof. He had touched things, moved things hidden in boxes, written about them.

"But I have promised Dr. Kawass a presentation. What can I possibly tell him?"

"Tell him nothing. Or tell him you changed your mind. Tell him the dating came back wrong and you were wrong about your original subject. Tell him you would like to talk about being an American working with the Cairo Museum. Talk about the crypts, about the thousands of un-identified artifacts crammed into those dark vaults. Talk about anything else. Please believe me when I say this is seriously dangerous."

"Seriously dangerous?"

"Yes. For you. Not just the statue. In fact you might want to send it back, Della. Someone might want it so much they would not mind hurting you to get it."

"I can't believe it is that bad, Nigel. I think you're exaggerating."

Nigel stopped, trying to decide what to say next. He almost spoke, but her piercing eyes stopped him. She knew he had lied again about their meeting previously. But he needed her to believe him now, to trust him. Instead he watched as she got a kind of determined look in her eyes, like, he imagined, the one that she had when she had fought her way through school, earned her academic accolades, proved herself in a field dominated by men. But this wasn't academia: this was the raw underbelly of the criminal world. The very lucrative criminal world. She would be a simple enough casualty, a small price for such a very profitable item.

The determined look made her eyes sparkle, and the wine had filled her cheeks with even more of a glow. He pulled his hand gently away. He would wait and try again later in the evening. "Would you split a dessert with me? I have heard they make a wonderful dish called framboises au chocolat en croûte. "

Looking down to adjust her napkin in her lap, Della,excused herself to go to the ladies room, after nodding agreement to dessert and to cognac.

Nigel checked his phone and the message was there, simple cryptic words: *Yes A's aware of it*. So it seemed that the people he suspected were just biding their time. He would have to try to talk to her again and to convince her this time.

She would be back in just a moment and then he had to succeed.

Nigel had tried to not think about this woman these many months. But his mind pulled him there, the force so much stronger than his good intentions, and he found himself reading any news he could find about the university to see if she was mentioned. If he found an article she had written, he could send a comment. If he could learn a type of artifact she was studying, he could contact her and tell he was writing about the same thing. It would be a coincidence. And now here he was in a restaurant in Paris waiting for her. After three days of being within inches of her shoulders, her fingers, her ears, her soft laugh. He had never been obsessed with a woman. And why this woman? Most of his women had been eager and forward, laughing too loud and ready for sex immediately and anywhere. Smart and brazen. This one was quiet and considered, even shy. And yet he couldn't stop thinking about her. A few more hours, maybe one more day. Maybe then she would see him they way he wanted her to see him. Understand about the desire. Understand that this was meant to be.

When Della returned, she sat quietly, ignoring the beautiful dessert but sipping at the cognac. Nigel watched her face, looking for clues to her intentions. But he was also struggling to see beyond the magnetic need to pull her to him.

They walked side by side in silence through the chilly Paris night back to Della's hotel and then rode the elevator up to the third level, also in silence.

Standing at her door, Nigel struggled to just tell her, once more, that she should change her plan for her presentation. She unlocked the door and was turning to say goodnight when he finally found his words.

"Della," he said, " I...."

She was looking up at him. He could see into the depths of her electric green eyes. He felt his face moving towards hers and as their lips met, a pulsing voltage ran through him and he felt both a charged release and the compelling need to fold her into him. The heat rose in his neck and he felt the firmness of her breasts against his chest and suddenly both of their mouths were open and they were deep in a kiss, his passion returned.

Della was surprised by the desire, a volcano flowing up within her. An out-of-control horse carrying her away. This flush, unknown to her, almost a panicky feeling, a kind of blindness, as though she were falling into darkness. Alarms were blaring in her head. "Oh" was all she was able to speak.

"Yes."

"I have to go now. Inside. Goodnight, and thank you…for your help."

Nigel couldn't let her go. He pulled away, but his arms would not release. "Della. For your safety please listen to me. Our kiss doesn't change anything about the presentation. Please. For your safety, change it."

"Thank you, Nigel."

"Wait.

"If I wait, Nigel…Good night."

"No one is here. No one will know."

"I'll know. Please leave me here, alone." Della seemed to be having trouble speaking. There was a little tremor in her fingers as they touched him.

He pulled back to look at her. She held his gaze, sure glowing pools of energy. He stood apart, only holding her hand for a long long minute, hoping for more words, other words. They didn't come.

"I'll go."

"Yes." Her voice was barely audible, a wisp of breath from deep inside her.

Nigel stepped back, finally releasing her from his embrace. He wanted to warn her one more time. And he wanted to ask her if she was sure she wanted him to leave, because he had never wanted anything more in his life than to hold this woman right now. She was leaning against the door, now looking down at the floral carpet, still holding on to one of his fingers.

Nigel separated his fingertips from hers and turned to walk down the hall to the stairwell.

Della pulled the door closed behind her and then clamped down a whimper behind her teeth. Tears began to seep out, silently, as she waited for the trembling to subside. She moved over to sit down in her desk chair. Later, when she calmed down, she would send some emails and then work on her new presentation.

She really did believe him, she realized, that she needed to change the presentation. His argument made sense. She even believed that she might be in danger. But right now she wasn't afraid of some hidden thief who would steal her little Wenut. She was afraid of Nigel. She was afraid of herself and Nigel together.

The next morning Della took a taxi early to the conference, where she checked in and signed up for other lectures. She looked around for Nigel now and then but she never saw him and was grateful for that. She wasn't sure what she would do if she did.

In spite of the last minute change of topic, her presentation had been well received, and as she had looked at the audience during the applause, she thought she saw him sitting towards the back. She wondered what he thought of her new topic. She hadn't asked for his hotel or his phone number, which was good, she realized. She spent the rest of the conference talking to other professionals, trying to meet anyone who was in active research on 2nd Dynasty items, and observing others' posters.

As she was walking to the boarding gate at Charles de Gaulle, Della thought she saw Nigel again, but she wasn't sure, and the man moved away quickly in the crowd towards another gate.

Returning to Cairo she was seated next to a very plump older woman, who was surprised to learn she was an American because she was wearing her abaya for the return trip to Egypt. The woman wanted to talk and so Della had to pull out her laptop and pretend to work.

Nigel called her the Thursday after she got back from Paris. She was surprised until she realized that she had given him the number in Paris.

He would be in the area that afternoon. Could he please stop by?

Della waited before she answered.

"Nigel, I'm afraid that if you do..."

"I promise you nothing will happen. I'll only talk, I promise."

Della didn't answer.

"Are you still there?"

"Yes, that will be fine. I'll tell the guard to let you in."

The little box on the wall squawked, then popped, as the guard switched off the connection. Walking out of her office into the hall, she stood breathing quietly by the railing overlooking the stairwell and waiting for the sound of the big double entry doors three floors below to bang open. She listened for his footfalls on the stairs. He must be wearing soft-soled shoes because they didn't echo very much.

She stood silently watching him as he climbed the stairs. As he started the last flight, he turned his face up to see her standing there, and she returned his wide smile as he came up the last few rises.

"As you see, elevators are not part of the thinking here. For visitors and workers, that is. The only one is reserved for artifacts. You need to be a couple of thousand years old to ride on it."

Nigel rose in front of her and came around to stand politely looking down into her eyes.

"I think I would rather not wait that long."

She noticed that he wasn't particularly winded.

"It is good to see you."

She didn't know what to say, exactly.

"Yes," she managed to say. "You too."

Della took Nigel into her office, which was really a collection of four rooms, originally intended to be a small waiting room, an office, a secretarial office, and a closet. Della had her desk against one wall in the front room, and work tables in two of the other three, and charts and large sheets of paper with her notes on most of the walls. In addition to this were three overloaded bookcases, several boxes in the corners with books piled on top of them, an old style PC and monitor on the desk and a red MAC laptop right next to it.

She told him about her current project, which involved the stylistic changes of 25th Dynasty canopic jars. Her usual area of focus was not canopic jars, but the study of Old Kingdom and intermediate period goddesses, and their development into other goddesses. Wenut, small and unassuming, had been brought out of hiding to show Nigel and was sitting on the one of the tables in the back room. Placed between books and stacks of documents one would never have guessed that she was so rare.

"You can see what I was so upset by the first dating report: looking at her, it is obvious it is wrong. The materials, the method of carving, and even the way the eyes are painted. The style is clearly far far older. And see, here? She has the remnants of a snake's head shape, inside of her rabbit head contour."

"I think that's the coup de grâce. It's like the sculpture has captured the goddess in transition from a more ancient form. They had to be wrong. However hard it is to believe that the Alpha Analytic Laboratory would make a mistake, I couldn't accept the results. I had to try again."

"Where did you send the second sample?"

"To the Thompson Morris Lab. But I sent it on my own, not through the university museum system. I paid for it privately."

"Don't you usually lock her in the vault?"

"No. I should. But instead I hide her in my office. I took her out to show you. Isn't she beautiful?"

Della showed him the little alcove she had created behind the paper in her cabinet, then wrapped the sculpture up lovingly, placed Wenut carefully, stacked some supplies in front of her, and removed her plastic gloves. Then she locked the cabinet and took him down to the vault for a tour of some of the artifacts that were stored here. Some were on loan from the Cairo Museum, some from other museums around the world. This was considered the safest place after the Cairo Museum, because it was an unassuming, well-guarded building, and most people were unaware of its existence. It was a vast underground room, climate controlled by a very modern electronic system.

"Why don't you feel that Wenut would be safe here?"

"I have always had a funny feeling about that. I would rather have her near me, where no one would think to look, where only I have the key, and where I can check on her. It is a dark, airconditioned space, so it meets most of the guidelines for storage."

"So, Della, I came to ask for your help." Nigel explained that he would like her opinion on interpretations of carved panels at Karnak that were supposedly related to the pharoah's invasion of what was now Syria. There was so much controversy, and both sides of the argument were so far apart. Perhaps she could go with him to see them and offer her opinion.

"I'm not sure I would be of much help. I haven't spent any time on that period. I'll go over there and see the panels one day soon and tell you what I notice about them. I think I know the section you're talking about."

"Perhaps we could go together," Nigel said, trying again.

Della didn't answer.

There were so many sculptures, stellae, and canopic jars that they only gotten through part of the collection, but the visit was growing long and they were both aware of each other's warmth in the cool quiet of the vault, so Della took Nigel back to her office and gave him a reference she thought he should consult on the Karnak issue.

"Thanks. This has been really interesting. It was great to see you in your own environment." He stood perfectly still, hesitating. "And I'm sorry if I was out of line in Paris. I hope this won't affect our friendship. Would you like to come with me next week sometime to visit Karnak?"

"Yes." She spoke softly, standing away from him.

Without more words, Nigel turned and reached for the door to the hall, as Della came around behind him, and as he began to open it, he turned around one last time and found her standing right next to him. She was looking up at him.

"Goodbye," he said.

"Goodbye," she said.

He turned again.

"Wait," she said.

He turned back and then they were embracing and kissing passionately. His hunger came back with an urgency he hadn't dared expect and soon they were grasping each other and leaning on the office wall, began to sink towards the floor. Della felt Nigel's hand on her hips and found herself leaning back so he could kiss her all the way down her neck towards her breasts, while she felt herself sinking into a desire she hadn't believed was there. Della began to make soft moaning sounds and Nigel lifted his head to look into her face, seeing that she seemed distressed.

"Do you want to stop?"

Flushed and wide-eyed, saying nothing, Della couldn't speak. She just stood and then, slowly, slowly, she pushed him away.

"I'm sorry, Nigel, I'm sorry."

"No, please don't say that. Don't be sorry. Please."

"It's my fault. I should not have invited you."

"You know that isn't true. I wanted to see you. And you wanted to see me. I think you know what is going on here, Della."

"Yes." Della heard the word coming from her mouth. She wanted to say it again.

Instead she reached for the squawk box on the wall and pushed the speaker button and said, "Mr. Sutherland will be leaving now."

Nigel hesitated for a full minute. Then he leaned down and kissed her softly on the cheek, chastely, like a man would kiss a beloved child. It was the opposite of how he felt. He then moved towards the door and left. He didn't turn around to look at her or to say goodbye. She didn't watch him go but huddled inside her office and listened as his footsteps descended the stairs, one level down, and then the next, then the next.

Della knew that she had just made a terrible mistake.

NINE

Nigel didn't call about going to Karnak.

Della started to come in early to the office and then to stay late to work on her reports. She kept her cell phone on the desk beside her wherever she was writing, or looking through her journals, or going through some of the out-of-print books of Egyptian antiquities that she had collected as resources. She jumped every time the phone rang. One afternoon she decided to go to the ahwa where she had first talked to Nigel, thinking that perhaps he would be having tea there. Of course he wasn't. She sat in the back of the little inside room, keeping her sunglasses on, sipping her coffee and watching the door. She sat for an hour and a half.

She realized she didn't know much about Nigel. She knew that he was living in Luxor while working on several writing projects for *JEA* and another journal, and that he had said he had an important deadline coming up. But how long was he going to be here? And what would happen after that? Would he move back to Cairo? Would he go to other locations to work? Would she run across him in Luxor, walking in the marketplace? She hoped she would at least have a chance to talk to him once more.

Della began to call Sameh every day, in the late morning, when she knew he would be getting ready to break for lunch. She asked him what he was working on today, and if he would like her to think of ideas to help. Perhaps she had been too distant of a wife during this stressful time in his life. They had had so much fun when they were students together and he'd always appreciated her input and opinions. When he had told her that he was going to be in negotiations, she would leave him voicemails telling him that she was thinking of him and wishing him well. He would call back in the afternoon to thank her, asking how she was doing. She felt like some of their old collaborative spirit was returning and that their marriage, which had seemed so tentative and distant lately, would really be alright.

Sameh was under a lot of strain, and they would get through this period and then he would spend more time at home, and things would be easier. Right now he was so busy, he was just trying to manage it all. Would it be like this if he was a spouse doing his surgery internship after medical school? Many wives had to sacrifice part of their early years of marriage to a career; they were no different from thousands of other couples. Lately Sameh had been staying in Cairo,not at home with his parents and siblings but with friends, for a few weeks, for convenience while he worked. This was easily done because he did most of his communication with his father and company by cell phone and laptop. He was avoiding having to deal with his father directly. He hadn't told his mother, so he asked that she please just keep it just between them. Of course, she would. Della loved Merina and admired her, but she suspected Merina would feel compelled to tell Omar if she found out Sameh was staying in Cairo and not at home in Luxor.

A week passed, and then another, and Sameh decided to stay in Cairo a little longer. He was waiting for word about a meeting in Syria, with the generals of the Assad regime, as soon as all the participants could attend. The contract would involve the shipping of large military equipment, and the clients liked to be sure their vendors could respond on a moment's notice. It was a kind of a war game they liked to play with their contractors.

Della suggested that she come up to see Sameh for the weekend. She would not let his family know and she would enjoy meeting his friends. Thanks, he had said, but these are business friends and I'm not sure they are good enough for you, my dear. I would much prefer that you stay safely in Luxor, near the work that you love. I'll be able to work as much as I need to if I know you're safe. If you come here, I'll only want to spend time with you and will get nothing accomplished.

Della understood. And it was better, probably, that she didn't have to deceive Merina. Sameh's mother was a warm, welcoming and intelligent woman, and Della didn't think she would like to lie to her. If Sameh hid some things from her, that was an issue between mother and son. Of all the women Della had ever met, Merina was probably her favorite, and she wanted Merina to feel she could trust her.

Nigel didn't expect to stay in Luxor much longer. He had planned to stay until he completed a series of articles on those war scenes at Karnak and finish up another piece on sonar in the search for new tombs in the Valley of the Kings. But now he wanted to leave the city, to be far away from Luxor and knowing that Della was living and breathing here. He expected to finish his interviews with local experts within two to three days and then he would have one more visit with the sonar expert before he could head back to Cairo, where he could finish working from his notes and tapes.

He hadn't heard from Gamal for over a month and that was great. His strategy was to write a few more really well researched and significant articles and then see if he couldn't earn a position with the *JEA* as a regular columnist and not have to ever do favors for Gamal again. He had tried to break off their relationship several times, saying he was too busy to help because of other obligations, but Gamal hadn't been too happy about it. He had tried to explain that he had been happy to help for a while, but his career goals were beginning to work out, and he would need to spend all his time on writing. Gamal had laughed, sitting across the table at the outdoor cafe. "You archeologists are all alike! You think you can live off of words! Ha!"

But what should he do about Della? He wanted to leave Luxor but he also wanted to see her once again. No, that was a lie. He wanted to see her much more than that. What was worse, Nigel couldn't stop dreaming about her. Her big green eyes would appear to him in his sleep and he would hear her saying "Thank you for helping me." And then he would wake up and stare at the ceiling of his temporary flat. Sometimes in his dream she would be looking up at him from a patterned rug when she spoke, and sometimes she would be hovering or floating above him, her red hair flowing around her head as though in water.

He would just call one more time. Just once more. Perhaps they could still be friends. She would be a valuable asset as a friend, he reminded himself, not believing for a moment that this was his real reason for calling. He sent a text and waited. Five hours later there was still no answer. He would wait until tomorrow and then call her.

Nigel dreamed of the green eyes again that night, but this time they were twirling around him in a flashing darkness. He felt her body, too, near him, and he woke up long before dawn and lay still, hot and fully aroused, waiting for the day to begin.

Della saw the text the moment it came in. She stared at it as she sat by her computer.

"Pls cld we meet for lunch. To talk. Miss you. N."

She almost deleted it but then decided not to. She wasn't sure she would be able to talk with Nigel. What was there to say? There was no way they should be meeting at all, and certainly not in this conservative city. For one thing, they would surely be seen. In Paris, no one would even notice them, a married woman meeting a man who wasn't her husband; but in Luxor they would. And he knew it, too. How dare he say he missed her. She thought about his kiss, about his face, about his smile. She missed him, too, and she couldn't, wouldn't, meet him.

Della had the driver pick her up early for a change. She took some books with her to review, thinking that she would be able to put Nigel out of her mind in her own home. But she found that she wasn't able to eat dinner. Silva had made soup, and she was worried that Della was getting sick again because she just sat and sipped her tea and stared out the window at the river. Della explained that she was just tired and that she would be fine tomorrow. She went to bed early, taking one of her dear old textbooks on the 3rd Dynasty to read, a sure way to fall asleep.

But tonight it didn't work. She kept thinking about Nigel being next to her. She could remember the smell and feel of his neck, his soft hair. When she finally fell asleep, she dreamed of making love, over and over, with a man with blond hair and blue eyes, and woke up to find herself bereft and alone in the big bed. She wondered where he was tonight. Was he sleeping?

The morning dawned bright and bleak. She would not see him today, or tomorrow, or any day, and so she would have to just get through it. It crossed her mind that she should feel shame and regret because of Sameh. But she couldn't find it in her. She would remember their embraces forever, and even if she never saw Nigel again, she would savor the memory of his touch. She had to admit that she hadn't guessed that this kind of passion was possible. In Hollywood movies, she had thought, was the only place that happened. It was a terrible thing to learn that it could happen to her.

She found herself at the office early, as usual, the next morning, determined to focus her thoughts into productive work, to give her physical being a distraction. It has been over a week since Nigel had asked for the lunch meeting. At 9 she began to prepare for her 10 o'clock phone conference with Dr. Yunus. She assembled her notes, including spreadsheets and lists of time she had spent on her projects. She was prepared and calm and ready when the professor called at 10:15. At around 11:15 her professor asked her to outline her plans and time going forward for the next month, and what additional resources she expected she would need to request, and what results he should expect. She had just begun her response when her cell phone buzzed. It had to be Sameh, she thought, fearing to look. But then, in mid-sentence, she glanced down at her iPhone screen, sitting to her right on the desk.

The message read: *Have a rm. 1877 Akbar, C-2. I'll wait until 3:00. N.*

She felt the heat rise around her head and stared in confusion at the desk, the notes, and the computer screen in front of her.

"Please, Della, repeat what you just said. I didn't understand you."

She must have stopped talking mid-sentence. A room? She knew that street wasn't one of the main cafe streets. Nigel must be crazy. She didn't know exactly where it was but it couldn't be far.

"What did you say? I didn't understand." The voice of her professor was getting annoyed that she had apparently ignored him. She struggled with her answer and began to fall back into her report.

After going through the rest of her professor's questions, she completed the call and then began to send the usual follow-up email. As she hit the keys, she knew Nigel was there, waiting for her. She could almost feel him.

At 1 Della made a cup of tea in the little kitchen below her office and saw two of her colleagues, who asked about her health. She found herself telling them that she had a bit of a sore throat and they might want to stay clear of her. She wasn't sure if she was coming down with anything, but they should play it safe.

She went back to her office and looked at her email. But instead of messages she saw Nigel's face in front of her on the screen.

It wasn't that she wanted to go to him so much as she knew she needed to resolve this issue. This simply couldn't happen. Sameh didn't deserve this. And surely someone would wonder. And she couldn't bear it if people were to suspect her of betraying her wonderful in-law family. This could only lead to scandal, great regret, and even social disaster. You never knew who was watching from within the little shops along the crowded market streets. In many parts of Egypt even the most innocent interaction between a man and a woman could be misinterpreted.

The best thing to do was to go and tell him this. She would explain it in person so that she would not seem so cold and heartless. God knows she didn't feel cold, but she had to become cold to prevent this. Perhaps it would be better if she didn't go. Better to let him think she was cold and cruel. Yes, that was probably best. But then how would she ever know about before, about what happened after the accident? She so much wanted Nigel to tell her where they had met before. It haunted her. She needed him to tell her, to help her to explain the wispy dreams she had with his face looking down at her surrounded by bright sun.

Della put on her abaya and hajib and gathered her string market bag and headed towards the fruit stand that she usually stopped at on the way home. Today she just walked by, however, and went across into the alley and down until she saw the printing on the side of the building, hidden behind flowing shawls and dresses: *Al Akbar* it read. She turned right and watched for numbers along the corners as she walked north.

Nigel looked at his watch. It was 3:30. She wouldn't come. He knew she wanted to, he knew it. It was better, though, if she didn't. Too dangerous. He should have found a woman and gotten laid last night instead of thinking about Della all night. It was crazy to even have talked to her that first time, much less those days they spent together in Paris. Nigel wondered what Gamal would do if he ever found out she had recognized him. Maybe her memory would come back and she would remember Gamal too. That would be a terrible thing. Nigel was sure Gamal wouldn't like that to happen, and Gamal was likely capable of doing something to Della. Nigel didn't want to think about what that might be.

He would likely run into Della somewhere later on, at a university event or a conference, and he would just smile, be gracious, and act as if nothing happened.

o He reached for his backpack and stuffed his water bottle in the side pocket and checked he hadn't left anything in the room.

He checked his pocket for the key and poked his head in the bathroom and checked his face in the mirror. He could see he was very tired. He splashed some water on his face, then his hair, and then moved out opened the door.

And there she was. Just standing there.

Nigel's heart slowed. He wanted to grab her. But instead he stood very still, and after a very long minute, he said, "Hello."

"Hello," she responded.

"Would you like to have some water?" For some reason this crazy question came out of his mouth. That wasn't what he had intended to say.

"No, thank you," she said, stepping across the threshold.

"You came."

She didn't answer. She just stood looking at him. Nigel took her hand gently and pulled her all the way inside and closed the door. He turned the key and led her down the little hall into the main room. She didn't look at the bed, or the faded drapes, or the dusty window. She just looked at him.

"Do you want to talk?" He looked at her face and couldn't read her thoughts.

This time she did answer. "No."

It was she who came to him, warm and lush with heat. He could barely breathe as they got their clothes undone, touching and kissing with an almost panicked fervor.

They made love all afternoon, exploring the geometry of their bodies, united in rhythmic pulsing harmony over and over again. Nigel was bewitched by the beauty of her creamy white skin, her lithe body, the tenderness of her touch. Their desire began to fade in the early evening, finally, as they lay resting, nestled tightly together enough to be one being. Now that the passion was quieted, Nigel was overtaken by a dreadful fear of losing her. He knew she would have to leave him here, but he was saddened by the grim feeling that his world would be barren without her.

Outside the tiny window, the evening filled the sky with purples and blues while Della, lying in this man's arms on rough sheets in a shabby room, stumbled through the knowledge of his body beside her. She knew she had crossed some great divide in her life, her own Rubicon, and she knew when she returned to her old life, it would never be the same. And she was suddenly terribly, achingly, afraid that Nigel would go away. She didn't know what she was going to do. He was part of her world now.

As Della left the room, she pulled her hajib around most of her face and walked down a set of stairs at the back of the building, not the way she had come in. Nigel had suggested this. She took a taxi home and went immediately to bed, telling Silva that she really had gotten the flu after all.

She called in sick the next morning and sat in bed and thought and thought. She felt like she had accidentally discovered a whole new world, or maybe a kind of drug, and she was both thrilled and terrified. There had been a hint of it a month ago in Paris, but to have this kind of physical relationship would have been impossible for her to imagine until yesterday. She understood how Pandora must have felt.

Nigel texted her about midday. "Can I call?" his message said.

Instead she called him.

"Hello," she said, quietly, so that none of the servants would hear.

"Please meet me. We should talk," Nigel answered. "Please."

"Tomorrow," she said.

"No, now. Please. I'll wait here for you. Please come."

Della gathered her books and had the driver drop her off at the campus. She took the books upstairs and then walked back down the back service stairs, avoiding the main entrance, left the campus, and followed the same route through the busy marketplace, north on the little side street, and up to Nigel's room. He pulled her into the room and they spent the rest of the day in the bed, making love, then resting, then making love again.

They somehow didn't get around to talking.

As the dusk came into the sky, Della said, "I won't see you tomorrow, or the next day. Nigel, I have to stop this right now. It is too complicated, too hard, to change our lives."

"I know."

"Thank you," she said, bending to kiss him again.

"But Della, here is a key to this room. I'll be here waiting. I'll bring my work here. Come any time you can. Don't answer me now, please, just take this key. I know this is crazy, I know this is hard, but please just take this key."

And she did.

He was surprised that she came to him so often. He learned that she tended to lose herself in her work, passing whole days hidden in her office, reading her research sources, analyzing styles and the chemicals in ancient paints, comparing them to charts and diagrams. She had told him she sometimes forgot to eat, discovering the lunch that Silva had packed for her in her kit bag, untouched.

"I found an unusual variant of the blue pigment today," she would explain. "I think that it implies a trade route farther south than we had thought."

But she came to him, in the afternoon, dragging her bag and maybe a book, and entered the room almost shyly, asking him what he was working on. Beneath all the analytical thoughts was a woman who had never known love like theirs, and Nigel was happy to wait patiently, while they talked about their writing, and their research, before he pulled her into his arms and they returned to the simple joy of touch, of smell, of the heated energy of the physical. Nigel wasn't sure exactly when he became aware then that he should be married to her, as they joined anew, and he finally fully understood the true import of being married. It hurt him to let her go in the early evening, her small figure flowing down the little hall and disappearing down the stairs. He missed the discussions they had, her insights on things he knew so well and yet was rarely able to share. He missed her smile, her laugh, and he ached for her in his empty bed at night.

They fell into a pattern of meeting every other day, at least three times a week. Della continued to call Sameh, and to go to work daily, but her mind now belonged to Nigel. Her mind and her body. When Sameh commented on one of their calls that she seemed to be happier than she had for a while, she didn't answer. But she wondered if everyone noticed this, if Sameh could sense it over the phone. She tried to be careful, to keep up her responsibilities at work, and to think of Silva with her timing. And she began to believe that she was successful and was managing this secret life, that she was unwatched, and un-suspected, as she went to work then took a late lunch and then disappeared until the next day. When you have been gravely ill people expect you to work a lighter schedule, expect your energy to be lower than before. Her colleagues, who she rarely saw because they were all on the floors below her, didn't say anything about her leaving early. She always covered up fully in her abaya, and hajib, always the same dark color, thinking that she would blend in with the many other women who were in the marketplace. But Egyptian men spend all their lives around women who are covered up, and they didn't find it difficult to distinguish the regular market women from the light small footed woman who came many afternoons to secretly meet the sandy haired English man who hid in the room upstairs. Several of the merchants snickered as they watched the woman pass by, thinking she was unobserved. And several of these same merchants knew very well that this information would be worth a goodly amount of money if it got into the right hands. It was simply a matter of finding out who would be interested in knowing about this, and then, of course, who was likely to pay the most money for the information.

TEN

Merina had once again changed the date for lunch with Gamal. She had done this many times, but he always seemed to understand, even though she chose not to give any explanation on the phone. Sometimes she did not explain at all. It wasn't something she felt she could discuss with him, after all, that she had to change their covert meeting because of her duties as a wife. She smiled to herself when she thought about this. Six months ago she would not have believed she would even consider this kind of friendship. And certainly she would never have believed she would be enjoying the secret challenge so much.

She had left for the spa on schedule and sent her own car home, then had checked in, gone into the private changing room, left by a back entrance, and met Gamal's car at the side door. His SUV had blackened windows, and she couldn't see inside in the bright sun, and for a moment she thought perhaps he had come to meet her, but he hadn't. Instead, after they pulled up to the restaurant's private entrance, a servant opened the door for her into the little back room and Gamal was standing there, looking gorgeous, holding a little box in his hand. She moved towards him and found herself being pulled up into his embrace, then his kiss, and wanting to continue, her hunger suddenly not for food. She heard herself murmur a little as his lips touched her mouth, as they felt the heat rise between them. He ran his hands over her breasts, and her hips and one hand came around to caress her all down her front. Then Gamal pushed her away tenderly, and clearing his throat, said in a whisper, "Perhaps we should have our lunch."

She turned and gracefully moved toward the little table and began to take a seat. As Gamal pushed her chair in for her, he bent and kissed her on the back of her neck. A long wet kiss. She was at the point of turning to meet his mouth when he moved back and walked around to the other chair. As they sat waiting for the waiter to appear, they didn't speak, only looked into each other's eyes.

After the waiter had served the drinks, he offered her his little box, across the table, calling it a token of their friendship. As he pushed the box towards her, their hands touched and lingered, and Merina knew that she would go with this man now if he asked. Without lunch, against all her better judgement. But he didn't ask, just waited for her to open the box. She wasn't sure if she was grateful or not.

The box contained a petite and delicate gold bracelet, with jewels studding it in reds and blues and greens.

"It is lovely, Gamal, but I should not accept such a beautiful thing. Is it a replica of an antique piece?"

"No, my lovely Merina, it is the real thing. Because you're the real thing. You're too precious for imitations. Please wear it and think of me. "

"Thank you so much, Gamal. It is beautiful. And yes, I'll wear it. When I'm with you."

If Merina hadn't been so distracted by the look on his face and the very present memory of his flesh so close to hers and his strong chest tight against her, she would have asked about the piece, which seemed to be expertly made and very intricate, and the stones were perhaps precious. But instead she found herself talking with Gamal about their usual subject, the most recent stories and rumors from the undercurrents of Egyptian politics. It was a topic they both knew a lot about and delighted in, and it was a refuge from their lusty thoughts.

Merina found the wine excellent, as always when Gamal ordered it, although he preferred whiskey, and he took several drinks straight up during the meal. Neither of them ate much of the beautiful food, picking at the lettuce leaves and the seafood.

After lunch was long past and they had finished the berries and the cognac, Gamal ordered the car for her and started to walk her to the door, but then stopped and remained by the table as the driver came to escort her to the door.

She turned, and seeing that he was waiting behind, went back to him, and stood looking up into his eyes.

"Will you ride with me back to the spa?" she asked.

"No, my dear Merina, that isn't a good idea. I think we would not go to the spa. We would go somewhere else."

"Where would we go, Gamal?" Merina stood very close, whispering her words.

"We would go to the Sofitel, to a suite, and stay for the afternoon."

Merina was suddenly flushed with desire, imagining the body of this man with his shirt off, his face over hers. She didn't speak a word.

She watched him wait for a full minute, standing close beside him, his scent floating into her nostrils, and then he said, softly "Would you like to have lunch at Sofitel sometime, Merina?" He was holding his breath.

She hesitated only a moment. "Yes, Gamal. Yes, I would."

His eyes glittered, and now it was his turn not to speak.

When Merina arrived at the payment counter at the spa, the clerk exclaimed "Oh there you are are, Mrs. We couldn't find you anywhere. Your masseuse was ready for your massage but she has already another client. So sorry. Please excuse the phone call."

"The phone call?"

"We called your home, Mrs., because someone thought they saw you leave in a car."

"Yes, I got a call from a girlfriend and dashed out to have tea with her. So sorry. I meant to be back much sooner."

"No problem, Mrs."

"Can you please find me another masseuse today? I really do need a massage. My friend is very frustrating." Merina listened to her lies and wondered if they believed her. She would have to be more careful from now on. And she would leave a big tip for the masseuse.

She would think of Gamal during her massage. She would ask the masseuse to push hard.

Omar called to say he would be home for dinner, but it would be late. Merina quickly ordered her head cook to go to the market and see what she could find that would be suitable. She wanted to be sure Omar felt that things were normal. Especially now. The girls were both studying for exams, so they would eat early in the kitchen, and Zaki had just left to go skiing near Davos, so Omar and Merina would share an intimate dinner. Omar would not be happy about the extra funds she had put in Zaki's account, but he would also not want his son to seem poor in front of his friends. It was really more that Omar would not want his son to seem poor in front of Omar's political colleagues, maybe enemies, of course, rather than concern about how his son felt. She laughed. Omar was like an addict. She enjoyed the political life as much as anyone, but Omar lived for it now, and he hated it when he had to return to business issues and put aside his intrigues and schemes. He was turning into someone she no longer recognized. He had discovered power, and there was no going back.

Merina took a bath and dressed in a long aqua silk caftan, with a tight teddy underneath and tiny gold sandals on her feet. She met Omar when he came in the door with a distracted smile, her hair flowing free in welcome. He accepted her hug in a begrudging husbandly way, but it was clear he wasn't in the mood for affection. There had been some kind of setback today, she gathered, and thought that perhaps he would share his problem with her over their dinner together. She had his chilled beer ready for him, and carried it to him herself, with his customary Johnny Walker Red chaser.

Merina had some wine and smiled and made supportive comments over the meal, as they sat next to each other at one end of the long dining table. She got him several more beers and had Hatim bring the bottle of Johnny Walker to the table, but Omar seemed quite preoccupied and took a long time to relax. She had seen him like this many times and knew that whatever was bothering him would come out eventually and that all she had to do was to be there to listen. He would often ask for her advice, trusting her knack for politics. She always told him it was that she just had enough distance from the problem to see it more clearly.

Tonight he was slightly drunk and it was 11 and he had still not brought up what was bothering him. Merina knew that waiting was the best way, so she suggested they retire.

Omar said he would join her later, that he was going to sit on the balcony and smoke a cigar, and have a brandy. She didn't ask to come with him but kissed him goodnight on the cheek and quietly left the room.

It struck her as she walked down the hallway to their bed chamber what a difference there had been today between her lunch and her dinner.

Shortly after 3 she realized that Omar hadn't come to bed, and so she got up and walked the length of the darkened suite and to see if he had fallen asleep on the balcony. But he wasn't there. In the old days he used to get up and go to the office, but that was usually not part of his political life. Puzzled, she went back to bed and opened her book.

Merina was still propped up on her pillows, her book in her lap, when Omar came to bed. She kept her eyes closed so he wouldn't know she had awakened. He turned off her light, moved her book, and slipped into the other side of the king bed. He twisted and turned for a while and then fell into a troubled sleep. Something urgent must have happened for him to leave his home, drunk, in the middle of the night. There were few who had the power to have him do that. In fact, Merina could think of only one person: the president himself. Did this mean that the rumors were true of civil unrest in the country? Would that mean a crackdown by the secret police? She wondered if Omar would even tell her if he knew. Did this mean that Omar would be helping with the crackdown? With a chill she realized he would find the thrill of such power irresistible.

ELEVEN

It had seemed like such a promising lead. But it had turned out to go nowhere, which was especially frustrating because it had been the only good lead either Manar or Wael had gotten so far.

It had started out like most police work: Manar had gotten a tip through one of his regular informants about a market vendor who had a little storage space for his clothing and pottery inventory in the same warehouse district where the American wife and the dead man had been found. He had told a friend that around the time that the woman must have been there, he had seen an old white van pulling down the street and into a garage and then later seen two men carrying some rugs down the street in the middle of the heat of the day. The man had told his friend that the odd thing about it was that the men carried the rugs back the same way they had gone. All in the hot afternoon sun. It was very funny. Stupid men to have to carry heavy rugs through the streets in the burning heat, and clearly they must have made a mistake or they would not have had to carry them back again a short while later.

Wael said that perhaps the carpets were a cover for the box they were looking for. Or that perhaps the carpets were wrapped around the box.

Manar went to visit the man in his market stall. He would ask him exactly where the men took the carpets and if they seemed to be struggling with a heavy load. But the market stall was closed and empty. The merchants on either side of the space said they hadn't seen him for a few days. Sometimes he went to visit his sister in Alexandria. Yes, it was true that usually he told someone he was going and had someone open his business for him while he was gone.

Manar thought it an odd time to travel, August being the hottest month, but it could have been a family emergency. Who could say? Manar left his card with several of the market vendors, one on each side, and one across the alley from the closed stall. Perhaps they would call him. Manar sighed as he walked out of the now crowded market street to the waiting police van. Another coincidence. He hated coincidences.

When Wael had called Cairo and discovered that the American wife was in actually right there in his precinct, in Luxor, he had decided to wait until he could talk to Manar. Soon, he had told Manar: he would call her soon. He felt sure that if he approached the meeting in an unhurried, matter-of-fact way, she would be more willing to talk with him, to trust him, and not feel like she was being investigated. He wanted her to think of Wael as a non-threatening and friendly resource. Everyone knew the police were corrupt in Egypt. Certainly this American wife would have heard the terrible stories. Alas, most of them were true. But he had a deep-seated hunch that she was connected to all these strange happenings. He had to learn what she knew.

But the real problem was the bomb. Manar complained that they were not qualified to deal with a bomb of any kind: they had no training, they had no equipment, and they would not know what to do if they found it.

"But what heros we'll be if we find it, God willing! We don't have to do anything with it, Manar, just tell them where to look. "

Manar wasn't convinced. He didn't like this international stuff, much less anything explosive. His preference was for petty theft cases and an occasional domestic dispute. Those he could handle with great skill. He was very good at intimidating stupid husbands who beat their wives and at locking up the right kind of thieves. Until they could pay a reasonable fee, of course, for their release. He had long since learned who was worth arresting and who was not.

When Wael had suggested that the dead man and the American wife could be connected to the bomb, Manar laughed at the idea. Why would an American wife want to be involved with a bomb? An extremely rich American wife, at that. And besides, she was alive. If she <u>had</u> been involved for say, funding, no self-respecting criminal or terrorist would have left her alive. It would have been much less hassle to just dispose of her in the desert somewhere where no one would ever find her. And as for the dead man, they were not even sure who he was and why he had been there, and even how long he had been dead.

In the dry heat of Egypt, it could have been a while. Police work was so much harder when there were no witnesses, which is why Manar preferred petty theft.

Wael had agreed to come down and help do interviews, and they had called in all the usual suspects and all the usual informants, one by one. They made it clear that a much bigger cash prize than usual was available for any information about a hand-built, heavy wooden box anywhere around Aswan. They explained that it might be hidden in plain sight: in a warehouse or one of the attic storage rooms. In fact, they had even offered to pay for information that was second hand, say if someone heard of someone else having seen something. And no, they couldn't share what was in the box. But yes, it was very dangerous. Please don't touch it, or move it, or try to pick it up, they told each man.

It was odd, to Manar, at least, that no one had come forward with any information so far. Wael said it was still early. He said they would kind of a clue soon. But Manar had instincts that had served him well over the years, and he wasn't so sure.

Della decided that today was the day that she would open the new dating report. It had been sitting on her desk for weeks. She was almost ashamed that she had put off opening it, but her mind had been in turmoil over Nigel. And maybe, she confessed to herself, she was afraid of what it would tell her. In the afternoon, during a meeting downstairs, she was really thinking about Nigel: his body waiting for her there, warm, hard, passionate, in the hidden room. She found herself sitting in front of her computer, one minute absorbed in the specific stylistic details of the carved lid of an 16th Dynasty canopic jar, and the next, with a rush of warmth she would be seeing his eyes looking down into hers and feeling his maleness hard within her.

She pulled the envelope out from under a stack of papers she had in one of the desk drawers. The report was heavy, consisting of a bound folder about an inch thick and then, beneath it, a set of papers in a large binder clip that was another two inches thick. These clipped documents would be the comparables, printed charts of similar artifacts and similar dating projects, with generalized names instead of the names of the real clients and the real artifacts. It was a little like real estate, she guessed, to choose a date. Although the carbon dating process was the most scientific method available, it still provided only a possible range. And so the laboratory had provided examples of similar projects that had similar data, items that were already dated, to help narrow down the likely date. And there was the problem of the wood, itself. The wood could have been harvested a long time before the sculpture was made and then recycled into the hare's head that crowned the goddess's body.

But none of these variables would account for the difference in dates between the 2nd and the 18th dynasties. That was a thousand years of difference. That was the difference between what the first report had said, and what Della knew in her heart to be true. Even in ancient Egypt, which highly prized standardization and regimented style, things changed over a thousand years. You could sense the devotion and reverence with which the earliest pieces were carefully wrought. Later pieces were more about glory and wealth, such as the amazing art work in Tutankhamen's tomb. A thousand years before King Tut, an artist needed to appease the deity itself, not so much the king. The earliest artwork was really a way of praying for good weather and rain for crops and protection from the ravages of famine and pestilence.

Della set the clipped documents to one side, placed the bound report on the desk in front of her, and picked up the report. Before she opened the folder cover, she looked at the little sculpture for one last time before finding out when she was made. She looked past the familiar shape of her old friend to try and see the sculpture as the maker had seen her.

In ancient Egypt, all artwork obeyed a strict set of rules. No one wanted anything different, no one wanted anything original. On the contrary, the most admired artist was the one whose work was closest to the beloved work of the past. It took an astute observer to recognize the subtle differences between the less sophisticated work of the more ancient pieces and the precision of the later ones.

The little sculpture of Wenut was a perfect example of this. Della believed she had been produced somewhere in the 2nd to 4th Dynasty, in upper Egypt, when the two countries, Upper and Lower Egypt, were still being melded together. This unification had begun in the 1st Dynasty, around 3050 BCE. Wenut was likely produced for one of the rulers from this period. This sculpture, in her coarse yet regal simplicity, would have belonged in the world when the great pyramids were being constructed, and when the amazing Imhotep lived, because he was the man believed to have built the first of the pyramids, at Saqqara, for the Pharaoh Djoser. That would mean the report should date it from somewhere between 2840 BCE and 2400 BCE. In spite of the figurine's age, in spite of the faded paint and roughened edges, Della could tell that the person who had made this did so with a deep reverence and love. It was that intensity that seemed to beam from the statue, in spite of all the long ages.

Sighing, she prepared herself and turned to page 5 in the folder. An hour later she called Nigel.

"Where are you?"

"Still at the office."

"Will you be here soon? I have something I have been saving for you."

In spite of herself, she smiled. Della thought she knew exactly what that might be.

"I opened the report."

"And?"

"You have to come and see."

"Bring it here with you."

"I shouldn't. Something might happen. Besides, I don't think you will read it if I bring it there." She could almost hear his smile.

"I can come to your office. What happened? Did the dates come back all wrong?"

"No. Something else. I'll show you when you get here."

"I'm on my way, but no promises to leave you alone."

Della smiled. She would not promise either.

"Half an hour?"

"Maybe a bit more."

In truth, Nigel loved to visit Della in her office. He loved to be surrounded by the artifacts of her thinking, the remnants that revealed her intense intelligence, just below the surface, an iceberg of insight. Sometimes he would stop by to see her when they hadn't met for a few days. Knowing both of their deadlines, he still was compelled to be close enough to feel the presence of her, to confirm that she was true. Watching her folded over her desk making notes, he would sometimes see, as she looked up and away towards her screen, a hint of a double chin. On one so thin and lithe, it was a surprise. Turning her head back to her work, she morphed again into the 30-year-old woman, the doctoral student, the careful scholar who contemplated ancient pottery and the minds of those who made them. But in those few glimpses of that chin, or rather, chin-to-be, he could imagine the softer, fuller woman she would become with age. It made him smile down in his soul to think of her then, white haired and still studious, an accomplished woman gracefully building her own history. He ached to be there to see her then, to know the lovely person she would grow into. He thought perhaps he would love her even more then, if that was possible.

Nigel hated seeing the text on his phone. He hadn't heard from Gamal since the incident in Aswan, and he had hoped that meant their business arrangement was over. No such luck, apparently. Nigel ran over the words he had practiced, over and over again, to tell Gamal that he wasn't going to do any more jobs for him. He knew Gamal wouldn't be happy to hear him say them.

The coffee shop in the Luxor market area was crowded, so Gamal motioned for Nigel to walk beside him into the market area. As they passed the street that led to his and Della's room, he didn't dare look up. Had Gamal had learned about their liaison? Best not to think about it: Gamal could read faces.

"I need for you to do a couple of things: a couple of reports, documentation, the usual thing."

"No, Gamal. I am not going to do that. I have decided that it is time for this business between us end."

"In fact, Nigel, it is not that time yet. I will let you know when it is time to resolve our arrangement."

"Look, Gamal, I have been a good partner. I have never breathed a word about our projects to anyone, and it'll stay that way. It's just time for me to stop, that's all." Nigel hoped that his words sounded firm and confident. In fact, he couldn't believe he had been able to get them out of his mouth.

They had paused in their walk along the busy street. Nigel raised his eyes to see Gamal looking at him, almost looking *into* him, his eyes deadly bright in his craggy face. "You seem, my friend, to be under the impression that you have a choice in the matter."

"Look, Gamal, let's keep this…"

"Which you do not."

"Gamal, there is no reason we can't be adults about this, and just let it go."

"Except, of course, for that one reason: that you will never work again. At the very least."

"Who're you going to tell, Gamal, the Minister for the Preservation of Antiquities? I think he might wonder how you knew about such things."

"You underestimate me, Nigel. No, I wouldn't do anything official. I would simply notify the security police that you have stolen artifacts in your possession and that your bank records reflect the sales of the same. Now that I think about it, the British government might be interested as well."

"But I don't have any artifacts in my possession, Gamal, and the British government isn't going to care about me freelancing for cash."

"Are you sure, Nigel? When was the last time you were home in your apartment in Cairo? "

"I have been working on several projects here in Luxor recently."

"Yes, so I understand."

Nigel felt a distinct chill in the hot afternoon air. Had he planted something in his apartment in Cairo to set him up? Did Gamal suspect about Della and him? Or did he know?

But if he did know, would he be talking? Or would Nigel be bound up in the back seat of some panel van on the way to be beaten – or worse.

"And, Nigel, both of our governments would want an explanation for a very large deposit, say 40K. Particularly if it happened to coincide with the mysterious disappearance of some artifact from the museum."

"You've set me up."

"You are surprised? So, we are agreed. I will send over photos of the artifacts and the dates and provenance I want you to use for your reports. Your work is always so convincing: clients are happy to pay more for such convincing reports."

"May I ask what happened to the box we moved?"

"No. There is no need for you to know. But because it was so heavy, the next time it was moved, we did it at night, when it is cooler. So you see, I have learned something from you."

Nigel continued to walk by Gamal's side, numbly, like a wooden solider, he thought, as Gamal was stopped and greeted by one merchant, then another, in the first hint of cooler weather in the September air. Everyone seemed to know him, and it was amazing that Gamal seemed to know all their names. He wanted to try again to tell Gamal he would not write the reports, but he could not think of any words that would work.

Wael was sitting in his office looking at the news on his screen. The newspaper had been delivered, and he had read it earlier, but now he was looking at news on the web. He was surprised that he had become so comfortable on the Internet. He had never thought of himself as very technical, but he had discovered that you can find out all kinds of things online. And he had also discovered that looking at things online was addictive.

Mrs. Makreim-Ebeid would be here within an hour. So Wael was looking up any news about her husband's company and about her father-in-law and his doings in the hot political climate of Cairo. And Wael couldn't help but be very impressed. She was an extremely well-connected lady. He thought that it was odd that she was living here, in Luxor, instead of in the family compound in Cairo. And apparently she had no children and mostly devoted herself to scholarly efforts. How sad, he thought. But maybe that was a new western way of living.

When Wael had first called her a couple of weeks before, he had told her that he was busy, but that some time he would like to follow up on her tragic experience, and perhaps they could schedule a time in the next few weeks.

Mrs. Makreim- Ebeid had hesitated but then had asked why, after all this time, did the police in Luxor need to talk to her. The incident, she had said, had happened in Aswan, and in no way was related to the police in Luxor.

Wael had smiled and explained that this was just a formality and that he worked closely with his counterpart in Aswan and because she was a citizen of his city, he felt that it was his obligation to personally introduce himself to her and to be at her service should she ever need anything. But of course there was no urgency of any kind, as this was just a courtesy and a formality.

"We can find a time later when you have some free time," he had said.

Mrs. Makreim Ebeid had softened after this, saying she would be happy to come by for an informal visit. Excellent, he replied, and of course, if they ever did figure out what happened in Aswan, he would at least know how to find her.

She wasn't at all what he expected. For Wael, most Americans were tall, blond, and considerably overweight. But she was a small and slender woman, almost short. Wael was surprised to see that she was wearing an abaya and hajib. He had expected western clothing. And she didn't have on much makeup and almost bare eyes, which was another strange western attitude. But she was very attractive, in spite of that, with creamy pale skin with a hint of freckles. She had clear green eyes, which shown like wide beacons out of the softness of her face. Wael had never much cared for the appearance of pale white skin, but in this case he could see that it was, in fact, surprisingly attractive, with the flash of those eyes and the long red hair peeking out from her headscarf. Especially when she smiled.

"It is a pleasure to meet you," he said, extending his hand across his desk. His English was a little rough, but it still worked.

"Wa alaykum e-salam."

Wael was impressed that she was replying to him in Arabic. Her voice was soft, even melodic. And her accent was barely noticeable.

"Wa alaykum e-salam."

They visited for about an hour and shared some tea. The American wife wasn't only fluent in Arabic and learned in Egyptology, but seemingly also very comfortable in the modern Egyptian culture. She clearly wasn't intimidated by a world so different from where she must have started out. But in spite of this she gave the impression of being quiet and somewhat shy. Wael learned that her husband traveled a lot, and that she spent most of her time alone and working. This seemed odd to Wael, for such a young woman, but he could discern no hint of unhappiness. But as she rose to thank him, he had the feeling that there was more here than what there seemed to be. In his many years of police work his gut had often told him things that his mind didn't recognize. Wael was sure there was something else important about her life, but he had no idea what it could be. Was he right to wonder if she had some connection to the bomb plot? He didn't think so. That was definitely not it. But it was something. He would do a little checking around. Perhaps some information would come his way.

"Mrs. Makrem-Ebeid, I do have one small question about your being in Aswan. You have said that you don't remember anything at all about being there, only waking up in the hospital in Cairo. Is that right?"

"Yes, that's right."

"When we were doing some investigating in the area, my colleague Manar, the chief detective in Aswan, and I, we found several long red hairs on the top of a pile of carpets in a warehouse. Here, let me show you. These are the hairs."

Della was fascinated. She looked up at Wael with a question on her face.

"Do you think they are mine?" she asked.

"Do you?"

"They could be."

"Do you remember anything about a carpet?"

"No. I have only one memory that might be part of that event, and I can't bring it to mind at will. It only comes back to me sometimes at moments when I'm relaxing, or thinking about something else."

"And?"

"There is no carpet in the memory. Only a face. A face looking down at me and telling me he will get me help and that I'll be alright. I think it must be a vague memory of the people who found me there, in the warehouse. But I don't know. That's all I can remember."

"Thank you for sharing that. If you remember anything else, I would be happy to know about it. Perhaps we would be able to find out who moved you, or found you, or helped you. There is so much mystery to your story."

"Thank you, Mr. Abbas, for your help, too. I'll be happy to tell you anything I remember."

"One more thing. Have you considered using hypnosis?"

"To help me remember?"

"Yes."

"It was suggested, but I decided not to do it. I wanted to forget the ordeal, and to move on in my life. I cannot see how remembering what must have been a horrible experience would help me heal. And there is no reason to believe that there was a crime committed, only that someone found me and got me out of the elements."

"I can certainly understand your desire to let it all go."

Wael was not so sure that a crime was not involved, but there was no need to speak of it to her.

Merina was sitting in the peace and privacy of her front salon. Omar had just left on a trip to Kenya to sign up some new clients. He had been in a rush and impatient with her when she had come in from shopping. He would have been much more than that if he knew where she really was. He needed her to call the president's wife and set up a meeting; needed her to find out if the -resident approved of Omar being chosen to be interviewed on international TV about the upcoming elections. She had smiled and said of course she would be happy to help. Omar was so intense about his political career. He was too obsessed to notice anything different about her at all. But there was something different, something very different.

She reclinged a bit more, stretching her legs, and then raised them to rest on the couch. She ran her hand down her thigh, over the silk of her long skirt, and then her leg, then her ankle and then slowly back, she brushed her fingers up the inside of her leg, all the way up to the most tender private silky surface. He had been there, kissing her, loving her, just a few hours ago. Even her skin felt different.

She had almost not gone. She had almost called and told Gamal she had changed her mind, even though she had planned very carefully, arranging for her day at the spa to broken with a long lunch and shopping trip with a good friend. The good friend had been an invention, of course, but she had left her name and her phone number with the receptionist in case she called. After her manicure and pedicure and leg massage, the girl had come to remind her that she needed to dress because her friend would be here soon, and suddenly, instead of calling to cancel, Merina found herself leaving as though to go to one of the restaurants in the nearby hotel. But in fact she got on a back elevator and rode up to the 20th floor, where she walked through the short empty hallway to Suite 2020. She raised her hand to knock softly but before she could touch the door it burst open, with Gamal standing there, pulling her gently inside. As he closed the door, instead of taking her in his arms, he almost bowed to her, kissing the top of her hand, and then kissing down to the tips of her fingers. She found herself tempted to lean over and kiss the top of his head, but she held back.

"My dear, I'm so glad you came. I wasn't sure."

"Neither was I, Gamal. But now that I'm here, I'm glad."

He led her over to the window, which overlooked all of Cairo, and showed her the table there, set for lunch. There was a rolling cart nearby with food under metal covers.

"I ordered several different choices and have them here waiting, so that you won't be hungry and so that we won't be disturbed."

"Thank you, Gamal. You think of everything."

"That's my goal, my dear Merina. I only wish to please you."

Merina had smiled at this.

Gamal got her some champagne and himself a whiskey and they sat on the couch and talked about politics and laughed together at the latest rumors as they sipped their drinks. Gamal seemed to be waiting for her, giving her the time to be sure that she wanted to proceed, leaving it all up to her.

And she did. She found herself leaning over to kiss him part-way through her second glass of wine.

She hadn't truly known what to expect, but in her wildest imagination she couldn't have anticipated the ecstasy of their love-making. Or his attention to her needs. Omar had been, and could still be, a good lover, and they had had lots of fun together, trying things as well as just playing with sex. But Gamal was a master of the senses. She didn't dare to guess how he had learned to do the things he did for her, but she found herself almost regretting reaching her climaxes, because she was so enjoying what he did to her and for her with his mouth, his hands, and his maleness. As they lay in bed afterwards, having finally gotten there after beginning on the couch, then the floor, she looked at his naked body and was thrilled at how classic it was. He was meant to be nude, she thought, as his clothes, though well made, hid so much well-toned shape. A Greek god, she thought, with just enough dark hair in all the right places. At one point she made him get up and stand in front of her, as she lay on the bed watching, and then made him turn around slowly so she could look at him.

He had been so sensitive and gentle after the sex, holding her hand as they went to the table to eat a little lunch. She had looked up with a mouth full of salad to find him staring at her with a kind of musing look in his eyes. She smiled back at him, her heart, already softened, melting down through her. And she knew she would have to try to remember to be the same with Omar. It would be an act. And she thought that maybe Gamal was changed, too.

When would she be able to see him again? It couldn't be too soon.

Gamal had the driver take him to his office. He would pour himself a drink and sit and watch the sunset out of his window and think. He would think about the amazing woman he had spent this afternoon enjoying. She was intelligent and educated and seemed to understand what was going on in their city and in Egypt and beyond. And she had an exceptionally beautiful body: womanly and ample but still supple and soft. And she knew how to use it. She was so very different from most of the women he had known, and from any of the women he had loved. Or thought that he had loved. With Merina, Gamal felt like he had met his equal. He wondered what kind of a life he would have had if he had met her when he was a young man. What could he have accomplished with her by his side, even though she wasn't a true Egyptian. Gamal knew that there were at least two pale red-headed pharaohs in the 18th dynasty: the wildly successful Ramses the Great was one of them. Ramses' father, Seti I, had had red hair as well. It was not lost on him that these powerful leaders, masters of their entire worlds, had apparently had redheaded partners at their side.

Dare he to think of such an alliance? Was there any way of convincing her to become his? Gamal knew that she had everything that she needed. Except me, he thought. She needs me now.

TWELVE

Omar was very pleased with himself. The kick-off meetings with the new Kenyan clients had gone very well and they were already calling to say how happy they were with their service. His company had delayed planes twice to be sure they loaded all the fresh floral cargo during the first two weeks of the contract because the cargo hadn't been ready on time, and the clients were not expecting the sensitivity of this extra service. They claimed this had saved them a great deal of money in storage and refrigeration costs.

The television interview was well received and the president himself had called Omar to congratulate him on handling the questions so deftly and for deflecting the one issue that could have been tricky for the government. The station management had reported back that their viewers had sent many positive email messages and that the comments were running heavily ten to one in favor of Omar's appearance. The station director mentioned that if Omar did in fact decide to run for the Shura Council, to please allow them to be the first to make the announcement. They would be very grateful for this privilege and would like to provide a few extra advertising opportunities at no expense to the campaign.

She and Gamal had agreed that the spa set-up would not work all the time, so sometimes she would go shopping and have his car pick her up at one of the malls and take her to their Sofitel suite. That was the one thing that they hadn't changed, always meeting in the same luxurious rooms overlooking the city. They tried to meet once every two weeks, and Merina always saved him tidbits of information about the political behind-the-scenes situation. Gamal was grateful to learn what she shared. Merina had gotten better at getting Omar to tell her things. These were her little gifts for Gamal. But most of all she counted the days until she could feel his touch on her body. She even found herself humming, while remembering their lovemaking. Omar had caught her once.

"What is the matter with you?"

"The matter? Nothing is the matter. What do you mean?"

"You seem somehow different. You never hum. And have you lost weight or changed your hair? What is it?"

"Nothing. I'm the same. I'm just very happy, that's all."

He had stood and looked at her, his eyes narrowing. "Well, that's good, I guess."

"Yes. It is good," she had laughed.

Merina had smiled at herself for taunting him, but she couldn't help it. She had never thought she was not perfectly happy. In fact she had thought of herself as very lucky and glad to have such a life. But now, oh now. She had never guessed about the sex. And the man. Gamal was uncommonly intelligent, which had become more and more apparent. And he asked for, and respected, her opinion and he listened carefully, always, to what she said. She was used to being consulted but not to having her intellect so respected. It was too bad he hadn't gone into politics instead of business. He would have been very very good at it. He was very good at the other things he did.

She found herself standing still and just smiling to herself again, and then she noticed that Omar had left and her girls were standing in front of her. They must have asked her a question, because they were waiting. Politely. Just like she had taught them. They were such good children. That was the only real problem, of course. The children. She loved them so much. She wondered if they would understand if she left their father. Not that she would ever do that. Not that Gamal or she had discussed such a thing. But oh, just thinking about it couldn't hurt.

The scandal hit from out of the blue. No one was expecting it. Of course there had been rumors of the liaison, but there were always rumors. If you listened to all the rumors that floated around Cairo, you would know 200% of the truth. But this time the rumors were not nearly as bad as what actually happened.

Of course it was customary for successful men to have mistresses. It wasn't outwardly talked about and it wasn't considered strictly proper in the more traditional parts of society, but everyone knew it was done. In fact even devout old-guard Islamists could arrange a secret marriage to second or third wives in order to keep within their faith. A faithful man could have four wives in total, but although it was the usual rule that the first wife had to approve the other wives, sometimes, with the approval of the imam, the first wife didn't have to be consulted. But no one knew whether this man, a devoted and religious family man, had, in fact, made the woman his secret wife.

What they did know was that he had had her murdered. And because he was a member of the elite Shura Council, he had immunity from prosecution for all crimes. He therefore had expected the whole thing to be swept under the rug. That was the traditional way, of course, so he was absolutely correct in expecting this.

What he didn't expect was the media. If he had murdered her in Cairo, he would likely have been just fine. There might have been a report or two, but it would have faded away quickly. But the woman, his mistress, was not the usual young unaccomplished woman, but one who had built up a reputation as a singer, with a number of successful albums. She had known better than to stay in Cairo. She had moved to Dubai, and that was where the man's employees were able to take care of the dirty business of getting rid of her. The media wasn't as well controlled in Dubai, however. And naturally the police were happy to sell some photos of the tortured body to the reporters to supplement their meager incomes.

The surprising outcome of the whole thing was that the council broke a long-time rule and voted to allow the man to be prosecuted. It was the first time that this had happened in Egypt in the 30 years of the Council's existence. But by the time the photos of the stunningly beautiful, bludgeoned, and nude woman were all over the Internet, it was impossible for the members of the ministry to do otherwise.

Omar was ecstatic.

"There will be a special election, of course" he said, pacing around their small family dining room, waiting for dinner, holding his glass of Johnny

Walker Red. He had already been through half a bottle. "He was stupid to be so blatant. He should have known that someone would sell him out. And in Dubai! What a fool!"

"It's very sad, don't you think, Omar? She was such a beautiful young woman."

"Sad? Sad for him, maybe. The woman knew what she was getting into. She should have done her duty and kept her word. She would have been fine."

"Do you mean she should have stayed as his mistress? Allowed him to torture her, beat her? But she had her own career. She wanted to be a success in her own right. "

"What kind of a woman wants that? And besides, she had agreed to serve him. She signed the deal. It was her choice to be there."

"But murder is so horrible. This murder was a terrible ordeal for her."

"My dear Merina, of course, murder is horrible. That's my point. She should have behaved herself and she would be alive today."

"I heard he liked to cut her."

"As I said, she agreed to be his mistress. It was her choice."

"It is all so sad, Omar. It doesn't seem like she really had a choice at all. She didn't even have the right to choose to leave him."

"Merina, dear. Don't grieve for this woman. You didn't know her, and she isn't the kind of woman you would ever meet. She chose to be a mistress, and then she didn't fulfill her obligation to her patron. So forget it. The thing that's wonderful, of course, is that I'll win the special election. The president has already put me in touch with my new campaign manager, and he is going to make all the arrangements. We'll need to come up with some payments, of course, but I have a fund for this because I hoped this day would come. I just never expected it so soon!"

Omar negotiated the amount of the seed money that was paid to this new campaign manager, some of which was passed to others "upstream." He had planned well and was able to pay all the requirements. It was a chance of a lifetime and he was very fortunate to have the opportunity to make those payments. He didn't ask the new campaign manager what the money was for or who else would be paid. He just promised to do as he was instructed.

Soon the posters were ordered, and radio and TV ads started, TV interviews were arranged, and Omar began showing up at ribbon cuttings and ceremonies of all kinds. At the Eid al-Fitr holiday, celebrating the close of Ramadan, he passed out a thousand kilos of bread and goat meat to the poor, with his helpers handing the meat in plastic bags over the heads of the waiting crowds, and Omar standing on a platform, also handing out some of them, his hands dirty from the blood. On the evening news the crowd seemed to be in the thousands, stretching through the streets, as the news photographers juggled their cameras.

Merina was surprised with the impression her husband was making on TV. She was very happy for him and hoped that he would win. However, she didn't entirely trust this new campaign manager, who had a habit of arriving unannounced at the residence to talk to Omar at all hours of the day and night. She wondered who he really reported to.

Once, upon coming home from a day of shopping, she found him in the vestibule, waiting for the servant to answer the front door. She wondered how long he had been there, as the housemaid was usually very prompt at responding to the bell.

"Good day, Mrs. Makram-Ebeid. How was your shopping today?"

She had stopped and looked at him full in the face.

"Fine, thank you. How is it that you knew I was shopping?"

"Ah, the Mrs. has lots of bags, of course!"

But she didn't have bags in her hands. She had, in fact, left them in the car to be brought up by the driver. And the bags were in the back of the SUV, behind tinted glass. What was going on here?

"In fact, Mrs., I know you enjoy shopping very much."

"Yes, I do. Thank you."

So had he been watching her? Or was he guessing? She was sure that the wife having a lover wasn't part of any campaign manager's plan to get his candidate elected. She was sure that if Omar ever found out, he would be beyond furious, and she was careful not to think about where that would lead. It was a risk she didn't expect to have to experience. She had been extremely careful and was becoming more so. She needed to keep Gamal in her life. But she had, in fact, only been shopping today, and she hadn't talked to Gamal for over a week. Merina told Gamal everything that Omar told her, and so he could make arrangements far more subtle and undercover than anything she could arrange on her own. The whole clandestine situation had made their lovemaking even more passionate.

Merina entered the door to her home with the campaign manager follow-ing politely behind. She turned and smiled at him and said, "I will order you some tea, directly. You can wait in the little salon, there. Omar should be home very soon."

As she watched him walk into the salon, she thought of Gamal's descrip-tion about the way campaigns worked in other countries, like her old country, the UK, or the US. And how different Egyptian politics was. And then she thought of Gamal's face and his lips and she remembered the way he liked to kiss her underneath her arms. Tomorrow she would see him again. It felt like it had been a month, even though it had only been a week and a half. She would text him about the campaign manager today, however, just in case they needed to change their plans. She hoped not. The underside of her arm tingled.

"You're sure?"

"Yes, sir. Ali was very confident about this."

"How long?"

"He didn't know, but at least three or four months. Likely more."

"Please pay a visit to our little friend, Khalid. He will know more. Let me know what he tells you."

Gamal watched as his man walked out of his office. He stood watching the door long after it had closed behind Ali.

He had been stunned when he had learned from Merina a month ago that her son Sameh was married to the woman his men had driven down to Aswan. When Merina had mentioned in passing that her young daughter-in-law was the woman who had been found in the Aswan warehouse, the alarms were so loud in his brain that he could almost not speak. How was it that this woman had been on the side of the road? He had a bad feeling about this. It was a coincidence, and Gamal had deep karmic suspicions about coincidences: they had always been bad luck for him.

He hadn't asked anything about her daughter-in-law so as to not seem interested in the subject, but he immediately sent his men down to Luxor to do some checking. And now he had just gotten back not only confirmation but much more. It was worse than he could have imagined. Gamal knew that

Sameh spent most of his time up here with Khalid, but he suspected his family didn't realize that. That meant that his American wife spent most of her time alone in Luxor. Sameh hadn't even had the sense to get her pregnant. But far worse, Gamal's men had discovered that Nigel had met with Della in Luxor just a few months ago. They had been seen together, openly, drinking tea together in an ahwa. His men reported that they were professional friends. They hadn't noticed anything but conversation. Gamal knew better. He didn't believe in friends between a young man and a young woman. That was a foolish western idea. As Gamal thought about these dangerous connections, he realized that his heart rate was going up, and that heat was rising in his neck, and he knew that he was growing red with anger. He would have to be very very careful about what he did next.

The young woman had been in very bad shape when he had seen her in Aswan, and he hadn't expected her to survive especially since he never called the police. He had told Nigel that he did, however, which should have been a sign to himself that he didn't trust Nigel even then. Still, it was extremely unlikely that the woman would ever remember anything about that day. But what if she did? What if she remembered a face, or a voice, or some of the words that were spoken? The chances that this could happen were exponentially increased by Nigel talking with her. And whatever else he was doing to her.

What the hell was that stupid Welsh infidel thinking? He should have never hired the young archeologist. He had thought that he would be smart enough to know better. He had clearly been wrong.

Gamal walked over to his rosewood bar and pulled down a crystal tumbler. He would have a stiff whiskey and sit down and put his feet up and consider. He needed to proceed slowly and to focus his thoughts like a laser – or a maybe more like a scimitar: sharp, clear, precise. He would, Allah willing, be able to solve this problem without having to change his big plan. It had taken two years to put it together. How could he have made such a huge mistake? God was testing him, surely. He would prove himself worthy of his project. He would fix the problem.

Perhaps later he would call up little Neela and arrange for a session of her kinky sex. Since he had been seeing Merina, he hadn't been with another woman. He should never have allowed himself to become so infatuated. Tonight, however, he felt like being rough, maybe very rough, and Neela had taken that from him before. He would maybe use the knife tonight. He had done that only once before and it had scared her, but she had performed anyway. He would give her a good tip tonight, of course. It was her duty to please him, after all.

His fingers were twitching in his lap and he remembered he needed to remain calm, and so he said a little prayer under his breath. God is Great. God is Great. Then he took a deep sip of his whiskey.

The guard buzzed her 20 minutes after she and Nigel had talked on the phone. He had come to her office quickly. After she answered the buzz, she went into the hall, leaned over the railing, and watched him as he skipped every other stair. He looked up at her on the last flight and smiled his big open smile. Della found herself warming inside, right there in the hallway.

"So what is the big surprise?" he asked as soon as they were inside her office.

"You know that I hoped that the dating report would come back between the 2nd and 4th dynasty?"

"Did it?"

"No. Much better. Look!"

Nigel followed her into the office and took the report from her hand and stood while he read through it and then, whistling softly, he looked up at her.

"This is amazing. It's even older. Pre-dynastic. What a find!"

"Yes. Can you believe it? I never would have guessed it possible that something so old would be in this excellent condition. And how often does anyone find a new pre-dynastic artifact? This piece brings the whole collection in all of Egyptology to about a dozen. And it means that the Goddess Wenut was being worshipped far earlier than anyone thought. I could make a whole career out of this and the implications."

Nigel read through the report with her for a while longer and then followed Della through the door at the back of the office into the dim and crowded supply room, where he helped her move the cartons of paper to bring out the little sculpture. In this most private place in the offices, the sculpture was only part of their need to be there. Wearing the gloves Della gave him, Nigel held the goddess gently in his hands and then lifted it up and turned it around, looking at the underside of the base. Then her lowered it and looked closely at the paint on the head. "It is amazing that this has such good color. It must have been in a dark and airless place for millennia to have retained the strength in the pigment."

"I agree. I know I need to get it into our vault soon, to keep preserving it. I wonder, too, where it has been all these centuries. Since I found it in the basement stored with the 18th Dynasty pieces, I wonder if it was passed down through the generations from very early Egypt and then finally put in Tutankhamen's tomb things. I like to imagine it would have been put there for good luck."

"That's an interesting theory. It could also be, however, that there is a whole group of very early tombs that have remained hidden from the world, buried somewhere unexpected, except for a few pieces that ancient robbers have been able to dig out and sell."

They were standing close to each other and Nigel put the little statue on top of the top box of a stack and pulled Della close to him into a gentle hug, but soon they were moving together past the early soft kisses.

"I hope you're not expecting any deliveries," his voice a smiling through his hoarse whisper.

"No," she murmured, closing her eyes and leaning back so he could kiss down her neck. "We would hear them on the stairs."

"Well, in that case," Nigel said, and pulled up Della's top. Loosening her bra, he began kissing the outside of her breasts. Della responded with her hands. She had small hands. They seemed almost adolescent and slender, with tiny delicate finger tips. Her nails were always clipped short. Nigel had never seen them painted. He couldn't imagine it. When she would hold one of her heavy books, her hands looked too fragile to support it, but he knew better. He knew because when she had missed him too much, she would wrap herself around him and grip him and he would feel the truth of their strength.

Soon they were lost in the ecstasy of their communion. Like a single moving thing they came together and ended partly leaning against one of the lower boxes, and then sat together on the floor, clothes a jumble, smiling at each other in their contentment.

"You're wonderful," he said.

Della said nothing in reply but leaned over to kiss him on the ear.

Nigel stood and straightened himself out and then started to reach down to pull Della up. But he stopped and let out a gasp. "Oh my God."

"What?"

"Damn, Della. I didn't even hear it fall."

Della had a sick feeling. And she was right.

Wenut had been knocked off the tallest cardboard box stack and was lying on the lid of the top of the box stacked beside it, two levels down. Because the cardboard had cushioned the drop, there was no damage, but Nigel felt like this was a signal of some kind. "I think she is in too much danger here."

Della smiled. "We'll have to choose a different location next time."

He kissed her on the top of her head and held her as he stood silently. "How long has that dating report been here?"

"A little over three weeks."

"Who else has seen it?"

"Only you."

"Who else knows that you ordered a second report?"

"I guess a few people. One or two of my colleagues, and the guard so he would accept it. I only told Sameh I was thinking about ordering it. Not that I did."

"Now that you know that the statue is pre-dynastic, someone else must know it, too. No employee in any lab would not be amazed at this. And you know what that means: it is worth millions and millions of dollars and it is no longer a secret. I can think of scores of high-powered tycoons who would love to get their hands on it, love to do whatever it takes to have it stolen and hidden away in their private collections. Della, when I say *whatever it takes*, I mean it. People have been savagely murdered for far less. It is not safe here, and you are not safe with it here. Anywhere, here. If you are lucky, she will disappear without a trace, and you will have not one clue as to who took her.

"I think you should take Wenut home and put her in the top of your closet in an old valise. Hide her in your lingerie drawer. Do it today, now, and tell no one. Put her someplace that no one ever touches but you. And don't tell your home guards, either. No one is above corruption when the price is so high."

She ended up hiding her in the back of one of the drawers where she stored her few winter sweaters. Della smiled to think that the ancient Egyptian goddess had probably never experienced the kind of weather that would require a cloak, much less a sweater. But it was September, which led to cooler weather in other climates, and so she was properly prepared, snuggled up in a white Shetland wool sweater from England, a gift from Merina.

When Manar had called to tell him about it, Wael had already heard. The Interpol contact had called Wael earlier that morning, to explain that he might be hearing some rumors of the raid, but that they were hoping to keep it out of the media. Please report if you hear anything other than a news report, the agent had asked.

The Egyptian shock troops had gone in the day before, just before dawn, with official permission from the Sudanese government and destroyed the training camp. If anyone ever asked, it had posed a threat to the citizens both of Egypt and the Sudan. Legally it was suspect, but no one would ever question it, so it didn't matter. And, of course, it was only terrorists who were killed. And also it was in the Sudan, so *killing, legal,* and even *government* had very different connotations than anywhere else. Than everywhere else, in fact.

Sadly, the Interpol agent had had to report, they hadn't been able to discover any evidence of a bomb in or around the camp. And unfortunately the terrorists had all been killed, so there was no one left to get information from.

Manar was excited when he called Wael. After hearing about the raid, and that no bomb was found, he had wondered if there had ever been a bomb in the first place. It was all just some boondoggle to make the Egyptian minister of intelligence look important to Interpol. Maybe it was even part of a plan to get more foreign aid from the EU.

But Wael didn't agree. He was convinced that the dirty bomb was very real, and he also guessed that it was still in Aswan, but he didn't say this to Manar. He wondered if it was meant to blow up the dam.

The fisherman eased his boat up to the dock, tied up with both of his ropes, and called to his nephew to help him unload the fish. Soon he would be making a little trip, and he wanted to sell as much fish as he could before he left. That way his nephew would have some money for food when he was gone.

The Big Man hadn't said when, for sure, only that it would be soon, and that someone would come to him the night before, very late, and that the fisherman was to put out into the water just after dawn, at the same time as he always did, and slowly make his way down the river. He must not tell anyone, not even his nephew who worked the boat with him. He would have to tell his nephew to take the day off. But he couldn't tell him until that morning just before he left.

The fisherman felt honored to have the chance to help, Allahwilling, in the fight against the infidel. To fight the Great Jihad. He had even offered to make the trip for free, but the Big Man had insisted that he take some money. The fisherman had accepted the money and would leave it in a canvas bag between his bed and the wall in the hut they shared, where his nephew would find it later.

The fisherman had just finished unloading the fish when it was time for mid-day prayers. Maybe tonight the man would come.

"God is great," he said out loud, lifting another canvas bag of fish. "God is great."

THIRTEEN

They were lying on top of the sheets, naked thigh against naked thigh, talking about Nigel's writing projects. Della was surprised that their lovemaking had become more and more passionate as the weeks passed. She had no basis upon which to imagine the escalating sensuality of their bodies intertwining. It was as if they were getting more and more in tune with each other, like two musicians playing music that they loved. She had discovered that even though she knew he was there, waiting for her, and that she would see him soon, she still found herself daydreaming about him.

Any guilt of betraying her good husband, or shame of being a wayward woman, had faded away as her feelings for Nigel continued to grow. They were a little frightening, it was true, because it was getting harder and harder to leave, and harder and harder to go more than a day without seeing him. They were texting often, but that was never enough. She had to admit that she talked to him about so much of her work that she had come to depend on his opinions and perspective on her projects. They had begun to turn into a good team, she thought, on so many different levels.

Nigel was waiting for her to say something, she realized.

"Did you ask about Sameh?"

"Yes."

Her head was on his shoulder, his breath whispering down over her forehead as she spoke. She didn't answer right away.

"I don't know if I can talk about him, Nigel, here, with you. Like this. "

"I just wanted to say, Della, that you probably know there have been rumors about Sameh."

"Rumors? From your friends? From where?"

"Yes. From friends."

"What about?"

"Think about it, Della. I think you can guess."

"Can't you just tell me what you have heard?"

He sighed, looking up at the ceiling, and hesitated, rubbing her bare arm with his fingers lightly, stroking the softness of her skin, trying to compose gentle words.

"I have heard that he keeps a male lover in an apartment in Cairo. And that he is very careful about the identity and location. And, I suppose, careful that people don't find out – so that it doesn't get back to his father."

Della lay very still snuggled against Nigel's side, looking across the floor to the window, and it was long minutes before she spoke. Nigel waited, breathing shallowly, fearing that he had threatened the trust that had been building between them. He wanted her to believe in him and in them, and he had taken the chance to speak now. It had to be said. Della needed to see the truth. He needed her to see that he was the one for her, not Sameh.

After a long quietness, she said, almost in a whisper. "I'm afraid, Nigel, that I may believe you. And I have sometimes had the feeling that Sameh is attracted to men, but I have also felt like I imagined it. I have watched men look at him – like that. But what are you saying, exactly, and why? Sameh has been a good husband to me, at least sometimes, and he has been my friend for many years. He has been kind and supportive in many ways. It is unfair to talk about him behind his back. Especially in these circumstances."

"Della, I know you care for Sameh. He is very fortunate to have that care. But don't you think it is obligation you feel, not love? Have you thought about how you really truly feel?"

"When you say 'you,' don't you really mean how I feel about us?"

"Yes. Us. You and me. Look at us, Della. See us."

"I don't know what I can do, Nigel. I know this must stop. And so do you. But I'm struggling. I'll miss you so much. I know you will be finished with your project and go back to Cairo soon, and that will be a very good thing. That will be the time to end this."

"I finished my projects two weeks ago."

"But then what are you doing here?"

"I'm waiting for you."

Now Della turned on her side and looked at his face, her chest pushed tight against his, her eyes peering into his.

"You can't wait for me, Nigel. I can't leave Sameh."

"Actually, I have to wait. Because I love you too much to leave. And yes, dearest Della, you can," he whispered.

"I think it is best that you leave here, as you planned."

"Really? Do you love me so little?I don't believe that I'm just an entertainment for a wealthy wife."

Della's face flushed, her heartbeat pushed up into her chest and neck. Nigel could feel it against his pectoral muscles. He had wanted to be cruel, but this was all he could manage. But he had to break through to her. He needed to have her in his world. Even more than that, he knew she needed him, too. He was more sure of it than anything he had ever been sure of in his life.

"Nigel, there is no point in discussing this. You know the truth."

"Then leave Sameh, and come with me, and let's live together forever. Let's make love together forever, and grow old laughing together. What reason would you give to walk away from this? An empty marriage? A famous name and lots of money and no one to spend it on or with?"

"You don't understand, Nigel. Sameh and his family have been very kind to me, and supported me and taken care of me and it is hard to just dump them. I don't have the nerve to abandon them after all their support. "

"They have been good to you, Della, but they have also taken advantage of you. You deserve so much more. You should have a house full of children and a man who hates to leave for work every morning. A man who dotes on you, loves your company, and will love you forever. A man like me like me.

"Nigel, this is a huge decision, and I need to have time to think."

"Della, this is your life, your only life. Think about the long years ahead. Is this all there is? Sameh gone most of the time and you alone reading in your bed until midnight? You deserve someone who loves you enough to want to be there all the time, who wants to hold you and listen to you and wait for you to come home. I want to do all those things. When I think about the years ahead, I see only darkness without you. So, yes, you should think a little longer. But, dearest one, we should begin our lives soon. We should go away somewhere together. Wherever you want to go. I want to take you to Wales to meet my aunt Bronwyn, the town of my childhood, show you where I went to school and even the old farm I started out on. In a month it will be Christmas in Wales: we could be all settled in time to enjoy it together. There is so much I want to share with you."

She put her head back down on his chest and snuggled under his chin loving the smell and feel of him. He hugged her tight as if to console her, and then she forgot everything but the feeling of him there beside her, then as almost a part of her, in the timeless heat of the afternoon.

Gathering her abaya around her as she walked home, Della knew that Nigel was right. It was time to do something. She had become aware of how empty her world would be without him. She hated having to hide, except for the few times they met for tea or he came to her office. She wanted to walk beside him in public, with the world seeing them together, knowing that they were a couple. She had never experienced a relationship where she was truly equal and so deeply loved. And they laughed so often, enjoying so many of the same things. It could be a good life. Yes, it would be better than her empty life with always absent Sameh, and far better than Kansas.

She would talk to Sameh. He had been her friend, and he was her family now, and she would just talk to him, to try to explain, and to ask for his forgiveness – and even his help. In their years as school friends, he had always been the one she went to for help and now she needed his help, needed his friendship, more than ever. And she owed him for taking her into his family, beyond the traditional Egyptian culture fealty and respect. Maybe he would be able to help her. In school he had always given her good ideas as to how to handle her problems: professors, papers, projects that didn't develop as they should. How was it that they had grown so far apart? Where was the young man she had so counted on to be her friend forever? Had he really ever been there?

Late that evening Della texted Sameh, saying she needed to talk to him. He replied that he was very busy and she should send an email. He would check for it. She realized he assumed that whatever she wanted to talk about wasn't that important. So she had texted back "important, must talk to you."

His reply had been "sorry, big contract, email best."

She knew he would be somewhere the next evening just before the dinner hour, even if he was with clients. She would stay at the office and call from one of the extra lines. If he was trying to avoid her call, he might not immediately recognize the number or at least he would wonder about it for a moment. Maybe he would pick up before he remembered it was her office. She had to admit that Sameh had probably been avoiding her for quite a while. Still, he was her husband and friend, and she told herself that her main goal was talk to him directly.

At 7:15 she dialed and was preparing to leave voicemail when she heard a voice. It wasn't Sameh's.

"Yes?"

She thought that perhaps she had misdialed, but then she was sure she hadn't.

"Is Sameh there?"

"Who shall I say is calling?"

"Who is this? This is my husband's private cell phone. Where is he?"

"He is indisposed."

"What does that mean?"

"You can imagine whatever you wish, Mrs. Makram-Ebeid."

"Why are you answering Sameh's phone?"

"Why do you think? You should be able to figure that out, dear. Stupid little red-haired infidel wife. Too bad he loves me better."

"Who is this?"

"Oh, I think you know!"

"Please, I need to speak to Sameh. It's important."

"No. He is very tired; he has been working very hard. He is taking a little nap right now and I won't wake him up."

Della didn't know what to say. She was surprised to hear her voice soften into the whimper of a little girl.

"I would be very grateful if you would please tell him that I called and that it is important that we talk."

"How grateful?"

"Pardon?"

"How grateful would you be, Mrs. Makram-Ebeid?"

Della again didn't know what to say and was trying to think of a response, but it didn't matter because the man hung up on her.

She sat very still for a long time, staring at her computer screen while her fingers hung in the air, not moving. The screen had long ago gone to sleep when she pushed her chair back and buzzed the guard to call the car. She would have preferred to walk. In fact, she wanted to walk for hours and miles and slowly ease away the sadness and confusion one footstep at a time. But it was too late in the evening now. And she knew that if she walked, she would not go home. She would walk to Nigel's room, and she would stay.

She couldn't do that because she needed to think clearly. With Nigel it was hard to think clearly.

The man who had answered the phone was there with her husband. Was he the man Nigel had told her the rumors about?

Della rode home quietly in the car, ate a light dinner, and went to bed early with a book. She didn't sleep until after 2 and her eyes flew open just before dawn.

She got up, had a little breakfast with coffee, and prepared to leave for campus. Just as she was going to the car, Sameh called. She thought at first that it might be Nigel, but her pleasure turned to anxiety when she saw that the number was Sameh's, instead.

"Della, you left a message for me?"

"Yes."

"I'm leaving for a meeting shortly but I have a few minutes. What is the problem?"

"Sameh, I really wanted to talk about this in person. But I have to tell you. I'm having a problem."

"With what?"

"It is hard to say this on the phone, Sameh. Remember, in school, when I always brought you my problems and you helped me? I wish we could do that now, Sameh, like we used to do."

"Della, I have a meeting. What is the problem?"

"I seem to have found a friend here."

"A friend."

"Yes."

"So?"

"He is a man, Sameh."

"A man? Wait a minute. What are you saying?"

There was silence as Della struggled with how to tell him more.

But Sameh continued. "And more, Della, what are you thinking? Are you crazy? This is Egypt, Della, not the university in the US. You need to uphold the family name and stay clear of anything that would give people reason to talk. You know that's a very small town down there. And it is much worse for gossip than anywhere in Cairo."

"Sameh, I'm afraid it has gone a little bit farther than that."

"What? I don't want to hear about it, Della. Do NOT tell me these things. And for God's sake, don't get yourself into any difficult situations. If you want to play around a little, you should leave the country. Go to Europe. Have a liaison, whatever, but <u>don't</u> do that kind of thing in Luxor. Do you understand me? I'm surprised at you, Della. I didn't think you were that kind of woman."

"But Sameh, please listen to me because…"

"No, Della, you listen to me. Do NOT tell me anymore about this and however far it has gone, stop it immediately. Do you understand me? You know that bad rumors can be the death of campaigns, much less family reputations. You're aware, of course, that this is grounds for divorce under Sharia law. I'm sure you don't need to be told."

Della caught her breath. "But you would not do that, Sameh. And I'm Christian, not Muslim."

"Do you really think it matters what religion an American infidel wife claims to be? Look, I'm not saying this is an Iddah, right now, at least, but I'm angry enough to do that. Perhaps you should go home to Kansas for a while. I'll send a letter to the airport telling them you have my permission to travel alone."

"But I love my work here."

"Yes. Good. Then do as I say."

"Sameh, who was that man who answered the phone?"

"Who answered the phone?"

"Yes, when I called yesterday evening, he said you were taking a nap and couldn't talk. I asked him to tell you I called."

Sameh's silence on the line was palpable. For a moment Della thought they'd been disconnected, or that he had hung up on her. When he spoke, his voice had annoyance and resignation in it, all at the same time. "Well, he didn't tell me, in fact. I was responding to your text. Who did <u>he</u> say he was?"

"He didn't say."

"Then we'll just leave it at that. It isn't necessary for you to know more than that. I have to go. Do as I say — in fact I insist that you immediately take my advice. After all, I'm sure you're free to leave your position at any time. The university will understand if you need to take a break after all you have been through. This is an order, Della, not a request. Get out of there and end whatever you have stupidly gotten yourself into. And let me know where you're going to be. I won't do anything legally without contacting you, but I require that you inform me of your whereabouts."

Della held the phone to her ear for a full minute after Sameh had hung up. Then she closed it and sat on the edge of the bed, stunned. So she was being ordered to leave Luxor. Ordered like a chattel. She didn't want to live her life that way. But she would also not let her anger dictate her action, and she wouldn't make rash and rushed decisions about her life. She would take the time to make sense of her choices. Sameh had a right to be angry, of course, and legally, under Egyptian and Sharia law, he had the right to order her to do just about anything.

She gathered her things and went to her office. She would stay there all day and work, giving her heart and her mind some time to think, analyze, and heal.

Work had always been her balm and her refuge, and that was what she needed now. She dove into the details, feeling a sense of relief as she looked at the structure and handwork of a new piece. She had been asked to evaluate a newly discovered canopic jar from a child's tomb, because she had become well regarded as an expert on the subject. If she concentrated and stayed with it, she could have the report back to them by early next week. It was a beautiful little piece, with the top of the jar resembling the head of a monkey, but not any monkey that lived today. It could have been mythical, like many of ancient Egyptian statuary animal forms, or it could be based on an extinct species of monkey. She especially loved the way the eyes had been painted. What had the ancient Egyptian artist been thinking when he painted those eyes? Had that artist loved his wife?

Nigel called three times, but she didn't answer. She needed the quiet to put her problems at a distance and to allow her emotions to calm themselves so she could be objective. She also needed to stop worrying, for it was unproductive. This problem wasn't really about Nigel, she realized, it was about her. What did she want her life to be like from now on? She would call Nigel later and tell him that she needed to take a break for a while. Tell him to go on back to Cairo and she would be in touch. But not yet. Not until she got to the next stage in her report. Then she would take a break and decide what words to say. Perhaps she would actually consider going to Kansas. Or somewhere.

Late that afternoon, she finished up the preliminary final outline for her report, and then made her list of what else she needed to do. At a good stopping place, she got ready to go home. She had called Silva two hours before and told her she would be late and to please put some food in the oven. She buzzed the guard and asked him to call the car, and then descended the front staircase, the one with the trellised stone wall. It was gracious and palatial and she used to feel like a queen descending the wide stairs beside the exquisitely carved stone work. Now, it made her feel sad.

In the slight cool of the early evening, she stood next to the guard station and then stepped forward a little to look past the walls on either side of her, up and down the street, looking for the headlights of the family SUV. Instead, as she turned back, she saw Nigel, standing directly across the wide street from the campus guard station. He was just standing there, looking at her through the few passing cars. She stood and looked back. She would not walk over and talk to him; she would not run to be encircled in his arms. She would not wave. Sameh was right. Who knew who was watching. She was looking into his eyes, between the passing of a few more vehicles and the few evening pedestrians, when the SUV arrived and blocked her view.

And at that second, as the SUV eclipsed his face in the twilight, it happened. From somewhere deep within the caverns of her mind, she remembered. The rest of the scene that had been whispering through her brain all these months came rushing back to her: the man, Nigel, was in front of her, then above her, as she was being carried from a car or truck. Beyond his face, which was crinkled with concern, was a warehouse. Filled with bags and slabs of stone. Marble? And the bags were huge. Burlap bags that were as tall as a man. There were other men, darker men, leaning over her, too, but it was his face. There was no doubt.

Oh my God. He had been there. Near where they found her. That was the only possible explanation. And she knew it was true.

The driver opened the back door for her and she climbed up onto the seat. She looked down at her lap as the driver pulled away. She assumed Nigel was still standing there, but she didn't look over to see.

Silva was shaking her awake. What time was it?

"Mrs, please get up. There is a man here and he says he must see you. I told him that he must come back tomorrow, but he won't leave. I told the guards to call the police but he says he only has a message for you. He seems very upset, Mrs."

It was only 11. She was curled up in the big chair in her bedroom suite, with the plush footstool in front of it, her book splayed open on the floor. After she stretched out, she had to wait a minute for her legs to thaw out and quit tingling before she could move them.

"Who is he, Silva?"

"He says he is Mr. Sutherland and that you know him. Should I call the police, Mrs?"

"No, thank you, Silva. I'll send him away. Is he in the front greeting salon?"

"No, Mrs. I made him stand in the entry hall. I would not let him sit down. I made the guard stand with him."

Della sent the guard back downstairs and took Nigel into the small reception room, near the entry hall. She told Silva to come back in exactly 20 minutes.

"Why are you here, Nigel?"

"Because I feel like something has changed."

"It has. I remember now."

"Remember what?"

"Where I saw you – before."

Nigel was silent, standing in front of her, looking down into her eyes, waiting. Neither of them had moved towards any of the chairs or the settee in the little room.

"And I talked to Sameh earlier today."

Nigel still stood motionless, looking into her eyes.

"I have to ask you, Nigel. Before – before we met again recently, did you help me? Did you help me or hurt me before?"

Nigel took a deep breath and then let it out slowly. "I found you by the side of the road and picked you up because you would have died out there. You had been in some kind of a horrible accident and crawled all the way from the river. We were going to Aswan and so I planned to take you to the hospital there, on the way."

"But you didn't."

"No. I didn't. The man I was working for didn't want the police to find out that we were there because of what we were carrying and so he told me he would put you in a building down the street and call the police. I heard him make the call. But I'm pretty sure he faked it and lied to me."

Della just stared at Nigel. "Why didn't he want to police to know? What were you carrying?"

"Smuggled artifacts."

"Smuggled artifacts?"

"Yes. I used to help this man date them sometimes, to supplement my income. But I don't do that anymore."

Della heard her voice, almost a whisper, say "You used to but you don't anymore?"

"Yes, I did, but only a few times."

"So you have committed crimes. Is that why you couldn't tell me?"

"Very minor crimes, only helping with dating, nothing else. And I couldn't tell you because I didn't know what you would do. But I've told you now."

Both of them were still standing, very still, facing each other, barely breathing.

"What else do I not know, Nigel?"

"The only thing that you don't know, or don't believe, is that I love you very much. I have probably loved you since that day I first saw you, laying there

151

beneath that tree, more dead than alive. I couldn't leave you then, Della, and I can't bear to leave you now. Please come home with me. Come with me and we can go anywhere you want."

"No,, Nigel. This is too complicated. I have a husband and you're a criminal. I can't believe it. How did this happen? It would be best if you go. Now. Go away and let me think."

"Della, please don't call me a criminal. I only offered my expertise on the dates of items."

"But you said you were driving a van to Aswan, and that it had artifacts in it."

"Yes, but only that once. And it was a very lucky day. Because I found you."

"I need to think, and I need to sleep. It's best that you go now."

"Come with me and sleep. Come and sleep by my side, or I'll get you a room of your own. All I ask is that you come with me. I'll tell you anything you want to know: everything you want to know. I only ask that you come, now. I promise that I'll bring you back anytime you want."

She looked up at his beautiful face, the cut of his jaw, the sandy hair loosely falling over his furrowed brow, his eyes so filled with pain. Those eyes that she loved so much.

"Please, Della, I know this is right."

This was a man who had always been wonderful to her, a man who she trusted with her most private thoughts, with the hidden reaches of her body. And he was the man who had saved her, found her and taken her out of the deadly heat. But he hadn't been able to tell her, to trust her, to let her trust him. In their many afternoons of passion, when she had trusted him completely, opened completely to him, what had he withheld? What else was there, hidden, behind those beautiful eyes? Was there no man she could believe in? Did all the men in her life have terrible secrets? Could she bear to learn any more of them. "Nigel, I need to sleep in my own bed, alone, and think. It would be best."

He didn't move.

"Good night."

He still didn't move.

She took his arm and he thought at first that she was coming into his embrace, but then he realized that she was steering him towards the door. She slowly walked him the few feet and opened it and gently guided him through it. He allowed her to do this, but then he turned back towards her, his face flushed. "I'll wait for your call. When you think tonight, remember how happy we are together. Remember our talks, our laughs. Remember us. I'll come within an hour's notice and get you, Della. I'll come tonight, tomorrow. We can leave Luxor and Egypt and go anywhere you want. Anywhere. You don't need to bring much, you can send for your things later."

She said nothing as she looked up at him.

"I love you, Della, more than life itself. And I know you love me. I'll be waiting." Then he turned and walked down the stairs, and she stood in the door and listened to the sound of his footsteps descending, followed by those of the guard. Soon the door at the bottom of the stairwell closed with a distant click, and Della slowly closed the front door and stood still, letting out her breath. Then she walked down the dark and empty hallway back to her room.

She didn't look for Silva to tell her that she was going to bed and so she settled down into her chair again, picking up her book to find the place she had left off. It was a very good book and very scholarly but quite readable, she thought, a perfect thing to concentrate on to settle her mind.

She had read some of Nigel's work and his articles were similarly well researched and well written. How had he allowed himself to become involved with smuggled artifacts? But she knew, as she looked around her comfortable room, that in this land of luxurious history, luxury was, in fact, scarce. Maybe he had strayed out of necessity. For the need to survive. And she believed him when he said that now he had reformed. What she wondered was whether he would ever do it again. Would he be tempted to work with smuggled artifacts again, if they were very poor? Could she love him if he did?

Her eyes began to ache from reading so much, with a few tears trickling out of the sides of her eyes. It wasn't that she was crying, only that she was tired from so much computer work and research. Truthfully, she probably needed to get some new reading glasses, as she had noticed that her eyes were tearing up a lot lately. She wiped the few drops gently with her sleeve, knowing that they would stop soon.

It was only in the wee hours of the night, with her face deep in the freshly ironed pillowcase that she was awakened by her own weeping.

FOURTEEN

She woke up early, still tired but with her choice made. She did love Nigel, and even more, she believed him. She believed *in* him. She might be making the mistake of her life, but somehow she didn't think so. Still, the leaving made her nervous. It was a huge step.

She dressed to go to the office and then went into to her closet and took down a small gold leather valise that she had bought on her first trip to Cairo. It She put in some clothing, toiletries, and shoes, then stuffed in her hairbrush and her extra glasses. She putWenut in, too, carefully wrapped in a bit of old soft blanket and an older pair of jeans. She checked her briefcase, as usual, but then added her laptop and her iPad.

She let Silva know she needed to have her things taken to the SUV and then taken to work. After her bags had gone, she stood in the room and looked around. The view of the Nile sparkled through the sheer curtains, a view she loved to rise to every morning. And the bed, with its plush percale sheets and pillows, was, as usual, rumpled only from her own body. She wondered how many nights Sameh had actually slept in this bed with her, but then decided she didn't need to know.

Silva accepted Silva's offer of a bagged lunch. She had come to love Silva's food and she especially loved the surprise of her bagged lunches, which could rival her dinners. She would miss those.

She rode to the office looking out the windows to enjoy the morning pedestrians and traffic, seeing them through the eyes of an almost-tourist, enjoying the colors and the cacophony of the slowly rushing flow of people and cars, the sight of mules and huge cargo baskets, the sounds of hawkers and car horns.

Her report was almost finished and she expected to be ready to edit it by lunch time. She would call Nigel when the report was ready to send. It was important that the university think she had fulfilled her promise. In other circumstances she would have asked Nigel to help her with a final edit, but today she just wanted to finish it. She would make arrangements for the jar to be shipped back to the museum. Would it be her last piece of work for them? Would she lose her position here, along with everything else? How would that feel?

She would have to sit down with Nigel and talk it all out, discuss all the details, how they would live and what she expected. She didn't care about the money, it seemed to her now, but she wanted very much to stay in Egypt and work. She didn't expect to be able to afford to stay with the university, but she knew a lot of people in her field and had earned a good reputation, so perhaps she could work as a consultant until she could find a job. She would insist on having a safe and clean neighborhood. She suddenly realized that they had never talked about children. She didn't know how he felt about having a child. She hoped he would want children.

She ate Silva's lunch at her desk, which was better than ever. She owed her an explanation or at least some notice. She would call her later this afternoon and tell her she would not be coming home. Silva was so good to her. She would ask her to pack up her things until she could arrange for them to be picked up and shipped wherever they landed.

Putting away the lunch container, and taking a last swig of her water, she decided it was time. It felt like a huge step, but she was ready to take it. For some reason she wasn't afraid. In fact she felt relieved. She wondered if maybe she had even loved Nigel since that first moment she saw him, staring down at her. And she knew he was right; they would have a good life together. A wonderful life full of laughter, love, and maybe family. It would be an adventure. She hit his numbers on her phone with a warmth in her cheeks. Now that she had finished her project, and made the choice, and she was ready to go.

The phone seemed to pick up, and then, after connecting, it suddenly disconnected. Perhaps he was driving or doing something else and hit the wrong button. She waited, but he didn't call back. She tried again. This time the call went to voicemail. He must be on the phone. She sent a text, so often faster, anyway. "Pls come to office this afternoon. Ready now."

She continued working while she waited, perusing through later pages of the report, thinking that it would be better to cut the pages down and put some of the material in an addendum. Her professors had told her more than once that they looked forward to reading her work because it almost read like fiction. She was proud of this, she realized. Perhaps she could find a job writing up things for other researchers.

It had been an hour now, and he hadn't called her back or responded to her text. Perhaps he was at some site or dig and was out of range. Although he hadn't mentioned going to any remote locations. Maybe he was working on a deadline and had turned off the phone. Except that he hadn't mentioned any.

After another half an hour, she decided to walk over to the room. She left her bag and briefcase at the office because there would still be time to come back before the night guard came on. Either way it wouldn't matter, she supposed, but it would be easier to just leave her office as usual at a normal time and then call and explain to everyone tomorrow. And perhaps Nigel would want to stay in Luxor while they got everything sorted out. It could be ugly, she thought, with the Makrem-Ebeids' influence with the Cairo Museum and the other political powers in Egypt. But being in Luxor had the advantage of being far away from the family's base in Cairo. She would call Merina personally and talk to her in the next few days. Della now realized that she had married Sameh in part because of his lovely mother. She would hate to lose that relationship.

As she approached her favorite orange vendor in the market alley, she noticed a large SUV stuck in traffic in the street that crossed the alley. Blocking it were a couple of cars whose drivers were standing out of their vehicles and yelling at each other. It seemed to have something to do with a knocked-over cart and a mule, who was quietly standing in the middle of the street. Della walked around behind the SUV.

Just at the moment the driver turned and looked at her full in the face. She caught her breath and froze in her steps. She knew him: it was Ahmad. For an instant she thought that maybe the man only looked like him, but no, this man's eyes were an odd golden color, like a lion's eyes. Ahmad's eyes were that color. They were frightening to look at, but also mesmerizing, like a snake's eyes, and Della was anchored to the ground, unable to take her eyes from the man, who was now staring back at her. She knew that he recognized her, and his expression was frightening. Why had she been told he died?

There was a sudden jerky movement, pulling her eyes away from his, and she saw that there was a man on the other side of the driver, in the passenger seat. He was involved in some kind of a struggle, reaching backwards, shoving something in the back seat. And then, with a loud slapping sound, the imprint of a hand appeared like a shot on the inside of the rear window. It was within a foot of her face. It was a large man's hand. Then the SUV seemed to shiver and lurch as if someone was trying to force their way out the door. The hand was ripped away and was gone as fast as it appeared.

The driver jerked his head up to look in the rearview mirror, cursed, and gunned the motor. The SUV lurched forward, just missing the mule, twisting around the angry men in the street, knocking down part of a clothing stand, and hitting a small dog, whose howl mixed with the scream of a mother as the SUV grazed a baby stroller she was pushing.

All this happened in a flash, but it left Della shaken. She knew it was Ahmad. And the expression in his eyes wasn't that of a loyal servant: it was the look of a dangerous man, of a killer. Tense and numb she watched the SUV disappear into the market traffic, leaving behind a wake of screeching tires and the shouts of angry people.

As the pedestrian traffic around her came back to life, she wondered what she had just seen. What had been going on in that SUV? Why was someone trying to escape from the back seat? Her sense of alarm was replaced with a deep feeling of dread. She suddenly had the sense that terrible things were happening all around her. It didn't bear thinking about. All she wanted to do was to go see Nigel and tell him about it.

She took a deep breath and went on, crossing the busy street, then going quickly through the market alleys and up the stairs to their room. There was no answer to her knock. Before reaching for her key, she tried turning the knob, and the door swung open. It was unlocked.

She knew immediately that something was wrong. The room was messy, like she had never seen it, and Nigel's papers were partly on the floor, partly jumbled on the tiny desk. His laptop was gone, however, so it was possible he had left in a hurry and didn't have time to tidyn up. Still, it felt wrong. Nigel was always neat. He would have stopped to pick up the papers, she was sure, no matter how rushed he was.

Della sat down in one of the cheap plastic chairs, noticing how small and empty the room was without Nigel there. She waited, apprehension growing inside of her, her fingers clammy in the hot room, looking at her watch two or three times a minute. Something must have happened to Nigel, but what? Had he tried to contact her? She had no texts or emails. Why would anyone want to hurt him? What was it that she didn't understand? Did this have anything to do with seeing Ahmad, with his fearful yellow eyes, and someone trying to escape from that SUV? She was imagining things, letting her emotions run away with her, conjuring up a crisis out of coincidental things. Ahmad's sudden appearance, his frightening look, her angst over taking such a big step, her dread of Sameh's anger when he learned she had left him. She must wait until she had some facts, something to go on. But she couldn't stay in the empty room any longer, there was an oppressive atmosphere about it. She had been there 20 minutes when she left a note on the desk, telling Nigel to call her. Then she walked back to the campus.

Back in her office she pretended to work on her report for another hour, and then tried calling again. It went to voicemail, again.

At 5:30 she called the guard and asked him to call her car.

By 11 that evening Della was deeply frightened. Had she truly rejected Nigel so badly that he had left? That was hard to believe. He had said he would wait, and she knew that he meant it. She had only really known him for part of a year, she told herself, and there was a lot she didn't know about him. But she *did* know him. He had been honest with her to his peril and he loved her, really loved her. This absence seemed so unlike him that she was sure something was very wrong. What could it be? And what could she do? If she had any idea of what the situation was, she would able to do something. She realized, with a tight fist of fear just below her diaphragm, that the only thing she could do was wait.

She kept her phone by her bed, and tried to sleep, but kept waking up to check the screen: 2:30, 3:45, 4:50, 5:25: no messages, no calls. With the dawn she sought the refuge of her regular routine. She bathed, dressed for work, had strong coffee, and had the driver deliver her to the office. It crossed her mind that Nigel would be there, waiting for her, to surprise her. He was so charming he might have been able to talk his way past the guard. But he wasn't. And the guard said there was no one asking for her.

She stared at her desk and wondered what she should do now. She didn't care about working on her report, or how it would be received, or her research, or anything. She tried to go through and sort through things she had been saving to work on later. But as she shifted through her papers, she could only think of Nigel and how he would enjoy reading through her to-be-filed pile. Had she ever told him about the Polish archeologist's crazy thesis about the Step Pyramid? Or about this tiny report on the theory of feeder tunnels leading into the bigger tunnels under Giza? It was packed full of new facts – so unusual for such a short piece. Nigel would love it.

By lunch time she had accomplished nothing. She had moved some paper around and made some neat stacks and but mostly she had been sitting in her chair and staring at the wall. She felt like crying, sobbing, except that she was too scared to do either one.

Late that afternoon, as she was sipping some tea, Sameh called on the office line. She was so preoccupied that at first she didn't recognize his voice. "Are you still in Luxor, Della? I thought you were leaving."

"I was preparing to leave, Sameh, but I have some things to finish up first."

"Good. Are you going to Kansas?"

"No, not Kansas. I'm not sure where yet."

"Look, Della, I'm sorry if I was hard on you yesterday, but you have to understand our –my – position. This is untenable. I don't know why you would involve yourself in something that's this sordid, but I don't really want to know. All I ask is that it is stopped. Immediately. "

"You made that very clear yesterday."

"Good, then we are agreed."

"Sameh, what about you?"

"This is about you, Della, not me."

"You're the one who is keeping a male lover in Cairo."

There was a long pause. "Look, Della, whatever rumors you may have heard, you cannot believe them – this is the rumor capital of the world. You just take care of your end of the bargain and I'll take care of mine."

'The 'bargain,' Sameh?"

"Yes."

"I thought it was a marriage. You're my husband, you used to be my friend, and you used to sometimes be my lover."

"Look, Della, this is hardly the time to discuss our relationship. And please don't be maudlin. I do care about you: in fact, I was calling to check on you and to let you know that if there is anything I can do to help you get out of this situation – quickly and quietly – let me know. And don't tell any of the family. Or anyone else, for that matter. This is just between you and me, as I'm sure you would prefer. "

"Sameh, I'm leaving you."

"I wouldn't do that if I were you."

"I can choose my own life, Sameh, and you're never here and you clearly love someone else."

"It's never a good idea, Della, my dear, to make big decisions in a state of emotional distress. I won't discuss this subject with you until you have come back from your vacation."

"What if I never come back?"

"Oh, you will come back, I'm sure of it. Now I have to go. I have to work so that you can live the life you have chosen, as you say. I'm sure you will keep this little issue to yourself. And if you need any help getting rid of this fellow, whoever he is, I might be able to help."

"What the hell do you mean by that?"

"Don't overreact. I just mean that I can arrange for someone to talk to him and make it clear that he needs to keep his mouth shut."

"How, by breaking his arms?"

"Della, you have seen too many episodes of your American *Sopranos*. It would only be a meaningful conversation. Please call me tomorrow so that I know where you are. And have a good trip."

She held the phone in the air in front of her after the click, aghast at the words she had just listened to. A "bargain." Get "rid" of the fellow. Just who the hell did Sameh think he was? As she sat in her chair, she realized that she knew exactly who he was. How long ago had she started noticing that Sameh was comfortable with whatever tactics he needed to use to win? She would have to tell Nigel that he was right, they would be better off leaving the country for a while. It might be dangerous to stay here. The Makrem-Ebeids could probably give the writers for the *Sopranos* a few ideas.

But she wouldn't leave without Nigel. Even if he had decided to leave, she had to know he was safe.

The days stretched on: one long laborious section of hours connected to another long section of sleeplessness. They all blended together while Della held herself in knotted waiting, every minute of every day, for the phone call, the text, something that would tell her where to look, what to do.

Sameh, after complaining that she was still in the country, started calling her at least once every day, often more, at home and sometimes at work, to check on her. She was able to get Silva to tell him she was busy a few times, but if she had to talk to him, she determined to say as few words as possible.

A week passed. Della settled into a drugged pattern of getting through the day, going home, trying to sleep, getting up and doing it all again. She kept her phone on at all times, charging it while it lay beside her on the nightstand. She would wake in the deep of the night suddenly convinced she had heard the beep for a text message and then find none. She tried to think of ways to find Nigel. She called the offices of several of the publications he wrote for and left messages there for him, knowing that it was at least something. She went to their room several times, but there was no change – it was just as she had found it the day he hadn't called back. Seeing more clearly what he had left behind was even more troubling. There was no question that he hadn't planned to go.

At the end of a week, Della called the detective, Wael Abbas, who had been so kind to her several weeks before. He told her to come down to the office, that he would be happy to meet with her.

Della began by telling the detective she was hoping he could help her find her very good friend Nigel Sutherland, her colleague, her fellow archeologist. Wael smiled, asked her if she would like to have some tea, and left the room to order it. When he returned, he sat down at this desk, and looked directly across into Della's eyes.

"Mrs. Makrem-Ebeid, please help me to understand. You have a very good friend who has disappeared, is this right?"

"Yes, almost a whole week ago. We were supposed to – meet – and he didn't show up. I cannot reach him by phone, and he isn't at his apartment, so I'm worried."

"You know where he is living?"

"Yes."

"Ah, I see. How is your tea, Mrs.?

"Excellent, Mr. Abbas. It is excellent. Thank you. Can you help me?"

"I don't know, but perhaps. Please describe this person to me, and then tell me about the last time you saw him. I'll take some notes while you talk. Please excuse me if I don't keep up. I have a slow hand."

"He is about 6 foot 2 inches, with short blond hair and sharp blue eyes. He is from Wales so he is what you would call a white man, but he has been in Egypt for many years so he has a very deep tan and sun wrinkles on his face. He is lean and wears khaki cargo pants a lot. He often wears a hat or keffiyeh when he is going into the sun. And aviator sunglasses."

"Ah, yes, very good details, Mrs. Thank you. And, Mrs., please tell me about the last time you saw him. When and where was that?"

Della took a deep breath. Detective Abbas didn't take his eyes away from her as she did this. He sat very still as he waited for her reply.

"He came to my office a few days before he – disappeared, went missing. I was just working on a new project for the university and I wanted to show it to him."

"And then you called him a few days later and he has not answered you?"

"Yes, that's right."

"Mrs., I'm sure he is fine. He has probably left the area to go to a dig site or do an interview, etc. You did say he a journalist, yes?"

"Yes. He is a journalist writing about Egyptian artifacts. But, Mr. Abbasdetective, we had made some plans and he would never have left without telling me, so I know that he has been abducted or something like that. I just know it."

"What kind of plans, Mrs.?"

"I would prefer not to say, Detective. But I can assure you that we had some very firm plans and he would not have left without notifying me."

"Mrs., I'm sorry to have to ask you this, but does your husband know about this friend of yours?"

"Yes," Della said, very softly. "He does."

"Does he know that he is missing?"

"Why does that matter, Detective?"

"Mrs., I'm happy to help you, but I don't want any trouble with the Imams. If you have not told your husband that this friend is missing, then I cannot help you. "

"Very well, Detective, I promise to call him and tell him this evening. He is in Iran on business so I won't be able to reach him until then."

Wael admired her determination, he had to admit. Although she was clearly an American if she thought he was going to let the issue drop at that. He put on his most pacific and comforting smile.

"Mrs. that will be perfect. I have enough information to proceed with my investigation, so all I'll need for you to do is to have your husband call me to confirm that it is approved for me to do so. Here is my card. He can call anytime. No need to worry you or take any more of your time."

Della knew she was being dismissed. But she had to accept the detective's decision, because it might mean he would help her. At least the detective knew about Nigel being missing in case he found something out. And she would call Sameh and tell him. Because she had to ask him to help her find Nigel. She would promise Sameh that she would not leave him if he would help her. She should have thought of that sooner.

FIFTEEN

Della waited for Sameh to phone her again, planning her words. She would steel herself, biding her time, and when he pleaded with her again to stop seeing the other man and to leave Luxor, she would make her offer: yes to both IF Sameh would help her find Nigel. When Nigel was found and safe, she would get on a plane and leave. And if Sameh didn't agree to help her, perhaps she would have to start talking. She would make this very clear to him when he called. Very clear. She would tell him she planned to talk to people about his male lover. She would not say who, of course, but Sameh would fear the worst.

But Sameh didn't call that day or that evening. She left two messages. Waiting and worrying was gnawing into her soul, reshaping her world with its blind fear, so she kept reaching for the phone, then stopping herself. Sameh had to see her as strong – that was the only possible way he would believe he had to help her. But as the last tangerine remnants of the sunset dissolved into vague evening purples, she gave up and called him again, dreading his lover's answer on the phone. Voice mail. Again she waited for his return call. Again it didn't come.

She wedged herself into her big chair and dozed while trying to read, napping fitfully between sudden waking dreams filled with fear. In the deep of the night she got up and went to her bed but didn't expect to sleep.

The phone on the nightstand beeped and she surged into heart-pounding alertness, grabbing it and answering before she looked at the caller ID.

"Nigel?"

"Della, you need to come to Cairo immediately."

"Sameh?"

"Immediately, Della. I'm sending a small plane. It will be at the airport in about an hour. When you land, you will be brought here."

"Why? What is going on? Where is 'here'?"

"The hospital in Cairo. I'll tell you when I see you."

"But, Sameh, I need your help to find my friend. He has disappeared and I really need your help. I plead with you, Sameh, please. I need your help."

"Della, this is serious. You must come here now. Do you understand? Now."

"Sameh, this is serious, too. I NEED your help. I'm willing to do what you ask if you will help me."

"Della, you don't understand. It is my mother. Just come."

As she heard the click, she realized that the cool and calculating Sameh had sounded distressed, maybe even on the verge of tears. She had been too upset herself to notice it right away. Sameh was rarely emotional. Whatever it was must be bad.

Silva helped her and she was in the car on the way to the airport within 30 minutes. She thought about Wenut, hidden in her closet, but decided it would be too dangerous to try and take her. The streets of Luxor were almost empty of traffic, so she arrived in time to watch the small plane touch down and taxi over to the small private terminal. A guard seemed to have been informed of the emergency for he was expecting her and helped to unload her brown valise and laptop bag. Hakim, the family butler in Cairo, walked towards her from the plane and then held onto her arm as she mounted the stairs. Silva had given her a small bag with dried fruit and nuts and she reached for them as she watched the flickering lights of Luxor descend beneath the wings.

An Egyptian man she didn't know was waiting for them at the private Cairo terminal, and he walked with Hakim and Della to the waiting SUV. They drove through the streets of Cairo in a rush, tearing around the few cars that were on the road at 4 a.m. She had asked Hakim on the plane what had happened to Merina, but he would not say, answering only that Mrs. would speak with her husband soon and he would make everything clear. His face was stoic, a block of weathered stone, but Della could see that he was working to keep any hint of emotion beneath his mask of propriety. Hakim had been with the family for many many years, and he knew how to keep things to himself, yet she could tell that he had had a shock.

The SUV pulled up at the Dar-al Fouad Hospital, at the emergency room entrance, and Hakim opened the door and motioned for Della to step down. She looked at him and was about to ask him where she should go, but just then she saw Sameh coming out of the door to meet her. He looked terrible: haggard, exhausted, and from his red-rimmed eyes it was clear that he had really been crying. He was wearing an old pair of jeans and a wrinkled shirt, and it was obvious that he had lost even more weight recently, since they had seen each other last, a month or so before. Had it been that long? No, it had been at least three months.

'Please come inside, Della. Follow me."

She lowered her head and went along behind him, her abaya and hajib carefully in place, knowing that western women were not welcomed in this hospital, as in many in Egypt. Knowing that the nurses would still suspect her of being an infidel, bringing bad luck, in spite of her proper garments, she kept her gaze focused on the back of Sameh's feet in front of her.

They went to a private room at the back of the emergency department and at the door, Sameh stopped and turned to face her.

"Please prepare yourself, wife. This is going to be hard. My mother has been in an accident. She is very badly injured."

Sameh led the way into the room and Della saw the woman whom she had last seen as vibrant and beautiful, lying on the hospital bed, connected to a snarl of tubes and wires that led to humming and beeping machines. There was the swish swish swish of a breathing machine, and three different screens signaling electronic reports. Della remembered how to read them from her own stay all those months before. The numbers were not good. The color of Merina's skin was remarkably pale, with only slightly more color than the hospital sheets she was lying on.

"What happened?"

"It was an automobile accident. The other person and the driver were killed."

"I'm so sorry, Sameh. Can she hear us?"

"No. She has to stay under sedation until they can operate. As you can see, her face is just barely bruised, but she has major internal injuries, as well as broken ribs, legs, and a cracked skull."

"Who was the driver? Was he our driver?"

"No. He was another man's driver. And there is more, Della. It's not good."

"What?"

"Not now. After my father arrives."

"Where is he?"

"He is on a plane. He should arrive in a couple of hours. Then we must decide what to do."

"Decide what to do? Is she in danger of dying?"

"Worse."

"Worse? What is worse than dying?"

"Della, I'll have to tell you the rest of the story in a more private place."

When Sameh thought of his mother he remembered her scent before he remembered her face. It wasn't her perfume or the scent of soap, but her own special smell, the smell of her hair, her skin, her flowing clothing. Even the smell of her hand reaching down to him from beneath the lovely oval face. She had always been young to him, a large warm smile looming over him as he looked up, hurt, from some unremembered scratch.

Sameh had always known he was her favorite. She had never confirmed this, to him or to any of his brothers or sisters, but he knew. Sometimes, even when he was in serious trouble at home, he would catch the sparkle in her eyes as she suppressed her smile: she seemed proud of him when he pushed the boundaries. He had learned early that if he had done something that was wrong, maybe knowing it was wrong, she would fix it for him – with his teachers, with the servants, with his father. And his siblings knew this, too, for they would never tell on him to his mother. They had each tried, in their younger years, to tell on Sameh to their father, but never their mother. And then they learned that they would have to pay for going around her. And so they learned to be silent.

As he gazed at her now, bruised and bandaged, connected to so many machines, her familiar scent wasn't there. This body in the hospital bed wasn't the mother who he knew, his protectress, his champion, and he could barely find his memories of her youthful smile. And he wondered how he was supposed to help her now. He wanted to help, but perhaps it was already too late.

Omar always exercised. He made himself do this even when he wasn't in the mood, which was rarely the case. He had discovered that a good workout would cure a hangover, bring on sleep when he had too many problems, and help him figure things out.

At home he had a room set aside for this devotion to the temple of the body. And when he traveled, he only stayed in places that had 24-hour access to the treadmills and stair-masters, and he had been known to request a rowing machine be brought in for his longer stays. Aside from forceful business sex, it was by far the most relaxing thing he knew how to do. And it lasted much longer.

They had found Omar there, pounding along on the treadmill, a little after 2 in the morning, alone in the gym and unseeing out the wall of windows on the 20th floor of the hotel. A man in a jacket with epaulettes and a red stripe down his slacks stood for several minutes before Omar even realized that he was there. He slowed the treadmill and came to a polite stop, preparing himself for the usual request that he be more quiet while he exercised. But that hadn't been the message.

The message had been from Sameh. He must call immediately. It was urgent. It was about Merina. There had been a very serious accident.

The crash had happened shortly before midnight, and, like the crash involving a famous British princess, it involved a bridge abutment and a compromised driver. But in this case the princess survived, although seriously damaged.

When the police and paramedics arrived at the scene, the driver's side of the vehicle was caved in, all the way into the middle of the SUV, which meant that the driver must have hit the pillar at full speed, perhaps 120 kilometers per hour. An investigation might have asked whether the driver was distracted by the activity in the backseat, between his two passengers, but there was never going to be an investigation. However, there were clues. The woman, the wife of a prominent politician who was the confidant of the president, was found wearing only imported French lace panties and an ancient Egyptian 18th Dynasty gold bracelet and necklace studded with rubies and emeralds and sapphires. Her matching lace bra survived unscathed, and was laying on the seat near her at the moment of impact. The male passenger was naked from the waist down, wearing only his opened shirt; his tie, slacks, and jacket partially burned before they were able to put out the fire.

The male passenger and the driver were dead at the scene. The paramedics at first thought that the woman was also dead, but as they reached in to decide how to pull her up and out of the wreck, she began to moan. The words were in English, and she was able to regain consciousness long enough to say her name.

The chief of police carefully put a call into Omar at his home while keeping the identity of the woman confidential. Mr. Makrem-Ebeid was well known in the region and in all of Egypt. It would not do well to have such a man for an enemy. And, of course, such a man would be grateful to reward the careful chief for his discretion. The chief had been in the police department in Cairo for 20 years. He recognized immediately that this was a rare and wonderful opportunity.

The night housemaid at the Makrem-Ebeid residence had explained that Mr. Makrem-Ebeid was traveling on business and couldn't be reached. The chief had explained, very delicately, that this wasn't an acceptable answer.

When the phone rang in their bedroom at 1:45 am, Khalid reached for it, harsh words for Della rushing to his tongue. Hearing the housemaid instead, he grunted a "yes" and without uttering a further word, shoved the phone towards Sameh, who unwound himself from his shroud of sheets and pulled out of his deep cavern of sleep.

When Sameh arrived at the hospital a little later, the chief was waiting for him, and Sameh followed him first to the room where the attendants were working on stabilizing his mother. He was stabbed by a deep knot in his gut: she looked dead to him. While they waited to talk to her doctor, the chief pulled him into a small quiet room at the side of the emergency department, a room that was heavily draped and chilled because it was reserved for the recently deceased. It was there that Sameh saw the lace lingerie and the jewelry laid out on the freshly sheeted hospital bed. The panties had blood on them, as did the bracelet. And it was then that the chief told him that the other passenger, a man, had been found also partially naked. The man's name was Gamal Muhammed Naguib.

Sameh had remained silent as the chief had spoken. He knew who the man was. The question was how was it that his mother knew him.

"When do you expect your father to arrive?"

"He is on his way now. Perhaps two hours."

"I'll meet you both here in two and a half hours."

Sameh nodded, still reeling with the sudden onslaught of terrible change. He almost forgot to say anything to the chief, but remembered just as the officer was pulling open the door to leave the room.

"Thank you, chief, for your excellent service. My father and I won't forget the help you have offered our family. We can talk later of some small kindness we can offer you in return. And of course I know you will want to keep this confidential until we have had a chance to talk further."

It hadn't been a question, it had been a statement. Perhaps he was learning how to wield power after all, Sameh thought, as he left to go find the doctor. His father would be pleased with him for how he was handling this shock.

As Abdullah Samir Said al Makram Ebeid stood at his mother's bedside, watching her now sedated form beneath all the plastic appendages and medical paraphernalia, he wondered what else he didn't know about his mother, and how so many things could have gone so wrong so swiftly. He was suddenly deeply sad, and he was surprised to feel a few warm tears trying to pierce his composure. She looked so bad, he thought, so far from the beautiful woman she was. He wondered if she would ever recover, ever be the same. But he knew the answer. Nothing would ever be the same.

He lowered himself into the only chair in the room to wait for Della and Omar to arrive.

Della was once again wedged in a chair. But this chair wasn't really comfortable. Waiting rooms never were, she supposed. She was wide awake but not really aware, feeling only numbness, in her limbs, in her mind, an aching in her throat.

She wanted to hear Nigel's voice, to know he was alive, to believe that she could find him. She wanted to sleep a little so that she could think what to do. She thought she should probably eat something or maybe drink some water, but she didn't have the energy just now. She dreaded hearing what had happened to Merina. It was something worse than a bad auto accident, she knew: she had sensed a deep fear in Sameh too.

Something nudged her knee and she muttered a kind of apology. Perhaps she had fallen forward again and hit some other person waiting. A nurse was leaning down and looking into her face.

"You must come now, Mrs. Please. Your husband says you can come now."

"Where is he?" she asked, rousing herself from what must have been a doze, but the nurse didn't answer, instead walking briskly away in her crisp green scrubs and then turning to look back at Della. Clearly she was meant to follow. For a moment her body refused to move. Then slowly she unwound herself and rose, tense from sitting so long, and walked slowly behind the accelerating nurse. As she turned a corner into a small private hall and followed her through double wooden doors into a private suite, she felt for a moment as though she might faint. She would ask for some water. But then perhaps her faintness was the sense of dread she felt rising before her, gathering like a tide around the two men, her husband and her father-in-law, as they stood, watching her approach over the deep carpet.

She was shocked by the decision. For the first few minutes she sat, mute, unbelieving. Could they really exile Merina? In the fog of her weariness she wondered if she had misunderstood. She was gathering her wits about her to ask why, when Omar turned and departed through the big wooden doors, leaving them there, she and Sameh, sitting across from each other.

"Sameh, I don't understand. Why?"

"You understand, Della. Don't pretend you don't."

"But she is your mother, Omar's wife of many years. How does she deserve this?"

"I have explained the situation, Della, in detail. How she was found, who she was with. I won't talk about it again. It is over and we must move on."

"I can see she has made a serious mistake, Sameh, but surely this is extreme."

Sameh didn't answer. Instead he looked past her, towards the wide windows where dawn was beginning to show.

"Sameh, if you expect me to do this, you have to help me. You must promise me that you will help me find my friend. Help me find Nigel."

He turned and looked her full in the face. His appearance of deep fatigue now matched how she felt, and she could see that this wasn't what he had wanted to do. She believed he loved his mother very much. But he was becoming more mature, she realized, more able to withhold and control his feelings. More able to do what was considered best even when he hated doing it. And perhaps cynical, too: comfortable with control. Comfortable with whatever cruelty was necessary. This Sameh was a mystery to her. Less and less the man she had thought she knew. But then there was so much she had thought that had been so wrong.

Very softly, almost in a whisper, he said, "Yes, I'll help you."

Della felt her eyes grow warm and the sadness welling up in them soften just a little.

"Thank you, Sameh. And so I'll help you. Or rather, you and Omar. But it is so sad. Perhaps he will change his mind later, after he has had some time to think."

"No, he won't."

She felt another wave of fatigue and yawned to pull herself out of the fog, which was settling down into her brain.

"There is one more thing, Della."

"What is that?" she noticed that her eyes were closing now, as she asked this.

"You must agree to let this man go."

Suddenly she was awake again, "What did you say?"

"You must agree to let this man go and remain in Egypt as my wife. In fact, I would like for you to move back to Cairo. Right away."

"Sameh, this is hardly the time to be talking about our marriage. You know it isn't working, and we both know it has not really been a marriage from the beginning."

"But we are going to talk about it now. And I disagree. My mother made an excellent choice for a wife. Until this recent problem, you have been an excellent spouse."

"Your mother? Merina chose me to be your wife?"

"Yes, she convinced me you would make a good one. She was right."

Della was wide awake now, her heart rate speeding up, her synapses connecting again, her eyes wide as she stared back at him. "I can't possibly stay in this marriage, Sameh. You know it as well as I do. Let's just get through this crisis and then we can work out a divorce."

"No. I have decided you will stay. But to show my good faith, I'll find Nigel for you. He will be safe and you will know it. Then we can talk about your role in our family. We'll need someone to take over for my mother, being in charge of the family and running of the household. You will be excellent at this."

"How does Omar feel about all of this?"

"He believes the family needs you now, and he feels that this is best."

"And your male lover? Does your father know about him?"

"My father didn't become so successful by being a fool. I have always assumed that he knows."

"And if I refuse to stay in this marriage?"

"Do you want me to help you find Nigel?"

"So that's how it is going to be."

"Ah, Della, the thing is that I trust you. In spite of your transgressions. I know that you will keep your word. And that's the deal. I help to find Nigel and you stay as my wife. This is best. You'll see."

Della felt a deep chill of understanding steal up through her. She could think of no words that would change things, so they sat there, silently together in the room, across from each other in the big plush chairs while the machines in Merina's room nearby worked to keep her breathing regular and her heart beating. Della didn't speak and neither did Sameh. No words could connect them now.

Perhaps because she was beyond tired, for one flickering minute Della saw the image of the field out her backdoor in Kansas, its wheat stubble glittering with frost in the winter sunshine. She got a sense of the smell of it, too, coming back into her memory with a kind of warm glow, woodstove smoky air, and the restricted breaths through cold nostrils, of crisp clean air, and then the sound of boots on the powdery snow on the back path. Her tears would freeze at the edges of her eyes, then, sometimes, when she walked there in the deep winters of her youth.

SIXTEEN

Ninety-six hours after Merina's accident, Omar knew what he had to do. He had been asleep on the couch in the apartment in his office, the whiskey glass still sitting on the low table in front of the sofa. He sat up, suddenly awake in the predawn darkness, with the sickening realization that the terrible events of recent days were true. He refused to acknowledge the nausea, the throbbing headache, the venomous sting of her betrayal. Like a Bedouin in a sandstorm, a battle-wounded pharaoh controlling his kingdom, now he must fight harder. And then, with the clarity of a piercing bright light, the plan came into his brain.

He hadn't seen Merina's betrayal coming. Not the smallest hint, even now, looking back, searching his memory for clues. Could there have been other men? Who knew about this liaison besides himself and Sameh? He wasn't worried about the police because they had been taken care of. But there had to be others. He would have to find them, take care of them, in one way or another. He couldn't allow himself to be in a position to be bribed. This information could bring his life's plans down like a crumbling wall, sending him back into the dreadful trenches of the freight business, away from the battlements of power and influence. Away from his true destiny. No one would ever trust him to be a political leader if he couldn't even keep his own wife under control.

He had given her everything. More than she could have ever wanted: the aristocracy she could never had experienced even in the most elite academic settings; the un-questioned access to whatever material things she needed – fashion, foods, the support of servants, leisure. And she had known how lucky she had been to marry Omar – he knew that she knew. She understood that she had entered the realm of staggering good fortune by being welcomed into his famous and wealthy family. He had truly believed she would be the most loyal and devoted of wives, the most enduringly grateful. But it seemed that she carried within her the evil seed of a western infidel. Omar couldn't believe that he was thinking these words, like an uneducated desert zealot, but there they were, loud in his mind. If he had taken an Egyptian wife, this could never have happened. It would never have occurred to an Egyptian woman to have dared such an infidelity. Only someone from outside his culture would believe it possible to have such an amazing life and still betray her benefactor.

Now, on this couch, hung-over and sleep deprived, Omar felt more awake than he had ever felt. He only wondered why: why, in the name of heaven, did she do it?

His rash nature, as she called it, had allowed him to attack like a bull and conquer so many enemy businesses, to build a massive freight empire that provided a vast flow of money. But now he would put that nature aside: he would become the calculating genius that Merina used to tell him he could be. In her Swiss convalescent hospital, as she slowly recovered and came back to life, she would know this. His revenge would be his enduring absence from her, but also the reports she would get of his amazing success.

The plan that came to him fully formed in the dark room was a subtle plan. But it was a proven plan, one that others had used before. It was said that an American president used just such a plan to engineer the success of his son. The son had followed in the father's path and also had become the president. The plan would build a dynasty.

As Sameh was ushered into Omar's office, he found his father sitting in one of the chairs at the corner of the spacious room. The vast desk was clean of papers, with only a small bronze calendar and speaker phone interrupting the extensive mother-of-pearl inlay. His father didn't look up at Sameh at first but kept gazing out the window. Then he rose and gestured for Sameh to take a seat. He seemed unusually calm. Calm and calculating. Not the irate father that Sameh had so often faced.

Omar began speaking softly and smoothly, his usual dramatic style set aside for once, and at first Sameh thought his father was beginning with small talk, circling around obliquely and working up to his subject. Then he began to hear the words more clearly. And he felt their chill.

Omar explained that there was a choice to be made. And the time was now. More than just business, it was time for Sameh to move into a political career himself. He, Omar, would continue to provide an excellent legacy and reputation, and Sameh would follow. It would become a dynasty. Sameh would have sons, and one son would follow this same plan and fulfill this destiny. It was a dream of many generations, to rise beyond the strong roots of a simple merchant to become a foremost family Egypt, maybe even the world.

"Sometimes, out of great tragedy, comes great gain," he concluded.

After the chaos of the recent hours, Sameh hadn't expected this to be the topic of their meeting. He wasn't sure where to begin. "Father, I don't see myself as a politician. I went to school to study economics and business, and I have worked hard to build a more solid behind-the-scenes structure for our business."

Omar looked at him, his eyes unchanged. Had his father even heard him?

"I believe you will make an excellent politician. And I'll be there to help. I have given this much thought, Sameh, and I have decided this is our destiny."

Sameh paused to choose his words.

"Father, this is your dream, your destiny, and you should pursue it with all your will and resources. But I would like to stay as your business partner and to support you in every way possible, from behind the scenes."

"No. That is not acceptable. It isn't enough. It is your task to carry our legacy."

"Perhaps one of my brothers can take this political role, perhaps Mohammed or Zakariya. They will both grow into capable and intelligent men."

"No. I have chosen you."

"What if I don't want to do this?"

"You will change your mind. You will enjoy this new role once you have started on the path."

"Father, are you saying that you're not giving me a choice in this matter?"

"Yes. You have a choice. This is your choice."

"And you expect me to have a son."

"Yes, you will have several sons. And in that regard, you need to take tighter control of your wife, and have her here, in Cairo, managing the household, helping you succeed. She is well known and respected in the academic circles here, and even beyond, and everyone will respect her if she gives up her career now to have children. It is time."

"What if she isn't happy doing that? What if she doesn't want to come to Cairo and have children?"

"Do you mean what if she wants to continue that little liaison with the journalist down in Luxor? No. Very few people know about that, and besides, he is, ah, gone."

Sameh sat very still, and then having forgotten to breathe for a moment, he took a deep breath. Then, he asked, very softly, "How do you know this?"

"I know many things that I don't reveal. It is time for you to bring her home to Cairo, to have children, and to give up your boyish pursuits of man-sex."

Sameh continued to sit, staring at this man who was his father, and wondering how much he knew and how he knew it.

"Sameh, that especially includes Khalid. Get rid of him."

"But arrangements must be made…"

"Now, Sameh. Today. Have someone make the arrangements."

Sameh felt like the building was shifting beneath him. He suddenly had the image of his father as a giant cobra, coiled in front of him, staring into his eyes. He had just felt the sting, and now the poison would flow through him, changing him into something else. Soon he would feel nothing, no pain, not even the loss of his beloved Khalid, only the sting of this destiny that had been thrust upon him. "I'm not sure I can do all this, Father."

"I believe you can. But if you're sure you cannot, you're welcome to leave, with my blessings, now, this afternoon. You will leave the Egypt, leave the region. I will not look upon your face ever again. You may have enough money to last one month. You will never contact me or anyone else in the family again. I'll have the documents drawn so you can sign them, and then give you a check before you leave."

Sameh sat very still and waited to breath. Who was this man? "May I ask why, Father? Why have you decided this?"

"No. You may not. You may draw whatever conclusions you wish."

"May I have one day to give it some thought?"

"No. You may not. It must be now. And you will sign this agreement now, accepting these terms."

It was Sameh's turn to look out the window at the low skyline. He had been in this office many times, but it was always to talk about some shipping or personnel problem, or to announce some new contract or good profit results. Never in all his life had Sameh considered that his father had wanted more of him than this.

"I'm not sure, Father, about Della. I'm not sure she will want to stay with me."

"You will find a way to convince her. Tell her that you will be a better husband and take care and protect her, as the Prophet directs."

"She is a Christian."

"I made that mistake with your mother. That must change. Della must welcome Islam and convert."

"What if she doesn't wish to do so?"

"Why do you continue to argue with me? This isn't a request, Sameh. You will be sure that this happens. And besides, I have come to the realization that we must both be far more devoted to the practice of our religion, and that it will be good for our business and reputation to be a more visibly conservative family. Only outside of Egypt will I tolerate any disobedience in this or any sexual deviation. Starting this day you will obey me. And so will your wife. The few people who were aware of her indiscretion have been taken care of; this won't trouble you in the future. Get her pregnant as soon as possible. And keep her pregnant for the next few years. She will forget many things when she has babies to play with.

"Also, Sameh, you must watch her and be sure she does only as you tell her. She is to have none of those western freedoms. I have learned where that can lead. You must make these changes, carefully, but you must make them. She is to be escorted everywhere she goes. I'll arrange for her to be accompanied and served at all times. Do you understand this?"

"Once again, you're telling me I have no choice?"

"I won't repeat myself. You understand your options."

He saw that his father seemed very composed. Even relaxed. He wasn't going to change his mind. "What about Mother?"

"What about her?"

"Do you know of her progress? Will she be coming home?"

Omar turned away, briefly, but then turned back with a fixed look towards Sameh.

"She is receiving excellent care in a facility that's better than anything we have here in our country. She will be taken care of for the rest of her life. We were very close to discussing her life in the past tense. It is all I'm willing to do for her. It is enough. She is being cared for and she is alive."

"Will I be able to see her?"

Omar turned his cobra eyes to meet his on's. "Are you sure you want to see her? Do you want to explain that you chose the facility in Switzerland where she will reside for the rest of her life? Perhaps you could write her a letter. She will be able to read again at some point."

"How will you know? Are you checking on her every day?"

"That's my business. Your mother is no longer your concern. You will know when I tell you."

Sameh sat in silence, stunned at the changes in his life.

"And now for the next step: your religious transformation. The most famous imam in all of Egypt is Abhallah El-Ebraheim and he is based at the Al-Quddous Mosque in Nasr City. He will come and sit with you to hear about your recent sudden religious inspiration, when you were overwhelmed by a vision from Allah. He will see that you have a deep desire to become more devout. He is very well connected throughout Egypt and beyond and will be the perfect guide to shepherd you through your reunion with our blessed Islam. In a country in the west the son of a president became a born-again Christian, and that was an important key to his rise in both business and politics. I'm sure you will be very good in that role. You should begin thinking of what you will discuss with the Imam. And when Della gets back from accompanying your mother to Switzerland, you're to have the imam meet with her and with both of you together. Counseling, I think they call it. I expect you to give this counseling a very convincing try. I would be good for your wife to have a friend too, and I'm sure Imam El-Ebraheim can arrange for her meet some other good Egyptian wives who are educated and also devout." He looked at his son. "Well?"

"What?"

"I must leave soon, Sameh. What is your answer?"

Sameh hesitated only a split second. Then he looked his father in the eyes and said, clearly and slowly. "I look forward to being part of this great destiny, father, and you can count on me completely."

"Good. You have chosen well. You will sign the agreement and then I'll leave for a cabinet meeting. There are rumors of protests, as in Tunisia, and we must arrange for that not to happen. I'll attend the meeting knowing that our plans are in your capable hands."

As he watched his father walk out of the room, Sameh wondered how so much could have changed in so few days. And the man who had caused that change, the tall man who was both his father and an utter stranger, handsome and powerful, walked from the room like a proud lion, never turning back to see his son's face. But if you watched him carefully, you could detect that there had been a great and deep wound from his mother's betrayal. Sameh knew that as with all wild animals, this had made him even more dangerous. He had only one advantage in this relationship, and that was his youth. He would wait. He would lead his father to believe he had accepted his destiny, that he would follow the new rules for a while. But Sameh knew that someday, when the old lion wasn't as strong, his, his own rules would take over.

SEVENTEEN

Della sat in a window seat in first class. As the jet reached cruising altitude, she had just told the flight attendant that she only wanted hot tea. She hoped that the woman had gotten the implied message that she wanted to be left alone. The man sitting in the seat next to her had briefly regarded Della in her abaya, then fumbled with his briefcase and newspaper and remained silent. She had carefully avoided looking at him, even though the two seats were separated by a shoulder high panel. She didn't want to talk to anyone. She hadn't talked to Sameh for over 48 hours: she hadn't taken his calls since she had left Cairo with Merina two days before. He would just have to wait until she returned.

She had no idea what was happening at home, with Omar and Sameh, and their attempt to suppress and contain any news of the accident, or rather, the circumstances surrounding the accident. And she didn't want to know. What she already knew was disturbing, but not as disturbing as the way the family had reacted. Right this moment she thought of both of these men, her father-in-law and her husband, as barbarians adhering to a primitive set of cultural mores. It continued to shock her that Omar would exile his wife and lifelong companion to a care facility in another country. Forever. That was what he had said. The family was forbidden to contact her. Was this how she should expect to be treated if something happened to her? Were all wives pawns in the political and business games these modern Egyptian men were playing?

Omar's ambition was clearly more important to him than his wife was. And now that she knew so much more about her husband, she could see that he was made of the same stuff as his father. Omar would probably be very successful, Della thought, feeling utter disgust. He might even rise to the pinnacle of Egyptian politics. Unless there was some political upheaval, which seemed unlikely. She wondered if these kinds of ruthless tactics were why he was so prosperous. Another thing she really didn't want to know. She had been so excited to join this family. So honored to even have the chance. Her dysfunctional Kansas upbringing had prepared her for the tension of constant family strife, but not for anything like this.

But she was keeping her promise and going home to Egypt. Sameh had promised to help her. She hoped she could believe him. But then, she didn't know who else to ask.

The private medical flight with Merina had gone well, leaving in the middle of the night from Cairo and landing at a private terminal in Zurich. Omar had insisted that two strong male attendants accompany her. To assist her with any transport issues, he had said. She had never seen either of them before. They were huge, like body guards or enforcers. But they had been polite enough and had stayed out of her way, even helping her at times. She hadn't talked to them except for basic instructions.

The Swiss countryside had been rich and green and there was snow everywhere as they accompanied Merina in the medical transport vehicle to a convalescent hospital nestled on a hill overlooking Lake Zurich. It had been sunny and cold, with Christmas decorations everywhere, and all the mountains dressed in sparkling white. She so wished Merina had been awake to see it. Merina would know where she was eventually. The doctors had insisted she was stable and would improve, although very, very slowly. They had explained that she would never fully recover. Merina had been in and out of consciousness since the accident, and the doctors had said that although it was all right to move her, keeping her sedated would minimize the stress of the journey. She seemed so fragile, not well enough to move at all, much less fly.

Della hadn't once left her side during the trip. She had been her true advocate, zealously watching every movement of every gurney and every tuck of every blanket and every adjustment of IVs and the breathing machines. She had only wished she could ask Merina why. Why had she done it? And why with that man, of all men? Sameh said he was rumored to have ties to the underworld of international crime, to have many mistresses, and to have been involved in drug trafficking, international theft, and even murder.

Gamal's family, from the Sudan, had flown to Egypt to take the body home for burial immediately in accord with their religious tenants. They had to get a special dispensation to even enter Egypt for this purpose, and then they had to leave as soon as they collected the body. How did the family even know he had died? The National Intelligence Minister had told Omar that his family was suspected to run a terrorist training camp in the eastern mountains of Sudan, training anti-Israeli shock troops. It would create problems with Egypt's allies if it was known that the government had even talked to anyone from this group, much less let them come into Egypt and not detained them. Sameh said tht Omar was trying to find out who had the power to keep it all hushed up. Della wondered what would happen to those people when he found them. One more thing she didn't want to know.

The authentic 19th Dynasty bracelet and earrings that Merina had been wearing had been stolen from a shipping carton being sent to the Chicago Museum for an exhibition. It had disappeared along with other priceless jewelry items including some ancient Roman jewelry from Britain. She wondered if Merina knew she was wearing stolen jewelry. She wanted to ask her if this man was charming enough to justify that. What else had he given her? Or was it just affection that she craved? Della was beginning to understand how empty her life must have been with Omar always gone or playing at politics. But why this man?

She would call Sameh when she landed in Cairo. She was just not sure how she was going to deal with Sameh and Omar, but she had to try. Sameh had probably not done anything to help find Nigel, she realized. The last thing she had done him before Merina's plane took off was to plead with him. Please, she had said, please keep your promise to find Nigel.

"I will. But you should realize that he is probably long gone, maybe out of the whole region." Then he added, "Perhaps, dear Della, he doesn't want to be found."

Then Sameh had said something about meeting the imam on her return, but she hadn't heard it all. She had jerked the phone out in front of her and stared at it as it burbled with cartoon noises. Then she clicked the OFF button. She almost sent a text pleading battery problems but decided he could wait. Della had considered calling her dad too but then decided not to do that, either. As soon as she got back to Cairo, she would have a private discussion with

Sameh about a divorce and then she would call her father. He would just worry if she told him now. He was the one person in the world she could trust, but she dreaded the idea of going back to Kansas. She would find an attorney and arrange to keep some property so she could keep living in Egypt. Near Nigel. It would be best to remain polite with Omar and Sameh until she had hired an attorney and knew where she stood. It was going to take all of her mettle to do this. She just wanted to scream at them.

Della looked down at her hands. Her cuticles were ripped and raw. She used to bite them when she was a young girl, and now, after years of having the clean smooth fingers of a scholar, she had started again. And she had added an acid stomach. In these tense recent weeks, her stomach had become more agitated. Being nauseous in the afternoon had been just one more little challenge to add to the load, and looking down at her fingers, the knot in her throat matched the warmth welling up in her eyes. She had been through tough times before, and she could get through this, too. If only she could talk to Nigel. She lifted her chin and looked at the padded ceiling of the cabin, willing the tears that were trying to form to slide back down into their ducts. They felt cool on the inside of her throat. Reaching for another tissue, she made a tiny coughing sound. She couldn't let the tears get started. She had to be strong. Because she knew Nigel was out there somewhere and she was going to find him.

The tray with the porcelain tea pot arrived, the attendant poured her a cup, and Della leaned over the rising steam before she took a sip. The plane now floated over the Dolomites, the sparkling white limestone section of the Alps, which were partially visible today through the ragged clouds below. Perhaps she would go to Bolzano in northern Italy. She had heard it was beautiful. And it wasn't a place that either Omar or Sameh would ever think of. If she could just find Nigel. If she could just find him, she would go wherever he was. Anywhere. She would live in a tent with him. Even in Kansas.

Khalid wrapped his robe around himsel with both arms and stood back. The two large men in the doorway looked at him, then their eyes traveled down

186

to his bare feet and back up to his face. The younger one, who had a body builder's torso and silky hair, suppressed a smile. The other man was holding a clipboard and a roll of blue packing tape.

"You're early," Khalid said.

"Our paperwork says 9 a.m. Should we come back another day?" asked the older man.

"No, now is fine."

Nasim brought Khalid his slippers and a demitasse as he positioned himself on the settee by the big windows overlooking el-Zahraa Avenue. He couldn't believe this was happening. Sameh had told him, of course, because Sameh never did anything without telling him. But then he actually did it. Khalid hadn't expected that.

Sameh thought he was being civil and generous about the break-up. He had arranged for another apartment, albeit in a much less glamorous area, and paid for the lease for a full year. Khalid had naturally refused to go and see it. He had told Sameh that he would come to his senses. But now he would apparently have to go. Either that or sleep somewhere else tonight. He would take Nasim with him because Sameh had said the apartment was large enough to accommodate his servant. But Sameh didn't know about the other one, his secret lover, the boy, his dear Jamel, who came to visit sometimes. The boy lived just a mile or two from here and Khalid had made an arrangement with his mother to pay for his visits. Jamel walked to their meetings now, and how would he get to the new location? Khalid hated to lose him; Jamel was precious to him. It made Khalid smile just to think of him.

Sameh, of course, would not approve of Khalid's arrangement with this young boy, but that was fine with Khalid. Jamel wasn't to be shared.

And so he sat and sipped his coffee and watched the workers who had come with the two men as they packed things and put them into boxes. Nasim hovered and fussed about everything being carefully padded and wrapped, and then not crowded into the moving cartons. Khalid watched with detachment, noticing only that Nasim was here in the salon, and now in the dining room, and now berating the packers in the kitchen. Usually his antics amused Khalid, but not today. Khalid didn't find anything about this move amusing.

Did Sameh really think he could get away with this? This move was going to cost Sameh a lot more than a year's rent. Khalid would have to be sure that the payback was particularly painful.

The fisherman sat down again to wait. It had been two days more than he had been told. But it was only time. He would not ask why or think. He would just wait.

The boats bustled by him in the busy harbor, docks all around him with their loads of cargo, box on box, and bag beside bag. He was an anchored pole in the center of the universe with painted spheres on long invisible strings that were circling and spinning and rotating around him. Wider and wider they spun, but he sat waiting, sure in his inner strength. He was the quiet sun with the heavens chaotic around him, but, devoted to the great Jihad, no dizziness would touch him.

The trip down the venerable river had been slow and full of peace. He had loved the soft warm air and small smooth waves as his boat gently pushed through them. He had loved the stars sparkling at night and the whispers of the insects as he passed through the vast delta, and then the easy rising of the tide as his boat flowed north and approached the great port of Alexandria. It had been a journey full of peace. And although the fisherman didn't know exactly what was in the box he had hidden in the bottom of the boat beneath the nets, he knew one thing: it wasn't about peace.

It was an ancient paradox: that there was so much peace when preparing for terrifying strife, for the turmoil of battle. His ancestors, those ancient great ones who had subdued the mighty Nile, understood this. The careful making of the shields, the arming of the chariots, all were small quiet steps of preparation, tiny increments of quiet to become ready. It was the peace before all battle.

It was a deep honor to the fisherman's soul to be part of the quiet before great terror, to be a part of a truly magnificent Jihad. For this he was happy to wait. God would provide. God would guide. Time wasn't important; it was only important that he was here, that he was ready, and that he hadn't been detected.

He rose and laid out his prayer rug on the tiny deck of his old boat, and rocking softly in the water of the busy harbor, kneeled to say his prayers.

Nigel opened his eyes in the darkness with a start. He could hear a soft shifting scrabbling sound. It seemed to be several meters away, but the darkness was complete so he couldn't be sure. He could tell from the change in the sound that it was moving: it was coming towards him. Nigel reached around him to find the flashlight. He had managed to shove it underneath his leg just before they left. They would've come back if they had remembered they left it. As he patted the floor beside him, the soft shifting sound stopped. Then there was a kind of breathy whipping sound, like a zipper being pulled. His legs were wrapped in chains that were bolted to the wall, so he made noise as he tried to find the metal shaft of the flashlight. He almost knocked it away but was still dexterous enough to catch it as it started to roll. He was surprised that he could move this fast after not eating or drinking for – how long? It could have been a day or several days. His heart was beating very fast. In the coolness of the underground tomb, he could feel the sweat rising on his brow.

Snake. It had to be a snake. Most likely cobra. Most likely King cobra.

He found the flashlight button in spite of the fact that his fingers were shaking. He clicked it on. It shone brightly at the wall opposite him, only two meters away, illuminating the carved scenes, which looked as though they had just been recently finished and were waiting for the painters to arrive. Nigel knew they were at least 3,000 years old. Maybe older.

Another sound. More of the soft zipper pull. Then a swish.

He moved the flashlight slowly around him, barely able to breathe, knowing that the size of a snake in this terrain would be large. They were famously large, in fact, and vicious hunters. Slowly he panned the light, down the long corridor to his right, back along the wall in front of him, now down the corridor to his left. But nothing was there. Unless. Were there two points of red light just at the border of the flashlight umbra? Two lights that seemed to move? Eyes? They were farther away than he expected. But then old Egyptian tombs were so tightly lined with fitted stone that they could echo. Wait. Now the little red lights were not there. Had he really seen them? He had imagined them?

Nigel sat holding the flashlight and not moving, except for the most shallow of breaths, and listened carefully. He heard no sound of any kind. But he knew he had heard something.

How long would the batteries last? Would they make it until the men came back? And would the men even come back – or leave him here, to die of thirst in this old tomb? Thirst or snakebite. The men would torture him if they came back. He had been held in a mud and wattle hut for a week before they brought him here. One of the men had been waiting to use his huge Arabian curved blade knife. He put it up to Nigel's throat several times. He seemed to salivate when he did this. The knife was at least 18 inches long and a curved tip. But the other man had said to wait. Said they had to check with the boss first.

Nigel assumed that Gamal had found out about Della and him. That was the only thing he could think of. But when he had asked them to tell Gamal he was sorry and would leave Egypt right away, they asked who Gamal was. They must have been playing games with him. If not Gamal, then who?

Oh God, Della. Would they go after Della, too? He felt the tears rising up inside him like a giant wave. Please, God, whoever you are, whatever happens to me, please please please don't let them harm Della. She would never know what happened to him. She would not believe that he had left her, but one day, after some time, her memory of their love would fade. She would have a good life. Oh please let that be the case.

He was tempted to ask them – if they came back. What about Della? But maybe that wasn't such a good idea. And maybe they would not come back at all. It would be easier, Nigel knew, to just let him die here and come back and move the body in a month or so. Or never. This tomb was probably a registered site with restricted access. Closed most of the time. Or, even worse, an undiscovered tomb that only these thugs knew about. These thugs and their boss. Who was who? He would ask them who.

If they came back.

If he was still alive.

Sameh didn't come to the airport to meet her. She hadn't expected him, of course. Hakim, after escorting her to the SUV, asked if she would like to go home immediately or wait for the luggage to be brought to the car. She chose to wait. Arriving at the family apartments in late afternoon, she immediately felt the absence of Merina. Her essence was like an unseen mist that floated throughout the compound. Della went to find the girls, who were in Nabeela's room, and told them how sorry she was about their mother. Both girls were oddly stoic. Silently, they nodded, but that was all. Della searched for sadness in their faces but it didn't look as if they had been crying. Perhaps they were bearing their pain better than Della was. Surely they were hurting, even if they chose not to show it. But Della wondered what Omar and Sameh had told them. The two boys were not home, and the girls didn't know when they would be back.

She learned that Nabeela and Nylla and Zaki were going horseback riding out by the pyramids the next morning with "Aunt" Zara and "Uncle" Faizel. The children all loved Aunt and Uncle, who were really not related at all but longtime family employees. They had been in the household whole the children were growing up, and were famously soft touches when their parents had been out, or too busy, or just said "no."

As Della stood there, not knowing what to say, Nabeela suddenly announced that she was going to get to ride a white stallion this time. Nylla followed this with a "me too!" Della then started to ask what their father had told them about their mother, but Faizel, who had come up behind them, interrupted her. It was time for the girls to take their shopping trip: they were to get new riding clothes for the trip and then go to a movie at the mall; the driver was waiting, he said, we must go now, as he ushered them through the door like a mother goose.

Della watched, mute, as the girls were escorted towards the entry way, with Zara right behind them saying something about having time to look at some make-up or new shoes before the movie started. She had never known that the girls to go to the mall, even escorted, in the evening. Merina usually insisted they go during the day. Of course the family was just trying to shield the girls from the sadness of missing their mother. But still somehow, it felt wrong.

Her nausea had passed, and suddenly very weary, Della went to her room and lay down on the bed. When she opened her eyes, Sameh was standing over her. As he looked down into her face, she thought she could see sadness in his eyes. Sadness and something else. Determination, resoluteness, she wasn't sure.

Was he preparing for their coming struggle over the divorce? She waited for him to speak, but he remained silent for several minutes.

"The imam will be here in the morning to meet with us. I have told him he could come at 10."

"Why do I need to see an imam?"

"Because in times of trouble a person should have someone to counsel them, to offer support, to help them through it. We know no Christian ministers that we can trust, but this imam is a good man, a holy man, and he will help you. Please be appropriately dressed and ready on time."

With this he turned and walked out of the room. Della was too tired to call after him, so she just lay there and listened for his footsteps disappearing into the Persian runners in the hallway.

Della checked her messages. The only texts were from Sameh. She just deleted them all. Then she texted Nigel. She hadn't texted him for two full days. "I'm here waiting. Tell me where to come to help you." The message was transmitted, and so she knew that his phone was still out there, somewhere, working. Perhaps someday, when she had stopped waiting, she would get a reply.

When she woke up again, it was late, and she called the kitchen and asked for some soup and a piece of bread. She felt a little better, so she sat at the desk in her bedroom suite, waited for the soup to cool and turned on the TV. It was almost midnight, time for the BBC World Service. This was BBC's Middle East broadcast, but there would be news from other places. The news was just what she needed to hear. It would be nice to think about somebody else's problems.

The news wasn't really new, of course. There were problems with the succession of the Labour Party taking control of the next Parliament in England, the Jordanian queen was having a fundraiser for her much-admired humanitarian project, the Israeli government had resumed building their hated wall, and Greece was managing to hold its economy together in spite of the riots about pension changes. There was yet another earthquake in an Italian hill town, and also in Indonesia, near Jakarta this time.

There was also a report that a fatal accident in Cairo several weeks before that had killed an international terrorist and crime lord, one Gamal Naguib, might not have been an accident after all. Well, Della thought, so much for Omar's efforts to keep this away from the media. But she watched, holding her breath, as the reporter continued without mentioning anything about the details. No mention of anyone else in the vehicle. The newscaster never even actually said where the accident happened or mentioned the type of car. Amazed, her spoon hovered over the bowl of cooling soup. Then the news anchor added, in his crisp British accent, *"There has been an international manhunt launched to find possible colleagues of this deceased criminal, and anyone with knowledge of the whereabouts of any of the following persons is encouraged to contact Interpol or your local police immediately."* As the reporter said this three photos, all head shots, were presented side by side on the screen. There were names beneath each one. She immediately recognized the photo on the right. Nigel Sutherland.

Della put her spoon down beside her soup. With a sinking feeling she knew she would not be able to get the food down. It wasn't tears that stopped her appetite, this time, it was fear. International criminal? Terrorist? What had she done?

Della didn't get up and dress appropriately for the imam the next morning. Instead she told her maid that she wasn't feeling well and would need to stay in bed and wished to be left completely alone. She felt like she was coming down with something. Perhaps flu. Then she rolled over and pretended to be asleep when she heard someone come to her door. Most of the day she lay on the silky sheets and stared at the soft draperies moving in the gentle breeze of the air conditioning. The white wispy fabric was misty through her tears as they slipped silently onto the pillow, unminded, untissued, uninterrupted. She wept for Merina. She wept for Nigel. She wept for the death of all her dreams.

Sameh sent word that he had arranged for the imam to come another day and that he hoped she felt better soon.

She awoke in the late afternoon, with nausea again, and requested mint tea. And then, as the kitchen boy, dressed in his crisp white gallibaya, was lowering the beautiful modern glass tea pot from the inlaid teak tray onto her table, it came to her: she was pregnant. She had assumed she had missed her periods because of all the stress. When she had had the accident on the boat, she had missed three months. Completely understandable the doctor had said. But there had been no Nigel then. Her life had been passionless. She would ask one of the maids to buy her a pregnancy test at the pharmacy to confirm, but she already knew. She hadn't recognized the morning sickness because it was in the afternoon. Every afternoon for at least a week and a half.

Della sat as still as a crane in the morning on the bank of the Nile. A baby. She was going to have Nigel's baby. Someone who would love her completely, someone to devote her life to. Someone she could teach and love unconditionally.

She had to think very carefully, very clearly now. She had to protect the life of her child.

EIGHTEEN

Wael was surprised to hear from Sameh Markram-Ebeid. Even more surprising, he called to ask about about the missing man. If Wael's suspicions were right, this was a man calling about the whereabouts of his wife's lover. Is this what an infidel wife did to a good Muslim man? Wael offered to share any information he was able to find. When Wael heard Sameh describe the man as "a friend and colleague of my wife's," he had smiled into the phone. It was strange, he thought, that Mr. Markram-Ebeid would contact a member of the public police. Typically people of his wealth and status conducted their inquiries through private resources. Which would explain the reports of several private investigator types in the area recently, also asking about this missing man.

Wael had seen the news report about the famous Gamal Muhammed Naguib being killed in a traffic accident in Cairo, and he didn't for a moment believe this was the whole story. Gamal was known to all the regional law enforcement as very powerful and well connected. Not exactly akin to a mafioso, Wael knew, because most Egyptians didn't believe he would be as ruthless. But Wael wasn't so sure about that. For one thing, no one in the intelligence and police community had been able to learn everything Gamal was involved in. There were many hints. Certainly artifact smuggling, certainly drug trading, and likely also weapons smuggling; probably sex trafficking, but was there terrorism, too? Perhaps.

It would seem that a person devoted to the acquisition of wealth would not be politically motivated towards terrorism. But Gamal was a mysterious character and the drive to acquire riches could be a cover for his true passion.

Wael had been hearing Gamal's name for years. He was always described as "up the line" or behind the scenes, and no one had ever caught him actually doing anything. Or, if they did, they never lived to report it. Except that someone had gotten to him now. But who?

Wael also didn't believe that the man, Nigel Sutherland, who was shown as a colleague of Gamal's and was also the missing "friend" of Mrs. Makram -Ebeid, was a terrorist or even a criminal. He was an archeological journalist. A simple man, really. Not such a smart man, of course, to have gotten involved with the likes of Gamal. And clearly a scapegoat for someone. But who? Who would have been powerful enough to have Gamal killed and Nigel implicated? Wael had given it a lot of thought and he couldn't figure it out. The only thing he had decided was that it must be someone high up in the Egyptian govern-ment. No one else would have the power and connections to get away with it.

Wael had almost shared with Manar that the young Mr. Makram-Ebied had called to talk with him. But before he could arrange a meeting, Wael's wife had had to be hospitalized. She had struggled to get beyond the death of their oldest son, a year ago. But the hospitalization helped and with the aid of antidepressants, she soon returned to being the wife and partner he had always loved. After she returned home, Wael called Manar to arrange a meeting, but Manar had disappeared. He had been out on an investigation, looking for any connections the recently killed Gamal might have had in Aswan, and had never returned. It had been almost three weeks and there wasn't a sign, or trace, of his person, his car, or anything at all. Wael knew immediately that he must be dead. Manar was very comfortable in his city, everyone knew him, and most didn't regard him as much of a threat. People involved in criminal activity usually just avoided him. It was widely reported that he took bribes, but Wael knew he was essentially harmless and would do the right thing when needed. There was no chance it was a mere mishap: Manar had been disposed of.

Wael drove down to Aswan to ask around. He learned that no one knew anything. No one had seen Manar or heard anything. In a place like Aswan someone should have seen something. And then Wael understood he most likely would only know who had taken out Manar if he was being taken out himself.

Were all these things connected: Gamal's accident, the warehouse in Aswan, the disappearance of Nigel, and now Manar? Each of these incidents were unsolved and without clues. Wael had learned from years of police work that when things were too neat, too "closed" that meant danger was very close. As he drove back to Luxor, he decided he would never talk about his suspicions to anyone. And he would never go looking for Nigel Sutherland. And if Sameh called again, he would say he knew nothing. Which was, in fact, exactly what he knew.

The maid who came to Della's room was new. She had been introduced to her a few days earlier, but she didn't remember her name. Della hadn't realized she was replacing Silva. This woman was older, she had a harsh face – Della hadn't seen her smile, nor could she imagine it. When Della asked what had happened to Silva, she was told Silva now worked in the kitchen full time. Why had she not been consulted? It was just one more small sadness: Silva had been with her since she first came to Egypt and had been a wonderful helper. Had she done something to Silva that made her want to leave? She would go down to the kitchen sometime and talk with her.

The new maid, Heqet, identified herself a second time, and told Della that the imam was here for her appointment. Della had been standing by the window, looking out towards the beautiful domes of Hosh al-basha, dressed and ready, for over an hour. The domes were especially magical in the sharp shadows of the early morning sun. Along with her beloved Luxor, Della felt closest to the true Egypt here, with so much of the glory of its history within view of these windows, and also stretching, like tendrils, back into the shimmering past. This ancient majesty was like an anchor in the recent nightmare of her existence. If only she could get back to the place where everything was magic. If only she could find Nigel. How could he be a terrorist? How could she believe this? Who was saying these things, and why?

For her meeting with the imam, she was wearing a simple off-white abaya and black hajib, with the red tendrils of her hair carefully tucked out of view. Della usually didn't wear eye make-up, preferring a simpler look that had some scholarly credibility, but today she had considered some deep charcoal shadow. Would it be better if she tried to dress more in the style of other young Egyptian women? If she tried to fit in more, perhaps she would disarm this unknown imam by looking more subservient and typical. But in the end she didn't. She chose only a little lipstick. She would be herself, at least for now. She wasn't sure what she would have to do to survive, but today she needed, now more than ever, to hold onto her own identity. An identity that seemed to be slipping from her grasp. An identity that now included becoming a mother.

Della followed Heqet down through several long parquet halls into the carpeted foyer of the Cairo residence. Mohammed, Sameh's brother, stood waiting with the imam. He would serve as her mahram, as it wasn't possible for a woman to meet with a man without a male family member present. Imam Abhallah El-Ebraheim stood silently waiting for them, his hands at his side. Della was surprised at his appearance. He looked more like a humble preacher from Missouri than a famous Muslim cleric. He was dressed in baggy khaki pants and an untucked, slightly wrinkled, button-down shirt. He had a short haircut. He had on sneakers. He looked into her eyes and there was a hint of timidity in his face, of hesitation, as though he was afraid she would not like him. She understood that the imam would not extend his hand, would not touch a woman, but this was more than just the hesitancy of a religious man. Della suddenly felt a little easier about the coming meeting. Perhaps he wasn't the threatening dogmatist she had dreaded.

She led Mohammed and the imam into the reception parlor and asked the holy man if he would take some tea, or something else, and carefully watched his mannerisms as he politely declined, saying that he had had tea earlier and didn't like to eat until evening. She thanked Heqet and sent her away and then waited for the imam to begin the conversation. He cleared his throat, and said, in a very quiet, almost bashful voice, "Mrs. Makreim el-Ebeid, I understand you have been under some terrible pressure of late, and while I don't need to know everything about those circumstances, except what you wish to share, I'm here to be your advocate, and to listen to your feelings, and to see what I can do to help you. I understand that you're a Christian, a great religion that I have the deepest respect for, but the family has asked that I, as a spiritual counselor for them, be here to help you. And so I am. "

This wasn't at all what Della had expected. The idea of someone she could talk to sounded dangerous. And yet it was true she had felt alone since Nigel had disappeared. She had wanted to ask her father for his advice, but she hadn't been able to get up the nerve to tell him about Nigel. She knew she would need her father's help to get out of this marriage, but first she needed to figure out what she could negotiate, where her possible strengths lay. Perhaps this imam could actually help. She had no intention of telling him about Nigel, but perhaps she could earn his support in her effort to divorce Sameh. For a flash, Della imagined having someone she could tell everything, share her sorrow and fear, her frustration, her desperate need to find Nigel, even her pregnancy. That moment passed almost as instantly as it had begun. Gazing up at young Mohammed, who was leaning on the arched doorway wall, she knew that she would hold all those secrets to herself. But if this imam were serious about being an advocate, she might as well start with a crucial issue. What the imam said about that would determine what came next.

Della lowered her head, and spoke just above a whisper. "Assalamu Alaikum Wa Rahmatullahi Wa Barakatuh, Imam El-Ebraheim. Thank you for offering your aid. My husband has a male lover. He lives with him and only visits me. I believe I'm entitled to a divorce. Can you help me?"

Mohammed didn't turn his head, but she was sure he had heard.

It was time to call her father. Della had found some attorneys in an Internet directory, but she wanted to talk to him before she made any calls. Her Egyptian family was so famous that it was likely that whoever she called would get the information back to Omar, and then to Sameh, no matter what she said, or paid, or the so-called rules of client privilege. Della had always been a very private person and the spotlight of fame – especially the scandal of an American infidel wife divorcing a handsome, wealthy man from a popular Egyptian family – terrified her. She hoped that her father would have a suggestion. An American attorney who could practice in Egypt would be ideal, but even then she wasn't sure. And there was Nigel. Sameh had promised to help her find Nigel if she stayed as his wife. But it had been almost a month since he had been gone, three and a half weeks since Merina's accident and Sameh's promises, and there had been no report, no hint that anyone had done anything.

Della dreaded telling her dad. He was so proud of her, being a successful archeologist and marrying so far above anything he could imagine. And he had always really liked Sameh. It would break his heart that things were turning out so badly. Because of his previous heart problems, she had to try to be upbeat when she talked to him. Still she had to talk to him. She would call around 6 on Saturday evening from her rooms. That would be 10 in the morning in Kansas, and she was sure she would find him either at home or on his cell.

Della rose late and walked outside around the fenced gardens of the compound on Saturday mid-day. In the afternoon she sat quietly in her faithful plush chair and read some publications on recent research. Her tea arrived at precisely 5:45 and Della gratefully poured the steaming liquid from the pot to the cup, enjoying the damp warmth on her face, taking solace in the little simple pleasures of life. She felt like she would be able to remain calm and positive when she called.

Her father didn't answer his cell phone. She sent a text and then waited for a response. She poured another cup and waited. She rose and walked around the room, thinking about what it must be like in Kansas today. It was December, so it might be snowing.

At 6:45 she tried the landline at the house. Her sister answered, and she felt relief that it wasn't her mother. Although her mother rarely answered the phone, Della really didn't want to talk to her.

"Hi, Sarah, how are you?"

"Della?"

"Yes, it's me. How are you?"

"I'm OK. Do you want to talk to Mom, She's right here."

"No, I want to..." But it was too late.

"You're probably calling to talk to your father."

"Yes, Mom, but of course I want to talk to you too. How are you?"

"He is in the hospital. Call him there. "

"Why?"

"Ask him yourself. He is on the cardiac floor, but he can talk on the phone just fine."

"Mom, what happened?"

"Really, Della, I would prefer you talk to him yourself. Here, Sarah can give you his room number."

And she was gone. Same old Mom. Suddenly Della was back in school wondering what was wrong with her, what she had done, why her mother hated her. But she stopped herself. She didn't have time for self-pity, not today.

When she dialed his room at the hospital, a nurse answered the phone.

"This is Della, Mr. Pieterson's daughter, calling from Cairo. Egypt. May I please speak to him?"

"Not now. We are giving him a bath and changing the sheets, so please call back in about 20 minutes." Click.

Twenty minutes crept by. Heqet came to the door to ask if she would take dinner in the dining room or in her rooms, but Della told her she wasn't sure yet and to bring more tea.

When she called back in 20 minutes, there was no answer. She tried again in ten more minutes. This time she got the nurse again.

"May I please speak to my father?"

"Who is this, please?"

"Mr. Pieterson's eldest daughter, Della, calling from Egypt."

"Egypt. Where? Missouri?"

"Egypt, Egypt. Cairo, Egypt. Please may I speak with him?"

There was a pause, while Della sensed that the phone receiver was being muffled.

"Yes, you make talk to him, but please don't talk long. Ten minutes at the most. He needs to rest."

"Della?" Her father's voice sounded faint. She felt alarm rise up in her throat. She had to be positive.

"What are you doing in there, Dad? No one called me to tell me anything was wrong."

"Oh, nothing is wrong, Della. It's just a temporary situation. I had to have a little angioplasty and things went a little sideways. You know me, I'm always causing trouble!" Nothing was further from the truth, and they both knew it.

"What does that mean, 'went sideways,' Dad?"

"Really, Della, everything is fine. They solved the problem and they tell me that I should be out of here in a few days, tops. Please don't worry about a thing. It really was a minor issue."

"Dad, how about if I hop on a plane and come see you?"

"Not now, dear. I would rather you wait until I'm a little more rested. It won't be any fun to have you visit if we can't do things. You know, more than me just sitting in a chair and resting all the time. So let's talk about you coming in a couple of months. Will you bring that nice husband with you, I hope?"

"I can't promise, Dad. You know Sameh works a lot. And we are having some, ah, problems."

"It will be great to see him. Tell him hello for me, okay?"

Had he heard what she had said? She started to say "okay" and then her dad was gone.

"The is the nurse, and your father needs to rest now, so please call back tomorrow. Thanks." Click.

Della didn't know what to think. How could it be so minor if he needed so much rest?

She had been badly injured once, she remembered, and it was true that basic sleep was the one thing that worked best. But something about the whole situation didn't sound minor. But her emotions were ragged and frayed, with the horrible month she had just experienced. Still.

She called home again, and again Sarah answered.

"Sarah, this is Della again. What happened to Dad?"

"Some kind of heart thing is all I know. Mom says we are not to talk about it, only pray."

"When did he go into the hospital?"

"Last week sometime. I don't remember. Mom wants to talk to you. Here."

"Della, did you talk to your father?"

"Yes, Mother. May I ask what the problem was or is?"

"No, you may not. Whatever your father told you is what you should know. Now please just let it be. Your father will call you after he gets back home. Goodbye."

Della sat still for a while. Something was clearly wrong. It was just like her mother to be in denial. She hated to deal with things. But Della had to find out. Maybe she could figure a way around the HIPPAA rules. If she called his doctor directly and maybe he would slip and tell her what was going on. If she called the nursing station in the middle of the night Kansas time, she could get the doctor's name. And see what else she could learn. She had never understood why her mother had never really liked her. She had learned the hard way, as the years went by, that it didn't matter what she did, it would be wrong.

She felt melancholy descend upon her like a fog, seeping into her being. Talking with her mother had reminded her of all those long afternoons when she had hidden in her room as a kid. Hidden with her nose in her books about ancient Egypt and goddesses and distant magical lands. She had practiced denial then, herself, she now realized. It was as if she was waiting, always waiting, for someone or something to rescue her. As she poured the last of the tea, she thought how funny it was, that now, after all this time, she was still hiding in her room.

Della found herself slowly beginning to understand the workings of the Cairo residence. Most of the staff had been with the family for a number of years, except for Heqet, and they helped her check the orders, deliveries, school schedules, meals, garages, and dozens of other things. She was surprised to learn that the family had 11 vehicles and a warehouse, and that they provided living quarters, food, and transportation for all 14 full-time and part-time staff and their families.

Less than a month after the horrible accident, Omar was back working or politicking most of the time. But Sameh wasn't. Sameh came home for dinner many evenings, and to Della's surprise, wanted to have dinner with her, and the rest of the family, in the dining room. She hadn't seen him for stretches of months at a time, and now he seemed to be always there. There were some evenings that he joined his father at an event or a meeting, but he had started to explain, in advance, that he would be going out or would be there for dinner. She looked up at him in wonder the first time he did this, and almost asked him why he was bothering to tell her. He could just tell the kitchen chief, as he used to do as a boy.

Sitting at the dinner table, she noticed that he was taking an interest in Nyla and Nabeela, and asked them about their school work and how they felt about their teachers. He began to organize weekend outings to futball games with Zaki, and to ask him about his studies and friends. She hardly recognized this family man as her husband. Della did her best to join the dinner conversation, at least a little, and then retreat into her rooms. She had agreed to stay in Cairo a little while longer, until the family had had time to recover from the loss of Merina, but why was she needed with Sameh there every day? She wasn't sure where Khalid was, or what had happened between them, but she really didn't want to know, either. She was ready to move on.

"Why am I here, Sameh? You're handling the household yourself. You don't need me."

"We do need you, Della. You're important to this family and we are all grateful that you have stayed."

"Those are nice words, Sameh, but what is the real reason? I want to go back to Luxor and resume my work. I'm sure you'll be fine without me."

"If you're thinking you will find Nigel, I can assure you, he isn't there."

"You know this?"

"I'm in contact with the chief detective there as well as others. One of them will call me the minute someone hears anything."

"But I have my work, and it is really important to me. More than ever."

"I have arranged for an extended leave of absence. Your position will wait for you. So there is no need to rush."

"What do you mean, YOU have arranged for an extended leave? This is my job, my career, and it is *my* right to make those arrangements. Or not!"

"Yes, of course. But you're my wife and we have some issues to work through, so I think it would be better for you to remain here for a while."

"Sameh, what if I don't want to stay here? I thought we agreed that we would discuss our divorce, and it seems to me it will be easier for everyone if you and I live separately until we can make those arrangements."

"I didn't actually agree to that. I DID agree that we could talk about it. Which is what we'll do. And, I think it is important to continue your visits with Imam el Ebraheim. In fact, he has asked if we would please have some counseling with him together, as a couple, and I would like to begin next week. Any day that suits you will be fine."

"Sameh, what are you trying to do here? You know this marriage will never work. What is the point? I'm in love with Nigel, Sameh, and you – you're clearly in love with that man. We both need to move on."

"I understand your feelings, Della. I really do. But since we have not found Nigel anywhere and since we ARE married, I think it would be best for you to remain right here, in the bosom of your family and your home. And Imam el Ebraheim thinks so, as well. I'll ask him to explain it to you when we see him next week. And there is one more thing."

"What?"

"I realize I have neglected you and not given you the love and respect that the Prophet teaches we must give to a wife. I want to make that up to you. I, as you know, have been taking instruction with the Imam and find myself growing closer and closer to the religious teachings of our beloved Prophet Mohammed. It deeply saddens me to think of the way I have treated you. I truly wish to change that, Della, and to show you that I can be a good husband."

Della wasn't sure who this man was who was talking to her. She wasn't sure what Sameh was trying to pull. But she was sure she knew he was up to something. She didn't trust a word he said. "What are you're saying, Sameh?"

"I'll come to your rooms tonight and show you that I can be the husband that you married."

"No, Sameh. Please don't. And why? After all this time?"

"Because I'm your husband and I want to show you I love you."

"Sameh, you love Khalid, not me. What are you trying to prove? That you're not gay?"

"I don't love Khalid. I have sent him away. It is you that I love. I have seen the error of my ways and am coming to you as a supplicant, asking for your patience and understanding. We are husband and wife, Della, and of course, you have an obligation to me as I do to you. I'll see you later this evening, after I return from the council meeting."

"No, Sameh. Don't come to my bed. Too much has changed between us. I forbid you."

"You forbid it? I understand, my dear wife. Of course I do. I don't want you to worry. Perhaps we can just continue the conversation later. The Imam has instructed me that I must earn your respect and your love. And so I'll continue to try."

He didn't come that night. But Della lay rigid in her bed and was afraid to sleep. But he did come the next. She awoke to find him in her bed, next to her, caressing her breasts. Before she completely woke up, she thought that Nigel had come back and with a cry reached for him in the darkness. But it was Sameh. He was taller than Nigel and more angular, and he was very insistent. "No," she said, "Sameh, no," but he kept going, reaching down between her legs to push his large fingers into her and then rolling on top of her, pinning her down in the bed. He was having trouble getting hard, so his legs were tight around the outside of her while he worked his penis with his left hand and pushed into her with his hand.

"Stop, Sameh, I don't want to."

But he kept holding her, and when she tried to move out from under him, he said, under his breath, "No one will come, Della, so just relax." She squirmed and tried roll away, but now he seemed more urgent, and his hard-on was finally growing.

"Be still, Della, and shut up! I'm your husband and I'm going to fuck you, one way or another."

His voice was an angry growl. This Sameh frightened her, so she just lay there, very still, open to him as he plunged into her, harder and harder. He began clutching at the skin on her arms and her back, she could feel him digging deep into her flesh, tearing at the muscles and the skin, and she whimpered a bit, but this had no effect on him, as he now began to curse in an angry moaning voice, calling her a little bitch, a dirty whore, and then finally, with a shudder and a cry, he reached his release.

When he was finished, he rolled off of her and lay still for a while, then turned to face her in the darkness. "Now that wasn't so bad, was it?"

Della just stared upward at the unseen ceiling.

"Talk to me Della. Tell me what you're thinking."

After a full minute she found her voice. "What do you want me to say to you, Sameh?"

"Are you crying? Della, that's absurd. I'm your husband and you just performed your wifely duties. Don't be absurd. Sure, I was a little harsh, but I don't think I really hurt you. You probably liked that when Nigel did that to you."

Della found nothing she could say.

Then he seemed to soften, becoming once again the new, kinder Sameh. "Della, I know you have been through a lot. I do understand, or at least I'm trying to understand. But I have been through a lot lately, too, and you must think of me, your husband. This is a good life. You're very lucky. Things could be so much worse. And I'll keep my promise to you. I will."

"That's not it, Sameh."

"What do you mean?"

"I'm pregnant."

Sameh was suddenly very still: he didn't sigh, or comment, and for a moment Della thought he hadn't heard her and she would have to say it again. And then, in a surprisingly strong voice, he said, "Are you sure?"

"Yes."

"For how long?"

"Over a month now, and you know what that means and so do I."

"Well that's interesting." Sameh rolled over and reached for the lamp on the nightstand and patted it to turn it on. Then he turned back towards Della and looked into her eyes.

She wasn't sure she heard him correctly.

"Did you say 'interesting'?"

"Yes. Very interesting, in fact." Sameh pulled the sheet up over her exposed breasts and tucked it gently around her neck, as though putting a child to bed. He was staring at the opposite wall, not looking at her anymore. "You're not to say anything to anyone in the family, or to any of the servants, or, of course, to my father."

"It would be best for me to leave before it becomes obvious, then."

"Leave? Now? I feel you will need the support of your family more than ever, Della. No, you should not leave. This is actually a very good thing. Have you seen a doctor yet?"

"I have an appointment for next week."

"Cancel it. I'll arrange for another doctor, a better doctor, the very best doctor."

Della clutched his arm, and making him look down at her face, into her eyes.

"Sameh, I don't want to have an abortion. I want to have this baby."

"Of course, Della. And that's good, very good. Now please rest. Rest is very important during pregnancy. I'll make arrangements for the doctor's visit tomorrow morning, and of course I'll accompany you for your first visit. Maybe for all of the visits. You need to have the support of those who love you, Della, during this time. Please just let me know if there is anything special you require. Perhaps you would like for us to order some special foods from the US? Whatever you require shall be provided. And one more thing: I would like you to wait before you tell the Imam about this. We should take one step at a time, as they say. I'll go now. Sleep well."

Della lay in the dark and wondered what was going on. Was Sameh really planning to pretend this was his child? She would have to ask him in the daylight. She couldn't believe his father would ever accept such a thing. Here in the middle of the night she realized that she had almost agreed to stay with Sameh, even after his cruel abuse, even not trusting him. Now that he was gone, she felt terribly alone.

As Sameh quietly walked down the dim hall to his own rooms, he felt a thrill of hope. Could it be that he had won the first round in his father's sordid game? Lately his luck had seemed so dark and foreboding, but things might be turning his way. And luck was just as good a way of winning as any other method. He could make his own luck, too. He would arrange for the doctor to announce a delayed due date. Della could deliver early, who cared? And now he could leave her to her own devices. He would not have to visit the bedchamber and deal with female sex. And he had a good feeling about this child being a boy, but, in fact, he was happy to accept the will of Allah. His father would see that Sameh had accepted the wisdom of his plan: he had gotten his wife pregnant, become more devout, and begun to take part in political events.

He would wait until after they announced the pregnancy before he scheduled a business trip with Khalid. His father had said, after all, that out of the country didn't count. It made him hard just thinking about Khalid's tight young body next to his. He would text Khalid right away. Perhaps a visit to a beach resort in Kerala, India. He had heard that they were very discreet there, very liberal. And even that they had invented hot oil massages there. Khalid loved massages.

NINETEEN

They found the body on the dock, wrapped in an old torn fishing net. A local fisherman had noticed the bundle of net laying on the edge of a little trafficked side dock, and thinking it abandoned, was going to take it to sell. From a little distance, the net looked like it might be a Me'adeya type of net, one with tiny holes for catching shrimp, but when he got close, he saw that it had been patched many times and was very old and handmade rather than modern plastic. But still, he might be able to get a few pounds for it. When he bent over to pick it up, he saw the edge of a hand, just a few fingers, extending from a fold in the bundle. They were blue and stiff and cold. He went to his fishing master, his me'alemeen, and the master called the police.

A detective arrived the next day to talk to the men who came and went on the boats in this part of the harbor, asking about the dead man rolled up in the old net. But no one knew him. Some thought that they may have seen him sitting in a felucca, a simple fishing boat from far up the Nile, but the craft was no longer anywhere in the area. No one remembered seeing it leave. Perhaps it had sunk in the harbor? The police found no identification on the body, and they were not prepared to dredge the harbor for what appeared to be a tiny and very old indigent who may or may not have been from another part of the country. The detective did notice that the man appeared to have a calm smile on his face, in spite of the rigor mortis, and in spite of the gaping flap of his severed throat. As if he'd welcomed his attacker, the detective thought. But then the detective forgot all about it and went on to things he could actually do something about. The Alexandria harbor had lots of very alive criminals to worry about.

The little felucca had in fact been sunk but not until it had sailed north, and was well out into the Mediterranean, and not until its secret cargo had been loaded onto a much larger ship. This was also a fishing boat, a marakeb garr, or pulling ship. This kind of ship would typically stay out to sea off the ports of Alexandria and El Deheila for 10-15 days before bringing in the catch. But this boat was different. It would change its ensign flag and repaint its home port under cover of darkness. It would switch from flying the flag signifying its Egyptian registry to flying the Israeli flag. Then it would quietly cruise north, fishing along the way, easing its way towards Tel Aviv-Yafo, as though going home.

Della called her family early in the morning Kansas time. It had been five days since she had talked to her father, and she needed to hear his voice. She would tell him of her pregnancy and then ask him to find a small house in her hometown tshe couldrent for a while. She had opened a new bank account with a bank that did business in the US and moved some money into it. She would keep that money a secret and not use it until she had to. Sameh could pay for her expenses until then. She didn't really care if he understood or cared about her. She needed to be out of this house and out of this marriage that was a trap.

She had finally come to accept that Nigel was really gone, and that after these many weeks, it was less and less likely that he would suddenly show up. If by some miracle he did, he knew where she grew up. He could find her if he wanted to. It still tortured her to think that maybe, that day in the street, she had seen the car that was carrying him away, that maybe she could have saved him. But how? What would have happened if she had tried? But was it really him in that SUV? Or was it a fantasy she had invented to help her understand? Would she ever know what happened? But now she had to move forward. She had to think of the child.

She reached her sister, who sounded even quieter than she usually did.

"Good morning, Sarah. This is Della."

"Yes, I know."

"May I talk to Dad, please?"

"No."

"No? Has he gone out? Should I try his cell?"

"He's still in the hospital."

"I thought he was going to be coming home a few days ago. What changed?"

"I'm not sure. I know he got worse."

"How worse?"

"I don't know. Mom just says to pray. We kids are not allowed to go to see him because he is in the CIU."

"The ICU?"

"Yes, that's it."

"Is Mom around?"

"No. She's at church. Mary Ellen took her over."

"Thanks, Sarah."

"Are you coming home?"

"I'm thinking about it."

"I think you should come right away."

She got the number for the ICU nurses station and when she called, she was directed to the nurse assigned to her father. Della explained who she was and that she was calling from Egypt, but the nurse refused to give her any information. She cited HIPPAA rules.

Della called her father's doctor's office and left a message asking to be called back. She waited for an hour and then called again. An office manager explained that the doctor was very busy and that he would call her back when he had the time.

She called Sameh on his cell phone, expecting to leave a message. To her surprise he answered.

"I have to go to Kansas, Sameh. My father is in the ICU."

"I think you should go right away, Della. Let me see what I can do to help."

"I can make the arrangements, Sameh, but thank you for offering."

"Actually, I think you should take one of the planes. It would be faster. I have to call and see which US-qualified pilots are available. I'll call you back in a few minutes."

He was right, of course. It probably would be faster. There would only be refueling and customs stops, and they would be in the private areas of the airports, so maybe they would be processed quickly. And the staff knew how to make all the proper international arrangements. Della was still a part of this family and her needs were important. Her father was important. Sameh was right this time. She would see if Silva could accompany her. Perhaps she could convince her to stay with her in Kansas for a while.

Della asked Heqet to call Silva. Soon Silva showed up at her door, as Della was piling things on the bed to be packed.

"Yes, Mrs. How can I help you?"

"I have missed you, Silva. Now I have an important question for you: will you come with me to Kansas, in the USA?"

"I would, Ma'am, but it is not for me to say."

"That's new, isn't it? Well, I'm telling you that you have MY permission. And I'll tell Sameh to have your papers put in order immediately. Please go and pack, as we are leaving very soon. And tell Heqet to come and pack my things."

Sameh called back just as Heqet went to ask for the luggage to be brought from storage. Della suddenly wished she had Wenut with her now. She had been trying to think of a way to get Wenut brought north from Luxor, but she hadn't been able to figure out a way to do it without anyone knowing. She had been separated from the little sculpture for a long time now, and she worried that someone would have stumbled upon her wrapped in the back of her closet drawer. If she was able to stay in the US, how would she ever see her again?

Sameh was there when she turned around. Had he been waiting long?

"All set, Della. The plane will be at the terminal in two hours, fueled and ready, with two pilots. We are planning a fuel stop in the Azores, I understand, but the next stop will be Kansas, unless the US insists we stop in Atlanta."

"Thank you, Sameh. I really appreciate this. I'll keep you informed of what is happening."

"Actually, I'll be going with you."

"I don't need you to go with me, Sameh. I can handle this myself."

"Or course you can, Della, but I'm still your husband, you're with child, and I don't want you to be upset. I know it has been difficult to find out what is really going on there, in Kansas. So I'll come along and have a little chat with the president of the hospital. That, at least, should insure that your father has the best possible care."

Della realized what a good idea this would be. Sameh was right again. He could be extremely charming and persuasive, and he would use it to her father's advantage.

Sameh went separately, but she was on her way to the airport within an hour. Silva had not been given permission to go. It was something about not having time to prepare papers. Amir was waiting for Della and Heqet at the curb of the private terminal, and they followed him, at a publicly polite and respectful distance, even though he was a servant. Della had learned to honor the traditions of Islamic male-female courtesy, even though she would have never imagined herself doing so even a few years ago.

To her surprise, Sameh was already there and had brought two more servants, one to drive for them and one to cook, he explained. The plane was bigger than she remembered. Sameh explained that the company had acquired two of these larger craft after they signed the African deals. "More fuel, you see, Della."

"What?"

"When we have to travel to distant places, there could be unexpected weather. In which case it is a good idea to have extra fuel. That's why we got the bigger jets. You can imagine trying to find a place to refuel in a strange county in the middle of the night. Especially some parts of Africa."

Della didn't care how her husband did his business. And she wondered why he was bothering to tell her this detail about the fuel. He seemed to be trying to reclaim their long-gone friendship, sharing his thoughts, his thinking. Too bad it wouldn't work. However, lots of fuel was a good idea.

The plane was equipped with bedrooms, bathrooms, and a galley, and Sameh had ordered food brought aboard. It was still too early to go sleep, so Sameh sat near her in one of the plush leather seats but left her alone to read an archeology journal on her iPad. After about two hours he asked if she would like to play a game of chess. And so, floating through the night sky, Della and Sameh moved their pieces around on the inlaid hardwood chessboard, speaking little, but each enjoying the peace of distraction. The game was equal for a time, and then it seemed as though Della would be the victor, until, when she thought she had only one more move to secure the win, Sameh suddenly check-mated her.

When they landed in Wichita, Della was somewhat refreshed, having caught one more short nap on the way over from Atlanta, where they had to land, after all, to go through customs. As they taxied to the terminal, Della realized she had never known there was a private terminal at this airport. It was still a two-hour drive to her hometown, but the jet couldn't land at any of the little municipal airports in between. Two American men met the plane and escorted them to the waiting SUV. It was black, just like the ones in Cairo. An American driver would take them to Granville, and then their driver, Akmed, would take over. It was the middle of January, and Della wondered if Akmed would know how to drive on the icy roads.

Sameh had reserved a set of rooms at the Crown Plaza Suites, and the SUV would continue there with the others, after dropping them at St. Jude's Hospital. The hospital had been remodeled and modernized, but nevertheless, as Della walked into the lobby, she was sharply aware of the difference between the palatial shiny white interior of the hospital in Cairo, and this smaller, low-ceilinged building carpeted in deep blue greens. She felt a twinge of fear. Should they try to get her mother to allow them to move her father to Wichita, to a bigger and more well-equipped facility? Passing framed awards citing the hospital as being a "Hometown Treasure" on the hall walls, she was even more concerned.

Sameh had changed into his power suit before they got off the plane, and as Della was taken to see her father, he asked for directions to the administrative offices. She knew he was going to introduce himself, on her behalf, to the CEO. She wasn't sure what he would say, exactly, but Sameh had a way of making people listen when he talked. He would not exactly commit to any kind of financial contribution, but the CEO would get the idea. As she watched him walk away from her, she was once again amazed that he had become so different from the young student she had married. He had learned many things since then, and she had a strong feeling that some of those things were dark and terrible.

She had to put on a protective gown, gloves, and a mask to go into see her father. The nurse explained that although his heart was the main problem, he also had contracted MRSA. He had no resistance.

Her father, although barely conscious, was able to recognize her. She felt the tears overwhelm her in spite of her decision to stay calm and positive. But then she saw the tears in his eyes, too, followed by what might have been a smile. The breathing tube made it hard to be sure. She sat by his bed and patted his arm and told him she loved him and was excited for him to get well so he could play with his new grandchild. He didn't respond to this as he had fallen back asleep. The nurse escorted her out of the room. She had used up her ten minutes.

"When can I see him again?"

"In 50 minutes. Ten minutes an hour. That's the policy."

"But wouldn't it better for someone who loves him, his family, to sit with him all the time? To give him moral support?"

"Sorry, miss. That's St. Jude's policy."

The nurse took her gown and mask, then gently guided Della into the small waiting lobby, pushing the double wooden doors closed behind her, the lock clicking.

Sitting in the little lobby, looking out the windows at a cement-brick wall covered with ivy, she waited. Soon she would go find the doctor and try to learn more. But for now, she just wanted to be here, near her father.

The cardiologist was willing to share lots of information. Her father's condition was grave, it was true, but he had seen many people come back from such crises and go on to lead happy lives.

Della visited every hour, for her full ten minutes, and then went home to the hotel after the 8 o'clock visit, where dinner was waiting for her. Akmed delivered her to the hospital at 6 the next morning, and she sat in the little lobby all day, reading magazines, sipping bottled water, making sure to capture all ten of her hourly minutes.

She expected to see her mother, but she hadn't come by the middle of the second day. Della called to ask her if their driver could pick her up and bring her. Your father doesn't need a crowd of people bugging him, right now, her mother had said. He needs to get well. And besides, Della, you're there, so why should I come? As she closed the call, Della had that same old question in her mind: Why was her mother always angry?

By the third day the nurses knew her enough to let her stretch the time just a little. Her father had improved and was taken off the breathing tube, and he was awake more and even smiled and listened as she told him about her work, and what was happening in Egypt, and how the baby would be born early next fall. She held his hand, with all the tubes coming out of it, and listened as he talked in a rambling, half-coherent way, and reminiscing about when she had been a little girl. Della would ask, now and again, if he knew where he was and what day it was, but he would just smile and say, "Yes, of course I do," so she left it at that.

Sameh did business from the hotel, via phone and iPad and laptop, and came to the hospital to see his father-in-law two or three times a day. Her father had always liked Sameh, from the very first time he wore his western style khakis to the barbeque in their yard. He grasped Sameh's hand once and smiled and said how happy he was that they were going to have a baby. He had understood, after all. Sameh smiled back and then looked at Della with a troubled expression. Surely he didn't expect her to keep this from her father.

At the end of that third day, the cardiologist found her waiting in the lobby, with 20 more minutes to go before her next visiting time. He sat down next to her. There was only one other person in the little lobby, and she was sleeping stretched out across three chairs.

"Your father is doing much better. I credit your visiting him. He is responding to care much more than before. It was an excellent decision to come."

"How much better? Will he be move out of the ICU soon?"

"Yes, tomorrow, most likely. Then, if he continues to improve, he will be moved to rehab after about a week and then released home. He could be home in as few as two weeks. I'm amazed at how much better he is after these last three days."

On the fourth day, mid-morning, Sameh came into the lobby in a rush, wearing his workout clothes. "Della, we have to talk."

She followed him into the hall, and he explained that a crowd of radical political Islamists had ganged up on and killed two dozen Coptic Christians in a little town just south of Cairo. There were plans for a massive demonstration in Cairo in Tahrir Square. This was looking like an uprising, almost a revolution.

"Oh, that's terrible, Sameh. But what has that to do with us?"

"Father has been given the responsibility of managing the security police forces. He is the one who has been put in charge of keeping the civilians quiet. As you know, Della, there have been rumors of political unrest among the people, particularly after the recent burning and riots in Algeria."

"Omar will do an excellent job, Sameh. Don't worry about that."

"Yes, of course. But he thinks it would be wise for the family to remove to Sharm el-Sheikh for a while. He says he has learned of some information that's alarming. He needs for us to organize the move. He says we should not delay. The family could be in danger. "

Della realized that this could be her chance to escape.

"You go, Sameh, go right away. I'll stay here for a while and then join you later."

"I understand how you must feel, Della, and I really do understand, but I also need your help. Father was keeping an eye on the business but now he has his hands full. So I need step in and run the company for a while, and that means someone else needs to take care of the family. There is only one person who can do this, and it is you. You can fly right back after we get everything settled. I'll even arrange for the same plane and pilot to be waiting for your call."

It took her a long time to answer. Something about what he was saying rang a bell in her mind. Hadn't he said these same words before? Hadn't she agreed to help out before and then found herself somehow still in Cairo, after weeks had gone by? But if the family was really in danger, then she should go. The girls could be a little careless and who knew if the boys were curious enough to go out and take a look at where the incident had happened. There was no question that people would resent their family, who were among the wealthy elite. You never knew what a mob of angry people could do. A mob of angry hungry people with no jobs.

"Do you promise that I can fly back as soon as I get them moved and settled?"

"You have my word, Della, my word. I'll personally instruct the crew to be ready for your departure. I would like to leave here within a few hours. Is that possible? You could be back by the weekend if all goes well."

"We have to go see my mother on the way out."

"I'll have everything ready. You just wait here. See your dad one more time. You can shower and rest on the plane. And, Della, thank you for helping."

Della's alarms went off. Why was Sameh being so kind to her? Was he trying to butter her up? There was somehow odd about this behavior, even though he had good reasons to be afraid for safety of the family. She quickly pulled up al Jazeera on her iPhone and searched on Egypt. The news about the riots and the killing of the Coptic Christians was true, and it looked like things were getting worse by the minute. He was probably right. But still, something felt wrong.

The driver was waiting for her as she walked out of the ICU waiting room. Della just nodded and followed him through the halls to the waiting SUV. She explained to her father that she had to go home for a few days but that she would be back. He had seemed to understand, then had fallen back asleep.

As she stepped into the waiting SUV, she saw Sameh talking to a man in a white coat in the hall. He handed him a piece of white paper, an envelope maybe, and then turned and came to the SUV.

"Who was that, Sameh?"

"He is a respiratory therapist. He has promised to get me information about your father. That way we'll be sure to be well informed."

Hardly necessary, Della thought. She had developed the respect of her father's doctor and and knew he would share all the information with her. So like Sameh, this conspiratorial way of seeing the world. But she didn't say anything as they drove towards her home.

She and Sameh were ushered into the house by her sister, but her mother, standing behind Sarah, had pointed to Akmed and said, "He can't come in. He can stay on the porch."

Della looked over at Sameh, who stood stiff, his eyes sparkling, his mouth turned now from his disarming smile to a compressed firm line. He didn't look at Della or her mother but nodded and then slowly leaned to whisper to Akmed. Della couldn't hear his words, but Akmed turned and walked toward the car.

Della told her mother that they had to go home for a few days, but that she would be back soon, all the while watching her mother's lips close into a grimace, her head lowered, her eyes peering out from under her brow. Like a bull getting ready to charge, she thought. Even after all these years, that look could fill Della with fear. What had she done this time?

Sameh must have recognized it, too, for he chimed in and told her mother that he and Della would be happy to contribute in any way they could. Perhaps they could pay some of the hospital bill? Della's mother didn't acknowledge this offer, but instead, stood up, and immediately moved towards the front door.

"You should get going. You have a long trip ahead. Please don't worry about us. We are just fine."

Della could see she her mother was hopping mad but couldn't figure out why. She stood to say goodbye to her sister and brother, who just nodded and remained strangely quiet, as though waiting for cues before they spoke, and then she and Sameh walked out the front door. Suddenly, letting Sameh continue to the car, Della turned back and re-opened the almost closed door.

"Mother, are you alright? I know this is hard stuff."

"I'm just fine."

"I want to help, Mother. Will you let me help?"

"No. I don't need your help."

"Surely there is something I could do to contribute. Even if I'm far away, I do have resources."

"Resources? You mean lots of money."

"Yes. I have some money."

"Well, you just go on ahead and be uppity, Miss Fancy. You just go on ahead with that dark husband of yours. Go back to that God-forsaken desert country with all those smelly Arabs wearing dresses."

"Look, Mom, I'm sorry if I have done something, I didn't mean to, and I want to ..."

"Don't call me 'Mom.'"

"I should have said 'Mother.'"

"No, not 'Mother' either. You're no child of mine, Della. Now get out of my house. You have never belonged here, never been anything like the rest of us. Always such a know-it-all: too good for us simple folk. Well maybe you are. So you're on your own, now: just go away. We'll be just fine without you."

Looking into her eyes, Della saw that she really meant it. There was no use in trying to talk with her now. Would this woman even care that she was going to be a grandmother? Would she think that any child of Della's would be as much of a threat to her as Della had always been? Without her father here, Della felt the coldness of her distance and knew the gulf was vast between them.

Della lowered her head, turned, and walked towards the SUV. Nothing had changed here. When she got back here, she would try again.

TWENTY

As the car left the Cairo airport, Della realized that they were not taking the usual route home. Although there had been a lot of military planes at the airport, things seemed calm. There were a many uniformed guards, but clients who used the private terminal expected high security. Della watched as Sameh talked quietly with the driver before he got in the back seat. She didn't ask him what they were talking about. Perhaps there were problems with access to roads, or perhaps he was going to be dropped off at his offices downtown.

It was usually about an hour's ride into town, and as the car progressed, things seemed almost normal, although oddly quiet. But then, 30 minutes into the trip, on the Geis al Sweis Avenue, Della began to notice barricades across the intersections they passed. She could see the people, in great numbers, behind them marching in the streets. They protested and told all the news agencies that they demanded a change in their government.

This was unprecedented in one of the most law-abiding countries in the Middle East. It had taken the world by surprise. Most of all it had taken the entrenched Egyptian regime of Hosni Mubarrek by surprise. No one knew what he was going to do, and it was unclear what changes the people would accept, but the protests kept growing, and it was rumored on al Jazeera that the army had sided with the people against the security forces and would not attack. This was very hard to believe. Della didn't trust such rumors. Having lived in Egypt for several years now, she, like most, had heard many stories of people being picked up at night and taken away, never to be heard from again.

A few prisoners were released, but they did not talk about their experience. Among most citizens, torture was assumed and never denied.

So now, though they were still far away from al Tahrir Square, the barricades made sense. Traffic was light, the few vehicles on the road were driving slowly, cautiously, not at all like typical Cairo driving. If it hadn't been so eerie, it would have been pleasant.

Della peered north to see if she could see any security police or military. It was reported that the demonstrations were peaceful and under control, which was amazing, as it was still hard for her to believe there even *were* demonstrations. The security forces must be permitting them. But they were better armed and stronger than the army, and were under the direct control of the president. As their SUV approached the access to the 6 October Bridge, they came to a stop behind a line of cars. Uniformed men with guns were walking alongside and talking to the drivers. Paper were being handed over for inspection. Just ahead, before the rise of the bridge ramp, Della caught sight of the outline of a tank. No, several tanks. And it looked like people were sitting on top of them. Ordinary people, not people in uniforms. Common citizens of Cairo were sitting on the tanks that belonged to the military? What could this mean?

Their driver had his papers ready and explained that he was taking his boss to work. They were directed down a side road, and Della turned around to see the officer speaking into his cell phone, never taking his eyes off them as they pulled away. Within a minute another military man on a motorbike pulled up and signaled the driver, then waved for them to follow. As they crept along behind their escort, zigzagging around blocked streets and men with short dark automatic rifles, Della looked for protestors, but could see only a handful of people walking. They were heading in no particular direction, and they were not rushing or carrying signs. Then, while waiting to cross the Abd al Salam Areaf where it joined al Tahrir Avenue, she saw it. To her right, maybe 100 yards away down the avenue lined with buildings, there were thousands and thousands of protestors. If she wasn't seeing it with her own eyes, she would not have believed it. A whirlpool of humanity, almost breathing in unison as it moved like a giant organism. It was far more massive than it looked on CNN or Al Jazeera.

Della was suddenly very afraid. Did those people realize what was going to happen to them? The Egyptian security forces could kill them all, brutally, without warning. And then she saw the cameras of the news media sticking up like flags. Just as they pulled onto another side street, blocking the view of the square, she saw a banner of the reviled al Jazeera. Perhaps this was their only protection against a bloodbath. She didn't believe it would protect them for very long.

Sameh was right: they really did need to get everyone out of the city. When the security forces decided to control the protest, which could be at any moment, they should be as far away as possible. The security forces were famous for their terrible efficiency. If you happened to accidentally be in their way, they would be sure you never had a chance to explain your innocence. It didn't matter who you were: you would simply disappear.

They pulled up in front of the company office building. The street was almost empty, but the escort jumped off his bike and pulled his gun up in front of him, watching as the driver opened the door for Sameh to step out. Sameh's phone buzzed, and he pulled it to his ear as he stepped onto the curb, looking both ways furtively while the guard watched his every move, his gun ready. Then Sameh turned around and looked back into the SUV directly at Della. He stared at her for a moment as he listened to the phone. His jaw was set in an intent expression. Did the call have something to do with her?

"Very good. Thank you." he said. He was speaking in English. And then, "I'll follow up, as agreed. No need to call. That's good."

What did that mean? Della didn't like the sound of the phrase.

"What is it?" she said.

But Sameh didn't answer. He quickly turned to look up the street again, as though he had heard a disturbance. Then he lowered the phone and followed the blue uniformed building guard to the double glass doors, which clicked open as he approached them, and then closed quietly and locked behind them. Della could see the outline of two men cradling a huge guns near the glass wall just inside. They didn't turn to watch as Sameh and the guard disappeared towards the elevator bank.

On the slow zigzag drive to the residence, she began to plan how to get the family to Sharm el-Sheikh. They should go immediately, in the early morning hours just after the curfew. She would have the staff spend the night packing and preparing four or even five SUVs and then they would convoy out of town, going directly by road, not air. It would be a long day, but it would be safer than trying to get a plane out of the airport. She would check with Sameh later. She'd like to leave before dawn, but they didn't dare violate the curfew.

She checked her phone and there were no messages, no texts. No news was good news. The doctor had promised to call if anything changed. She would check with Dad from the car tomorrow when they were well away from the city. Soon all this would be behind her and she would back in Kansas, by her father's side.

The Cairo residence was calm and silent, belying the tension. The four children were quietly watching live news of the protests, but they all turned to look up as she entered the den. She saw the fear in some of their eyes, but something else in Zaki's. They had been watching al Jazeera for days, even though Omar and Sameh hated the network. Zaki was on his iPad checking Facebook and using Twitter. Mohammed, the family nerd, peered over at the iPad screen, but he seemed disconnected, curious but not really engaged. He was playing games on his tablet. But Zaki was excited, enthusiastic, as though he was watching an important soccer match. It seemed like he might yell out a cheer any minute. Who was he cheering for? The staff had been adamant about everyone staying inside, but Zaki had managed to sneak out and to go to Tahrir Square. One of the garage men had gone after him and brought him back before curfew. Thank goodness for that.

Della told them to start packing their casual clothes because they were going to go on holiday. She could see in Zaki's eyes that he resented her. And she suspected he didn't want to go. For him, leaving was like running away from a party. She put him in charge of helping the kitchen staff organize the food and water for at least a two-day trip for everyone, which included the five family members and 11 of the staff. In the desert, you had to be prepared. Sameh and Omar, in the apartment in the office building downtown, would both be too busy to help them. Two men from the garage would stay behind to do double duty as guards. She assured them they would be paid an extra bonus and suggested that they prepare an escape car in case things became too dangerous. She knew, even as she spoke the words, that they would disappear and blend into the crowds if the protestors came this far. But Della did not think that would ever happen. With Omar behind the scenes, something would happen soon. Perhaps as soon as he knew they were gone. Would he have his troops disguised as the army that was so beloved by the Egyptian people?

At 3:30 that next morning, she looked up at Silva and realized that they were as ready as they were going to be. Setting her alarm for 5, she lay down in her clothes and was almost asleep when she suddenly thought about Wenut. If the country was sinking in to revolution, how would she ever get her again? Would the unrest spread to Luxor?

When the alarm went off, she was dreaming of Nigel, seeing his face floating above her smiling, and saying, *"It will be alright. Don't worry."*

It was a full hour after the convoy had crossed the Suez Canal, two and half hours into the six-hour trip, that Sameh called her. His voice seemed different. Cool and composed in spite of the craziness of managing a business during a political unrest. He was back in control.

"I have some bad news, Della."

"Is the building okay?"

"That isn't it. And yes, father and I are both okay. We are both quite good, in fact."

Only Sameh could see himself as good in this terrible crisis. No doubt Omar was reveling in his behind-the-scenes power role, and Sameh was enjoying not having Omar around to second guess him. She looked forward to the time when she didn't have to think about what reprehensible things they might be doing.

"What then?"

"I'm sorry to have to tell you that your father has died."

She was suddenly aware of the barrenness of the landscape outside the speeding car. It was perfect for the feeling of doom that rose up inside her. "No! It can't be, Sameh. He was getting better when I left. Wait, how do you know this?"

"I received a call. Yesterday. I didn't want to upset you until you were safely out of the city."

"Yesterday! But why you? Why did they call you? And who called?"

"Calm down, Della. There isn't anything you can do now. I'm so sorry for your loss. I really liked your father, as you know."

"Sameh, who called you? Why didn't you tell me?"

225

"The doctor said he couldn't reach you. I'm not sure why. Probably the problems with reception that the foreign radicals have caused. Who knows? But I'm grateful that you're safely away from Cairo before you have learned this sad news. Your protection is important to me."

In spite of fighting an eruption of despair, she instantly recognized this voice, this demeanor: this was the same old manipulative Sameh. And he was lying. About what she didn't know because he would not tell her this about her father unless it was true. But there was more to the story. And now she was heading into the desert, to be in and out of cell service for hours to come. Had Sameh known she was just there on the edge of reception? She would not put it past him to have tracking devices in the SUVs. Della felt as if she was speeding into a barren future, going farther and farther away from her hopes and dreams.

Instead of answering Sameh, she closed her phone. She couldn't speak. Her throat was frozen, locked in a vise grip to hold back the flood that was inside her. More than sadness, a deluge of rage, of screaming, and of terrible weeping for another loss. For the loss of the one person who had loved her unconditionally. The one person left that she could believe in.

It occured to her then that only an iron will could save her now. She clamped down and allowed not even one scant tear to escape as she stared ahead. Outside, through the tinted windows, the desert scenery around the little convoy became a blur in the bright sunshine, as she was swept headlong to the south, towards who knew what.

"Sarah?"

"Yes, Della, it's me. I knew you would be calling. Do you want to talk to Mother? Because she's not here."

"No, to you. Are you doing okay?"

"Yeah. Fine."

"What happened? Just before we left the doctor told me Dad was doing a lot better. They said he would come home soon."

"He died, Della, that's all I know. He had another heart attack."

"When?"

"A few hours after you left."

"How is Mom doing?"

"She is fine. She's at church. They are helping her with the funeral plans."

"When is it?"

"Day after tomorrow. Saturday morning."

"Sarah, I don't think I can come. It is hard to travel now, from here. There are a lot of problems with protests and civil unrest."

"You shouldn't come, anyway, Della."

"Why do you say that? I loved him so much. And he was my father, too."

"Dad is gone. There isn't anything here for you now. Stay there."

"But I'll miss seeing you."

"Maybe you will."

"Sarah, would you come and visit me here in Egypt, after things settle down?"

"Maybe, maybe not. I really belong here, Della. You got out, and now you belong there, not here. You were so different when you came to visit, we hardly recognized you. You really aren't like us anymore."

"I wish you wouldn't say that."

"You know it's true."

"I want to send flowers. Sarah, is the funeral at church?"

"Yes. But Mother says no flowers. Only donations to the church."

"When will she be back?"

"I don't know. But I wouldn't call her right away."

"Why, is she having a hard time?"

"She blames you, Della. She thinks Dad would have gotten better if you hadn't come to visit."

"But that's not true!"

"I don't believe her, Della, but don't call. Just don't. Maybe you could call her later. Like in a month. At least. I have to go."

"But Sarah..." Della realized her sister had hung up.

Della placed the little square of the black phone on the table, then folded her arms in front of her and lay down on them. Her eyes were hot and there was a lump in her throat, but she kept her tears firmly wedged inside her mind. Was Sarah right? If I don't belong there, I don't belong here or in Cairo either. The only place I ever really belonged was in Luxor at Nigel's side.

227

The anger came up quickly, like a tsunami wave from the deep. She sat up straight in her chair, looking at her luxurious surroundings with new eyes. She had to think of a new plan now, of a new way forward. The anger was growing within her, becoming stronger. With clear dry eyes, with perfect posture, Della pushed it down inside, so she could think clearly. She was really on her own now, and she had to be very careful.

She sent flowers to the funeral anyway. She ordered online, and chose the custom white easel bouquet for $400. She didn't expect to ever hear if they were received, so it was no surprise when she didn't. She knew the flowers were for her really. And to let everyone know she was still there. To let herself know she was still there.

The days went by slowly in Sharm el-Sheikh. Della found herself sitting and looking at the beach from the veranda and napping in the early afternoon after lunch. There were a number of other families from Cairo and Alexandria who had taken up refuge there, and there were invitations to join them for lunch and dinner. To talk about the situation, and share ideas, no doubt. Della let the young people see their friends in the compound, but she declined all invitations. During the first few days, she had trouble sleeping, because plans and ideas raced through her mind, but as the warm quiet days stretched forward, she began to think less and less and to just stare at the placid waters more, empty minded, unquestioning. She had arrived eager to be finished and gone, but after a week, she could barely reach any sense of urgency. The protests continued, she heard, when she remembered to check the news.

During the second week, she came out of her stupor and called Sameh. "I have done as you asked, Sameh. Now I need to leave. I would like to go back to Luxor to live. I'm going to go back to my job. You could come and visit the baby now and then, if you would like."

"I understand, Della, and you have been wonderful with the family. And I know how much you love Luxor. Perhaps it would be best to wait until after the birth to make the transition. It would be better for both of you. But let's talk about it when you come back to Cairo. In a couple of weeks. I'll see what I can find out about the job in the meantime."

Della wondered, as she hung up the phone, if she should try to call the Director of Antiquities's office again. But there had been looting at the Cairo

Museum over the last few weeks and he was reportedly beside himself and had threatened to resign in live video on international news. Then he had disappeared. When she first called, there had been no answer. Was everyone hiding out? She would wait for a better time.

Although Sameh called every day or so to update the family on the situation in Cairo, to everyone's great relief, he didn't come to Sharm el-Sheikh. Della usually handed the phone to one of his brothers, talking with him as little as possible.

Half-way through the second week, when the household was settling into a routine, Imam el Ebraheim arrived. He came unannounced and unaccompanied. But he came with luggage. He explained that he had been advised of Della's loss of her father and wanted to offer comfort to her in her time of sorrow. The residence at Sharm el-Sheikh, which was one level but large and rambling, had several wings of bedrooms for potential guests, and, as was typical in Muslim homes, there was a wing for just males. Wondering if the imam was also trying to escape the turmoil in Cairo, she invited him to stay in a room near Mohammed and Zaki.

Several weeks went by and he was still there. He seemed to be a calming influence on the youngsters, challenging them to conversations about the upheaval in their country. An admiration slowly grew in her for his skill at counseling and rational discussion about these volatile issues. While the girls held their opinions to themselves, Zaki wanted to argue loudly about the rights of the people and the oppression of Mubarek, and the Imam was happy to both listen and talk late into the evening with him. Della would go to bed early leaving the two brothers and the Imam sitting around the table, Zaki challenging, the Imam calmly responding, and Mohammed silently watching them both.

Della and the Imam developed a routine of talking together in the later afternoon about how the children were adapting and how Egypt was analogous to that transition. Sometimes the discussions moved in the direction of religious philosophy, but the Imam was careful never to push her on these topics. At first they asked Mohammed to sit with them while they talked, but soon the Imam became comfortable enough to be alone with Della and the staff. He was a good listener and slowly, slowly, she began to tell him about her former life in Kansas, about her hopes for the marriage to Sameh. And one day she realized that she could trust him.

After almost five weeks at Sharm el-Sheikh, and more than four weeks after Mubarak resigned, they returned to the Cairo residence. Sameh had called to say it was safe to return and alluded to the fact that he and Omar had helped to "bring things under control." Once again in a caravan of SUVs, they arrived in the early evening.

As they traveled into the city, it felt like things had almost returned to normal. There were only a few remaining barricades, and the military, although present, was keeping a much lower profile. It only took a day, however, for Della to appreciate the tension all around them. The servants were exceedingly careful to be orderly and not to stop on the street, but to move about their business. The curfew was still in place, and although Omar could arrange a pass at any time, he had made it clear that the family should observe it to the fullest. In spite of no formal government, the country was rigidly stable, proving what Della knew were ruthlessly tight controls behind the scenes. How was this different, Della wondered, from Mubarak's regime? The security forces were still sudden and vicious, and they seemed to be omnipotent. But now no one was sure who was behind them. Now there was no figurehead to blame, no face to put on signs. People didn't know who to hate now. But they remembered how to be afraid.

Omar and Sameh came together for a welcome dinner the day after the return to Cairo. They assured the household that things were under control. Della remained polite and non-committal, and bowed slightly to accept the personal congratulations from Omar on her bravery in her condition. Clearly Sameh had set the stage while she had been in Sharm el-Sheikh. She excused herself to go to bed early and recognized that this was permissible because she was expecting. In other circumstances, Omar would have considered it rude. In fact, Della was beginning to feel the weight of her pregnancy now and had found the trip back to Cairo much more exhausting than the trip over. She welcomed the ability to nap and order what she wanted for food and to read alone in a parlor in the afternoon sun. She had no stomach for hearing the stories Omar wanted to tell about how he had been able to bring the radical-sponsored protests under control or confound the corrupt western media. She had no illusions about what he had been doing with unchecked power. She wondered if Zaki realized what his father did for a living. He would soon enough.

Soon Della missed the discussions she had in Sharm el-Sheikh with the imam, in the lazy afternoons, with the lovely coastal view out the windows. After a week back in Cairo, the imam called to request an appointment to visit her at the residence. She looked forward to seeing his friendly face.

The chief detective of the 13th precinct in Cairo was awakened by the call at 3:00 a.m., and regaining his composure after screaming invectives into the phone at his lieutenant, he finally understood. He had always told his men never to disturb him at night unless it was a very serious emergency. This was.

When he walked into the apartment just before dawn, he had been astonished to see so much blood. In his 25-year career, he had never witnessed such a scene. It was on the drapes, the windows, the screens, the floors, in the crevices of the decorative friezes over the arched doorways, and even splattered wildly across the 12-foot ceilings of three rooms. The director's analytical nature, always his defense against the horrors he encountered, caused him to wonder how it was that so much blood could drip downwards into the carved flowers 10 feet off the floor. After refocusing his attention, it became clear: dismembered body parts. They had most likely been chopped off with a machete or some sharp tool. Probably while still alive, which would account for the blood canopied overhead. With a kind of vertigo, the director had felt like the room was slowly revolving, spinning backwards in time to the brutal murder of the famous singer-mistress in Dubai. He had seen crime-scene photos of that event, and this scene looked just like it, though much more horrific for the putrid smell and the cloying sticky feel of slaughter in the air. Flies had already found their way in and it was still very early. They were multiplying rapidly.

It was a full 20 minutes of standing amidst the vermillion gore and viscera, watching his crime team work, before the detective began to suspect that there were too many pieces. It was 3 in the afternoon, after everything had been bagged and tagged, that he knew for sure. There wasn't one, but three, mutilated bodies.

The next day he learned that the name of the primary victim was Khalid Zakki Yaseem, a relatively recent tenant with society connections, whom neighbors reported entertained a lot. The other body was a slightly younger man, believed to be the man's servant. But before they could establish an identity for the last corpse, a young boy, the word came down from his superiors: hands off. No more investigation. Clean it up and forget it.

The director called his superior, the governor, to complain. This was too terrible to hush up, even in Cairo. But to his surprise, his boss simply invited him out to a late dinner. That night, over whisky and kabobs in a private nook in the El-Bialy Restaurant, the director got the message. His boss was an old political war horse, grizzled and sure of himself in his cruel determination. But the director recognized the fear in his visage immediately. It seemed to ooze from his pores, an undeniable scent. And he knew he would never mention the terrible event again. As much as he disliked his boss, he knew that whoever could put fear into him was beyond dangerous.

The thing that nagged at the Director was that there had still been no report about a missing boy. In had been over a month now, and no mother, no father, no person had called about the young victim. And he had been a handsome boy, too, which was perhaps why the killers had left only this one head intact, uncleaved, lying in the middle of a soft pillow on the bedroom floor. The detective had seen the tubular packet of flesh stuffed into the boy's mouth when he first observed him, but later when his workers were bagging the head, he saw that it was no longer there. That scene: the soft curls of the perfect head with its surprised eyes looking up from the young and beautiful face, surrounded by the pale pink pillow: it was an image he struggled to bury deep, to keep from rising to haunt his dreams. Even when he was awake.

Half-way through her seventh month of pregnancy, Della recognized the ambush. She had been back from the beach for two months and she had continued to live simply, finding it easier and easier to be waited on and to be served. Sameh had left her alone, been kind to her when they did talk, and praised her when he was home for dinner. He was trying to get her to stay. She knew she had to do something or she would never be able to escape from her invisible but terrible bonds.

She was waiting for him when he stepped through the front door in the early evening. Omar was just behind him.

"We have to talk."

"Of course, Della. Can it wait until after I get a drink?"

"No. Now. "

"Let's go to your room."

"No, right here."

Sameh turned towards his father and said something, quietly, that Della didn't hear. Omar continued down the hall towards his den, and of course, the bar.

"What is it, dear wife?"

"Don't 'dear wife' me, Sameh. You promised me and it is time to honor your promise."

"What is it, Della, that you want me to do?"

"I want you to order the house in Luxor to be opened and prepared for my arrival. I'll take a car down tomorrow or the next day, with Silva. I'll live there, as we agreed, until the baby is old enough for me to move."

"Move where?"

"I'm not sure yet."

"Please calm yourself, wife."

"Don't do that, Sameh. I mean it. You promised you would do this."

"Actually, Della, I only said I would look into it. In fact, your job in Luxor is no longer available. I spoke to the director. He has found a young man to take that job. He thinks it is better to have a man in the position, anyway. Safer."

"You have no right. I'm not your chattel! But I still want to move."

"But you have been treated very well here, and we'll all miss you so much. I will miss you."

"Sameh, we have been through this. This isn't a real marriage and I'm not happy and I'm leaving."

"So, in that case, what will it take?"

"What do you mean?"

"What will it take for you to stay?"

"Everything always has a price for you, doesn't it, Sameh? This isn't about money, Sameh. This is about love, and honor, and marriage."

"Is there someone else, Della, that I don't know about?"

"You can be as cruel as you want to, Sameh, but I still want to leave."

"But you have not told me what you want."

"I want my freedom, Sameh. That's what I want."

"In Luxor?"

"Yes."

"You want to be free from me and this family in our ancestral home in Luxor, with your maid and other servants, which is to be paid for by us?"

"You owe me that."

"Really? Would you be interested in having the baby's paternity tested?"

"Sameh, don't be cruel. You know the truth. You agreed to let me go."

"No, actually, I agreed to consider it. I have. I have decided that you will stay."

"Well then we might as well tell your father and get it over with."

"And you think that will help you feed your child? Do you think you will be able to find a job anywhere in Egypt, even the world, when Omar gets finished broadcasting the 'truth' about your betrayal? And the artifact, the one you have been saving with you all this time. Do you think you will be able to get a job if the world knows you have 'borrowed' it from the museum?"

"You wouldn't."

"I would. But more than that, my father would. Shall we call him?"

Della stood looking up into this man, her husband's face. She felt surprisingly calm and only slightly frightened. But then suddenly she felt like she might faint.

"I have to sit down."

"Please, sit here on the settee."

"Please call for some water, Sameh. I feel faint."

"No. Not until you tell me."

"There is nothing that you can give me to make me stay. Nothing."

"Yes. There is. I recommend some insurance. You want to have something that no one can take away from you. Something that's entirely yours. In case things go badly."

"What do you mean 'take away from me'?"

"I mean exactly that. Things can be taken away. Lots of things: freedom, property, even babies."

She stared at him. Sameh had turned into his father.

"Della, for once in your life, listen to me as an old friend. In this volatile world, you need something that's all your own."

"What would that be?"

"I have an idea. I'll show you tomorrow."

Della wondered, as she sat perfectly still, if Sameh would always outwit her. Someday, somehow, she would win.

"I'll look forward to seeing it."

"I'll call for some water."

Della held his eyes, with their malicious sparkle, and didn't turn away. She would not answer him. She would have the small victory of having the nerve to hold his gaze.

The following afternoon an envelope was delivered to Della. She was in her home office, doing some research on the Internet, when Heqet brought it to her. Inside was an odd-sized folded paper. Not paper exactly, but thicker and pliable, like a kind of vellum. She pulled it out and unfolded it. It was a large rectangle, maybe 10 centimeters by 16. There was a legal description of physical property towards the top, and then more language about rights to receipts from that property, part way down, and at the bottom there were several signatures, Sameh's and others she didn't know. The legal language was in Arabic, but a kind of formal Arabic that Della had only seen in textbooks. And an embossed seal with the date. Today's date. She read through it carefully. It appeared to be both a deed and a contract. Attached with a paperclip was a business card and a note. The note was from Sameh and it said she was to meet him at the Arab African International Bank in downtown Cairo two days from now, on Friday, at 10 to set up the account. The business card was for a man at that bank. The title on the Card was Executive Vice President for Personal Accounts.

Looking at the paper in her hands, Della realized she didn't understand what the deed was for or where the property was located. She wasn't sure she was going to a meeting at the bank. How would owning a piece of property be insurance anyway? It had to be a trap, another one of Sameh's tricks. He still believed everything had a price, that she would stay with him for his wealth. Look how well that had worked out for Merina.

Nigel had thought there was more money in his account. He was shocked to learn that it had been four months since he had checked. Because he had been in the old house before they moved him to the tomb, he had lost all sense of time. He had no idea why they hadn't killed him right away. He hadn't expected to live beyond the first day, much less those long months. There wasn't much money. He hadn't been able to remember, exactly, but he would have sworn it was more than he found. He cashed it out, however, because the bank knew him and didn't ask for ID, which he didn't have. To explain his appearance, he told them he'ed had a bad fall at a temple site. He assumed they didn't ask for ID because they felt sorry for him. He'd managed to buy a ticket to Sharm el-Sheikh and charge it to one of his publishers, on Thursday afternoon, late. It was a holiday in the UK Friday and Monday. So he would land before they figured out that it wasn't authorized. But with or without traveling money, he had to get the hell out of Cairo. He had spent the last four nights with old Mrs. Ahra, who still managed the building he used to live in. He wasn't sure she believed his story, but she had always liked him, so he was hoping she would let it go for a couple more days. He hated to even be on the street in the light of day. You never knew who was watching

He had walked to his bank indirectly, through back streets, watching everyone around him. His stealth mode was on high alert: whoever was behind all this had long ago found the two dead men and would be looking for him. After he had overcome the men in the tomb, to his surprise, he had been able to jump-start the van and drive it to a small town nearby. He abandoned it near the garbage dump. They would expect him to go immediately to Cairo so he didn't. He hid out in vacant areas and slowly made his way north, hitchhiking short distances.

He was counting on the fact that whoever had imprisoned him did not expect one man to overpower two thugs. They would assume he had had help. Nigel hadn't expected to succeed: he'd figured he'd rather die in a good fight than of snakebite or thirst, so when he saw his chance, he attacked. Then he got a lucky hit with that dead flashlight that they had forgotten. A head shot. The surprise on the other man's face was all he needed to go in for the kill. They should never have unchained him.

He had been sleeping most of the time since he got to Mrs. Ahra's. He was still limping and sore all over, but the biggest problem was the knife cut that ran the length of his face. It had partially healed and he hated to look at it. He wanted to go to a doctor, like Mrs. Ahra said, but he just wasn't sure. Whoever did this would have thought to alert local doctors that a payout would be provided to anyone who reported a man in his condition. No. He had to wait. So he slept and let Mrs. Ahra feed him soup and clean and salve his scarring wound. It wasn't deep, but it was going to be there for the rest of his life. Which might not be very much longer.

Nigel had had lots of time to think about who had done this to him. It wasn't Gamal. Nigel had seen the article in the al Jazeera about the death of Gamal in the accident. He had seen his own name there, too, as a person of interest. He couldn't figure out what the hell was going on. Someone more powerful than Gamal would have dug up his name. He was just a red herring to distract the security forces from the real culprit. Which scared the hell out of him. All he wanted to do was get to Della and get as far away from Egypt as possible.

Della's family's phone was unlisted, but he found the address of the family residence and went there, but when he saw some of the goons behind the tall metal fence with the concertina wire across the top, he decided not to barge his way in. He found someone nearby who knew one of the garage men and got him to ask about her. And learned that Della had gone to Sharm el-Sheikh.

Sharm el-Sheikh should be easier than Cairo. There would be lots of guards and locked gates, of course, but he might have a better chance of passing for a workman and sneaking in. That was the only way he could think of to reach her, and it had to work. He had called her on her cell phone and texted too many times. At first there was nothing, but now there was recording saying the number has been disconnected. He had to reach her before they found him. All he wanted was to just see her again. She was the only thing that mattered anymore.

ɛ bank, he conducted his business swiftly, thankful he had a small sav-
ʌunt. There was more money than expected in this one. As he stepped
down ʟ..e last step onto the sidewalk, his cash in his jacket pocket, he saw the
big black SUV. This kind of vehicle sent a chill through him, so he stopped,
pulled his hat down over his brow, and lowered his head and only looked out
of the corner of his eyes. A woman was being helped out of the car by a uniformed man. It was Della. She was right there on the street, forty meters away
from him. She wasn't in Sharm el-Sheikh at all.

She looked different. Very thin, almost fragile, but rounder in front. And
suddenly he knew: she was pregnant. Feeling stunned he realized what that
meant. It had to be with his child. He wanted to run to her, but his feet wouldn't
move.

As she disappeared through the gold filigreed glass doors into the huge
bank next door to his, he finally stumbled forward: he couldn't let her get
away. Keeping his head down he walked by the driver, who was waiting by the
SUV with a second uniformed man. He moved as quickly as he could without causing suspicion up the four wide steps she had just used. Through the
doors, he entered a huge ornate vestibule with marble floors. In most places
this room would be bigger than a whole bank. On the other side of the room
he saw two more filigreed glass doors closing slowly and realized that those
were the doors into the main bank lobby. He opened the second set of doors
just in time to see Della being ushered through an inlaid wooden door at the
back of the vast room. The escort stood by the counter, waiting. The bank
was cathedral-like with 30-foot ceilings, carved friezes, and gold fixtures.
There were Persian rugs on top of the marble floors in several places with
ultra-modern leather chairs arranged on them. These arrangements didn't
soften the space, which echoed with metallic sounds rising over the hum of
hushed voices. Nigel chose the seating arrangement farthest from the door
Della had gone through. He picked up a magazine and opened it, looking up
every few minutes to watch the door she went in. A man crossed the marble
floors and was invited into the same room. This had to be Sameh. He had
found photos of him on the Internet. He was a taller man than Nigel thought
he would be. His expression was extremely serious. Formidable would be
another word to describe the set of his jaw, and the look in his eyes. Nigel

realized this man would be a terrible enemy. The door closed behind the man. Nigel waited.

Della felt out of place inside the large bank office. It was ostentatious and a little intimidating. She felt sure that was the intent. She met Ramzy Ezzeldin Pasha, who was a senior bank official assigned to her account, and she knew immediately that he was part of the scheme to intimidate. The man was stiff and formal. He looked like he never smiled. After Sameh arrived, he produced paperwork and Della pulled out the folded paper deed and contract. Mr. Pasha commented that ordinarily he would have requested some identification but that Sameh had vouched for her.

She learned that the deed was for a tenement building in Dubai that housed visiting foreign workers. The proceeds described in the contract were rents coming directly from large construction companies, who employed the workers. The funds would be deposited every month by wire. Mr. Pasha would arrange to have any proceeds Della didn't need invested in conservative instruments, paying modest dividends, which would be reinvested. At some future time, after her child was born, she should come in to discuss the structure of the portfolio. Listening to his stiff formal voice, Della got the strong impression that he didn't think she was up to the task, and that perhaps the machinations of advanced investment science were too complicated for her. Sameh did not meet her gaze. He simply stared straight ahead. He was nervous. It was clear that the bank official didn't approve of any of this, but was Sameh ashamed? Perhaps because everyone in the room knew what was really going on here: it was a pay-off. She had agreed to stay and he was giving her something to seal the bargain.

As the meeting dragged on, Della became uncomfortable, felt pressure, and asked to use the ladies room. Alas, Mr. Pasha explained, the bank didn't have a ladies room. Della's insurance was to be held in a bank that didn't even plan to have women on the premises. When she had come in, she hadn't looked around, but she now suspected she was the only woman in the place.

Abruptly, she rose, took her deed and envelope, and in one swift motion, thanked Mr. Pasha and announced that she would be leaving now. She was surprised at how fast she was able to move out of the office and through the two sets of doors. Her startled escort had to run to catch up with her. She moved across the vast lobby like a shot, with quick staccato steps, flinging the doors aside as she bolted through them. Approaching the SUV, she spoke in a clear loud and unusually forceful voice, telling the driver to take her home immediately.

She didn't see the tall blond man with a limp stand as she rushed across the lobby, or notice him follow her through the doors. He looked as if he wanted to shout something, so the two guards, alarmed by his face, grabbed him and pulled him to the side of the hall. The doors of the SUV closed and pulled into traffic. The man stood looking out the door, ignoring the questions of the guards who were holding his arms; he could just see the tail of the SUV as it drove up the avenue. Sameh came next, his angry look punctuated by his tight lips and gritted teeth and brushed near Nigel, unconcerned with a man being held by guards, perhaps accustomed to such a sight.

Della didn't know that Silva had carried a message for her from a man in the market place. Silva remembered the foreign man, and she knew he meant something to her mistress. It didn't take a genius to suspect that her mistress was in love with him. Which was very dangerous considering what was said about Sameh. One of the new guards offered to carry Silva's groceries up to the kitchen. When Silva looked for the message, which had been tucked away in the pocket of one of the cloth bags, it was gone. Silva prayed that the guard didn't show it to Omar or Sameh. They would not be pleased. She had been a fool to take it. They would fire her and give her a bad reference. At best. She would have to move far away to find work. Nothing happened, however, except that Silva was again re-assigned to the kitchen. Heqet was returned to service of her mistress Della. Silva was grateful to still have a job and was careful to avoid Della anywhere in the residence. From then on, one of the new house guards accompanied Silva to the market. She never saw the man who gave her the message again. If she had, she would deny she knew him.

Della had been having trouble with her iPhone, so Sameh ordered her a new one. He said it was a special personalized version. It didn't look much different, but it was faster. She still had trouble making some calls. The new military government might have been intervening into the network, however, so she didn't say anything.

She used the landline when she called Kansas. She had spoken to her mother once since her father's death, and the conversation was very short. Her mother didn't want to talk. The next few times she called there was no answer. She hadn't called for a while now.

When Della had talked to her father's cardiologist, he told her the same thing he told her when she called him from Sharm el-Sheikh: a sudden unexpected heart attack. These things happen, he told her. She still found it hard to believe he could have looked so good when she left him and then died just hours later.

Sameh was very solicitous during the final months of her pregnancy. The staff worked to get her whatever she wanted: fresh strawberries, pistachio ice cream, orange sorbet. He encouraged her to rest, and had a yoga teacher come in a couple of times a week. The yoga teacher had been recommended by the imam and was a nice young Muslim woman beginning her own business. Della was happy to help support her entrepreneurial venture, even though she wasn't very good at yoga.

Her only real visitor was the Imam, who came many afternoons to have tea. They spoke of many things, such as how the country had begun to stabilize after the protests, and Mubarak's departure, how the blessing of a baby could help you see the hand of God, and how the family seemed to be so much happier with her here. Slowly she found herself talking more about Islam with him.

Della had of course learned during her studies that for hundreds of years the Muslim world was the epitome of civilization. Muslim cities had sewer systems, hospitals, libraries, and universities while Christian Europe was still in the Dark Ages. The knowledge from the Greeks and Romans was kept alive by the Muslims. Ancient Muslim scholars wrote texts on medicine, astronomy, mathematics, algebra, human rights, education, and the deeply important obligatory charity to the poor. It wasn't until the Renaissance that the center of civilization got to Europe. But the imam taught about the

Quran based on the modern interpretation of a living scholar, a woman who had translated the ancient words more accurately. She said that the "great Jihad" was the internal human quest to control base instincts such as greed, lust, and cruelty and to seek spiritual purity. Della began to realize she had much more in common with modern Islamic theology than she had with the narrow-minded rural Christianity she had experienced as a child. Above all, she was grateful for the imam's company.

Oliver Mohammed Robert Makram-Ebeid was born on May 2. Sameh was on a business trip but flew home in time to visit Della while she was in the final stages of labor. Then he waited in a private waiting room for her to finish. In an effort to demonstrate his commitment to being a family man, he had considered attending birthing classes with Della and a few of the more modern young couples in Cairo, but in the end he had been too busy. He had suggested that Della take Heqet with her. He was happy to wait until the nurses had cleaned up both Della and the baby before entering the room.

Baby Oliver had a full head of dark hair and deep green eyes.

Della, who had converted to Islam during the eighth month of her pregnancy, had the imam come to bless little Oliver on the day of his birth, to read the Quran into the new baby's ears, and then the family participated in the naming ceremony soon afterwards. She was grateful that the imam, so familiar and kind, was there to bless her new son. The new grandfather, Omar, at the naming ceremony, held the child in his arms, looking down into his eyes. Della watched Omar to see what he would say about the baby's very pale skin, but as he raised his head, she saw what seemed to be a softening in his eyes. They were not tears exactly, but still, she bowed her head, not wanting to look upon this moment of intimacy.

During the first months after the birth, Omar sometimes called to have the baby brought to him. Della was distressed the first time this happened, because she wanted to go with her baby. But the nurse told her no, that she couldn't come, as she had been instructed to bring him alone. He was returned within 20 minutes, at most, and seemed unchanged. Still, Della undressed him and checked him to see if anything was amiss. What would he have done to him, she asked herself? She didn't think about what she would do if she found anything wrong.

One evening she sought out Omar in the dining room, at the late hour he ate dinner. He didn't expect her to walk up to him as he sipped his liqueur and, not looking up, assumed she was one of the kitchen maids.

"Why don't you allow me to come to you with Oliver, sir?"

Sitting stock still, his eyelids heavy with the balm of drink, he raised his eyes to look at her and then gave a short hard laugh. "I don't wish to see your face, Della. There is too much of Merina in you. Don't try my patience. You will regret it. Now leave me to my reverie."

As she looked into his face, where once she had seen a handsome prince from the stories of the Arabian Nights, now she saw the features of a monster, the gnarled roughness of a man who was both her benefactor and her master. All in this home bowed to his will, even Sameh, in spite of his partnership in the business. Nodding in deference she began to back out of the room, only to find Sameh coming up behind her, just arriving.

"What are you doing here, Della?"

"I was just speaking to your father."

"About what?"

"About little Oliver. And his wishes to spend time with him."

"What is she talking about, Father?"

"Surely you're not asking me about how I interact with my family, Sameh? Surely you have other things to discuss that are more important."

As Della tiptoed down the hall towards her rooms, she heard Omar asking Sameh if he had taken care of the problem. Sameh had said that yes, it was finished. She was sure that the problem'was probably a person and shuddered to think of what might have been done.

Perhaps because of that evening, or perhaps not, a trust fund, with Omar and Sameh as trustees, was set up when Oliver was three months old. It was customary in the Makram-Ebeid family to wait until a child had reached 1 or even 2 years old, but for some reason they decided to move ahead sooner. Sameh brought a copy of the paperwork to her room to show her one evening. She hadn't been invited to the lawyer's offices.

"I have called three times, Della. You're always too busy to talk."

Sameh had come bursting into her room and accused her of ignoring him. She didn't even attempt to give him an excuse. She suddenly noticed that Sameh seemed taller than he used to. It felt like he was towering over her.

"When I call you, Della, you are to take my call. Is that clear?"

"Yes, of course, Sameh. Of course."

"The museum called. The university wants its sculpture returned."

"I don't have it."

"Yes, you do. Where have you put it?"

"I left it at Luxor, Sameh, in my office there."

"Don't equivocate with me, wife. I know all about your plan to go around the university for a second dating report. Now tell me where it is so I can have it picked up."

Steeling her eyes, and her body language, she coolly and calmly answered, looking directly up into his dark eyes. She had only recently noticed how frightening they could be.

"I'm telling you the truth. I left it there. When Merina... I left it in a rush to come up to Cairo when the accident happened. And I have not been back, as you're well aware."

"Where in the office? Better yet, you call them and explain it. I want no part of this dispute. And do it tomorrow. I'll let the director know you will be contacting him."

"He is back?"

"The new director. The old director's whereabouts are unknown."

She almost asked what that meant. Della knew what that term used to mean: that the police had put him in a secret prison somewhere and he would never be heard from again. But things were supposed to have improved after the change of government.

She took the business card with the new director's name on it. "Yes. I'll call tomorrow."

And she did call, at 4:30 in the afternoon. She left a message saying she would phone again in a week. It would give her a little time to think.

She had sent for some things from Luxor but had specifically said to leave the winter clothes and the lingerie there. She hoped it hadn't sounded too suspicious. The staff would probably not have riffled through her closet drawers, but it was possible. Everything was possible if Sameh suspected her of hiding the sculpture there.

She should just call and tell them to pull it out and pack it up and send it up to Cairo to the Antiquities office. And it would vanish into some wealthy mogul's private collection. The only chance she had to have the little sculpture acknowledged for her true status in the art world would be to get it into a reputable museum. But not in Egypt. Not now. She had no idea how she would do such a thing. If only she could just wait.

"Why next week, Della? It is only Tuesday?" Sameh asked.

How had he found out what she had said on the phone call? Was someone listening into her calls?

"It was the assistant's idea, Sameh, not mine." She didn't think that he believed her, but he let it go, and that was enough. For now.

TWENTY-ONE

The army continued to maintain order in Egypt. With a few differences, things seemed to return to the way they had been before the massive demonstrations.

Public elections on a referendum to amend the constitution were held shortly after Oliver was born. People queued up in orderly lines to put their folded paper ballots in the wooden boxes. There was a lot of video coverage of these lines. The army generals running the country were rarely shown in the news, holding to their low-profile policy. Della thought all of this might be orchestrated with the media so that people felt like they had a voice. Many people talking on news program seemed to believe things were really going to change. But they didn't know Omar.

Omar now worked directly with Essem Sharaf, a former transport minister under the Commanding General Tantawi. General Tantawi had been a key confidant of former President Mubarak and was very conservative. He had great respect for the importance of strong Egyptian businesses and their economic value to the country. Omar assured him of his devoted loyalty to the army, to Egypt, and to making Egypt a powerful force in the Middle East. He also provided the general with a luxurious mansion and staff to run it. And a few other small things, perqs, which included private entertainment that would only appeal to an older military man who had come to appreciate the harshness of life.

While Omar was moving higher behind the scenes in the shadow government of the new Egypt, Sameh had begun to supply secret and secure transport services for the army leadership. This insured that Sameh knew what was being shipped and to whom. By special request he arranged for some "packages" of funds to be set up, privately, for several army generals, in banks in neighboring countries, such as Jordan and Saudi Arabia. When moving these funds, Sameh discovered that other funds could be attached, to go to other accounts, for other purposes, such as for the purchasing of contraband high-tech weapons. Stumbling across an opportunity to sell a cache of weapons, Sameh discovered that the profit was amazing. Everything was paid in cash at delivery. Even the highest profit margins on freight couldn't come close to the mark-up on these weapons. But even more than the extortionate profit, there was a little danger involved and he discovered that made it even better.

Della discovered she loved being a mother. She rose each day to the joy of playing with Oliver. During the first month, when she was very tired, the wet nurse spelled her during the night. But since then she always heard him fussing first and couldn't sleep knowing he needed her. He was a good baby, although he was always hungry, and it soon became apparent that he was going to be a big boy, unlike his diminutive mother.

She had just fallen asleep after putting Oliver down when she felt a rough hand on her shoulder. "Is something wrong? Is the baby okay?"

"You must come now. Mr. Makram Ebeid requests your presence. Now."

"Please ask my husband to go to his father. I'm going back to sleep."

"No. Your husband isn't here. Your father-in-law says you must come now. He says now."

It felt like it was the middle of the night. And she was being summoned. This couldn't be a good thing. She gathered her robe around her and followed the clearly disheveled Heqet out of her suite and down to the den. Her clock on the night table read 1:30.

As a houseboy opened one of the double doors into the den, a room she only been into once, she instantly remembered why she didn't like it. The walls were covered with armor and spears and some weapons she didn't recognize, all artifacts of ancient battles. But instead of being interesting from an archeological perspective, they gave off a threatening feeling, a feeling that the person who had decorated this room felt very comfortable with the implements of violence. Maybe more than just comfortable.

Omar was sitting in his black leather chair. His face was flushed and the look in his bloodshot eyes brought Della completely awake and alert. The bottle of whisky was almost empty on the tiny pedestal table by the ornate crystal glass. The word "Waterford" passed through Della's mind. So did the word "heavy."

"Sit down, daughter-in-law."

"No, thank you, Omar. I prefer to stand. It is late and I would like to go back to sleep as soon as possible. Why did you call for me?"

"Sit down! Now! Or I'll show you a thing or two about the respect owed to a father-in-law in my culture. I assure you, you won't like it."

Even though he had obviously been drinking, his words were very clear. Chillingly clear.

She sat down in a chair across from him.

"No! Move closer. I don't intend to yell across the room."

She pulled the chair towards him.

"What did you want to talk about?" She was careful to keep all emotion out of her words.

"I would like to tell you a small thing, just one simple thing. Can you guess what that thing might be, daughter-in-law?"

"No, sir. I cannot."

"Please, try!"

He gestured genteelly now, extending his hand in a graceful motion sideways, and ever so slightly nodding his head. It was as though he, a consummate gentleman, was asking a lady to choose which horse she would ride today.

She struggled for an answer. "I can't guess, sir. Could you give me a hint?"

"A hint?"

"Yes, sir, a hint."

"Ah yes, infidels don't like surprises: they like a hint."

"I'm not an infidel, sir. You know I have converted to Islam."

"Don't toy with me!" His face flushed red and he reached for his glass and swilled down the last drops, then lifted the bottle to refill it.

"But I will give you a hint. The hint is Oliver."

"Baby Oliver?"

"Yes, but with a slight twist, a subtle difference."

"I can't guess your meaning, sir. Do you want to know of Oliver's well-being? He is progressing well and is healthy. He is a happy baby, sir."

"The hint is Oliver gone. Oliver never seen by your eyes again. Is that a good hint, daughter-in-law?"

Della's fingers were suddenly very cold in the midst of the over warm room. "Why would you say this, sir?"

"Ah, I never discuss why. But here is the thing – the small simple thing – that I'll tell you: if you do anything to embarrass this family, you will never see your child again."

She sat very still and tried to breathe.

"You may go now. Go back to your bed. Leave me. And Kozam, send in Marta."

As Della walked along the hallway towards the stairs, she caught a glimpse of a female form, naked beneath a sheer caftan, carrying what looked like ropes, walk past her towards the den. The girl didn't look at Della,, but just passed by keeping her gaze straight ahead. She looked very young, Della thought, maybe in her early teens.

It was a late morning on a Friday when Heqet asked her to come down to the reception salon.

"I'm busy, Heqet. Whoever it is can come back another time."

"They say they have an appointment with you."

"Who says?"

"Two men from the university."

"Made by whom?" But she knew who must have set it up.

Gathering her hajib around her she flashed through possible words, excuses she could formulate as she followed Heqet slowly down the back stairway. She waited to be announced and then watched as Heqet stepped aside. One attendant remained by the arched entryway to the salon. When Merina was here there were no attendants, who looked more like guards than serving staff. They were another one of Sameh's paranoid ideas.

Two men were standing with their backs to her gazing out the salon windows onto the leafy suburbs surrounding the compound. One of the men was short and muscular, and the other much taller. She noticed a large red leather embossed case on the coffee table. They had come prepared, it seemed, to take their property back.

Finding her voice, Della, in her most polished and aristocratic Arabic said "May I be of some assistance to you gentlemen?"

The shorter man turned to look at her, but the other seemed to hesitate. And then slowly he rotated to face her.

She felt the room begin to spin and was suddenly sure she would slide down onto her knees. She grabbed for the carved wooden arm of the chair nearest her and pulled her body towards the seat. She only managed to perch on the edge of the satin cushion, but she felt some stability flow back into her. She looked down at the one hand in her lap and then up again.

It was Nigel. The taller man was Nigel. He was deathly pale. And she could see by his eyes that he was very afraid. He was holding his breath. He had a big scar across his face. But most of all she could see that it was truly, truly Nigel.

Her stomach turned over suddenly and she realized she was going to heave. She was seeing Nigel again and she was going to vomit on the floor! Hearing her fast breathing she tried to slow them down, to take a deep breath, and to not think about what might come up. She needed a distraction.

"Please, some water!" She waved towards the attendant and used her angriest voice. The shorter man with Nigel rushed towards the attendant and started demanding water also. They both disappeared down the hall.

She was alone with the man she thought she would never see again. And at the pivotal moment in her life, she heard only banal things coming out of her mouth, in the whimpering voice of a little girl. It was all she could do.

"Oh my God, Nigel. Oh my God. You're alive."

He was beside her instantly, his face down by her neck, kissing her now, his smell his real smell, his touch his real touch. And then he pulled away and stood back, farther back than when she had first seen him.

"Listen carefully. We only have minutes."

"Take this number and memorize it, then destroy this paper. Make an appointment to see a doctor with the baby and call and leave a message on this number as to when and where. I'll be there. I'll rescue you. You and our son."

She wanted to rush into his arms and hold him to her and weep at his just being alive.

But instead she heard questions come pouring out of her. "But why did you go? Why the scar? I can't go Nigel. I promised Sameh."

"Yes, you can. You're a prisoner here. I have been trying to reach you for months: your cell number has been disconnected and the staff report that you don't live here anymore. Think of Merina. They won't be as kind this time."

"But how..?"

"We'll talk about it all. All of it. Together. Later. Now take this. They'llll be here with a towel and water soon. You need to seem sick. I will say we'll come back another time when you're well. Don't look in the red case until you're alone."

As she stared into his beloved eyes, she could remember those eyes next to her, close, passionate, even as the attendant came in with some towels and some water in a carafe. Heqet followed, carrying a damp cloth, which she offered to Della for her face.

Nigel's tone changed as he assumed a crisp official Arabic. "Mrs., we are sorry to have disturbed you. We'll call for another appointment in a few weeks. If you locate the item in the mean time, please place it in the case and call the museum. We'll send a courier to collect it. It will be no trouble for you. No trouble at all. Good afternoon."

And then he was gone.

Della accepted assistance to her rooms where she lay down on one of the couches with the wet cloth over her face. It was a perfect way to hide both her joy and her terrible fear.

She hadn't had time to ask Nigel about the report of him being a terrorist. Was it true? Did the staff say she didn't live here?

She took only tea in the evening and went to bed early. At first she asked the nurse to help with Oliver, but then she felt the need to hold him until time for his bath and bed. She lay down and kept her eyes closed, but sleep was as far away as Hatshepsut's tomb.

In the middle of the night, while most of the household was sleeping, she unlatched the red case and looked inside. It appeared to be an empty container, carefully lined with stiff foam, with a middle divot the length of it designed to hold a small piece of sculpture. It would fit little Wenut if she had her. But then, sitting with it on the bed beside her, she felt like something about the thickness of the cushioning seemed off, and so she found herself trying to dislodge the foam piece by piece, even though it was glued to the sides of the case. A little after 1, she found, beneath the bottom layer of foam, the hard edges of something. And soon she lifted the carefully wrapped and diminutive Wenut out into the dim light of her table lamp.

As she examined the tiny goddess, she knew that it was the original, and not a clever copy. How had Nigel gotten her?

She had to hide her again, here in her rooms. But before Della wrapped Wenut up, using one of Oliver's white cotton baby blankets and a shaw, to make her into a diminuative mummy, she first put her on a nightstand and gazed into her lovely eyes. They were the eyes of an old friend. An old friend who had brought Nigel back to her. Without her customary plastic gloves, touching the ancient surface directly, she felt the connection she had felt the first time she had seen her. A kind of magic. Then she carefully laid the little mummy inside a large Louis Vuitton bag and placed it back on the shelf with her small collection of purses. Della hadn't gone anywhere to need a purse for many months now. Who would think to look there?

Della sat down and thought for an hour. She had made her deal with Sameh. He had trusted her. But she realized she was lying to herself if she thought she could count on him. If she stayed, her child would be raised by men for whom honor and ethics had no meaning. To whom brutality and trickery were business as usual. The more she knew about this family, the more she was afraid of them. And how long would it be before they got rid of her? She had provided a male child, so Sameh really didn't need to keep her around much longer. And it was true she never went out anymore. Her every need was provided, brought in before she even finished requesting it. Would anyone outside of the household even know she was gone if they took her away – or worse?

She loved Nigel. And he loved her. Just that. It was so simple. Somehow Della knew it would all work out. Nigel really would have everything planned. And they would be happy.

It took Della a week to come up with a workable plan. Sameh would insist that the doctor, whichever one she asked to see, come to the residence. She had been aware that he controlled her access to the world, but now that she was trying to get out of the house, she realized how far she had allowed things to slide. So she had to devise a reason to leave.

Would blood work be good enough? But why? It had to be something a little alarming.

She took a pin and pricked her finger and dribbled a few drops of blood in Oliver's diaper when she changed it. Then she put the dirty diaper in the sealed bucket. She only used cloth diapers and the staff took them away to wash twice a day. She continued to do this almost every time she changed his diaper for three days, and then she told Sameh that she was taking Oliver to see a specialist because she had noticed blood in his urine. She explained that she had called the pediatrician and he had recommended a specialist. In fact, she had really done this, although the pediatrician had said to wait a couple of weeks before she did anything. She had told him she wasn't going to wait. Sameh would believe this and agree. She assumed he would check with the laundry maids and the doctor. He did, but when both stories checked out, he agreed that the baby should be checked.

Della made the appointment and arranged for the driver and her usual guard to accompany her. She called the number Nigel had given her to leave the name of the doctor and the time and date. The number didn't go through. The message said she had misdialed. She tried calling the number on the house phone and she got the same message. Now she was getting scared. Had Nigel given her the wrong number? Or was it somehow blocked?

She called the garage and asked to see the new car seat and Hamid accompanied her down to the garage and showed her the new model they had ordered. She pretended to push it and check it, pulling straps and moving the inserts, all the while looking around for one of the garage men's phones. Pointing to the new Mercedes to distract Hamid, she was able to grab one. Hamid escorted her to the elevator, and she thanked him and went quietly to her rooms. There she tried to call, one more time, on the cell phone she had pulled out of the jacket hanging on one of the hooks near the elevator entrance in the garage. The call went through this time. Which meant it was true. Her phone calls were controlled. So she really was a prisoner. Had they tracked the owner of the number she had tried to call twice? Would that lead them to Nigel? No, she told herself. Nigel was too smart for that.

After leaving the information on voicemail, she turned off the phone and walked down one level to the kitchen. Seeing no one around, she went into the walk-in pantry and left the cell phone on the very edge of a top shelf. They would find it, of course, but not right away.

The next day was the appointment. When Sameh arrived to accompany her, he asked Heqet to take the baby and then said,

"Della, you will stay here. I'm taking Oliver to the doctor."

"But Sameh, I need to go. I'm his mother!"

"Heqet and I will see that he is given the best care possible. Please don't distress yourself. You will learn everything the doctor says when we return."

She couldn't believe it. He wasn't even letting her go with her child to the doctor.

"Sameh!" she screamed as Sameh and Heqet carried Oliver down the long hallway."

She felt the hands of one of her guards on her shoulders. The hands were firm, holding her in place as much as consoling her. But then she heard the soft words behind her.

"Shhh, now, Mrs. Don't be upset. It will be fine. Your baby will come back."

Della realized that she was utterly at Sameh's mercy. And for one horrible moment she wondered if she would see Oliver again.

When Heqet brought Oliver back later that afternoon, Della was sitting by the entrance, waiting for them to arrive. She scooped him into her arms and hugged him with a knot in her throat. Oliver was cooing and smiling, as if he had had a good time. It made her even sadder.

Della lay awake for night after night. What should she do? Had Nigel come to rescue her and thought she had changed her mind? How was she going to try again? Would Nigel even be checking that phone number if she could find a way to call him? She desperately wanted to leave, to flee, to run away, but she would not leave her child.

Slowly, over a week's time, she came up with a new plan. It was daring because it had to be. But if Sameh thought he was going to get away with keeping her prisoner, he had another think coming.

She succeeded in slipping and falling in front of both of the guards and Heqet. Walking across the room, holding her tea cup, she suddenly tripped,

ıg the cup and spilling the hot tea on the parquet floor. At exactly that
ıt her leg slid into the puddle and then out from under her. She came
down hard, her head hitting the hard, wet, floor. She lay there, faking unconsciousness, for as long as she could, hoping it was at least two minutes, and
then opened her eyes and looked around with confusion. A guard leaned down
to help her up, but she kept losing her footing. With her peripheral vision, she
could see that Heqet had not been convinced when she first fell, but then, as
she kept trying to stand up, concern crept into her face. Della had correctly
judged that none of the three of them would want to be responsible for her
being injured. Even if Sameh would be happy to be rid of her, they would
surely be punished.

She assumed Sameh had been informed of her fall that afternoon, so now
she went into her full plan. For the next two days, she carefully faked dizziness,
disorientation in her speech, and the inability to walk straight. She was betting
that Sameh would at least want to find out if she had a head injury. Which
meant a CT Scan or an MRI. Which meant going to a hospital. She wasn't sure
how she would get away from her guards then, but she would have a better
chance than she did here.

It was in the middle of the fourth afternoon after the fall, while she
was supposed to be taking a nap, that she was able to talk to Silva. She had
struggled with the words to ask one of the guards to get Silva so she could
try to ask her to prepare a special dish. The guard must have felt sorry for her,
because soon Silva was standing at the foot of her bed. She explained what
she needed, tearfully making promises she didn't know if she could keep.
Would Silva follow through? Della only knew she needed to believe that she
would.

She packed one of her larger purses with some diapers, wipes, bottled
water, the envelope that Sameh had given her, and, at the bottom, wrapped
in diapers, Wenut. Sameh now kept her passport and her bank cards, so she
packed $20 in cash. If one of the guards or the driver inspected her bag she
would be instantly in trouble.

She tried to call and leave a message for Nigel, but the number he had given
her still did not work from this phone. There was no way she could get to the
garage again. Then, feeling desperate, she tried his old number, the one she had

called some many times. She sent a text. The words "MRI" were all she dared to say. It seemed to go through and encouraged, she tried to call. The number began to ring and then suddenly stopped. It would have to do.

She was given no notice about the trip to the hospital. She was told to get dressed and that she would be taken in an hour. Della prayed with all her mind that the word would pass through the household, to the kitchen staff, that she was being taken. It had to work.

The car took her to the imaging annex, and Heqet and a guard accompanied her into the lobby, where she was immediately escorted into a room to undress and put on a hospital gown.

She looked carefully all around her hoping to catch a glimpse of Nigel, hoping he knew that she was going to be here. All she saw was softly carpeted halls and draped cubicles with lockers.

The MRI seemed to take forever. The banging sounds the machine made were intimidating, even scary, and her fears were running rampant in her mind now. She was so close but also so far from getting away.

After the test, she was instructed to dress and wait while the radiologist took a preliminary look at the findings. She decided to stay in the little cubicle, because it was a refuge from her guards and Heqet, who were hovering on the other side of the hall door in the lobby.

One of the radiology aides found her sitting quietly on the bench. "Please come with me, Mrs. The doctor will see you know."

As she followed the woman wearing purple scrubs down the hall, she was flooded with despair. It hadn't worked. She hadn't gotten away. She tried to prepare herself for a discussion with a doctor who would tell her that nothing was wrong with her.

The aide opened the door to the doctor's office, and she stepped inside. The office was empty, so she sat down and waited.

And then she heard his voice. "Now, Della, now."

She swiveled around and there was Nigel, dressed in scrubs, looking like a surgeon just out of the operating theatre. She rose to go to him, but he turned away, pushing open a side door, and whispered, "Now, we have to go now."

Della explained to Nigel about Oliver as they were hurrying to the elevator. She didn't look at his face, afraid of what she would see there. They were both silent as they rode the elevator to the top of the parking garage and then rushed across and down the elevator into the main hospital. It only took a second to flag a taxi. Nigel told the driver that they wanted to go to the airport, but then, after they were away from the hospital, changed the destination to the bus station. He had gotten her messages, he said. He had been coming here every day, knowing this was the best imaging center. He had prepared everything he could think of. His bag carried disposable diapers, bottled water, snacks, wigs for both of them, and a long coat for Della. When they got to the bus station, she put on the wig and the coat and sat down next to Nigel to wait. They did not touch, or talk, or look at each other. Nigel did not ask about Oliver. Della hoped that this meant he trusted her.

The minutes passed like hours, and Della began to have terrible thoughts. There was just one more bus going north today, and it would be boarding in 25 minutes. They had to take it or wait until tomorrow. And they both knew that would be too late.

With five minutes before departure, Della turned to Nigel and gave up.

"Go, Nigel. I will go back. Get away while you can."

"No, I am going to wait with you."

"No, it has been too long. He should have been here by now. It is too late. I love you, Nigel, and I always will. So go, go now, and remember us."

Della reached for Nigel's hand, to take it into hers for one last touch before losing him forever, but just then she saw the imam out of the corner of her eye. He was standing in the crowd, holding Oliver, looking lost. He had not recognized her in her wig.

She ran to him, her friend, and took her baby from his warm arms. He did not smile, but instead reached over and placed a hand on her head, saying a blessing.

"Thank you, thank you, dear friend, for helping me" was all she could think to say.

"May God be with you, Della. Do not forget your God."

And then he turned and walked away, and Nigel was beside her and the three of them were boarding the bus.

Within three hours they were on their way north, in coach, a sweet young dark-haired family, Mr. and Mrs. Nils Svenson and their son Olen. Nigel had false papers stating they were Swedish citizens, in addition to the wigs, and he explained that Della was to act as though she couldn't speak or understand either Arabic or English. Della nodded.

She felt a combination of terror and serenity, all at the same time, like prey running away from a gaining predator, as though they would be discovered at any moment and everything would come to a horrible end. She found she had no thirst, no appetite, and no desire to speak. She only wanted to take care of Oliver and to keep moving. Her reality existed only here and now. There was no past or future, just their seat on the bus and the landscape rolling by outside the window. Nigel sat beside her, also frozen and silent, staring ahead down the aisle of the bus.

Arriving in Alexandria, in the late evening, they took a taxi to the harbor, where Nigel walked them to a gate near a cargo loading area. A man met them, greeting Nigel with a huge bear hug. Nigel spoke with this man for half an hour, in Arabic, while Della stayed on a bench beside the office. She had begun to feel dizzy and hoped the fresh air would help to restore her equilibrium. She didn't want to faint with the baby in her arms. Her sense of danger had faded some and a kind of resignation had come over her. Whatever happened, she wanted Oliver to be safe.

Abruptly, Nigel approached her, "It's time. The ferry leaves in a few minutes."

Looking up into his eyes, Della saw in them urgency and love and something else. There was so much for her to learn about this man.

The ferry to Crete was for cargo only, but somehow Nigel had arranged for them to sit in one of the little lobbies for the overnight transit to Greece. They hadn't been out of the harbor more than an hour when they hit rough seas, the ferry ploughing through the huge waves and rocking and rolling from side to side. Nigel moved a few of the dirty chairs up next to the cigarette smoke soiled walls, Della fitted Oliver tightly between them, and they held on to each other as they rolled through the night, wondering if they would ever see land again. Della's heart and stomach fell again and again, and she would have been seasick except that she hadn't a thing in her to lose. As she gripped Nigel's arms and clasped the baby close, she was surprised that Oliver remained calm and happy, peacefully enjoying the wild ride.

Somewhere deep in the night the rough waters subsided and all three of them fell into a gently swaying sleep. They were a tangle of family huddled in the tiny lobby.

When Della and Nigel came up on deck to go through customs at the Heraklion port, the steaming August heat of the Mediteranean hit them like a blast. The water sparkled in the bright sunlight and for just a moment the world was completely different, containing only the two of them and the dozing baby, as they stood and gazed around the peaceful harbor. But the moment didn't last and they were both wide awake as they approached the customs booth, trying to hide their fear.

The power of the Makram-Ebeid family was vast and by now there would have been enough time to alert all the family's allies in the shipping business and offer a hefty reward for the recovery of a kidnapped grandson. They were both trying to breathe normally as they moved up to the customs official in his glass cage. Somehow Nigel managed to pull off being Swedish, which amazed Della. If she hadn't been terrified, she would have laughed. Then, just as they had been given their stamps, and waved through, Ollie cried out and Della, before she could think, said, "Hush now, my sweet."

She knew what she had done before the words were out of her mouth, and she felt the heat in her cheeks rise up as she stumbled with some way to cover her English. She heard some nonsense words that sounded sort of Swedish coming out of her mouth, as she and Nigel continued walking slowly. She didn't look up at Nigel: she didn't want to see his face.

Later Nigel would tell her how real it had sounded, and how well she had done to change the impression that she spoke English. She never told him that she almost fainted at that moment. She didn't want to think about where they would have ended up if the officers had taken her to a private room to ask her questions.

They were both exhausted, from the travel, from the fear, from the danger, so as soon as they could take a taxi away from the port, they went downtown and found a small hotel, bought a few groceries and bottled water, and huddled in their room at the back. Oliver, who had proven so far to be an easy traveler, was wide awake and wanted to play, and so they put him on the bed and played with him a while, before laying him to sleep in the bureau drawer they lined with two towels and set on the floor. Nigel and Della, even though they were beyond tired, made love in the little bed and then again, and then fell asleep in each other's arms.

When Nigel awoke, Della was sitting in the chair nursing the baby in the pre-dawn darkness, and he could see that she was crying softly in the dimness of the little room. He went over to her and, his arms around her, kissed away each tear, without saying a word, as he knelt beside his madonna and child. Tears came into his eyes then, too, and soon it was only the soft and peaceful Oliver who wasn't weeping.

They spent the day in the room talking, catching up, asking questions, and then sleeping and making love until early the next morning, before leaving for the airport for a flight to Athens. They arrived in London as Mr. and Mrs. Smythe. Nigel expected Della to ask him about this second set of false papers, but she just nodded when he handed her the new passport. "Nice name, Nigel. I like it. Della Smythe. Almost like an old *Perry Mason* show."

Ollie was now Olivier, like Sir Lawrence Olivier. Nigel thought his name should be a bit more pretentious to fit with Smythe.

The streets of London were frightening. Stepping out of a taxi Della had to stifle a scream as she looked up to see a tall man dressed like an Egyptian walking towards her at Kensington Station. Nigel grabbed her hand and was prepared to run into the crowds of the station, pulling Della and Oliver with him, but the man continued past them, unaware of their presence. He was pulling a roller suitcase. Della was shaking all over as Nigel took Oliver and held her hand tightly, urging her towards the trains.

"I can't, Nigel," she said. "I can't. They're everywhere."

"Yes, you can. Come along and you can sit in a corner while we wait to board."

They did find a quiet corner to hide in while they waited for the train to arrive. And then they boarded quickly.

At the first train change, Nigel stepped down onto the platform and looked in both directions before turning to nod to Della. "It's all clear. Just the locals."

But she was frozen on the step. Her eyes were wide with fear.

"You have to come off, now. Really, it's all right."

When she still didn't move, Nigel climbed back up onto the train with her and hugged her to him, and they walked back and sat down again in their corner seat. He held her then, with Oliver between them, as they rode to the end of the line. It was two full hours later that they were able to get to the same stop, after the train had reversed its route.

They got to the station at Machynlleth just before it closed for the night. The inky darkness was a boon to Della, who this time hopped off the train with Oliver in her arms and ran for the cover of shadow on the far side of the little station, away from the floodlights. Nigel, pulling their one bag off with him, had to rush to catch up to her. She stood shivering in the gloom, her fingers to her lips telling him to remain silent.

"What happened?"

"It's too quiet. Something is wrong."

"It is always quiet here, my dear. There are only 2000 people in this town and they are likely all safe in their beds." He leaned down to kiss her then, gently and slowly on the forehead. It was his way of saying you're safe now, you're almost home.

In spite of the late hour, they were able to find a driver to pick them up, and so, in the deepest part of the night, they came at last to the little town in Wales where Nigel had been raised.

For the first few days they couldn't believe they hadn't been followed. The caretaker's cottage was cold and small, and a vast difference from the places Della had become accustomed to, but in spite of all of it, she felt a tiny sense of freedom ignite in her. After several weeks they moved to the old stone house in the town proper that Nigel had inherited from his aunt. There was a back alley entrance that Nigel used, wearing what he called his Sherlock Holmes disguise, to get groceries, and they continued to keep the shutters closed tight, but they no longer tiptoed, and instead found themselves laughing over a game of cards or hanging laundry across the sitting room or watching Nigel making soup with Ollie on his shoulder. It turned out that Nigel made excellent soup. Sometimes in the twilight, they would sit quietly in the tiny overgrown garden behind the house. Nigel set up new accounts for Internet access, banking, and email. They never once checked their old email addresses.

They fell into a kind of routine, like an ordinary couple, taking care of the baby, cooking, washing, cleaning, and talking about ordinary things. Nigel would bundle Oliver up in his blue cap and sweater, and take him in his stroller to the local grocery store, leaving Della behind. She struggled to overcome her fear, worrying every minute they were gone that Ollie was in trouble, wondering at each tiny noise she heard. It was so different from when she had first moved to Cairo and wanted to go to the market every day, and so much more like that last year in Egypt, when she never left the house at all. Della was afraid of her fear, feeling its paralyzing chill as she sat in the house alone and listened.

One late fall day, crisp and clear, with Nigel's help, she dyed her hair a deep dark brown and cut it off to above her ears, and wearing black rimmed reading glasses, she went with Nigel into the village. It had been more than two months since they had come to Wales. They were only gone an hour but it felt like five. All the way home she couldn't help assessing each person they passed: did they look Egyptian, or Arabic, or armed? When Nigel pulled the front door closed behind them at home, she wondered if they might really be safe, after all. She just couldn't quite believe it.

One day Della realized she felt almost normal. With that realization she jerked her head around behind her to be sure no one was following her. When Della became pregnant again, Nigel was thrilled. Nigel loved getting down on the floor to talk with Oliver as he was beginning to explore on his knees.

They both found small contract writing jobs. Della wrote articles on Egyptian archeological issues and reviewed others, similar to Nigel, as an expert working under a name and a company name she had invented. Only her agent knew her real identity. The museum community loved her work. Her only fear was that someone in the Cairo Museum would recognize her expertise, so she shyed away from writing about her favorite subjects, even though it was tempting.

Nigel and Della married in a quiet civil ceremony in mid-winter, and since they didn't know many people in town, two of Nigel's second cousins and Oliver were the wedding party. At Nigel's insistence Della agreed to take the surname of Llewellyn because it was an old family name. There was never any discussion of her asking for a divorce from Sameh. To file any papers anywhere would have instantly alerted the Makram-Ebeids to her whereabouts.

Over their dinner out, their honeymoon, sharing a dessert, Nigel asked, "Do you ever miss Egypt?"

"Only the politics," she joked.

"And it is kind of strange to not be there now with all the changes going on. I feel like I'm missing something important, do you?"

"I know. I think about that. If I could be sure that the Makram-Ebeids were forever out of my life, I would go. But not now. But you could. One of your clients would likely pay for it."

"No. Until things change, I will miss the Egypt that I came to love from Wales."

Della did miss Egypt. So many things: the smells of the food, the feel of the air. She missed working at the museum, touching surfaces of the amazing historical artifacts, and the so many other things about the rich, complex, fascinating, Egyptian culture. She wondered how Silva was doing, and if Zaki had gotten into trouble yet. Sometimes, in the lazy afternoons when Ollie was napping and she was working on an article, she thought about the imam. She could almost see his face, his caring expression, as he patiently allowed her to share her feelings. He had been a friend to her, in spite of everything. She would not have survived without his kindness. She wished she could talk to him, to ask how he was managing with all the political upheaval in his country. In their country. In the depths of her soul Della knew she would return to Egypt someday: it was part of her now. But not yet.

She couldn't believe that Sameh and Omar had let her go: it was not in their nature. They didn't like to lose. Especially to a woman. She felt like there was something she was missing, something she should have figured out but hadn't. And even though the political landscape had changed in the eyes of the world, she knew both Omar and Sameh were still there, behind the scenes, wielding their dangerous power. In fact, mostly likely they were even more powerful than before. More in their natural element of fear and brutality than they had ever been before. She often woke up in the middle of the night listening for any furtive noise. What was Sameh up to? What was he planning? Would she recognize the danger in time?

There was no need to worry Nigel with all these thoughts, however. No need to upset the balance. And Della began to think of herself as happy. She wanted to try to re-connect with her sister, and so she and Nigel agreed that, after a year, Della would call her sometime when they were in London.

There were a few other things, however, that she found she couldn't share with Nigel.

For some reason she had never gotten around to telling him about the contract that Sameh had set up for her. She called once, in late January, from a payphone in the lobby of a little hotel in town, and spoken to Mr. Pasha at the Arab African International Bank. He said that her account was accruing rental income, and it had grown to a considerable size. How much would she like to have sent to her, he asked, and which bank should he wire the funds to? She could access the account online from anywhere and send email instructions for any changes.

She took the email address he gave her and said she would get to him after she got back from her holiday. But she hadn't. Mr. Pasha had mentioned nothing about Sameh, nothing about her being out of the country. She knew Sameh had kept the whole affair hidden from his father, and it was unlikely that he would want to admit now, after losing Della, that he had paid her to stay. She would wait until after their second son was born, in late May, and then she would deal with it. It had waited this long, it could wait until then. She would tell Nigel that there was a large sum of money in her name. She wasn't sure why she had waited, but perhaps it was because she was afraid it could be a trap. If it wasn't, then the portfolio would just grow, and if it was a trap, she would have time to figure it out.

Nigel would probably laugh when he learned about the money. He would be surprised but he would understand. He had become accustomed to her habit of looking for strangers doing surveillance, for odd coincidences that could be an ambush, for possible observers behind walls and around dark corners.

Nigel always listened to her, never once telling her she was over-reacting. When they were walking in town, she would often hesitate, and pull Nigel's arm and whisper "Who is that? I don't remember him." And Nigel would put his arm around her, hugging her, and say, "Not to worry, my dear: it is only a mild case of paranoia. I recommend a glass of ale and early to bed tonight." She would laugh along with him, then, and sometimes, using her professorial accent, would say "Thank you, doctor, for your diagnosis. I look forward to the therapy." But other times she would lower her face and hang back behind Nigel as he pushed forward, pulling her coat around up around her neck, gathering her scarf around her so as if to fend off the cold wind.

EPILOGUE

One crisp October afternoon in 2013 the Office of Acquisitions at the British Museum received a visit. Mr. Oliver Wellesley phoned up his superior, Marian Babour-Jones, and explained that a young couple had brought in an ancient Egyptian statue they would like to donate to the useum. Mr. and Mrs. Rutherford indicated that although they wished donate it to the museum, they required no compensation or tax credit and only requested that the museum put the item on display for the British people and then, later, offer to return it to Cairo after things settled down there politically.

"Is there any provenance?"

"Yes. Some. A dating report or rather a copy of one."

"Dating? As in carbon dating?"

"Correct."

"So you think this is a genuine article, Wellesley?"

"Oh, yes. Most decidedly."

"Bring the couple up to my office and let's talk together with them."

"That's the problem, Marian. They have gone."

"Well, phone them up and ask them to come back."

"They didn't leave any numbers, I'm so sorry to say. In fact, they said that it would not be possible to contact them."

"Did they say why?"

"No. They simply said it would not be possible."

"We'll have to trace them back through the laboratory, then, I suppose. Whoever ordered that report will know who they are."

"I'm afraid the report was done at the Thompson Morris Lab. They closed their doors two years ago."

"Well, Wellesley, what do you think? Sounds a bit odd to me."

"If this report is correct, and I believe it must be, this piece is the find of the decade, maybe the quarter century."

"That good, eh?"

"Maybe better. In fact, I'm being quite conservative."

"Well, let's get our own dating report ordered and see what we have."

Mr. and Mrs. Rutherford had a lovely lunch near Hyde Park and spent the night in a modest hotel. Then they spent the next day enjoying London and were going to take in a show but decided instead to return to their room and go to bed early. They were delighted to be away from the children for a little while, but of course, as young couples do, they missed them terribly and decided to go home to Wales a little early on Sunday.

EPILOGUE II

Submerged in the rotting wooden bones of an old fishing boat, in six feet of water under an old dock at the outer edge of Tel Aviv harbor, there rests a handmade crate. Inside is a device that could be described as "a speculative radiological weapon that combines radioactive material with conventional explosives". It has been very carefully, some would say beautifully, crafted and its watertight seal has not yet been breached. There was one man who knew about it and its whereabouts, but the Masood, in its efforts to get him to tell them, accidently killed him.

It sits quietly, waiting for one of the small metal clasps to rust just enough to allow the dirty salt water to trigger its detonation.

Made in the USA
Charleston, SC
02 April 2014